Karen Harper is a former English teacher who taught literature and composition at Ohio State University, as well as ....terest in both the .... and the history of the Elizabethan period. As part of her classes she encouraged her students to put on an Elizabethan Festival each year which included performing Shakespeare, learning court dances, jousting and always culminating in a (mock) beheading.

Praise for *Shakespeare's Mistress*, also by Karen Harper

'The novel's chief pleasures derive from the easy intersection of Shakespeare's work, the history of Elizabethan England, and the life that the author imagines Shakespeare might have had . . . The Bard's language infuses the story with life'

Publishers Weekly

'Harper . . . knows her period well, and it shows . . . in sure handling of the details of politics, theater, and daily life, including some harrowing passages featuring childbirth and the plague . . .'

Booklist

'A delicious and intriguing historical novel . . . Expertly researched and woven with the pageantry of Elizabethan and Jacobean history, *Shakespeare's Mistress* gives us a rare glimpse of real persons from hist............................tives that will entertain and de.............................ders'

.ction

The Queen's Confidante

KAREN HARPER

EBURY
PRESS

1 3 5 7 9 10 8 6 4 2

First published as 'Mistress of Mourning' in 2012 in the USA
by New American Library, a division of Penguin Group (USA)
Published in 2012 by Ebury Press, an imprint of Ebury Publishing
A Random House Group Company

The Random House Group Limited Reg. No. 954009

Addresses for companies within the Random House Group can be found at
www.randomhouse.co.uk

A CIP catalogue record for this book is available from the British Library

The Random House Group Limited supports The Forest Stewardship
Council (FSC®), the leading international forest certification organisation.
Our books carrying the FSC label are printed on FSC® certified paper. FSC
is the only forest certification scheme endorsed by the leading environmental
organisations, including Greenpeace. Our paper procurement policy can be
found at www.randomhouse.co.uk/environment

MIX
Paper from
responsible sources
FSC® C016897
www.fsc.org

Printed and bound by CPI Group (UK) Ltd, Croydon, CR0 4YY

ISBN 9780091947330

To buy books by your favourite authors and register for offers visit
www.randomhouse.co.uk

For Don
Thanks for your companionship on all the trips to
England and for putting up with the endless
manor houses, castles, and museums.

IMPORTANT EVENTS BEFORE THE STORY BEGINS

August 1483	Disappearance of the princes from the Tower, Edward V, and his younger brother, Richard of York.
August 22, 1485	Battle of Bosworth Field. Henry Tudor defeats King Richard III after lengthy civil war. Viscount Francis Lovell flees the battlefield and goes to sanctuary at St. John's Abbey in Colchester. His lands are confiscated.
October 20, 1485	Coronation of Henry VII
Jan. 18, 1486	King Henry weds Elizabeth of York
Sept. 19, 1486	Birth of Prince Arthur
1486	Lord Lovell, age thirty-two, escapes from Colchester Abbey and leads revolt against Henry VII. Defeated, Lovell escapes to Europe.
1487	Lovell travels to Ireland to meet with others hoping to topple King Henry with Lambert Simnel plot.
June 16, 1487	Lovell is defeated in Battle of Stoke and disappears.
Nov. 29, 1489	Princess Margaret Tudor born
June 28, 1491	Prince Henry Tudor born (later King Henry VIII)
1492	Princess Elizabeth Tudor born
1495	Death of Princess Elizabeth
March, 1496	Princess Mary Tudor born
Feb. 2, 1499	Prince Edmund Tudor born
June 19, 1500	Death of Prince Edmund Tudor

PART 1

PART I

"She perceives that her merchandise is good,
And her candle goes not out by night."

—PROVERBS 31:18

"Alas! When sleeping time is, then I wake;
When I should dance, for fear, lo, then I quake;
This heavy life I lead for your sake,
Though you thereof in no wise heed take."

—"A COMPLAINT TO HIS LADY,"

GEOFFREY CHAUCER

CHAPTER THE FIRST

LONDON
October 20, 1501

"*J*ust think on it—us making candles for the royal wedding," my brother-in-law, Gil, called to me from the door of the wax workshop.

"Us and six other chandleries," I reminded him as I sat behind our shop's counter, which was cluttered with stacks of candles. "Four hundred tapers for the thanksgiving service, the mass and wedding banquet. I'm so excited that the marriage itself will be out on a public platform for all to see. I do so adore weddings, especially when I've seen so many funerals."

Gil shuffled all the way into the shop, which fronted the street and which I oversaw. He was a short man but with a powerful upper torso from hefting metal molds and bales of woven wick from the days when he had his own small shop out by Wimbledon. I think his far better position in "fancy London," as he always called it, went to his head, though he had not yet been admitted to the Worshipful Guild of Wax

Chandlers. It was one of my goals for him, since women could not belong and my deceased husband had been so prominent in the guild. Gil did a fine job for me here: Our four apprentices jumped when his piercing voice ordered them to tasks he once had to do himself.

I myself had jolted at his voice and stabbed the wing feathers I'd been carving on a wax angel. I would have to smooth it over. It was entirely possible to correct mistakes in wax, at least. Dear heaven, how I rued the ones I'd made in life. Why, if I hadn't been so careless, perhaps my dear Edmund might still be among the living.

I slowly slid the half-carved candle under the counter so Gil would not see that this angel, like the others I'd carved, had my dead son's face again. Maud and Gil thought I was weak for mourning him so deeply, but they'd never had or lost a child. It was my sister's cross to bear that she longed desperately for one, but Maud had never conceived.

"The 'prentices were talking 'bout seeing the Spanish princess enter London," Gil said, wiping his hands on his waxy apron. "So, by the by, you going to walk our own Arthur home from school or want me to? I thought Christopher'd be calling on you again afore we close up, and I know you want someone waiting for the lad the moment he comes out the door."

I was, as usual, tempted to go myself to greet and accompany my boy home, though most of the lads walked by themselves. But Gil was right about my possible visitor. Like many a widow with a prosperous shop, I had been courted by several men, and Christopher Gage, an officer in the Worshipful Guild of Wax Chandlers, had emerged as the most determined. I was in no rush to wed again after a year alone. Though there would be much profit in our shop's assets being merged with his, I wished he would do more to make my son Arthur like him. Such a union with another chandler had helped me once, when I wed after my family died, but then, as ever in a merchant's marriage, it brought my money and skills to the Westcott Chandlery too. That had been my dowry to my husband, Will, and my dower from him was this fine house and larger shop—and most of all, a kindly husband who gave me my two sons, though one of them was lost to me now.

In truth, I was not prepared to deal with Christopher again, so I was about to say that I would walk to fetch Arthur. Then, through the shop window—panes of real glass, I thought proudly, not just thin horn—I saw a fine ebony stallion ridden to a stop just before our door. No, two fine horses. A well-attired couple dismounted, and the man, tall and broad shouldered, gave a street boy a coin to hold their horses.

"You'd best go for Arthur," I told Gil, standing up and shaking out my burgundy wool skirts. "Well-heeled customers, I warrant, ones I don't recognize."

"So I see," he said, stooping to squint past me.

And then the great adventure of my life began.

On that momentous day, I, Varina Westcott, was twenty-six, a wax chandler with a fine home and shop, a widow with a son named Arthur, after England's Prince of Wales. My other son, a two-year-old boy, my dear Edmund, had died but four months past. Of course, I had suffered losses before, for my parents and brother had died of the sweat seven summers ago. My husband's death more recently was a great blow, but, by the blessed saints, how I had loved Edmund.

He had so resembled me, with his curly, golden hair, green eyes, and slender frame, while Arthur favored his stocky, chestnut-haired father. Sweet Edmund had looked at me so piteously upon his bed, as if to cry, *I beg you, save me, Mother.* My summoning the apothecary, a barber-surgeon, and paying much for herbal cures, bringing in a priest and saying prayers, prayers, and more prayers could not save him. Had I not kept him warm enough at night? Had I accidentally fed him something rank? Should I have seen signs of his ailment? I lit ten perfect candles to bathe him in light at the end, but he still stepped into the valley of the shadow of death.

Since then, I have carried on as best I could, tending the front shop of the Westcott Chandlery while my sister, Maud, and her husband, Gilbert Penne, moved in with us to oversee the workshop. I put one foot before the other. I employ a solemn voice for our customers in mourning, for many of our wares are funeral candles or wax-soaked shrouds. In our shop window and on our wooden shelves, I display votives to be burned on London's many altars for the masses of departed souls. When I take pity on a grieving mother, I show or even give a candle I have carved, an angel with wings furled, its face looking upward in heavenly hope.

And at night I sleep with a braided circle from Edmund's ring-toss game and his deflated bladder ball, the latter of which rolls out of bed during my own tossing and is found in a corner of my bedchamber each morn as if I had cast it off.

All that morn, when no customers came by, intent, my head down, I had been savoring the silence and the solitude, despite the hubbub outside on busy Candlewick Street. Perched on a stool behind the counter with its scales and measuring sticks, I had begun to carve my boy's angelic face into a foot-tall, four-inch-thick candle. I would not burn it, for I could not bear to see dripping, curling wax cover his face as had the shroud I'd wrapped him in, then the coffin lid and the upturned soil of the burial ground in nearby St. Mary Abchurch, next to his father's grave. After losing him, I'd acquired a horror of small, closed places.

I have sold carved candles for a goodly price, but the ones with Edmund's face as the angel I neither sell nor burn, but keep them stored in my coffer or linen chest, just as I hide my hurt deep in my heart.

"All right then," Gil said, interrupting my agonizing, "I'll go for the boy and tell the 'prentices not to leave the grounds while you see to our fancy customers."

The grounds consisted of this half-timbered shop fronting the street, with storage and our living quarters in two stories above and in an L-shaped building running back along two small gardens, and a cobbled courtyard to stables and more storage at the rear. I wondered what our edifice looked like to the handsome pair coming in the front shop door, for they were gentry at least, nobility at best. The little bell over the door jangled to announce their arrival. By the saints, I wished I'd smoothed my tumbled bounty of hair back under a veiled headdress or a proper widow's hood, for the lady looked most fashionable.

And the man looked simply overwhelming.

First, he was so tall he had to duck his blond head to enter. He was dressed well but not ostentatiously. His jerkin—imported Spanish leather, I warranted—seemed molded to his shoulders and chest. His cloak, black as ravens' wings, was thrown back on one side. His face, broad with a high forehead, emphasized his taut-lipped mouth and compelling eyes, a most unusual clear gray.

I hardly regarded the pretty woman at first. Of course, they must be man and wife and here to buy either feast or mourning candles, but why would ones of their carriage and rank not send a servant?

"Mistress Varina Westcott?" the man inquired.

I ducked them a quick curtsy. "I am. How may I serve you?"

The couple—I would guess he was not yet thirty years of age, she a good bit younger—exchanged a fast glance I could not read. Perhaps it conveyed, *You go first. No, you!*

"Let me make introductions," the man said. His voice had a low timbre to it, both comforting yet arousing in a way I had not felt with Christopher's avid wooing. "I am Nicholas Sutton, and this is Mistress Sutton. At least, that is the way of it for the ears of others, for we would speak with you privily and ask your promise that what we say here will go no farther."

I stared at them, my mind racing to find reasons for such a statement. Was either of them who they said they were?

"I can offer candles for private weddings or votive

candles for secret masses for departed souls, with all discretion," I said.

"Actually, we came about this," Nicholas Sutton said, and produced from beneath his cloak a candle very much like the one I had been carving, not with Edmund's face but rather with a smiling cherub's. Indeed, it was an angel candle I had made. But did these people want to buy one, or were they wax guild sponsors, come to scold me as Christopher had for selling an item the brotherhood had not approved or priced?

"The person who purchased this says you carved it," he went on. "I think it is much too fine to burn, and so does the lady at the palace, who sent us to inquire whether you would visit her on the morrow so that she might employ your very talented services privily for a short period of time."

By the saints, he spoke well, once he got going. I prayed I did not gape at them overlong like the village idiot. The lady at the palace?

"'Tis true," the woman put in, and I really regarded her for the first time. She had russet hair and a comely face, perhaps enhanced by rice powder and cochineal on her cheeks and pert mouth. She sported a long, classical nose but balanced features and pale blue eyes. "One of the queen's own ladies," she said, "wishes to meet you and perhaps have you carve a large death candle for her, per her instructions."

"A death candle," I said. "Yes, I admit that's what they are, a memorial for someone lost."

"The thing is," she said, standing quite apart from the man, as if they were not a couple as I had surmised, "if you can slip away on the morrow, we will call for you early morn, soon after sunrise. You may tell others we are taking you to our home, where we have lost a child—just a story so this can remain among the three of us and the lady. She will pay well for your time and talent, and we will be your escorts and your story—our secret."

I wondered whether they knew I'd lost a child and were playing on my sympathies. "Why would my telling someone be forbidden or dangerous?" I dared ask, wondering whether some lady dear to the queen had been delivered of a bastard child who had died and her reputation was to be protected at all costs. Perhaps I could also get an order for candles to burn at masses said for the deliverance of that child's soul, all the sooner to be released from purgatory to heaven.

"We can only hope you will agree to our regulations," Nicholas Sutton said. "I promise that your well-placed trust will be profitable to you and your chandlery." For the first time, my gaze locked with his. Strangely, everything else faded. Even his words bounced off me a bit, and I felt a foolish maid, a green girl, when I had been wedded for five years and borne two children. Though I was tall, I had to look up at him. He made me feel small but safe, so I nodded.

"I understand," I said, my voice shakier than I would have liked. "I shall trust you in this and be ready on the morrow. But are we actually going to the palace, *into* the palace?"

"Not Baynard's Castle or the palace at the Tower, but Westminster. We are indeed," he said, and added a few parting words as they purchased four plain, foot-long beeswax candles. Perhaps those were their excuse for being here today, for they overpaid my price by half and made a quick exit.

I stood in the middle of my shop, where nothing seemed familiar anymore. I had been invited into huge Westminster Palace, which sprawled along the Thames across the fields between the city and the great gray abbey where kings were crowned and buried. I, Varina Westcott, would walk where jousts, feasting, dancing, and huge, earthshaking events had happened. I was thankful too that I was going to a place where I wouldn't imagine my lost child toddling about in every room.

I jumped back to reality when the shop bell jangled again and my five-year-old, Arthur, bounded in from school, with Gil behind him. "Mother, Mother, we're learning Latin but also sums and subtractions, so I can help in the shop and sell the candles. Wait and see!"

I hugged him hard and kissed the top of his uncapped head. "I knew you would be a big help to me!"

He squirmed a bit, but I hugged him all the harder, anxious, as ever, to keep him close, especially as I saw him growing up and sometimes pulling away from me. Like the Tudors' Prince Arthur, he was my and Will's heir, and I fretted for his health and safety. I might have lost my Edmund, but by all that was holy, I would die before I would lose Arthur too.

How I would have loved to tell him—Maud and Gil too—what strange fortune had just befallen me, but, still holding Arthur to me, I said only, "Gil, I'll need to have Maud tend the shop tomorrow morning, for I promised that couple I would visit their home and see about some candles for their chapel, and they are coming to fetch me." Then the shop bell over the door rang, for coming through it was my suitor, Christopher Gage.

He was a good decade my elder, in public a hail-fellow-well-met, popular in our parish ward and at our church and important in the wax chandlers guild. He looked suddenly short, after I had met Nicholas Sutton.

Christopher was of broad build but carried his weight well, his shoulders back, his head always held high. His cheeks bloomed with health under his carefully combed brown hair that so perfectly matched his clear brown eyes. He dressed plainly but richly, and favored large, gem-set rings, one of which, twice, he had tried to give me as a betrothal gift. Christopher Gage was an intelligent man, a widower with two grown children. He was going places, and Maud and Gil thought I should be going with him. Well, I must admit my business merger with Will had turned out well in our personal lives, and our marriage had been solid.

"Ah, my dearest!" Christopher cried, and seized and kissed my hand as if he were some chivalrous knight and I his lady. "Arthur," he said, ruffling the boy's hair until it resembled a bird's nest. "Gil"—with a nod and a single pat on his shoulder. "I bring good tidings of great joy, as the gospels say."

The man was ever cheerful when he had an audience, though strangely that did not lift my dark moods of late. He was not attuned to my grief, telling me we could simply make another son to take Edmund's place if I'd but wed him. Still, Christopher had not only been a friend of my husband but had known my father, Simon Waxman, which went far with me, for I had adored my well-traveled, urbane, and talented sire. When I was a child, I yearned to travel with him, but I'd barely been outside of London.

"Tell us then, Master Gage, if you please!" Arthur begged.

"Should I fetch Maud then too?" Gil asked.

"Of course," Christopher said. But the moment my brother-in-law left the room, he told us, "The wax chandlers have purchased land for a new guildhall, over on Maiden Lane where currently stands the Cock on the Hoop Tavern. God as my judge, the location is as fine as those of the major liveries, and we'll build a grander guildhall too. It will benefit us to be nearer to the guilds with noble and royal patronage, like the broiderers and the haberdashers, away from the tallow chandlers, with their lesser candle products for the poor—smelly, dirty stuff," he said with a wrinkled nose.

"It's all some folk can afford for lights," I protested. "I've known one or two who saved all their lives to buy our good candles for their funeral processions and masses for their loved ones' souls."

He shook his head almost imperceptibly and went on. "In addition, King Henry has granted our new motto, 'Truth Is Light,' to replace the old 'Loyalty Binds Me' granted by King Richard—ah, God rest his Yorkist soul," he added in a whisper as he made a swift sign of the cross. "To top all that off, the guild is to have a new coat of arms, and the artist wants you to sit for it, Varina!"

"I . . . That's wonderful, but who is he?" I asked, feeling

too many people I didn't know were pulling the strings of my life today, however much bounty was bestowed. Besides, I wanted to create images, not become them. I truly longed to be an artist, like my father, and not only an artisan.

"He's the Italian who bought votives from you the other day. I suggested he come by. I believe you told him your father had been to Italy, and you discussed the wax effigies the wealthy Italians pay to have carved and clothed to their likenesses. That's one way to stand near the holy altars to curry favor with the Virgin and other saints, eh?" he said with a sharp laugh. "But if that would catch on here, instead of only with our royalty and nobility ordering such effigies, the price of our beeswax would soar, I'm afraid."

"You mean the artist is *Signor* Firenze?" I said, finally getting a word in. "But why didn't he discuss it with me when he was here?"

"After he saw you, he needed the permission of the governors of the guild, of course."

"Including yours?"

"I would be deeply honored to have my future wife's beautiful face on our new coat of arms."

"Are you two wedding for certain then?" Arthur asked as Maud and Gil ran into the room.

"Oh, is that the news?" Maud cried, clapping her hands, her pale face alight.

"No," I insisted. "We are getting ahead of ourselves. Christopher has brought us word of a new guildhall site and coat of arms for the company, and he asked me to pose for it."

"That's all good, at least," Maud said, though she looked

less than enthusiastic now. She was my younger sister, and, I warrant, had had her fill over the years of hearing I was the pretty one, the clever one, when all I ever wanted was for her to love me. And now that the shop was mine, and I'd borne two children when she yearned for her own, her green-eyed envy was an unspoken barrier between us that I longed to somehow shatter.

As they ever did to give Christopher and me time alone, she and Gil hustled Arthur from the room. I suggested we stroll in the herb garden at the edge of the courtyard, but he gently pushed me back onto the stool while he leaned against the edge of the counter, towering over me.

"There is something I didn't want your family to hear, because you are the one who must decide to cease and desist," he said. "The guild council has ruled that you are to stop carving and vending those angel candles until we can decide on the pricing and distribution."

"But I'm offering them only to trusted customers—or once, when a grieving mother noticed several on the shelf but could not pay for one."

"See what I mean!" he said, smacking his knee with his fist, looking as if he'd stage a snit, the way little Edmund used to try to get his way. "You do not heed my helpful advice. My dearest, you know the guild governors set all the items and prices, and no one shop is allowed to strike out on its own, else the strength of our body be weakened."

"But I—any woman—am not admitted to guild membership, and Gil is only being considered now. I long to donate benevolences to our fraternal guild of the Holy Name of Jesus at St. Paul's." I hated my wheedling voice.

Wishing I had some sort of power to bargain with him when it came to business, at least, I said no more.

"All of which are reasons you need me," he said, bending down to capture my hands in his. "You still must answer to the guild, of course, so I shall represent your efforts, and keep this chandlery in line and in the guild's good graces since Will's loss."

And, I thought, if we wed, this man would also control one-third of my assets. My shop and money would come under his aegis, even as I would pledge to obey him in bed and board. Until Arthur's majority at age fifteen, or when his stepfather decided the lad was ready, Christopher could control another third of the worth of this store and of our family fortunes, that which was pledged to Arthur. It was a good system, I warrant, to build up a business, but I was not ready to entrust Christopher Gage with all that, or with myself. Not even this influential, avid man—not anyone right now—could sway me to wed, and it was the loss of my child as much as of my husband that made me feel so.

Then too, of course, I was expecting on the morrow to receive a lucrative offer for the newly forbidden angel candles, either from my mysterious visitors or from some unnamed lady. After all, carving candles had not been forbidden to me when I agreed to visit the palace. Wouldn't Christopher love to hear of that visit, if not my future sales there?

"I can give you only my usual answer right now," I told him, "despite your kind offer and support. I thank you for keeping me abreast of the guild's opportunities and practices, which the Westcott Chandlery, of course, considers of utmost importance."

I felt my neck and cheeks flame, my fate with such a fair complexion when I was vexed or did not quite tell the truth, as now—or when he gaped at my breasts as if he could see right through my bodice when I'd merely used the word "abreast." If Christopher and the guild learned of my secret visit on the morrow, I'd take their censure, but, by the all saints, I was going to the palace.

CHAPTER THE SECOND

The next morn I waited, pacing in the shop, just after the sun came up. I could hear our apprentices, who had cots in the storeroom overhead, beginning to stir. More than once, I had ripped through my clothes coffer, in a fret about what to wear to the palace. Something plain and dark, though not black, to show I knew my place as a merchant of mourning and funeral goods? Something with a bit of flair, to suggest I was an artist and not just a waxmonger? Father had told me once that white was the mourning hue in France, but that would hardly do and might get smudged. Indeed, whatever I wore, I was still in mourning for my son.

I had finally decided on my tawny gown with brown piping and an edging of squirrel along the shoulders. The bodice was the newly fashionable square cut to show more of my gathered lawn chemisette beneath. My hair was gathered in a netted snood under a small green-and-white hat—Tudor colors. My best girdle dangled about my waist, the one of silver chain links, Will's wedding gift to me. My skirts swished as I walked back and forth, with my cape rustling too. I kept tugging at my sleeves, full at the shoulders but tight to my arms from my elbows to wrists.

Why didn't they come for me? I wanted to leave before Maud opened the shop or Gil brought Arthur down to walk him to school. Surely this had not been some sort of clever hoax, perhaps some test of Christopher's or the guild's to see whether I would tell him about this when they had forbidden further angel candles.

No, there were the Suttons, reining in before the shop, and with a third horse, a dappled gray with a fine leather sidesaddle. My heartbeat picked up. Careful not to be seen gawking out the window, I bent my knees to watch Nicholas Sutton as he dismounted, leaving the woman ahorse. I hurried to unlock the door before he could knock. I even held the bell so it did not sound.

"I see you are quite ready, Mistress Westcott," he observed as his gray gaze swept over me. Though it annoyed me when Christopher ogled my body, my insides cartwheeled at this man's merest glance. I warrant I earned his approval, for he smiled, flaunting strong white teeth, and for a silent moment our eyes met.

"I am ready indeed," I told him, though the truth of that could be disputed.

I joined him outside—the breeze, even here, was brisk—then closed and locked the door behind us. Though we had a three-step brick mounting stair for our customers, he evidently did not see it or was in a hurry, for he cupped his hands for my foot and gave me an easy boost up. I settled my skirts and took the fine leather reins in trembling hands before I realized I should have worn riding gloves.

"Good morning," Mistress Sutton said with a nod. Soon I was to learn her name was really Sibil Wynn. I must admit I had surmised they were not wed, and I was somehow glad of that. "We shall ride to the water stairs near the Steelyard and take the river," she told me.

We turned south, riding single file in the increasingly crowded street, as cart vendors and shoppers flowed into the parishes that sold London its goods and flaunted its merchant guildhalls: mercers, grocers, drapers, skinners, tailors, and ironmongers, haberdashers, broiderers, and more. As we neared the river, brewers' and fishmongers' smells permeated the air.

I had taken hired barges on the river before, but never a private one, and of a certain not one so fine as that which awaited us and our mounts. The six oarsmen were not loud and raucous, as the hired ones were, and they were attired alike in forest green livery. A green-tasseled canopy protected three stationary padded benches from sun and rain. I had a hint then that the lady who had sent for me was very dear to the queen.

"Against wind and high tide," Nicholas Sutton remarked as he sat me between him and Sibil, and our horses were stowed in the rear onboard pen.

Against wind and high tide, I thought. When Nicholas Sutton said such, did he think of that in deeper terms, that we must all suffer loss and trials and yet carry on? Or was that just my melancholy nature now, and he meant naught by it?

"My name really is Nicholas Sutton," he was saying as he turned slightly my way, "and you may call me Nick."

Wondering whether such familiarity meant he was not a courtier after all, I nodded. As we pushed out from the Steelyard water stairs, I held on to my hat. Already my wayward curls were blowing along my temples. Mistress Wynn's coif seemed perfectly in place, mayhap, I mused, a requirement of serving with the queen's ladies at court.

Queen Elizabeth of York was known as Elizabeth the Good for her generosity and charities. I had glimpsed her twice on London streets as she passed in procession, beautifully arrayed, each hair in place when my strands kept blowing in my eyes and mouth. It was her union with King Henry VII that had helped to heal the wounds of the long civil war between the Lancastrians and the Yorkists, for she was the eldest daughter and then heir of King Edward IV, and sister to the poor boy, briefly king, Edward V. Her Majesty boasted more royal blood than did the king, for he had a slim claim to the throne through his forebears, and those considered by some to be illegitimate. At Bosworth Field, Henry Tudor had won the kingdom by might as well as right when the previous king, Richard III, was slain.

I saw people along the river pointing at us and shading their eyes to catch a glimpse. Was this recognized as a royal barge, even without its pennants and crest? I tried to enjoy the journey, telling myself that the entire city of London was laid out before me on this day. The Tower loomed to the east, and London Bridge, of course, bustled with life, for shops and houses lined it. St. Paul's was visible to the north, where soon Arthur, Prince of Wales, would wed his Spanish princess, Catherine of Aragon, who had not yet arrived in England.

As we were rowed farther past the city itself, I fancied I could see the square stone tower of St. Mary Abchurch on the gentle rise of the hill, my parish church where Will and Edmund were buried, and which I had endowed with monies for their masses. More than once, despite the pleasantries of what light conversation my hosts provided, I craned my neck to look ahead toward Westminster, but we had not yet traversed the broad bend in the river.

Still, despite gawking at the panorama of passing London, I was very aware of the big man next to me. Even had he not worn a flat velvet, feathered cap, he was at least a head over me. His booted feet were one and a half of mine, which I drew back under my skirt hems. His thigh pressed into my skirts, and though I could not feel his finely muscled leg, I almost wished I could. Each time he shifted or turned my way—or when pointing something out and he took my elbow, making it tingle—I had to force myself to look at aught else.

Then there it was, over my left shoulder: tall, stone Westminster Abbey, with the vast Palace of Westminster huddled at its stony skirts. It looked not heavy and cumbersome, but as if it were floating between the river and the morning mists from the fields. I'd walked around its walls and scattered-timbered two-story buildings before. Who in London had not, perhaps dreaming of the glorious, golden folk within? I was almost as entranced by the mere sight of it as I was by my hosts. For the first time in months, I felt my spirits lift.

We disembarked at one of the two water gates, the one nearer the palace proper, and walked along a wooden pier guarded by fantastical carved and painted creatures: a unicorn, a dragon, a—

"That's a griffin, half eagle, half lion, one of His Majesty's symbols of his Welsh heritage," Nick said, as if he could read my thoughts, which did not set a good precedent. Again he took my elbow lightly to steer me along, and something akin to the feel of hot, melted wax there made me break out in a sweat. I knew I must get hold of myself. I must remain calm and careful. I must look and speak my best.

The tall, halberd-wielding yeomen at the gate wore beautiful tunics that snagged my artist's eye; embroidered with the red rose of Lancaster encircled by gold vines, they almost glittered. Within these walls, I knew, also lay the law courts of Chancery, King's Bench, and Common Pleas, as well as Parliament, but my belief that I'd be able to glimpse any of that soon changed as a long wooden corridor blurred by. It was a maze in here. Turn, another turn, then the traversing of a large room empty but for messengers or servants scurrying through it. I realized I was biting my lower lip, and made myself stop that and unclench my fists.

"This way, Mistress Westcott," Nick said, and we turned again. More servants rushing by, some with trays or other burdens. Plain torches in sconces along the walls, no longer polished pewter or bronze ones. We climbed a narrow, curving stone staircase. It was only then that I realized they were bringing me in a back way. Because I was not to be seen by important people? Because I was merely a merchant here on an errand? Again, it seemed Nick Sutton read my mind.

"Don't fret," he said, his voice calm. "We are taking the servants' staircase only because, as we mentioned, the lady wants your visit and services to be kept private."

In a dim corridor we stopped, and Nick rapped his knuckles on a door once—then gave three more knocks. A lady dressed finely, much like Sibil, opened it and peeked out. "The wax woman?" she asked.

"Yes. Mistress Varina Westcott, née Waxman," Nick told her.

They knew my maiden name! So perhaps my being here had something to do with the reputation of my parents' chandlery, my father's talents. Yet they had said the lady had admired the angel candle I had carved.

As for my carving ability, years before, while my father made the faces and hands of life-size waxen funeral effigies for London nobility, he had taught me to sculpt faces in wax, the perfect color of a corpse, though he employed herbal dyes to create fleshy hues. Since then I had carved only faces in candles. But how I recalled that Father's effigies looked as if they could breathe and move. Sometimes as I'd watched him work in flickering candlelight, I was sure that they did. Those figures coming to life like ghosts or phantoms was my childhood bad dream before I knew what nightmares really were—death, the deaths of those dearly loved and tragically lost.

As the woman stepped back, Nick gestured that I should

enter. I prayed he and Sibil did not desert me. I clutched his arm that held me yet by the elbow as if I would bolt.

"This way, if you please," the woman said, and I reluctantly loosed him. My new guide was pleasant-looking and wore a gabled headdress with a veil over her hair. "Your companions will wait for you here and escort you home later," she explained. "I am Lady Middleton, at your service, Mistress Westcott."

Was that what I should say when I met the lady who had summoned me, I wondered—that I was at her service, just as in my shop?

But then, for the first time, an inkling of who might be behind all this stunned me. I nearly tripped over my own skirt hems when I saw the fine tapestries in this elegant room we were passing through—real woven tapestries, not painted canvas. No plain rushes on the floor, but here and there a Turkey carpet. Chairs with the cushions fitted directly into the wood, a polished table with a carved onyx chess set and painted playing cards strewn on little parquet tables. It was well-known that the queen's painted face on cards was that of King Henry VII's lovely Elizabeth of York. A golden goblet tipped on its side beside ivory dice gleamed in the morning sun streaming through the window. We roused several little lapdogs with silken ears from their pretty, embroidered pillows and—

Lady Middleton knocked and put her ear to the next highly polished oaken door we came to. "Enter then," came a woman's clear voice, barely muted by the door. It opened, and I was in the presence of the queen.

* * *

Queen Elizabeth of York

I vow by the holy Virgin, but I did not expect the wax chandler I had sent for to be so young or well favored. But then, in truth, it had been eighteen years since her wax-worker father had sculpted the lifelike effigy of my royal sire, King Edward IV, for his tomb. In my soul's eye, I can yet see that fine waxen figure in the abbey, with us frightened children gathered 'round it and Mother in tears, surrounded by bishops, abbots, and priests with their long, black, flaming candles. As if Father were yet alive, his wax image was propped up to seem standing, painted and bewigged, robed and crowned, holding in one hand the scepter and in the other the orb of silver and gilt. Yet we knew that our dear father truly lay nearby in his leaden coffin, quite dead.

Varina Westcott dipped me a steady curtsy, more power to her, for I saw her hands were trembling, and what must she know of meeting royalty? I stepped forward and touched her shoulders to raise her. "I thank you for coming. The death candle my information says you carved is exquisite."

"I thank you in return, Your Majesty. I am at your service."

"Lady Middleton, that will be all for now," I said to dismiss my last attendant. I was seldom alone and meant to be for this endeavor. As Lady Middleton curtsied and backed from my presence, I indicated that Varina should accompany me to the window. The view was lovely from it, for the courtyard beneath had been spared the early frosts. Leggy roses still sported random blooms—entwined Yorkist and Lancastrian roses, I always told myself—and water splashed in the two-tiered fountain. Despite the crisp air, I had set the casement ajar. Of course, this skittish young woman could have no way of knowing that I was as on edge as she.

I wanted what I said to her to be unheard by someone who might tarry at the door. Or His Majesty's all-seeing mother, Margaret Beaufort, Lady Stanley, could sweep in unannounced, as she was wont to do, though she was overseeing Prince Henry's tutor this morn. Unlike our always obedient eldest son, Arthur, Henry had a mind of his own.

"As I said, I greatly admired your candle," I told her, "and wondered, especially since your father had the skill of not only producing fine faces in wax but also of making their likenesses so uncannily resemble a particular portrait, whether you had that God-given gift also."

I could tell Mistress Westcott was uncertain whether her eyes should meet mine or remain lowered, so I said, "This is of great importance to me, so I pray we can converse face-to-face."

Canny young woman, she took my hint and raised her gaze to meet mine. She had fine, arched brows and eyes as green and restless as the countryside Thames at Richmond where the tide turned.

"Yes, Your Majesty. I have carved people's faces, ones I knew from life, if not from a particular portrait."

"Your father carved my father's waxen image from a plaster death mask someone else had made, but I have naught of that for what I need," I told her in a rush. Oh, my hopes soared then, to think I might possess more than the tiny portraits of my own angels I had lost, my little Elizabeth and my Edmund, just a babe.

"Let me show you what I mean," I told her, and, from the top of my writing table, I produced the joined oval portraits of my dead children. I held them out to her. "My daughter was but three years old and my dear son Edmund only four months, and this is not enough for me to hold to, and . . ."

I saw Varina Westcott waver on her feet and put her hand to the wall to steady herself. Tears sprang from her eyes and speckled her cheeks. But I'd heard she dealt with funerals, with death's decorations. What had I said? She looked both distraught and appalled. My hopes fell.

"What is it?" I demanded. "Can you not carve wax faces?"

"I— Forgive me, Your Majesty," she whispered, swiping at her cheeks with her fingertips, "but I lost a son Edmund too—not four months of age, only four months ago. My son Arthur is quite well, and yet I have carved my Edmund's face over and over, and still his loss haunts me."

"I . . . I understand," was all I could manage. I had wanted to keen and tear my hair when my children died, just the way my mother had when she learned her two young sons were missing in the Tower. Yet now I, daughter, sister, and wife of a king, almost pulled this stranger into my arms to comfort her when I was desperate for that very thing. My lord was strong and stoic in his mourning, and so I pretended to be also. But I was truly tormented by the deaths of my two children. Even worse, I vowed by the holy Virgin, I was smitten to the depths of my soul by something else. I feared the Lord High God was punishing me for the loss of two other royal children I mayhap could have saved, my beloved brothers, surely murdered, and by whom? I had secretly spent the last ten years trying to find out, and I would yet do anything I must to discover who had killed them.

Mistress Varina Westcott

As I gaped at the queen—she too fought back tears—I realized what she wanted from me. Surely I had been summoned not to carve just cherubs or angels in candles for her, but candles with the faces of her two deceased little children. Bless our queen, for she had lost two, not one, as I had. Perhaps in doing this service for her, I could find solace for my own loss. Indeed, Edmund was a common name, but it had taken me by surprise to realize that I'd had sons Arthur and Edmund too, named, of course, as was the practice, for members of the royal family. Feeling the fool for exploding in tears, I carefully examined the two oval, gold-framed miniature paintings she had handed me, neither longer than the span of my hand.

"Of course, you have not the profiles here," the queen said as she bent her head close to them too. "But I could describe those, or perhaps a glimpse of my other children would help, for my Mary's nose is much like Elizabeth's, and Henry's is similar to Edmund's, the chin too."

A floral scent wafted from the veil that hung from her gabled headdress beset with jewels winking in the spill of early-morning light. I could see the desperation, the wretchedness she sought to hide, in her pale blue eyes and the tiny crow's-feet that perched at their corners. She was a blond, roses-and-cream beauty, but this close I could see that her mouth, lush as a Cupid's bow, was drawn together like tight purse strings. I believe she was in the midpoint of her fourth decade, but she looked worn and older. Could not the approaching nuptials of her firstborn son and the health of her three living children help to allay her grief?

"Yes," I told her, "I believe I could carve such candles for you, with your help. Of course, I could not presume to take those portraits away with me to work at my sh—"

"No. No—I was hoping you could work here at least part of each day. We can arrange for you to be escorted to and from the palace, of course. Nicholas Sutton is entirely trustworthy, discreet, and loyal. I have a quiet work chamber for you nearby, even much fine, expensive beeswax laid aside. The thing is," she said, her voice such a whisper now I almost had to read her lips, "what I wish to have—to reward you well for—is not candles but life-size effigies of the children. Not for their tombs in the abbey, but for myself alone. There is more, but I would show you. Not here, but in the room I have prepared for your work, if you will come to see."

If I would come? I thought, when this woman could merely command me. "I am at your service," I said again.

To my surprise, Her Majesty led me not out the door through which I had entered her suite of rooms, but through one hidden by a large, woven arras, one with a scene of the Virgin cradling the crucified Christ beneath the cross. We traversed a short corridor glowing from a torch toward a small, open doorway beyond.

My pulse began to pound. The walls here were blocks of heavy, thick stone. Two torches burned low athwart a doorway at the end of the hall. I could see that within the well-lit chamber beyond, the ceiling was low, the walls close. She entered, but I hung back. At least the room, perhaps twelve feet by ten, had a second, small wooden door in one corner, and I yearned to flee through it. Stiff armed, I braced myself in the doorway. Sweat beads leaped out on my forehead. I could hear my heart hammering. I feared the entire palace would crash down around me, shutting me in forever.

"I—I am bothered by small, enclosed places," I gasped out, hoping I did not sound like a coward, not to this queen who had spent years of her young life enclosed in sanctuary or held against her will during the civil war.

"Then we can keep this far door open, the one you stand in too," she said, and grasped my hand as if she were an intimate friend, a sister. "You see," she said, pointing with her free hand, "four blocks of fine wax for faces and hands, and I shall take care of the clothing, stuffed bodies, the hair—I shall cut my own hair for a perfect match."

"F-four?" I stammered, honored but horrified by what she expected. Did she want two effigies of her lost children, or extra ones made lest she lose more? There was something terribly amiss here that I could not quite fathom.

"Two for my lost children—and two for my murdered royal brothers. I must have them all with me, sacred, safe at least this way, since I could not save their lives. I shall guide you on the likenesses of my poor lost brothers: Edward, who was our rightful king, and little Richard, Duke of York, who should have reigned if aught befell his older brother. And all this must be a secret between us; swear it!"

Wide-eyed, with my back against the solid stone, I could only nod. Even should she bestow honor and fortune on me, by all the saints, what had I gotten myself into? A chill snaked up my spine, for she wanted much more than I could create with a simple candle. Was our dear queen—was I—devoted or demented?

CHAPTER THE THIRD

*B*undled in my robe with warm wool mules on my feet, I paced my bedroom that night. I could not believe my good fortune—or was it to be misfortune? Could I abide laboring long in that chamber like a tomb wherein would lie the waxen forms of four dead children?

And did I have the skills? What if my work did not please the queen? I had no doubt I could carve the faces, the hands too, but they must not remain the waxen hue of death. Elizabeth of York wanted sleeping figures on beds, not corpses on biers. I still had my father's handwritten herbal of what roots could stain wax to lifelike shades. Although I had watched him tint wax, I had never tried so much as a colored candle, other than the black ones we sold daily for funerals. Or I could arrange for someone else to paint my wax to lifelike likeness. Perhaps the Italian artist *Signor* Firenze was a possibility I could broach with the queen. Then too, Christopher's chandlery made the best wax for sealing letters, and he added colored powders mixed with oil to molten mixtures to create reddish hues. It could be that just a touch of his vermilion would turn that fine *cera bianca* the queen had bought into a healthier flesh hue. And how was I to keep all this from my family and friends—and from Christopher? I must cobble up some sort of excuse, one even those closest to me would credit.

When I heard the midnight bells toll from St. Mary Abchurch and St. Swithin's, I blew out my candle and made myself lie down in bed. I drew the bed curtains tight against drafts, pulled little Edmund's ring-toss rope and ball to me, and stared up at the dark underside of the tester while all the queen had said plodded through my mind again ... of the loss of her dear daughter and son. . . . I saw my Edmund's face. . . . I must not carve my own child's countenance for the queen.

And then her two young brothers, the so-called lost princes in the Tower. Their uncle Richard, Duke of Gloucester, brother to King Edward IV, had put them there supposedly for safekeeping after their royal father died. The true heir, King Edward V, was but twelve then. Soon Gloucester had himself named king as Richard III, claiming the boys to be illegitimate, since their father had supposedly signed a marriage precontract with another woman before he wed their mother.

The boys' mother, the widowed queen, and their sister, the current queen, had fled to sanctuary at Westminster Abbey after Edward V had been taken to the Tower. Our present queen was the eldest child and a protective sister to the rest of the brood, a spate of sisters and the other son who was still with them, Richard, Duke of York. But King Richard's councilors and bishops had coerced the royal family to allow the younger prince to join his brother in the Tower as a companion.

Then disaster, the mystery of our age. Both boys simply disappeared. Rumors ran rampant, claiming their uncle Richard had them dispatched to clear his way to the throne. Yet enemies of Henry Tudor, the current king Henry VII— and there were still many, despite his God-given victory at Bosworth Field over King Richard—whispered that Henry Tudor had ordered the boys murdered, so that they did not stand in his way. He wed the boys' sister to unite the warring factions of Lancaster and York, and that was that for the lost princes. But obviously it was not the end for Her Majesty. Or now, for me either.

Queen Elizabeth of York

After everyone in the palace had quieted—I could hear my ladies' slow, even breathing from their trundle beds across the room—I arose and wrapped a cloak about my night rail. Like a barefoot penitent, I went in the darkness toward the small stone room I would henceforth think of as another bedchamber. As the arras whispered closed behind me, I shuddered to think what would happen if I were discovered missing and my ladies set up a hue and cry and called for the king. How I wished that such a panic and search had ensued when my brothers had disappeared from the Tower. But for days no one had so much as said that they were missing. By that time, we knew they were gone for good—that is, gone by someone's murderous hand.

I kept a single, huge candle burning in this chamber, with the wax blocks laid out on boards that I would later transform into three small beds and a cradle. I regretted that this was once a garderobe with a chute that dropped human refuse to the Thames before this new era of close stools replaced mere chamber pots. But, saying I would use it for a private chapel that no one else was to enter, I'd had the chute blocked and the walls scrubbed and a back entrance hewn through from the servants' hall. That way the wax woman and her guard—I should use Nicholas Sutton, for he was eager to earn his way back into our good graces—should enter and depart. Poor Nicholas, for, like others, his people had cast their fortunes with the losing side in the war, and I knew he was ambitious to make amends and rebuild his family's future.

I stroked one of the blocks of fine beeswax, smuggled in by some contact in the countryside Nicholas had found for me. Smooth as a child's cheek, which, mayhap it would become. I prayed she was good, Varina Westcott. I knew her chandlery produced excellent wax-impregnated cloths for winding sheets and smooth, smokeless votive candles she could carve so cleverly that, gazing upon the one I was given, I could almost hear that angel sing.

In this private sanctuary my dear ones would rest where I could guard them . . . but again I saw my brother Richard on that last day. In danger of our lives with our father dead and the kingdom in chaos, we had sneaked into sanctuary in the abbey with our jewelry in bedsheets. Everything had gone down, down from there. Only two sons among us seven daughters, precious sons who should have had the throne. The eldest boy, Prince Edward, proclaimed the new king, had been brought back from Ludlow Castle in Wales and put in the Tower by Uncle Richard—for his protection, it was said. Alack the day! Lies, all lies. We huddled in fear, all of us women—Mother, me, my sisters—around young Richard when they came for him, saying he should join his brother, be his playfellow.

"I cannot let my last son leave my care," my mother had insisted, her once lovely face gaunt and white as she faced the bishop and the guards our uncle had sent. "Bess, what shall I do? Whatever shall I do?" she whispered to me, for as the eldest child at age seventeen, I was the best she had for counselor and comforter in our isolation after Father's death. "We cannot allow Richard to go too."

"But they are right to say Edward will be lonely there," I had argued. "We must keep his spirits up, for he is the rightful king. How it will cheer them to be together!"

Richard had pleaded too. "Yes, Mother, if you please, I want to go. I beg you, do not be afraid." He had blond curls and was blue eyed like all of us children, the inheritance from both of our handsome parents. At age ten, of course, his voice had not changed. I could hear it yet, sweet, almost a piping sound as he said, "I will help Edward, protect him, study and play with him, and when he is released to rule, I will be at his side."

"Bess, I cannot bear it," Mother said, as if he had not spoken.

"We have been given the bishop's word, Uncle Richard's word," I told her. "Should not the boys be together to comfort each other, even as you and I do for each other here?"

That decided it for her, I vow. More fool I to trust my uncle, to trust a man, especially one ravenous for power, especially one who had made himself, even as my husband later did, the king.

Mistress Varina Westcott

The next morn, just after dawn, I was surprised to see that only Nick Sutton awaited me outside—with one horse. He was dressed more plainly too, in scuffed riding boots and a wool jerkin and short cape. Had something changed? Was I not to go today? I darted out with my leather satchel crammed with carving and smoothing tools. A copper kettle and coals to heat it would be my first request, for Her Majesty said I could have anything I needed.

I felt myself flush at that thought, for I needed someone like Nick Sutton. Strong, handsome, daring, like Lancelot in the Arthurian tales, I fancied. At least in my wildest, most foolish dreams, I wanted someone like Nick Sutton to be courting me, not Christopher Gage.

We bade each other good morning. He explained straightaway that Sibil was indisposed and Her Majesty wanted no one else to know where to find me either at the palace or in the city, so he alone would be fetching me from now on. I saw he simply assumed that the queen's word—and his—was to be obeyed, but then, I understood her need for secrecy. Was she keeping her passion for a privy memorial to her children and her brothers even from the king? I did see, though, that I would have to give my family, mayhap my friends too, a better story of why I was riding off each day with a handsome man of obviously good breeding, however he had dressed today.

Nick stowed my goods in his saddle pack and boosted me up to ride behind him. I was a bit shy to hold on to him as I mounted behind him and he said with a deep voice, "Let's away!" Strangely, in that small moment, I didn't give a fig whether Christopher saw us, for I'd thought of a story to cover the truth, though I'd probably pay the piper one way or the other. But, truly, riding close behind this man, my thighs tight to his rear in the slanted saddle as we bounced along, I was not only content but thrilled.

"You know the truth of why I've been summoned?" I asked as we turned toward the river.

"I do, for I'm to lead you in and out of your work chamber the back way and guard you. I'll try not to distract you while you work."

Was he jesting? Surely he did not know how he affected me. Or perhaps he just knew how he moved women in general, for indeed he must. I wondered whether he was wed, if not to Sibil Wynn then to some other woman. Deciding to change the subject, I said, "You are dressed far different today."

"Attire borrowed from a royal stable groom. Depending on the task for Their Majesties, I dress up, I dress down, I ride to the country or stay in town." He chuckled and I felt his ribs lift, then fall.

"You serve them both and not just the queen?" Though I

KAREN HARPER

spoke to his broad back and the street hubbub was increasing, he seemed to hear me well enough.

"Mostly the queen, though it is His Majesty's goodwill I admit I covet. But that is a long story."

At the Steelyard water stairs, he helped me onto the same barge as before, though now stripped of its fringe.

"You are young to be so skilled," he said, turning toward me as we set out on the river. His perusal was so intense that I almost missed speaking to his back. But if I blushed the more, he might think it was from the sharp autumn wind.

"I learned much of chandlery and wax sculpture arts from my parents, especially my father. Do you have a family?" I blurted, before I could stop myself.

"To put it plain, Mistress Westcott—"

"You may call me Varina, for you said I should call you Nick."

"So I did. My family was on the wrong side in two battles against the king. My father and uncle died at the Battle of Bosworth Field. I was only thirteen at the time and so was summoned to court as a mere page, perhaps as surety of my family's future good behavior toward the Tudors. But I have learned well and served loyally."

"And have risen far?"

"Not far enough by far," he said, looking quite serious despite his wordplay. "I hope to earn my way in this Tudor world, for, however His Grace came by the throne, I believe he unifies the past warring factions and makes England stronger. This coming marriage of our Prince of Wales with Catherine of Aragon will help shore up the realm and show

France we have the powerful kingdom of Spain as friends. Of course, the Tudor throne yet has internal enemies of whom we must be wary—disgruntled Yorkists, fervent loyalists to King Richard, however dead he lies in his grave."

"And you are a fervent Tudor loyalist?"

"I admire a man who can pull himself up by his own bootstraps, as did our king, and it seems to me God's guiding hand is on him. So, for now, I am guard and guide for the wax woman, as the queen has called you. But you look fair flesh and blood to me."

I knew not whether he meant that as a tease, a compliment, or just more wordplay, but by the saints, that mere turn of phrase pleased me more than had all of Christopher's pretty endearments and vows of love.

I labored long that first day at the palace. *Tempus fugit*, as my father used to say. I was ever aware of Nick's presence and his gaze upon me. Though he made it clear the queen had asked him not to speak while I worked, it surely helped me to have him there, to keep the walls from closing in. But when I began to carve the first face, that of the princess Elizabeth, I became lost in the shaping and smoothing. As I worked, sometimes he watched me; other times he hunkered under the array of candles that gave me good light, and wrote letters, to whom I knew not, mayhap his lady love. His presence there—our physical closeness—felt both reassuring and awkward.

As though he were the tavern keeper of Westminster, Nick disappeared only to bring us both food and drink or to leave me if I needed to use the chamber pot in the corner of the room. We spoke briefly as we ate, but he took that time to go out and tell the queen how things were progressing, so I was soon back to work.

Her Majesty came in but once, for Nick said she was busy being apprised of the final preparations for the entry of her future daughter-in-law to London for the royal wedding. "Oh, yes, you have the shape of the head there," Her Majesty told me with a tremulous smile. She was beautifully gowned and bejeweled, so did she dress that way every day? "Nick will have the kettle and coal fire for you to melt wax on the morrow. And I have not forgotten that you shall have your glimpse of my younger children, so that you can copy noses and chins. I know I am asking a great deal of you when you begin to carve my brothers, of whom I have no portrait to show you, have no remembrance of them to share. . . ."

Her words drifted off; her clear gaze misted over under her furrowed brow. Suddenly she was not here, but in some distant memory or imagining, until she shook her head and stroked the cheek of her deceased daughter that I had carved, however yet roughly hewn and uncolored.

"I shall see you are paid each week, and I do understand you have another life and your own child, your Arthur," she said.

"Yes, Your Majesty—about that. When my family and fellow chandlers discover I am to be sent for on many days, I fear they will ferret out to where, and the false tale of Nick and his wife having lost a child will be found out. May I not say you admired the angel candle and are asking that I carve wedding gift candles for the Spanish bride's household— flowers, birds, and such?"

"Yes, perhaps a better idea, and the fact that it is a royal request will help protect you too. Tell them you are carving the roses of York and Lancaster and the pomegranate of Spain, for it is Catherine of Aragon's emblem and the symbol of fertility. New princes and princesses for the nursery soon, I pray," she added with a glance again at the blocks of wax. "Nicholas, you take good care of her for me," she threw over her shoulder as she departed as quickly and quietly as she had come.

"I shall, Your Grace," he said, though we were then alone, momentarily frozen in a bow and curtsy that seemed, suddenly, only for each other.

I soon had the dressing-down I had been dreading. I had delighted Arthur, Maud, and Gil with my story of carving candles at the palace, but Christopher came storming in at the shop's usual closing time that afternoon. I was on edge already. My back and neck hurt from reaching and bending, and my right hand was numb from handling knives, spoons, and spatulas. Indeed, I hated myself for lying to my son and kin, although the truth would have been even more remarkable than my fabrication. And if gossip flew about that the queen was yet tormented for the loss of her brothers, who had more right to the throne than the last and present king, I could be completely undone. Yet I managed to walk calmly around the counter to put it between Christopher and me and leaned against it to steady my knees.

He dared to lock the shop door behind him. He was red in the face, as if he had run miles. "By the rood, a little bird tells me you were not here when our artist *Signor* Firenze came by to set up the time for your first sitting!" Facing me across the counter, from his left hand he took the large ruby ring he had offered me twice for a betrothal and dropped it on one side of our large scales. The balance trays bounced slightly askew. "And," he added, "you rode off with a man. I'll not have you looking like a common woman, a doxy, not the woman I wish to wed! Others know I favor you, and they will think you have rejected me."

"I did ride to the palace this morn with a courtier and royal guard, and now have permission from the queen to explain why."

He gaped at me like a beached fish. "The queen. The queen? Leave off!"

"It is true. Yesterday she sent one of her ladies with that courtier to fetch me and asked me to carve candles for the new Spanish princess's wedding gifts. She desires to have them carved at the palace, a special, secret gift."

"Angel candles?"

"No, but finely decorated ones. I assured her that though I am, as a woman, not permitted to be a member of the Worshipful Guild of Wax Chandlers, they would understand and support my efforts, and I knew when I told one of the governors of the guild, who was my friend, that he—you—would respect her privacy in this matter."

He had not yet blinked. May the Lord forgive me—for I was already deep in lies, but I decided to push my great good luck even more. Not to request admittance to the guild, for I knew full well that only a few guilds, such as weavers, broiderers, and brewers, permitted female members. Besides, that plea would give Christopher another reason to insist how much he could do for me in wedlock.

But how I had yearned to be permitted to donate votives for the guild's secret, prestigious religious fraternity that worshiped in the crypt of St. Paul's Cathedral, below the very site of the mass to follow the royal wedding. Everyone knew a bounty of blessing befell anyone who contributed to the Guild of the Holy Name of Jesus. Christopher had been holding it over my head that if I would but accept the betrothal ring that weighed down my scales right before my nose, I could, through him, donate alms and benevolences in support of the rites of that guild.

"I'm afraid," I said to him, "that I told Her Majesty a bit of a lie. In speaking to her about the wedding at St. Paul's— and, of course, she knew our—your—guild is furnishing candles for that—I implied that I also made candles and gave alms for the Holy Name guild that met in the crypt there."

"Oh . . . ah, yes. I could care for that—you could be included. And why not suggest to her that the guild provide more candles for the prince and princess's gifts? I hear they will go to live at Ludlow Castle in Wales, where he had been before as Prince of Wales. Rainy, dreary, I hear—much light needed. Tell her—or I could go with you to suggest it—we could contribute candles for their Welsh castle. And, yes, yes, I repeat, I will see to it that your chandlery can donate to the secret rites of the Holy Name."

"She has given me a room in which to work at the palace, but she is very busy and I see her seldom. I can promise, though, to speak to her on the guild's behalf. I'm to come alone to the palace, though. And word about my carving there is not to go beyond the guild's governors."

"God as my judge, I can see to that. But the wax for it. Do you have enough good wax for the extra candles? Can I be of help there?"

"I do not know her source, but she has provided *cera bianca* for me. If it is not too much to ask, could you donate a bit of the vermilion you use to color sealing wax?"

"Red candles? Perhaps a Spanish custom, eh? Of course. You'll need a bit of Venice turpentine for the mix too. It's my chandlery's secret yellow-green resinous extract from larch trees. It's precious, but then so is this task you have been given—and so are you to me."

He picked up the ruby ring, and the scales bounced back to their balanced position. For once, I felt a bit of power over him. I was not so in thrall to his wishes.

"A partnership in all ways, my love?" he asked, extending the ring to me across the counter.

"I cannot promise that now," I said, no doubt a bit too hastily. Then, mayhap because all this had gone to my head, I added, "I hope the guild has decided on the distribution and pricing of the angel candles, since the queen owns and values one that brought me to her attention."

"Ah—oh, yes. But now that we can tell buyers that the queen quite favors that candle, I'm sure the guild's governors have set the price too low, so I will let you know of that soon. At close range, is our queen as beautiful as she looks from afar?"

"Beautiful and kind. A noble woman with deep loyalties beneath the crown and gowns and trappings of her power."

"I want you to wear this ring to the palace," he insisted, when I had hoped he was going to put it back on his own hand. "Not a betrothal ring then, but a promise of partnership."

"I can promise only that I will try to make you and the guild proud. And if you send *Signor* Firenze to me at this time on the morrow, I will be pleased to either sit for him or set a time to do so."

"I've arranged for him to paint you at my house, before that fine new oriole window for which I paid a pretty penny—lots of late-afternoon sun. As for angel candles, your angelic face, and our new motto of 'Truth Is Light'— how blessed I am to be a part of all this and in your life!"

It did prick my conscience again that truth and light were not things I had clung to today. Rather the old motto, "Loyalty Binds Me," fit better—and that had been the one suggested by our former king, who might have dispatched Her Majesty's brothers.

I cleared my throat. I decided I had argued and won enough today and would forgo complaining about how Christopher had cleverly maneuvered me to sit for the portrait at his house.

"I know," I told him, "that I am blessed to have this trust of the queen, as well as your support in my sitting for the guild's new coat of arms."

"I swear you will be in my arms too, and soon," he vowed as he took his leave, backing a few steps toward the door first, as if I were the queen herself. I reckoned he could not wait to rush to the other guild governors with his news.

Somehow his play on words pleased me not half so much as did Nick Sutton's. I knew I would have to confess my lies to the priest before I dared to place one candle on the altar of the Holy Name of Jesus, our savior from Satan's wiles. Yet how sweet it was that the queen's name had saved me, for now at least, from Christopher's demands.

CHAPTER THE FOURTH

Queen Elizabeth of York

$\mathcal{A}$t midmorn, my husband summoned me to his withdrawing chamber. I could but pray nothing was amiss with the wedding preparations or the elaborate plans for the triumphal entry of Arthur's bride into London. And, by the Virgin's veil, I hoped there were not more storms to keep the princess from our shores, for she had been forced once to return to Spain after setting out, and we had not yet been informed of her safe landing.

I nodded and smiled to curtsying and bowing courtiers clustered in the presence chamber. My lord's councilors were huddled here, so my stomach twisted tighter. Ever since the troubles in my father's reign, when he was once even driven from England and had to fight his way back, I dreaded dangerous dynastic news.

In the sixteen years my lord husband had sat upon the throne, two insurrections and much murmuring had proved there was yet opposition to the house of Tudor after years of Plantagenet rule. Some who had been defeated at Bosworth Field had not given up the fight, and we feared that after several years of silence from those who had escaped capture, something dreadful was brewing. We knew full well we still had enemies lurking at home and abroad who would go to great lengths to topple the Tudor throne.

So my lord husband's claim to the kingdom must be shored up by continued vigilance and, however tight the purse strings, by a grand show of public events such as this coming wedding. I'd been praying for hours on my knees that, especially with the open-air wedding and parades, naught would befall any of us.

I'd also preferred, since our Arthur was but fifteen and his Spanish bride barely a year older, that the marriage or at least their living together be delayed. But that could not be. We needed the security of many heirs, and England needed every national foreign friendship we could forge.

The yeomen guards swept open the double doors for me, and, leaving my ladies behind, I entered. To my delight, Henry had plucked Arthur from his strenuous regimen of studies. They sat together, both behind the large writing table. Arthur's face, as ever, lit to see me, and he stood to bow and then came to me for a hug. Ah, how much he resembled my father, whom the people had so loved. I held him to me one moment too long. He would soon be a married man—indeed, he had already been wed by proxy.

Arthur had been born before the proper time, just eight months after our marriage. I suppose the tongues of those who deemed Henry Tudor a usurping blackguard wagged on that, though it was the truth that our heir arrived early, not that we bedded before our vows. My firstborn had ever been a bit frail, and oft looked either too pale and solemn or too rosy-cheeked and feverish, like now, but I knew he was excited by his coming nuptials. I ever carried in my small pomander a copy of the sweet letter he had written to his future bride, because it always bucked me up. In a world where royal marriages had naught to do with love, I prayed that the two of them would find great affection for each other and not just duty and resignation.

"Good day, my dear lord," I greeted the king as he too came around the table. At age forty-four, he was nine years older than I. Lean, gaunt, and tall, he had to bend to kiss my cheek. His prominent nose dominated his small mouth and narrow, gray eyes. He'd taken to wearing day caps, since his once-reddish hair was graying and thinning. Even in our most intimate moments, he had ever seemed guarded and watchful. But he hid an aggressive nature; he was prepared to keep his lofty place by pouncing on his prey and tearing it limb from limb if he must. Still, he had ever been good and kind to me. We were loyal and loving to each other for our children's and the kingdom's sake and not only for our own.

"My dearest, we wanted you to know that when we hear the *Infanta* has safely arrived on our shores, we—Arthur and the council too—intend to greet her," His Majesty informed me, and Arthur nodded.

"But we have written Ferdinand and Isabella that we would receive her and her entourage here in our capital," I reminded him.

"And so we shall. But we both want a good look at her,

to be certain she is all they say. We shall trust other kingdoms only to a point, eh, Arthur?"

"Trust but verify," the boy insisted, and I wondered whether he'd heard that from his brilliant tutors or at his father's knee. No one said more for a moment, as Arthur coughed into his hand and then his handkerchief. He was ever prone to suffer from drafts.

"But," I said when Arthur had recovered, "it could dismay the princess to have all of you suddenly riding in, and I hear she goes veiled in public." Actually, I did not want Arthur riding out in cold weather or to be out where he and the king could be attacked by some lurking enemy. "Will you snatch away her veil and examine her like a new horse or a book—even inside its cover?" I argued.

"You'll not gainsay us on this, my dear," the king said. "Then we will return to London to await her arrival, but I must be certain this is the woman to bear our name and our grandchildren. We are taking a full contingent of courtiers and guards. I just thought you should know, that's all." He kissed me on the other cheek, as if that were my cue to leave.

"I do long to see her, Mother," Arthur put in. "And Father and I are going hunting this morn to make the lagging time hie itself apace."

I knew better than to protest that too. I nodded and hugged him again, even though the king had warned me not to coddle Arthur. Henry, our second son, liked my kisses and cuddling too; I know he did. Well, to have a mother as formidable as did my husband—she yet ruled the domestic roost here at the palace. I could see why my lord was not used to my being sweet and soft to my sons. My husband's father had died before his birth, and he had been mostly reared by his beloved, stern uncle Jasper Tudor. So when his mother, then remarried to the powerful Lord Stanley, came back into his life to support his claim to the throne, he tried to make up for years of separation by giving her too much power over my own family. Or so it seemed to me. Though I never said so, I vowed my mother-in-law was a demanding, strident she-wolf even now.

My son and husband bade me farewell again and went off in a flurry of talk about shooting roebucks. I could hear the men of the court clattering behind them across the oaken floors to mount their horses in the courtyard. *Bought like a new horse or a book*—my own words rang in my ears. I glanced down at my lord's writing table and saw that a book of household expenses lay open there. He had again been toting up sums, records, numbers. How much my own father had loved books, but ones with stories and fables. The only fiction Henry Tudor favored was about Welsh kings of his own heritage, or of King Arthur, for whom he had named our heir.

I sighed and gazed out the window, which was half covered with thick ivy now gone bloodred in its autumn hue. One of the happiest days of my young life was when my sire, the king, took me on his big horse to the new printing shop of William Caxton in the city. People cheered us all the way. Then there were no worries of assassins or revolts. At the shop, Caxton showed us how a book could be reproduced in many copies by a big stamping machine without one stroke of a man's pen. My lord father bought two books that day, and I cradled them to me in the big saddle with his arm around me as we rode back to the palace, I so proud to be his child, his beloved firstborn, though I knew I was a female and would never rule. We could not wait to show our treasures to my mother, the beautiful Elizabeth Woodville, whom he had chosen for love and not for power.

I shook my head to clear my thoughts and started back for my own apartments. Four of my ladies fell in behind me, chattering about the coming wedding. When we reached my privy apartments, I bade them stay at their embroidery frames in my withdrawing room, saying I wanted to read and pray alone. That was true and, as I closed them out of my bedchamber, I leaned against the door and took out Arthur's letter, which he had written over two years ago to Princess Catherine. He had given me a copy of it, asking me to look it over for "proper wording to show my respect and love."

It was addressed to "my dearest spouse," for he had written it after their proxy marriage, and once that was accomplished, only the physical consummation of their bodies was needed to complete the contract. He wrote at first that he fancied he embraced her, though she was then still living at the fabled Moorish palace called the Alhambra in Spain.

My favorite part of the epistle read: *I cannot tell you what an earnest desire I feel to see Your Highness, and how vexatious to me is this procrastination about your coming. Let it be hastened, that the love conceived between us and the wished-for joys may reap their proper fruit.* Their proper fruit, I thought, from the young woman with the fertile pomegranate for her personal badge. Their proper fruit, like Henry and my own sons, like my two lost brothers had been to my parents.

I stuffed the letter back in my silken pomander. I must wipe my tears and blow my nose, and then I would call upon the wax woman and my stalwart Nick in my hidden carving chamber. With the king away and my mother-in-law keeping a vigil today in the abbey with our daughter, her namesake, Margaret, praying for the coming safe arrival of the Spanish princess, it would be a good time to introduce Varina Westcott to my clever Henry and my little Mary.

Mistress Varina Westcott

"So, both Her Majesty and I have losses to mourn," I told Nick as I brushed on melted wax to a make delicate raised eyebrow for the effigy of Princess Elizabeth, eyebrows I would have to either dye and fuse or have someone paint. Named for her mother and grandmother, the young child had emerged from beneath my knives and smoothing spoons—slender shoulders, neck, now her face.

Despite the heaviness of this mazelike palace and the sadness that hung in this small stone chamber, the loss of my Edmund was somehow eased by my work, and I had shared that with Nick. Tears clumped my eyelashes together and blurred my vision as I had told him about my son's death. Indeed, I would not have been here had not the queen lost children too. Misery loves company, the old saying went, but it was more than that. Despite the chasms in gender and rank, I had found a commonality of heart between Her Majesty and me.

"Though I have no children, I too have lost loved ones to cruel fates," Nick said suddenly, when I thought he might shift the subject. "My father and uncle died opposing this king at Bosworth Field, and my older brother died in the Battle of Stoke."

"The Battle of Stoke?" I repeated, feeling the fool that I could not place that event. So—this man had suffered too. He'd been watching me and talking more today. Mayhap it was my telling him of my deepest wound that had made him share the same.

"Yes, Stoke," he said. "Two years after this king took the crown at Bosworth Field, Stoke was fought in June of 1487 in Nottinghamshire near my ancestral home. Do you remember hearing of the uprising in favor of a young pretender, Lambert Simnel? Tudor enemies were trying to pass him off as Richard, one of the princes in the Tower, saying the two boys had not been killed but rather escaped."

I had walked several steps toward Nick in the small chamber. I could see his nostrils flare in repressed anger and the pulse beating at the side of his throat. I swayed slightly toward him before I caught myself and stepped back, but how I yearned to put my arms around him.

"I warrant," I said, my voice catching, "that I was too young to remember that."

"Then let me tell you how it was," he said, his voice crisp and cold. "At the Battle of Bosworth Field, where my father and uncle died fighting against this king's forces, their commander, Francis, Lord Lovell, simply disappeared. The next year, Lovell led a poorly organized revolt which was put down, and again he escaped. The next year, Lovell led rebels against the royal forces at Stoke in a stronger effort, where my brother Stephen fought and died at his side, and still again Lovell disappeared. His body was never found, though I heard the king had men searching for it day and night among the wounded and fallen. Later, some said they saw Lovell fleeing the fighting by swimming the River Trent. Some said he escaped on horseback. Some said he vanished into thin air."

I gasped, and when Nick paused, frowning, I said, "Rumors. People always love rumors, the stranger, the better."

He seemed not to heed what I said, but plunged on. "Lovell became a damned legend—a heaven-rescued hero to some, a vengeful ghost to others. But where did he go? He hated the Tudors with a passion, so the fear is that he will try again, return again. Three times he's evaded the king's justice, and twice he left my family dead in his wake. But all that mattered to me after the Battle of Stoke was that my brother and hero, Stephen, was dead, and all the menfolk of my once proud family were gone—I alone survived."

I leaned forward and put my right hand over his clenched left fist. Lightning jolted up my arm as he opened that fist and clasped my hand. I almost winced at his strength. We seemed to hang suspended for a moment as his gaze, previously distant, as if he imagined the battle scenes, took me in. I vow I could feel his grip and devouring stare even when he let me go and I stepped back a bit from him.

"I understand your grief and loss," I said, my voice not my own. Our gazes stayed locked until, in the screaming silence between us, I forced myself back to my task. I had to continually dip my small horsehair brush into heated wax set in a dish over the copper kettle on the rack above the coals, because I could not trust my trembling hand to form the other waxen eyebrow. I could feel his eyes yet upon me, as hot as the coals.

"I was bitter toward everyone for years," Nick went on, when I thought he would say no more. He sighed and slumped onto the bench with his back against the stone wall. "Bitter against my dear grandmother, with whom I lived in dire poverty after our ruination; against the Tudors, even when they took me in and gave me a chance to earn my way—my family's way—back. Especially bitter against that devil Lovell. He deserted his men, and 'tis said—rumors on the wind, Varina—that he and his minions still work covertly in Europe and in England to overthrow the Tudors, that he remains a dyed-in-the-wool, pro–King Richard Yorkist. I am waiting for the day . . ."

His voice trailed off, but it had been so menacing that I turned to stare at him again, my brush in the air. "I am waiting for the day," he repeated, speaking through gritted teeth, hitting his fists upon spread knees, "when the king will hearken to my petitions and give me leave to hunt Lovell down like the damned dog he is!"

Petitions? Was that what he'd been bending his blond head over for hours at a stretch? Such a thirst for revenge was outside the realm of my thoughts or understanding.

"I owe revenge and restoration not only to those I lost but also to my grandmother," he went on, his voice almost a whisper. "She yet lives in sad straits but for coin I send her. My family's misplaced loyalty cost us our pride and property near Nottingham, and I mean to have both back—for myself and for her who reared me and has sacrificed so much. And who knows how many years she has left, and if I cannot . . ."

We were both startled when a voice—the queen's—said from the hallway, "I am waiting for that day too, and other retribution for certain heinous acts. Some say—you may have heard, Nicholas—that Francis Lovell could have been a party"—she put a hand on each side of the doorway as if to brace herself—"to the disappearance of my brothers, to help prop up his liege lord King Richard the Third."

Nick jumped to his feet, and I curtsied. "I did hear that about Lovell and his ilk, Your Majesty," Nick said, rising from his bow. "But, of course, there have also been other names whispered in connection with that dire deed."

"Such as?" she demanded, stopping in midstride and rounding on him. He looked surprised at her vehemence.

"It was said King Richard's henchman, Sir James Tyrell, knew something of it," Nick told her. "But he must have had his name cleared, since he was one of the few Yorkists pardoned and he now serves His Majesty. I know he's been a loyal servant ever since, so I took it for rumor. I hear Tyrell's still in France, guarding a fort in Calais for England."

"Yes, but I believe His Majesty has summoned him back for the royal wedding. Ah, we shall see—and I am pleased to see this beautiful carving."

The queen bent to peer closely at my work. I slanted Nick a glance and saw that he stood silent, his eyes narrowed, his lips pressed together as if to halt himself from saying more.

Her Majesty glanced at the block of wax that I had been carving, and she said, her voice quiet, "We shall speak no more of these things today or in this joyous wedding season. Both of you, come with me. We shall visit the royal nursery, for my youngest, Mary, is at her lessons there, and Prince Henry, since his watchful grandmother is not here today, is with her."

"Prince Henry is blessed to have his grandmother near," Nick said, but I saw he missed the royal frown sent his way for saying that, and I knew not why. I hastily removed my canvas work apron and, picking cooled wax from beneath my fingernails, fell in behind the queen. Nick followed, and I could only hope that Her Majesty had not overheard him claiming how bitter he was yet about his losses from his family's stand against the Tudors.

It seemed strange to walk the wide, adorned hallways and rooms of the palace proper, for Nick had always brought me in through the warrens of the servants' realm. Two of the queen's ladies trailed us, Sibil Wynn and Sarah Middleton. But the queen left everyone but me outside the guarded door as she led the way into a spacious, sunny room.

Two ladies and a man, the latter evidently a tutor, leaped to their feet and genuflected to Her Majesty, as did a beautiful blond girl of about five years, no doubt the princess Mary, baby of the royal brood, and a tall, robust-looking redhead, who must be Prince Henry, around age ten. I curtsied to both children. While I stood back, during greetings and introductions—I as Mistress Varina Westcott, an artist—and hugs from the queen for her offspring, I observed both of the young, vibrant royal faces.

Though I had seen Prince Arthur in procession through

London's streets, I had never beheld the second son, Henry, Duke of York. The two brothers seemed as different as night and day, the Prince of Wales, unfortunately, being the night. This boy emanated strength of body and character, whereas Arthur was so thin he seemed frail. The little princess was one of the prettiest children I had ever seen.

"Mistress Westcott is an artist who works in wax," the queen told them. "She carves angel faces in candles, and I believe I shall have her create ones with my well-favored and well-behaved children, so I wanted her to see you. I shall expect you to act like perfect angels hereafter," she added with a little laugh that seemed to light the room even more.

"On my candle," Mary piped up with a wide grin that flaunted her loss of baby teeth, "I should like to be smiling, but not with the gaps in my mouth showing, if you please, mistress."

"And," Henry said, his voice steady and sure, "I would like to be ahorse and—"

"But you are a prince and not a horse," his little sister interrupted.

"No, poppet," he said with a frown that silenced her, "*sitting* on a horse in my first set of armor. Mistress Westcott, make it a tall candle that will burn with a big flame—if you please," he added with a glance at his mother's face. But the order definitely was to me. "And, my lady mother," he added, hands on his hips, "I think it unfair that Father and Arthur went hunting without me, even if Arthur is the bridegroom and will be king someday!"

I kept quiet but observed each child intently, noses,

chins—and personality and behavior. If I really were to carve candles of these two, Mary's would be sweetly scented and Henry's would be boldly burning at both ends.

"*Signora, bene, bene!*" Roberto Firenze, the Italian painter, told me again, this time as I was finally allowed to move from the pose I had been holding for far too long in the upstairs solar of Christopher's fine house.

The artist was most adamant about catching me in the late-afternoon light. So far I was not only intrigued by his rendering of me from the tip of my head to my hips, but also enchanted. Although he did not ask that I kneel, I was doing so in the painted sketch he'd done so far. There I was upon a wreath of pretty posies with a garland in my hand—none of the beautiful blooms were actually present in this room—with my hair flowing free down my back and my face turned slightly to the right. It felt strange to pose without a widow's cover over my hair, as if I were a maiden or a bride again. With his magical oil paints, in place of the green gown I actually wore he had created a tight-sleeved gown of cloth of gold lined with ermine, the fur of royalty. By his talented hand I was not only a virgin again but also a queen! And more than that, for he told me that many who saw the portrait would think of the blessed Madonna.

Christopher, however, was beginning to remind me of Her Majesty, in that he darted in and out of the room to study the results. I was hoping to be left alone with the man he called *Maestro*, so I could question him about painting or coloring wax. Finally, here was my chance, for Christopher had made a grand exit to oversee the packing of crates of candles to be sent to three places the Spanish princess was expected to stay on her journey toward London when she landed. With much ado, Christopher had twice announced the places to me and *Signor* Firenze: Dogmersfield in Hampshire, a royal manor in Berkshire, and Lambeth Palace across the Thames from London.

As I sipped a glass of claret with the wiry, short artist, I said, "I wonder if you could give me some advice on either painting wax or coloring it with paints. I've been looking over my father's notes for such. I have happy memories of watching him prepare herbal dyes and then writing down his concoctions for him, but it is hardly the season to be finding such things as the fresh leaves of alder, saffron, or betony that I would need."

"Ah, *si*, I have painted wax figures in my native Firenze. The ones we spoke of before that your father saw on his journey, all those life-size wax effigies wigged and painted standing close to ze altar at the church of Orsanmichele, *chiesa della santissima*, many of the great family of Cosimo de' Medici. Almost all of ze figures are men, *signora*, ze important men who want to buy their way to heaven. The power of seeing that, dead men yet standing, I cannot tell you, but that is why your papa tell you that and you remember, *si*, because he so impressed by ze waxworks. Did you ever hear of Caesar's stab wounds?"

I stopped drinking the red claret. "Caesar's stab wounds? In a painting, you mean?"

"Painted on a waxen effigy, is true, is true! After he was assassinated in ze senate chamber in *Roma*, his friends hired a wax *artiste* like yourself—only a man, I wager—to make

63

Caesar's exact form with all twenty-three bleeding wounds painted crimson. Put on display in ze public square, ze effigy create a riot with ze people. The *Romani* revolted and burned ze chamber where he was slain! Oh, ze power of art, of paint and wax!"

"Yes, I know," I said, trying to wipe the image of bloody wounds from my mind's eye.

"Oh, but you ask about painting and tinting wax," he plunged on, his dark mustache bobbing with his words when he became excited. "*Signora* Varina, how you use paints to dye wax is leach out some oil from paint on parchment or cloth overnight, then mix the remnants with hot wax."

I nodded. If the bit of vermilion, larch, and oil Christopher had given me today didn't work, I would try to buy some paint from this man. And if that was a lost cause, if I could only trust that Roberto Firenze would not talk too much and tell the queen's secret, I would suggest to her that he paint her effigies. That is, if my work suited her. If I could create four children I had never seen, if everything I was trying to balance in secret, including my growing interest in Nick Sutton—if, if, if!—did not just all blow up in my face.

CHAPTER THE FIFTH

"Thank the Lord, you are here," John Barker said the moment I entered the shop where the two barber-surgeons were bent over, embalming a corpse. John was a skilled embalmer; he had tended to both Will's and Edmund's bodies. "'Tis bad business," he went on, "a death just before all the royal wedding festivities. And I was expecting your sister with the wax cloth."

Thomas Merridew, a wealthy haberdasher, had died suddenly the day before the Spanish princess was to make her grand entry into London. I could hear muted sobs and wailing from the upper floor of the Merridew house. Even his shop, where they had laid him out on the counter for embalming, was draped in black cloth.

"You might know," John went on, "that his family and guild will have to postpone his burial until after the wedding three days hence. Death may abide for no man, but the king has decreed that funerals and grieving are not welcome now, and what this king decrees, he gets," he said with a small shudder. His helper, another barber-surgeon whose name I could not recall, did not speak a word or look up from his task of dressing the body.

Indeed, the city was shivering with excitement as well as a biting November wind. My sister, Maud, usually delivered the wax-impregnated shrouds to the Worshipful Company of Barber-surgeons, the guild that prepared corpses for the grave and of which John Barker was an influential member, but Maud was ailing with pain from her monthly menses. And, sad to say, ailing because once again she had not conceived a child.

Today was Thursday, November the eleventh, and the royal wedding would be on the fourteenth. This was also the first day in weeks, but for the Sabbaths, that I had not spent hours at the palace, working on the effigies for the queen. I was grateful for the break, but truth be told, I missed Nick.

"Will you help us wrap him, then?" Master Barker asked as I stepped closer.

I was not squeamish around a dead body, for I had seen many in various stages of preparation for the grave, but I did not wish to spend much time at this task today. I was to meet Christopher and several other chandlers at St. Paul's to help oversee the positioning of the two hundred and twenty tall tapers for Princess Catherine's thanksgiving service. If we were to have sunshine then, the light would be suitable inside the vast stone cathedral, but if it were cloudy like today, we must have banks and boards of candles, let alone the ones on the altar.

I carefully unrolled the three ells of Holland cloth that

we had soaked in wax at the chandlery. It clung to the corpse, kept any fluids in, and, at least people liked to think, it kept the mold and cold of the grave out. It took real skill to imbue the wheat-hued flax with just enough wax at the right temperature, to stretch it straight until it dried, and then to store it so it would not crack.

As they rolled and lifted the body, I wrapped and tucked the cloth around it, fitting it snugly, keeping the arms to the torso and the legs together, tending carefully to the corpse's head. Some families wanted the faces kept unwrapped until the coffin was closed, but farewells were best said before embalming.

I was grateful the barber-surgeons had done their work before I came today, for they were not only healers of the ailing through bleedings and cuttings. Unless it was plague times when many died, or even during the sweat disease such as had carried off my family, each body buried in the city must be eviscerated and the soft organs of the abdomen and chest removed. Sometimes the organs were buried with the body in an urn. In the case of important people, the organs might be interred elsewhere.

The corpse was washed inside and out and often stuffed with herbs and spices, depending on the wealth of the family. Major blood vessels might be seared before the body was wrapped in layers of our waxed cloth, most oft called cerements, for the Latin word *cera* meant wax.

Even today, by the saints, this task brought back too many bad memories, so I was grateful Maud had lately taken it on. With Will's and Gil's help, I had wrapped my parents' and brother's bodies; Gil and Maud had not let me help with Will's. But Edmund's little frame—I had wrapped Edmund and then held him in my arms until they pulled him away. . . .

"The other bad thing is," John Barker was saying—he ever looked for problems—"that Their Majesties plan to view the princess's passing by with her entourage tomorrow from the window of the haberdasher William Geoffrey in Cheapside, and he's the one who will head this man's burial procession. Wrap him good now, because he's going to have to wait for burial at least until the day after the wedding, and then mayhap in secret, since there are to be jousts and revels at Westminster for several days, and all that following the banquet at Baynard's Castle. Physicians and barber-surgeons are to stand at the ready lest any knights are hurt at the tilt rail."

I said naught about those festivities, though Nick had told me much of them and had promised I might have a glimpse. I accepted my payment from John and Clement— yes, that's right; that was his name—and took my leave. This house was not far from Walbrook, which was hard by St. Mary Abchurch, where my family was buried. I had visited their graves frequently after each funeral, then less often, the same with even Will's and Edmund's, because I could not bear the pain. But today I would go, then hie myself to St. Paul's.

My parish church was situated on a slight rise in the southwest section of Walbrook Ward. With its turfy graveyard curled around it on three sides, the old gray stone building abutted Abchurch Lane and Candlewick Street. My people were buried on the south side, for by tradition the north was the domain of the devil, the burial site for unbaptized infants, suicides, and criminals. Tall, thick yews hunched over the mossy stones, for those trees were evergreens, to remind us of eternal life, and their red berries to recall Christ's blood shed for us. I passed through the stone wall, using the lych-gate with its roof-covered seats where the bearers of coffins oft rested out of foul weather.

The gate creaked, even as I closed it carefully. Though I had not been aware of him before, I saw a man I did not recognize coming close behind me. He nodded, entered also, and, with his hooded black cloak flapping in the fitful breeze and snagging on his sword, he walked around the church to the north side. No one else was in sight in the graveyard, though it was midmorn and others passed by, so I had no fear.

I slowly approached the single, small headstone that marked the Westcott plot: WCOTT, it read, for many of the smaller stones had shortenings of the names. The one marking the Waxman graves where my parents and brother lay had praying hands and WXMN. In faith, I supposed it hardly mattered how earthly records read, for human bones might lie here, but their spirits had long since flown away.

So why could I not let Edmund go from my thoughts? I agonized as I knelt by his grave. And why was Her Majesty yet haunted by her losses, especially those of her brothers who died long ago? Though if they were indeed murdered, of course, she could yet seek justice or revenge.

Despite the past summer season, the grassy turf above my child's coffin had not yet regrown. I had thought that carving the queen's effigies of her children had helped me to pass beyond grieving, but kneeling there, I felt the crushing weight of loss again. How I wished I had Nick to listen to or talk to now—just to know that he was near and—

"I beg your pardon, mistress, but you seem familiar with this area."

I sucked in a sharp breath, then steadied myself and rose quickly to my feet. It was he who had come in the gate behind me, and I had not heard a sound of his approach.

"Yes, sadly. Are you looking for a particular grave?"

"I am. I'm from the country, in town for the great events. I believe my cousin, last name of Stoker, is buried here. Have you seen such a grave? And permit me to introduce myself— Alan Bainton from near Colchester."

"I'm sorry, but I know of no one by the name Stoker, even in this parish," I said, deciding not to give him my name in return.

Alan Bainton was tall and thin, but he emanated a certain strength. His hood, pulled up against the wind that snatched at our garments, shadowed his face with its grizzled beard, but his aquiline nose and dark eyes were prominent. Though it was hard to tell because of his hood, he seemed to have silvery hair. I could not guess his age. As if his throat were sore, his voice was hoarse, almost a whisper, but strangely, it commanded my attention. He was attired in plain garb but for his shined boots, which flaunted spurs, though I had not seen that he had a horse when he entered.

"Perhaps it is my mistake to search here," he said.

"The other parish church is St. Swithin's, just down that way," I told him, pointing. I needed to leave now. I should head for St. Paul's.

"I will try that and inquire within of both priests," he said. "I have a very ill cousin and will want to bury him with the other."

He wore riding gloves, ones that also were too fine for the rest of his garb. He must have money then. "If you need votive candles or waxen shrouds, my family owns the Westcott Chandlery on Candlewick Street, at the sign with the blue candle. It's an area of chandleries, but our sign has the blue color," I repeated.

He made a stiff little bow. "I shall remember that, and I thank you for your present and future assistance." The moment he turned to go out through the gate, I realized I had been holding my breath. Once he was in the street, I hurried out the gate and stretched my strides toward St. Paul's. I looked back once to be sure he was heading in the direction I had indicated, but he had vanished.

Much ado at St. Paul's Cathedral had already begun when I arrived. Outside, the huge, elevated wooden platform on which the marriage service itself would be solemnized had been completed, and common folk buzzed around its base like bees. Inside the cool cathedral, I hurried through the nave, where wooden seating had been erected for the nobility, then through the choir toward the high altar. Christopher and Robin Longfellow, head of the wax chandlers' guild, seemed to be giving directions, as others I recognized scurried about. The best beeswax tapers we London chandleries had to offer were being set in or spiked to wood-and-iron supports called candle beams, and the pulley ropes that hoisted them aloft were being tested.

"Ah, Varina, my dearest," Christopher called, and motioned me over. "If you could review the tapers in the candelabrum on both sides of the altar—be sure each stands erect—that would be a great help."

"Our lady of the new coat of arms," Robin welcomed me with a nod and a smile. He had looked as if he would kiss me in greeting, but with a glance at Christopher had obviously changed his mind. Our voices echoed even when we spoke in whispers here. "I've taken a peek at it—almost done, though I plan to petition for some sort of heraldic beasts to be added too, perhaps unicorns, appropriate with the maiden of the painting."

"Did you not think that with the new 'Truth Is Light' motto," I said, "the lady should be holding a candle or lantern?"

"If beholders of it don't know it's our company's crest, that just shows their ignorance," Robin said huffily, and Christopher nodded, though he also gave me a quick hand motion that said silently, *Get busy!*

So I did, scrutinizing and aligning the tall tapers near the high altar, where the royal couple would join hands and lives—and countries. Nick had told me that Prince Arthur spoke no Spanish and Princess Catherine no English, so until they learned each other's languages, scholarly Latin would have to do between them. How many spouses, I mused, had problems really talking, even when the couple both spoke in the same tongue? Will and I had had our share of small disagreements, though he had almost always won in the end. Sometimes, when I was fretting over being scolded or overruled, I used to think to myself that I would choose my own husband next time, one who would heed my thoughts a bit more—and that was hardly Christopher Gage.

When I finished my assigned task, I stood against a pillar that joined another in a sweeping arch overhead, and felt very small. I planned to take my son and, with Gil and Maud, join the throngs in the street to catch a glimpse of the princess's parade tomorrow and then to find a place from which to view the ceremony itself on Sunday.

"Varina," Christopher said, appearing suddenly at my side, "since no one is below in the crypt, would you like to go down with me to see the chapel of the guild of the Holy Name of Jesus? I promised you might donate some of its votives, and I shall try to keep that promise—but only if you would make a certain promise to me."

He took my hand, and I did not protest. I would much rather see the chapel than discuss the possibility of our union, and I should have paid better attention to his words. Granted, I saw clearly that marriage to this man would be the best business decision for my family, my shop, my own prestige. Yet my own stubbornness held me back.

He led me away from the altar where the choir joined the great nave, and, looking around, evidently to see that no one was watching, he unlocked a small wooden door with a rounded top. He took a lighted lantern from a huge hook just inside and, holding it aloft so both of us could see the narrow, curving steps, led the way down.

I was impressed and intrigued. Down, around we went. I prayed silently that we would not be going to a small chamber, for these stairway walls seemed to close in upon me. The stone stairs were worn to grooves by generations of feet, and someone had swept the staircase clear of dirt and cobwebs. At least it was not dark below, for wan light greeted us. Was a guard kept here?

Yet when the stairway narrowed even more, I hesitated and slowed.

"What is it?" he asked, turning around and looking up at me. The shadows on his face from his lantern made him look spectral.

"I just . . . Lately, small, enclosed places make me anxious."

"Nonsense. The chapel itself is domed and the crypt beyond is vast. It has some ancient burials and monuments, but that usage had been halted of late. I am with you, Varina. There is naught to fear."

I did so want to see this place where the prestigious religious guild connected to the Worshipful Guild of Wax Chandlers met. I had concocted a theory, however whimsical, that if I could provide votives for the altar here, even pray within its realms, the Lord might ease my mind over Edmund's loss. Had He not already bestowed blessings upon me with my duties at the palace, memorializing lost children for our beloved queen?

Though the temperature was merely cool and seemed constant down here, my teeth chattered and my pulse pounded. Then, in a brighter burst of light—from four lanterns someone must keep burning—we stood in the chapel of the guild of the Holy Name of Jesus.

It was deserted, silent—as a tomb. But it boasted wall hangings, padded seats on eight wooden benches with kneelers, and a painted triptych behind the ornate altar with its golden crucifix. "Come," Christopher said, and, putting his lantern down, he recaptured my hand and led me forward.

For a moment I felt lost in the beauty of it all, the stunning richness, yet the delicate details. Behind the crucifix, painted on the triptych, were soaring angels filling the sky over the humble manger in Bethlehem. Amazing angels with gilded wings and halos and shimmering skirts soared, holding harps and golden trumpets. Lost in my thoughts and prayers, I did not protest as Christopher pulled me down to kneel at the prie-dieu before the altar.

"In this holy place," he said, his voice a whisper, "I ask you, Varina Waxman Westcott, for the fourth and last time if you will be my wife."

That jolted me from the realms of reverie. He had the ruby ring off his finger again and was holding it up between us as if it were a sacrifice. The stone glinted bloodred in reflected light.

"Above us at the high altar," he went on when I kept silent, "Prince Arthur will wed his Princess Catherine, and I likewise ask you to be a helpmeet to me. Will you not make that sacred vow here, before the Lord, before these angels you so like to carve—and so much will be given you?"

He meant this for the last time then, the proposal here. Was it truly now or never with him? If I turned him down, would he become my enemy?

"Varina, wear my ring, for I wear my heart on my sleeve for you."

"This . . . this finality is so sudden. I admire and respect you, but cannot you give me more time?"

"Sudden? I've been on bended knee for months! Will's been dead a year, and you know he would want the best for you, Arthur, and the Westcott Chandlery. And that means, whether we talk business or hearts, an alliance with me."

"I know."

"Do you? Yet you dither like the weakest of your sex, Eve wanting the fatal apple and the tree of knowledge when she should have trusted Adam and obeyed God."

"And I would be obeying God to wed you?"

"Must you argue like a lawyer? St. Paul said 'tis best to marry, and 'tis the natural way of things."

"If you truly want what is best for me, you will give me just a bit longer. To sort out some things."

"Wed me and I will help you sort them out! You must stop clinging to your grief over Edmund, for I will give you sons to take his place, make you forget him."

I thought I said, "Never!" but I must have said it only inwardly, for he plunged on.

"You need a man in your life to tell you which way to turn, lest you wander from the path."

Wander from the path—the temptations of Eve and my weak sex. Yet I dared to dream, to desire someone else, to think I could control my own shop and perhaps just a bit of my own life.

"How much more time will you need to decide?" he asked, jamming the ruby ring back on his own finger. "And if I give you so much as one fortnight more, my patience, when I am not a patient man, must convince you how much I want you—esteem your favor—and is that not love?"

"Until yule," I blurted. Surely, I thought, I would be

nearly finished with the effigies then, and my time at the palace near the queen and with Nick would be over soon after. "Until yule, for winter is a good enough time for weddings."

"Then we shall seal that bargain," he said, reaching over to clasp my chin with his beringed left hand. He kissed me hard, heavily. It had once been comforting to be mastered thus by Will in our bed. Yet it dismayed me that I yet did not feel the sweeping rush—like the swoop and soar of those angels over our heads—as when Nick Sutton merely looked at me.

Ah, more fool I, I thought as I followed my disgruntled suitor up the twisting stairs to the real world again.

CHAPTER THE SIXTH

*S*inging and strumming a harp, the angel descended from above our heads. The cheering crowd hushed, and I could clearly hear Catherine of Aragon say something in Spanish. I stood on my tiptoes until my legs cramped to see her as her entourage paused in the street for a pageant, this one presented by the powerful grocers' guild.

Ah, we had been wise to stand here waiting for two hours, even amidst the elbowing, jostling crowd. Arthur had begged to see the pageant with the red Welsh dragon and the painted canvas castle, but I had taken him there yesterday to see it being built, because I knew we'd never fight our way that far through the throngs today. The beast had even belched smoke while we had watched, so Arthur had been as enthralled with that as I was now with this flying angel.

As our future princess and queen had entered the city across London Bridge, we had heard the ovations swell. We, who knew her route, could tell exactly where she was, and word of that spread through the crowd packed in the narrow streets like herring in a barrel of brine. We heard her welcomes as she turned down Fenchurch Street to Cornhill, then to Cheapside, where, beneath the Eleanor Cross, she was formally welcomed by the lord mayor of London before proceeding toward St. Paul's for her Thanksgiving service celebrating her safe delivery here in England. How I wished I could await her there, but only the governors of the Worshipful Guild of Wax Chandlers were in the cathedral today to light needed tapers.

Fortunately, the princess rode not in a litter but on a brightly bedecked mount, so we could all see her. Maud and I—Gil, too, who had Arthur on his shoulders—gaped at the fantastical costumes of the *Infanta* and her Spanish courtiers. Though, as we'd expected, their garb was adorned with exquisite goldsmith's work and bold embroidery, their skirts and sleeves were huge and bell shaped, so foreign-looking to us English of the draped gowns and close-fitted sleeves. Then too, the princess wore a little hat with a flat crown and a wide brim, like a cardinal's. She was short and seemed nearly swallowed by her costume.

I'd heard she always wore a veil in public, but not today, for she showed her pretty, plump face framed by two huge coils of hair covering her ears. More than once, folks in the crowd whispered that her fair complexion, red-gold hair, and blue eyes were the heritage of her royal English great-grandmother, a Plantagenet. It made us love her all the more. What a fine wife for our dear Prince of Wales!

Amidst the floating banners and tapestries hung from

windows, the yet-suspended angel—it was a handsome blond lad—stopped strumming his parchment harp and gestured for silence. His bare feet must be cold dangling beneath his white woolen robe, because he sneezed. His metal halo went askew, yet stayed propped up by a wire from the bulky corset that must hold his wings—a white chicken feather floated past my face. Yet all that did not spoil the illusion for me. Was that what my Edmund would have looked like at that age?

The Spanish retinue, the English prelates, dignitaries, nobles, and knights accompanying the princess, even the raucous crowd, all hushed and looked up. Sadly, the angel spoke in Latin, which meant that few in the crowd, including me, could grasp his words, but I caught that he was portraying the angelic messenger Gabriel.

Fortunately, a fat priest behind us whispered to his companion, "The archangel has reminded the princess of Gabriel's words to the Virgin Mary, 'Blessed be the fruit of your womb.' I translate that to mean that the princess's chief duty is the procreation of children to stabilize the Tudor throne. Producing children, Gabriel explains, is why the Lord God has given mankind the capacity for 'sensual lust and appetite.'"

"Oho!" the other man behind me said with a chuckle. "So these days the body's passion is not only permissible but blessed? Now, why did I think lust was one of the seven deadly sins?"

"Only outside marriage, my son," the priest said, but he was chortling too. Free wine had been flowing all day, and I warrant he'd had his share. "Most of my flock," he went on, "might never come to that venerable estate of wedlock were it not for the gift of 'sensual lust and appetite.' Speaking of which, let's away to sample more of that imported wine Their Majesties have provided, eh?"

Though I'd never deign to argue with a priest, I could challenge the so-called wisdom of those men. The desire to wed, in my opinion, could also be spurred by a passion to possess a fine second wax chandlery and a hardworking widow's resources. I could see a widow wedding to give her children a good father. Or in Nick's case, perhaps a wife of rank could help him regain his family's property and prestige. Had he not considered that, instead of clinging to his lust for blood revenge against the traitor Lovell, who truly might live today only through rumors and bitter memories?

But I did not need to conjure up Nick Sutton the way I had my lost son. No, for there Nick was in the flesh, some distance away. Decked out in Tudor green and white, he sat mounted on a huge black destrier that knights rode in the lists. Amidst rising cheers as the entourage went past, I realized Nick was with those who would be jousting in the tournaments that would celebrate the wedding during the next three days. He sat among other strapping men, holding a lance upright, from which fluttered a green banner with the stems of red and white roses entwined with that of a pomegranate.

I fancied I caught his eye in that sea of heads and hats between us. I sucked in such a sharp breath that Maud looked up at me and asked, "You all right then?"

I nodded, touched by her concern. Unable to break my

distant gaze, I waved at Nick. He nodded straight at me; that is, if he saw me at all and it was not mere chance.

Queen Elizabeth of York

Despite the glorious event of our son's marriage, the queen's crown was heavy and cold upon my head that day. My purple velvet robe trimmed with ermine was welcome in the chill wind. Although we were outside, our seats at St. Paul's Cathedral were far better than had been our perch in a second-story window of a haberdasher's house in Cheapside from which we'd seen Catherine's entry into London two days ago. The timber scaffold on which we now sat, twelve feet square and four feet high, covered with red baize, was adjacent to the north transept of the cathedral, so we could easily progress inside for the coming mass. Within, on wooden stands, awaited the nobles of our land and many from Spain.

Of course, my lord's mother, Margaret Beaufort, Lady Stanley, sat on the king's other side, severe, regal, as if she had as much right to oversee this ceremony and later festivities as I. Scolding myself for not being grateful we had most of our family here, I blinked back tears as the mid-November sun glinted off our Arthur's white satin garments. Our eldest daughter, twelve-year-old Margaret, sitting directly behind her grandmother's chair, and recently betrothed to King James IV of Scotland, was all eyes. Little Mary had been allowed to attend and had been schooled on sitting still, yet I heard the occasional creak of her chair behind me.

But all eyes were on our second son, Henry, too, for he'd

seldom been seen in public. The boy looked older than his ten years, and the pride with which he held himself as he stood behind Arthur as his supporter made me realize again that Henry would never make a good priest, however avid he was at his studies. Indeed, Henry was quite full of himself today, for it was his duty, once these public rites were concluded, to escort our new Spanish daughter-in-law down the aisle of the vast cathedral to join her husband at the altar for a formal mass. Until both this ceremony and the mass were accomplished, the wedding would not be complete, and the festivities—three days full of feasts, dancing, and tournaments—could not begin.

The princess looked both demure and enraptured today. My hopes that I could be a second mother to her had partly been dashed by our having to speak through an interpreter, but she must, of course, learn English soon. She too wore white satin—the Spanish style, she had told me—with puffed sleeves and a huge, pleated skirt over a large cage called a farthingale. Whether or not Spanish style caught on here, I believed that Catherine would, for the crowds seemed to adore her already.

Henry Deane, Archbishop of Canterbury, and William Warham, Bishop of London, conducted the ceremony. I tried to follow the familiar Latin of the rites, yet my mind wandered. Our two lost children should be here. And if my two poor brothers were, I would be yet a king's sister, not wife, and not have to ever bear this huge weight that sat in my stomach in my guilt for their loss, Richard's, at least.

I had believed that the wax woman's creation of their effigies would help ease my grief, but I realized now that nothing except justice would ever appease me. "Justice is mine, saith the Lord," but I must know the villain who caused my brothers' deaths, for I craved revenge.

Their murderer could be some Yorkist zealot like Lord Lovell, who had raised rebellions and battles against us, then disappeared. If he was still alive and could be found, I would spur my husband on to see that he was executed. His very name sounded wicked to me: Lord Lovell—not Lord Love but Lord Evil. My stomach turned at the thought of him, and because I'd heard from reliable sources that he might be back in England. Rumors still? Seditious Yorkist lies? I knew not, but I feared. . . .

If my uncle, King Richard, were to blame for my brothers' deaths, at least he was already dead, with those mortal sins upon his black soul. I had also been pursuing the possibility that Sir James Tyrell, who had once been King Richard's henchman, had actually done the deed. Yet how could that be when my husband had pardoned Tyrell and granted him the command of Guisnes Castle in our holding at Calais? Twice he had been pardoned, though I must admit he had not fought against the Tudor forces in the Battle of Bosworth Field. But to invite the man back to England to joust in honor of our heir's wedding—what was my husband thinking?

Trumpets blared. I started. The king smiled as we rose and offered me his arm. Arthur bowed to us, and Catherine curtsied in a huge whoosh of skirts. Arthur went first into St. Paul's through the east entry, and my son Henry followed with Catherine on his arm. Oh, but we'd had a row, the king and I, about whether Arthur and Catherine should be bedded, but, of course, my lord had prevailed. I did not know if our frail Arthur could yet perform the marital act, but after all, with these rites and the mass to come, they were truly wedded. Now, in unison, the king and I waved and nodded to the cheering crowds and turned away to go within too.

It was then that the hair on the back of my neck prickled and my knees went weak as water. I felt a sharp pain between my shoulder blades, as if I had been struck there. Someone hateful, someone evil wished us ill among all the hurrahs. Though royalty was watched by many eyes, this felt far different.

As the king turned to wave again and I followed his lead, my eyes skimmed faces I could see from this height. The warmth of the crowd washed over us like a river, and yet, even at this moment of triumph and joy, dark fear nearly swamped my strength.

Nonsense, I told myself. On to the mass and the banquet at Baynard's Castle, on to a blessed, charmed life for our Prince of Wales and his new princess. Yet I trembled as we walked into the shelter of St. Paul's.

Mistress Varina Westcott

The next morning, I was most distressed to see my escort to the palace was Sibil Wynn and a guard I'd never seen. He seemed a brooding man but well favored, introduced to me as Jamie Clopton. Like most of the palace guards, he was tall and strong, though Sibil later said he'd lost his right thumb at swordplay and had retrained his left hand to hold sword or lance. She also told me he always wore black gloves with stuffing where his thumb would be so no one would know—though everyone did.

"Is Nick unwell?" I asked Sibil as I mounted the third horse they'd brought. "I saw him in the parade yesterday."

"Glorious, wasn't it? The banquet and dancing lasted till all hours," she said with a yawn and watering eyes, as if to prove her point. "The queen didn't want you to miss a day at your task, though she'll be busy with the festivities. No, Nick is jousting in the lists at Westminster this afternoon, asked at the last minute by the king in person, so he was happy for that. He asked me as a favor to take you up to the parapets so you can watch a bit of the joust—before I return to the queen's stands, of course."

She heaved a huge sigh, whether in annoyance at having to tend to me or just from weariness, I did not know. At least I could see Nick joust. Even in his excitement at the king's attention, he had thought of me. But what if he were injured? The barber-surgeons had told me they were to be at the ready if anyone in the tournament was hurt.

"Speaking of favors," Sibil went on as we boarded the barge, "Nick will be wearing mine today—my scarf—on his lance, and of course that of the queen and the new princess too, but mine is bright yellow, so if I forget to mention it later, you must look for it when he tilts." She sighed again.

When he tilts . . . Her last words echoed in my mind. Nick Sutton had tilted askew my head and heart, but I was foolish to think he gave a fig for me. Had this woman set her cap for him, or was she just pleased he'd wear her colors before the court?

I tried to force my thoughts back to the business at hand, the only reason, no doubt, that I was of any consequence to the queen or, sadly, Nick either. Today I would begin the effigy of Her Majesty's brother Richard, Duke of York, for I wanted to leave for last the boy King Edward. A week ago, I had received permission from Her Majesty to ask *Signor* Roberto Firenze if he would paint the wax faces and hands. I had sworn him to secrecy—only the queen, I, Nick, and Sibil knew of the effigies—and the artist had already painted the waxen flesh of Princess Elizabeth and Prince Edmund to fine effect.

In high praise that I valued more than the generous money Her Majesty gave me through Nick each week, she had claimed that I had sculpted perfect corpses in repose and the *Maestro* had given them life.

That midafternoon, when Sibil summoned me from the door to my work chamber—how I hated being there without Nick to keep the walls from closing in—my silly dreams of him took flight again. Sibil, obviously in a rush to complete her task so she could return to my betters, led me up curving stairs to a flat, crenellated portion of the roof. I had never seen her so beautifully gowned before. But then, she'd been garbed only to go outside the palace. Today, her matching bejeweled necklace, rings, and earrings sparkled, and I realized that beyond serving the queen, she must have a wealthy family. Or perhaps a besotted suitor who showered her with gifts. She seemed enamored of someone in the crowd below, blushing, waving, to whom I could not tell, but at least it could not be Nick, who was not now in sight.

"Nick bade me explain things to you," she said with a sweep of her arm at the panorama in the tiltyard below. The hubbub of voices reached my ears before I peered over at the stands and jousting area with its gay tents and fluttering flags.

It was brisk and windy up here, but I didn't care. How far I could see, as if I were a bird about to soar over the Thames. The city lay behind us, and the great gray-green river like a wide ribbon separated us from the Southwark forests cloaked in their brown and yellow leaves clear to the fertile fields beyond. But what a vantage point from which to behold the glorious pageant below!

"You cannot see the king and queen from here," Sibil said, "but just as well, as they'll not see you. I'm sure Nick did not ask permission for this."

Her voice was dismissive, even snippy. She resented, of course, having to take time with me and perhaps away from whomever she kept eyeing and waving to in the crowd below.

"I hardly think anyone will see me," I told Sibil, "for I will simply stand behind this projection and watch for a while. I'm sure you would like to return to your friends."

"Yes, I shall, but, as I said, Nick asked me to give you a bit of an explanation. Have you seen jousting before?"

"Only when boys played at the tilt rail in the streets."

"Well, then," she said, wrinkling her nose at that, "those tents are where the knights are armored. Though Nick is not a knight per se, he's filling in. You won't be able to pick him out until he removes his helm at the end, but I'm to tell you he will wear a red-plumed one and his cape will have a swan on it—something to do with the family coat of arms of the man he's replacing."

Poor Nick, I thought, to have his people so disgraced and to be so hastily included here that he could not represent his own family. Sibil's voice droned on, but I came alert again when she said, "He's to joust with a man who used to be a York loyalist but now serves this king, Sir James Tyrell, summoned from France for these festivities."

Was that not the man Nick and Her Majesty had mentioned as possibly having been involved in her brothers' murders? And the queen had said that His Majesty had invited Tyrell home to joust for this occasion. Oh, if only Nick could pin him down, force him before the entire court to tell all he knew of working as King Richard's henchman, whatever that entailed. No doubt I would not be the only one cheering Nick on over Tyrell today. Would not he be much more skilled than a younger man?

Then, though Nick was still nowhere in sight, came the rush and clash of the first jousters. On their third pass, a lance splintered against a shield. One man was unseated, crashed to the ground, and writhed under the weight of clattering armor. But all was well, as squires helped him to his feet and both jousters stood to bow in fine fashion to the royal box and the cheering crowd.

"Has Nick had much practice at this?" I asked Sibil.

"They all do, of course. Well, then, I'll away. Are you certain you can find your way back down? Nick said you should stay here but a little while, as Her Majesty is anxious for your project to be completed."

She started away, then turned back. "And Nick is too, of course, so he can return to more manly pursuits."

I glared at her back as she flounced away, but I did not

want to miss the excitement unfolding beneath me. Wait until I told my Arthur of this! How I wished he could be here with me.

I stood entranced for at least an hour before I could force myself to go below to my little room and the creation of wax children of the lost, those who would never ride a horse or cheer at a joust. Besides, I was fearful someone would see me on the roof or stairs and question what I was doing in the palace. But I must say, when Nicholas Sutton rode out in chain mail and armor, which gleamed like polished silver in the sun, and charged Sir James Tyrell and unhorsed him at their very first pass, I shrieked his praises like a fishwife.

I was beginning to wonder whether Sibil would return to escort me home from the palace when I heard the clink of spurs. Nick, divested of his armor, stooped to enter the little chamber. He was bareheaded, and his thick blond hair was mussed and damp. My insides cartwheeled at the mere sight of him. He bore a tray of food—cheese, meat pies, a flagon, and two wine goblets. I smiled broadly but for a moment was tongue-tied.

"Your cheeks are rosy," he said, "so I think you were up on the parapets for a while."

"Oh, yes, it was wonderful. My thanks for sending Sibil to fetch me. You were magni—did so well."

"I bested him smartly, did I not?" he said, beaming like a boy. "The queen was so pleased to see bested a man she mistrusts, she sent a purse of coins back to the tents, even as my squire removed my armor. But I pray the king doesn't mind that I unhorsed Tyrell. I wanted you to be watching, lest he did me in and I needed a waxen effigy for my funeral," he added with a shouted laugh. I could see he was ecstatic. His mere presence lifted my spirits. "Here," he said, setting the tray down. "I did forget to tell Sibil to feed you. You must be famished."

"In truth, I am." I sat down on my familiar end of the bench where we always ate. He poured us wine, sloshing a bit of it on the cheese. "I—I suppose you need to hurry back."

"True, but I'm exhausted with everything," he said, and flexed his big shoulders. I longed to rub his sore muscles, but I took the goblet he offered and downed a swallow of the delicious wine. "Those Spanish women the princess brought with her don't dance like we do at all," he told me. "I had to watch I wasn't trampling their feet and those bushy skirts— 'keep away,' they seem to say."

"And so you should," I dared with a little laugh. Our eyes met and held—always a thrill and a danger for me— before I looked down and sliced the bread. "And how do the bride and groom in all of this festivity?"

"People are talking, wagers being made about whether or not they bedded last night," he said, his mouth half-full of cheese. "I mean, they had the bedding ceremony, the bishop blessed the bed, and they were left alone, but the prince is not the most robust of men. He boasted a good deal this morn about wanting wine because he had had such hot work and had spent last night 'in Spain,' but odds are they did not perform 'the conjugal act,' to put it in legal terms."

"But if he so boasted . . ."

"Still doubtful," Nick said with a shake of his head. "I heard the bride looked untouched and told her maids so, though the two of them had best get to it, since the king needs not just a family but a dynasty. If the prince and princess are sent to big, drafty Ludlow Castle in Wales, I can't picture that being a snug spot for newlywed lovebirds."

"But the winter wind makes it best for cuddling and bedding," I blurted.

"Does it?" he asked, turning toward me. His eyes widened, and he looked me over as he sometimes did. "I'd like to prove the truth of that, but I rather favor lying on the grass under the trees in the lusty month of May with a willing wench."

He grinned like a lad with his hand caught in the sweets jar, so charming and alluring. I smiled back, and then the unthinkable happened. He leaned closer, slowly, slower, as if giving me time to bolt, while I sat stock-still, gripping my hands in my lap around a piece of bread I smashed, mesmerized by the depths of his eyes, where I could see myself framed by his fringe of eyelashes, sinfully thick for a man's.

"Today," he whispered, his face so close to mine that I could feel his breath, "I was given several ladies' favors to wear in the joust. But this is the favor I covet, the joust I would like to have."

I sat stone still in anticipation. His lips touched mine, coaxed them open a bit. He did not need to take my mouth, for I surrendered it freely, and even tipped my head so we missed noses and fit perfectly, moving, tasting, exploring. I forgot to breathe. Besides my mouth, he touched only my cheek that day, stroking my skin there with a calloused thumb that sent shivers through my entire body and made something hot as melted wax settle in the pit of my stomach. Neither of us moved closer—at least, our bodies did not with the tray between us—but it was as wild a move for me as if I'd thrown myself off the parapets of the palace before the entire court.

CHAPTER THE SEVENTH

*A*ll was silent in the house one night about a week after I'd left the palace for the last time. The dead children opened the curtains of my bed and hovered above me like angels in the cold December night. Surely they could not be the waxen effigies I had made, because they moved; they breathed. Their wings fanned my face, and their bare feet dangled as they held out their arms to me beseechingly. Unable to budge or scream, I lay horrified yet mesmerized, staring up at them.

The heads of the last two effigies I had done, the little princes, wore small gold crowns like halos. How fine they had looked when I had finished with my work. Only then, though bedecked in their fine satin and velvet garments, they'd been lying on their little beds the queen had made.

But now I saw five children crowding in above me, not just the four I had carved and which *Signor* Firenze's paints had brought to life. The fifth one—my Edmund! His sweet mouth opened so slowly and he cried, *Mother, Mother, help me, Mother. . . . I don't want to die. . . . I want to live, not to leave. . . . But farewell . . . Farewell . . .* Then they all cried out as in a roaring crowd at a parade or a joust: *Help us; save us! We don't want to die—to diiii—ee. . . .*

Soaked with sweat, I gasped and sat up. Church bells were clanging, clanging—twelve tolls, midnight. I was alone. No children, no voices but those in my head and heart. A nightmare, just like those I used to have that my father's waxen effigies had come to life.

I put my head in my hands and sobbed. I had held back tears for four days, since I'd been returned from the palace with a full purse and an empty heart. And not escorted by Nick, whom I might never see again, but by his substitute, Jamie Clopton, who knew only that I carved candles for the queen. How I treasured my talks with Nick, our single kiss that day of the jousting before he had to return to the lists. *This is the favor I covet,* he had said, *the joust I would like to have.* Had they been mere seductive words or a strange good-bye?

Now this nightmare had assailed me when I had hoped to move past Edmund's death. It was well-known, Christopher had said, that overmuch grieving was unhealthful and showed a lack of trust in God's will. Another clock was clanging in my head, marking off the days before I must give Christopher my answer to wed him or not. Some stubborn core in me screamed, *No!* but my head knew it would be best for my future. The Westcott Chandlery's future, at least.

What a jolthead I had been to fall for Nick Sutton or to think that the queen might buy a huge supply of candles from my shop. Though she had praised my skills, and I'd seen tears glaze her eyes as she beheld the finished faces of her fallen family, her last words to me had been stern, almost as if I were a child: *I want you to vow you will tell no one what has happened here or what you leave behind in my care. Lest someone from the palace or anywhere should question you, this must go no farther than Nick*, Signor *Firenze, Sibil Wynn,* and *you. These thick castle walls will keep the wax cool and preserved in summer or in winter, but you must forget what you leave behind here. Swear it!*

I swore not to tell, but I would never forget. How deeply it had disturbed me that my final farewell to my finest work seemed to be under the weight of not a vow but a threat.

Queen Elizabeth of York

As I lay in the royal bed, I thought I heard a child's voice calling me. Even the words were distinct enough to awaken me: *I don't want to die. I want to live.... But farewell. Farewell! Help us; save us!*

My first thought was to calm myself by running to the little chamber where the four beautiful effigies lay, but I was sleeping with Henry this night. When we bedded together—as now, usually in his chamber, not mine—he was always Henry to me, not the king. I would be thirty-six at my next birthday, but my body yet responded to his lovemaking. Perhaps there would be yet another prince or princess, though never ones to take the place of those I'd lost.

My heart still hammered in my ears from the echo of

little voices I surely must have heard only in my head. Henry still slept, though fitfully, tossing, moaning, breathing hard in spurts as ever. From his earliest years, he'd confided once, he'd never had a sound night's sleep, not even with trusted guards at the doors, not even when, at last, the throne was his. *Especially* not then. In our earlier years, he had even slept with his crown by the bed, fearful lest someone would come and snatch it.

Although I knew it would be unusual if I left him before morn, I carefully extricated my hair, which was caught under his shoulder, and edged toward the far side of the bed. I could tell the guards in the hall I had a queasy stomach and needed my own chamber. I vow that was nearly the truth.

"Are you all right?" came Henry's sleepy voice. "Is all well?"

"Yes. I was just awakened by worries," I told him, deciding he might insist on sending for a physician and make much ado if I told him I felt unwell. I wondered what he would say if he ever learned what lay in the secret chamber off my bedroom. I could not stifle those little voices in my head demanding, *Save us . . . help us!* Perhaps, though they were long lost, I could help myself. But first I must mention something I would give in to before asking for a great favor.

"You're not fretting again that we should stay here for Christmas instead of Windsor?" His voice came slowly, dragging out his words. "Tradition is important in establishing the Tudor name."

"Not that," I told him. True, I had not wanted to leave my secret chamber for so long, but I did love Windsor all decked out for yule, and hoped the change of setting would help to heal my heart. But I had to get this precious and precarious moment back on track. I'd capitulated on Windsor and now must give in on something else.

I told him, "I admit I'm still fretting about Arthur and Catherine leaving us before yule and riding to the Welsh border in this bitter weather."

"Is that it then? I told you, my dearest, it's best that they establish themselves in their own household there. He's not called Prince of Wales for nothing. Besides, you know I named him Arthur to remind our subjects that the Tudors claim a heritage from King Arthur of Camelot, that good and glorious kingdom of yore in that very area where Ludlow now stands."

"I know. But our Arthur is thin and has that cough." Though I had meant this already settled issue as a diversion, I shuddered at the thought of Ludlow Castle with the winter winds and sharp spring off the Marches that divided England and Wales. I lay back down in bed, feeling overly warm instead of chilled. Now. Now, I told myself. I must broach the issue I had wanted to for weeks, indeed for the sixteen years we'd been wed, and especially these last long ten years when I had covertly pursued my inquiry. Seeing my dead brothers brought to life had made me bold and desperate.

I cuddled back against his warmth, and he put his arms around me so that we lay spoon fashion, as we oft did after our union. I did not have a loveless marriage, for this loyal, clever man truly cared for me beyond the blending of our blood and lineage—I knew that and must trust it now.

"Of course you are right about Wales," I said in a rush before he fell back asleep or was tempted to take me once more. "But there is something I need and want very much, I beseech you, Henry."

He kissed my naked shoulder. "And not this?" he asked, his voice teasing.

"No—that is, not yet. I bear a burden you could ease, though I know you would rather leave the issue buried—I mean not deal with it, as busy as you are."

I turned in his arms to face him, to whisper even more quietly, as if some evil being would hear my plea, however much we lay in a curtained bed in a room and palace guarded to the hilt.

"Speak, my dearest, if I can do aught to ease your mind and heart."

"It yet haunts me that my brothers disappeared. No doubt they are dead, but there is no one to answer for it— murder and regicide."

I felt his body stiffen. I held my breath.

"So long ago," he said.

"But new to me each day. I still blame myself for counseling my mother to let her second son go—and I should have told her to protest little Edward's being taken to the Tower, son of a king—a king himself!"

"Yes, yes, but King Richard, who no doubt had them harmed by one of his lackeys, is dead and buried, and I'd like to keep it that way. Some Yorkist wolves are still on the prowl, and we don't need another uprising with a pretender to my throne, which could happen if I stoke those fires of Richard dispatching your brothers again."

"Such rebellions could be cut off by proving the boys are dead—bodies or bones found, a murderer's confession, something! Could you not make more inquiry in a privy way? It would satisfy me—and the justice on which our Tudor kingdom must be established—if it were handled secretly, but I must know."

He knew I was distraught, yet I held back the depths of my vehemence. If the boys' murderer still lived, I would see that he or they were assassinated or executed—send Nicholas Sutton secretly to do the deed, if need be. Lately, though, he had gone from my service to the king's, and had been assigned to Prince Arthur's personal guard for the coming journey to Wales.

It haunted me too that there were Yorkists the king had taken back into his good graces, such as Sir James Tyrell, who helped to hold Calais in France for us. Even our Lord High Treasurer, Thomas Howard, Earl of Surrey, had once stood for the Yorkist cause. Since Henry needed their talents and services, he had given reprieves to both men, but they might indeed still be on the prowl. I vowed that, whether my brothers' murderer hid inside or outside of our court, I would be a she-wolf to discover him!

Henry pulled me closer, tucking the top of my head under his chin. I could feel the pulse in his neck, the very thudding of the heart that had the power and ruled this kingdom. He had not said no. He was weighing all the options, as he always did.

Mistress Varina Westcott
Because Christopher had gone on a journey into the shire of Kent to bargain with the beekeepers who provided all of us

with wax, he had allowed me to deliver candles from my chandlery to the chapel of the guild of the Holy Name of Jesus in the crypt of St. Paul's. Ah, he was trying to tempt me with all the good things he could do for me and mine if I would agree to wed him.

I took two of our apprentices along—over Gil's protests that he should be the one to go with me—because it would have come to a spat when I told him he could not accompany me down into the crypt. Christopher had been adamant about that. The lads would guard the horse and cart I had loaded with the longest tapers we sold. These were black ones, thick four-foot-long candles priests usually carried in funeral processions but which the guild of the Holy Name of Jesus had ordered for their secret ceremony on this day. Christopher would be back to attend, so I wanted everything to be set up just right.

I was not nervous, for I knew I would not be alone in the chapel. According to Christopher, the increasingly popular *Signor* Roberto Firenze had been hired by the holy guild to paint soaring angels on the ceiling. Hoping those did not remind me of my nightmare, I was anxious to see them. Christopher had also said that he had no doubt that the *Maestro*, as he oft called Firenze, would use my face for at least one of them—and he'd bribe the man if he did not.

"We ought to get a cut of his fees from assignments to which your portrait has given him entry," Christopher had said. "I hear he's painted some very important people of late." I had almost laughed aloud; he would have erupted had he known the little Italian had painted wax figures for the queen—ones I had made.

"You lads, wait here and guard all well," I told John and Piers, fifteen-year-old twins, in their second year of apprenticeship to us.

"But those big ones be heavy," John said as they handed me two of the six tapers and I balanced them in my arms.

"Yes, but you can't enter the chapel with me, so I'll be back—twice."

Fortunately, I found the door unlocked and the stairwell well lit, though closing the door behind myself took some doing. As I descended carefully, I fancied I could hear Firenze below singing or humming. What a blessing to be happy at one's work, I thought. I could cling to that in the future if I found the courage to turn Christopher down. I prayed that he would not hurt our chandlery from spite, since he had the power of the guild behind him and we had no representation there. Just to show me how much I needed him, he must be delaying acceptance of Gil's request to join.

"*Signor*, it's me, Varina," I called as I neared the bottom of the stairs, not wanting to startle Firenze and have him spatter paint on an angel's face. But he was not painting angels and not on the ceiling; on each of the side walls he had sketched outlines of five women, all holding lanterns, five thrusting them forward, five sadly holding them down at their sides.

"Ah, *mi bella* Varina," he sang out, turning away from his task. His curled mustache tilted up in a welcoming smile. "I did hear you might be coming."

"But I heard you were painting angels on the ceiling," I said, looking up at it before I laid the two long tapers carefully on the floor.

"Later. Right now ze five wise and five foolish virgins

from ze Bible, eh, from the Lord's own parable. Half of them had their lamps lit, prepared for when ze bridegroom come, ze others not and want to borrow a light, but too late, and they are left behind, calling, 'Lord, Lord,' in the darkness. Has something to do with the guild's secret rites in this place, eh?"

So far, only the outline of the maidens' faces and hands holding their lanterns were completed. They looked like ghosts emerging from the white plaster, as if they'd risen from their graves out in the crypt and were able to pass through walls. Strangely, it popped into my head that Nick had called the detested Lord Lovell a ghost, but I thrust that thought aside.

"I hope you're doing the wise ones first," I told him. "Christopher said you might use my face. If you do, I hope it's one of those."

"Of course, of course! But, speaking of being prepared, I must ask you something." He came closer. His face was streaked with smudges of paint, just as he'd looked when he painted my portrait and the queen's effigies. It rather gave him a wild look, I thought, and I somehow liked him the better for it. Besides, I was forever burning myself with wax, getting it in my hair or clothes or under my fingernails. I knew how it felt to be totally absorbed in one's work.

"What is it?" I asked him when I saw how distressed he looked, yet how he hesitated. "Does working so far down in this small place bother you too?"

"Not that. I think I been followed. And someone outside my door at night—ze hall floor creaks. I look out through ze keyhole and only see black clothing. I call out and open ze door and someone running down ze steps at the inn, but no one below seen a stranger. Ze lady who hired us lately—she was so—ah, what is ze word?—adamant I keep her secret, I fear she sends someone to keep their eyes on me that I not talk. You have anything like that?"

A shiver shook me. By the lady, he meant the queen. "No, but I've been preoccupied. I admit I haven't been watching. Yet I can't imagine that—"

"You know what happened to ze Egyptians."

"The Egyptians? You mean in the Bible?"

"No—just heard about it," he said, lowering his voice to a whisper, though we were quite alone. "The pharaohs, their kings and queens, they build small burial chambers hidden in huge stone buildings. But to keep ze location of their bodies secret from grave robbers, they kill ze ones know about it, ze ones built it for them, seal them in a crypt too."

"What? You don't mean that the—the lady—wants to silence you for what you know?"

"Just my imagination, *si*, but I got a good one—you too, I bet. Artists must have that or not artists at all."

I tried to reassure and calm him. He went back to work as I hurried upstairs and went outside to the cart to carry down two more black tapers and then, when I saw Firenze was working like a madman, went back up for two more without bothering him. The boys were blowing on their hands and stamping their feet in the cold, so I sent Piers to buy hot spiced ale and roasted chestnuts for us. I told them I would take longer this time because I needed to set up the candles. But when I went back down with my last load, the artist was nowhere to be seen.

I feared Firenze was upset that I had not sympathized with him more about his worries. Had he just not been speaking to me on my second trip down because I'd ignored his talk of Egyptians? Was he playing a trick on me? Not only was he not in the small chamber, but he had snuffed out all but one of the lamps in the room, though the stairwell was still brightly lit and threw light within.

I put the heavy tapers down. I looked for him under the benches, then behind the glorious triptych screen with the soaring angels. There was room for someone to hide back here. How I'd like to secrete myself to hear what really went on in one of these males-only rituals, but I saw nothing but spiders there.

"*Maestro? Signor* Firenze? Roberto Firenze!"

My voice echoed. Surely singing or chanting would carry just that strangely down here. I saw that the side door to the huge crypt area itself, which Christopher had mentioned, stood slightly ajar. Was Firenze hiding out there? I did not put it past him to jest with me, but he had not seemed in the mood for that today. Yes, his things were still laid out here—paint exposed to the air, even a big horsehair brush dropped hastily on his large palette, with its handle as well as bristles in the paint.

Dared I look out into the crypt? Perhaps he had just gone out to relieve himself or even to explore. I could imagine the coffins and monuments of yore resting there in the vast, silent darkness. I shivered again. I could go for help, though to whom I did not know. Or at least I would take the lantern at the bottom of the stairs with me and call into the crypt for him.

I shook my head at my foolishness. I was obviously making much ado about nothing. The volatile little man had evidently gone up to get some drink or food, and I had simply missed him on my way back down. I should have asked whether he needed something from upstairs. He could have gone out any of the cathedral doors and not wanted to leave all the lanterns burning while he was away for a respite.

Without anyone else here, the walls seemed to close in on me. I stood frozen, trembling, almost unable to get myself to move toward the staircase. My pulse pounded, and I could not catch my breath. I could see why they wanted to have the ceiling painted down here. That would at least give the illusion of space. To think of all those dead bodies just beyond that partly open door to the crypt, enclosed forever, just as my dear ones, my Edmund had been. And to think that Firenze had feared he was being followed and I had refused to credit it . . .

I heard footsteps on the stairs. Thank heavens, he was coming back. As he approached, the light that curled from the well-lit staircase into the back of the chapel dimmed as his form blocked it out. His shadow, somewhat shapeless in a cape perhaps, cast itself upon the wall and then disappeared.

I realized the person was too big to be Firenze. Whoever it was had been putting out the lanterns on his way down the steps. Was it the one who had been following Firenze, and the artist had gone upstairs, seen him, and fled back down here and into the crypt to hide? Should I call out or hide too?

A long, black-sleeved arm with black gloves reached out to lift the lantern at the bottom of the steps off its hook. The intruder shuttered the light so that only a single, narrow beam shot into the room, for all had gone dark behind and around him.

His steps slowed. As I pressed myself back behind the edge of the triptych, I heard him shuffle into the room. He could trap me here. I dared not cry out to question or challenge him.

Staying in the shadows, I bent over and tiptoed toward the door to the huge crypt under the cathedral. Some said it was as large as the building above. I cursed the door when it creaked as I opened it farther and darted out into utter blackness.

CHAPTER THE EIGHTH

I feared I would be pursued, and I was right. How had everything so swiftly gone so wrong?

I heard the man come out into the crypt. His narrow lantern beam swept the area by the door, back, forth, along the walls, the floor. I heard him close the door to the chapel firmly; I knew that would be my only way out. If I fled farther into the crypt, I could wander in the darkness for days and be lost down here forever in this pitch blackness. I knew I must work myself back to the door and flee upstairs, but then, my pursuer knew it too. If I was gone too long, would the apprentices summon help or send someone to look for me? Why had I told the lads I would be gone for a long while? I should have heeded Firenze's warning about being followed. And where was he?

Bending low, I tried to feel my way along, but I bumped into stone tombs or even metal coffins here and there. One resounded with a muted boom, but the man must not have heard it. With his lantern beam still a narrow shaft, playing it back and forth before his feet, he slowly worked his way closer to me. He must know I had not the courage to flee into the depths of the crypt. So did he know me? Was this someone I knew?

I was horror-struck at how closed-in I felt, despite being in an immense area. My blood pounded like drumbeats in my ears. I had to remind myself to breathe. The air was stale. Dust shrouded everything I touched. Spiderwebs laced themselves across my perspiring face and snagged in my eyelashes. I heard a rat scurry away and wished that I could too.

Behind a big stone monument, I knelt and peered out. It was pitch-black but for the man's shifting stab of light as he methodically came closer. Who was he? Surely not Firenze in disguise with huge, padded shoulders to teach me a lesson about being followed, though he had mentioned the foolish women he painted who were lost in the dark. Had that been a clue that he would play this macabre trick on me?

Christopher, who had of late become more desperate about possessing me—had he hired someone to frighten me so I would realize how much I needed him? Or had he come back to town early? It could be one of the members of the holy guild who didn't approve of a woman so much as stepping into the place of their secret rites. *Holy Mother Mary*, I prayed, *please don't let Firenze's fear come true that the queen sent someone to ensure that we keep silent.* Nick? No, of course it could not be Nick, however much this man's height seemed to match his.

Tears speckled my cheeks when I blinked, but tears or

not, eyes closed or not, the blackness was all the same. I felt the weight of the massive stones above me, the weight of my fears pressing me down. I had to bite my lip not to scream out in abject fear, even if that gave away my position.

From time to time I heard the man's sword scrape against stone or ding a metal coffin. Was it still in his scabbard, or had he drawn it? And for what purpose against an unarmed woman?

He suddenly lifted his lantern aloft. I ducked, hitting the floor on my belly. He spoke in a whisper, but even that echoed.

"Varina! Her Majesty has sent me to fetch you. The master painter is already on his way. We must make haste."

How could this man know about the queen, unless she had sent him? I did not answer, did not move, only breathed, shallow and slow. If he came closer, I must crawl farther away, find shelter in this place I could not see.

I prayed that death and purgatory were not like this. I must leave behind more money for masses said for Will's and Edmund's and my souls. I must donate more votive candles, more— Was I mad? I must keep my mind on the here and now.

I forced myself to crawl slowly, feeling the way before me lest I bump into another tomb. My skirts under my knees dragged me back. I pulled my front hems up and held them in my teeth and crawled upon my bare knees on the dusty, hard stone. The next tomb I reached was carved, some sort of large sculpture. I had dared to go back closer to the chapel door—at least I thought so. If I hadn't lost my bearings, this was an area the man had already searched. I stood to feel the carving with both hands—a stone effigy of someone in armor? I think a stone-hewn dog lay at his feet. Yes, his wife's effigy lay stretched stiffly out beside him, but with enough room for me to climb up and wedge myself between the two of them.

I could only pray my pursuer would not find me here, that I was hidden by the stone or the shadows. I lay as still as the dead, as still as the wax effigies I'd carved. The fact that my pursuer did not speak again must mean he was afraid I would recognize his voice—or that now, since I had not answered, he knew that ploy would not ferret me out.

Surely he would not search the entire area. If his lantern gutted out in the erratic drafts here, he could be lost too. I warrant he was thinking I would make a dash for the chapel door. That I longed to do, but I was smarter than that, not a wise virgin with a lantern but a wary widow in the dark. Even if he went back into the chapel and locked me in here, I could bang on the door when the guild members met late this afternoon—if I did not lose my mind by then.

If this man thought he would go out and leave the chapel door ajar and wait inside to snag me, he was much mistaken, but what had he done with *Signor* Firenze? The hastily abandoned brush in the paint palette now made me even more fearful for the artist's safety. Could he be on his way to see the queen and had thrown his brush down in all haste? No, if that were true, would not my pursuer have identified himself?

The man was moving slowly back toward the chapel. Dared I hope he was going to leave? I was shaking so hard my shoulders bumped the stone shoulders of my hosts. Oh, no, he was coming close. But he seemed to be projecting his beam low, to guide his own feet or to flush me out like hunted game. How I longed to leap at him, to scratch his eyes and tear his cap and cape away. *Who are you?* I wanted to scream.

He paused near where I lay. I could see some of this tomb now in the wan, reflected lantern light, stone emerging in shades of gray, a tall, carved monument around and above me. Of the man himself, I dared not shift myself to try to catch a glimpse of him.

My nose tickled. I could not sneeze or all was lost. Though I needed to stay as still as stone, I slowly raised one hand and jammed a finger under my nose. Yet I was going to sneeze. He would find me, I— Ah . . .

The sensation passed, and he did too, walking faster now, going out the chapel door and banging it closed behind him. I heard him lock it; the metallic sound echoed. At least that proved he had actually gone in, not just pretended to, then waited in the dark for me to move.

Tears of relief ran down my temples into my hairline and my ears. Yet I had never beheld such utter blackness. Fearing I would lose my bearings and miss the direction of the door, I sat up. My snood snagged on something and my hair spilled free, but I did not stop. I climbed down and started in the direction of the sounds he'd made. I must make straight for that but not go too close, lest he suddenly throw open the door again to seize me.

But I did go a bit closer, praying I was on track. It would not be too long—maybe several hours—before the holy guild members, including Christopher, would be inside, and then I must knock for help, explain some of what had happened. But time, space—everything here was out of joint. The air was not good, and I felt so drained ... my body shaking with fatigue from holding myself so still and quiet ... fears, emotions, and exhaustion sapping the remnants of my strength. ...

Hiding under an elevated bronze coffin, despite stirring up a nest of mice there, I must have fallen asleep.

I jerked awake so fast I banged my head on the bottom of the coffin. Lying back, slightly stunned, I heard sounds— singing. By the saints, the service in the chapel must be under way!

I edged out from under the tomb, amazed I could pick things out around me a bit now. Had my eyes finally adjusted to the dark? No, for whatever reason, the door to the chapel stood ajar. Despite how long I must have been in here, should I wait for them to finish? What would it do to my reputation—or Christopher's—if I were to spring out, filthy and wide-eyed, during their solemn service?

I decided I would bide my time. Surely the man who had sought me was gone. Or if he was one of them, he would not dare to harm me after their service. If they should close or lock the door again, I would have no choice but to bang on it and tell all—without saying my pursuer had mentioned the queen and the palace. Perhaps the queen had sent him just to test me. But surely it wasn't true that Firenze had gone ahead.

I picked out a place against the wall, one tomb away from the door. Sitting in the shadows with my back against the carved stone tomb, I put my hand out.

And touched cold flesh.

I gasped and scrambled a bit away. A person, but alive or dead? I could see little in the dim light and with my hair spilled in my eyes. Was it my pursuer still waiting for me in the chill? No, not moving, and too small to be him. I made but a little cry, though I wanted to scream my soul out. The small man's head lay at a sharp, unnatural angle. A broken neck? And on his face a mustache, paint smears I could even feel—he was not breathing and his limbs had begun to stiffen—*Maestro* Firenze, sprawled here, dead.

Queen Elizabeth of York

"I am sure you will like Wales," our son Arthur told his bride as the newlywed couple supped with the king and me in our withdrawing room at Westminster Palace. I saw color come to Arthur's already rosy cheeks. "A great adventure, Catherine! The people are almost as wild as the scenery, you know."

"I learn . . . all I can," Catherine said in her halting English. "I like meet . . . the England people and Wales."

"I applaud your quick learning, daughter," I told her, and raised a goblet of Rhenish to her, and the king followed suit. "The people love you, and they will love you all the more when you learn their language and their ways."

In Latin, Arthur repeated to her what I had said. She smiled and nodded. Arthur clearly adored her, though I had heard from my ladies who had spoken to Catherine's Spanish ladies that the happy couple had not yet truly consummated the marriage. But, heading their own household in Wales, there would be long winter nights for them to complete their union—and for me to miss him.

With kisses all around, Arthur and Catherine took their leave, hand in hand, heading for Baynard's Castle, where they had lived since the wedding. We would see them off from there just four days before Christmas. I greatly disliked the timing of that, but had not argued with the king. And then the court would travel to Windsor for the holiday season.

"They are getting on exceedingly well, I'd say," my lord observed as the yeomen guards closed the door behind them, leaving us alone. "I know the word is they have not yet sealed their union, but I spoke to Arthur about it, and I predict the word from Wales will be productive by spring or summer. Elizabeth," he said, turning me toward him and encircling my waist with his arm, "I have decided I will look further into that matter we discussed the other night."

"Oh, my lord, I am so grate—"

"But on the condition that you not continually inquire how it goes or what I must do to ferret out answers—or from whom. I will tell you what I know of import when I know it."

"Yes, I understand. And I thank you, whatever means you must use."

"We all use our own means from time to time, do we not, my dear?"

"Indeed, we do and must," I countered, wanting to agree with him in all things for this boon he was giving me. I suppose he meant my asking him for this great favor when we lay abed together, but I prayed he knew naught of my privy plans and necessary scheming.

Mistress Varina Westcott

Leaving Firenze's body where it lay, I crawled closer to the door of the chapel. Should I burst in, crying, "Murder! Murder!"? Should I wait until they were greatly dispersed to send one of them—Christopher, if he was there—for the sheriff or crowner? By the saints, what if they thought that I had killed the artist? Or could he have come out here to relieve himself or look at something, then fallen and hit his head? No, I knew in my heart that the man in black had killed him as he would have me, and I knew that however stringently I was questioned, I could not say all I knew about who could have meant us harm.

As I huddled outside the door, through which I could now clearly hear the service, my mind raced over terrible possibilities. Had that tall man truly been an assassin? If so, surely he'd not been sent by the queen. Wouldn't she need both of us alive, lest she wanted repairs on her precious effigies? The portrait Firenze had painted of me—and the effigies that I could never mention—were the two things that bound the artist and me together.

But unless I had been followed, just as Firenze said he had been, Christopher could be the only one who knew where I and *Signor* Firenze would be, and quite alone. But that man who had pursued me in the crypt—he could not have been Christopher any more than he could have been Nick Sutton.

My distracted, scattered thoughts finally settled enough to make sense of the service on the other side of the door. No doubt my six black candles burned before the angel triptych, casting light on the virgins with their lanterns that would never be finished by Firenze now. I wiped tears from my cheeks, despite knowing my filthy hands would smear my skin gray. I shook and my teeth chattered as I waited for a pause to knock on their door.

Although the lead voice and some of the singing had been in Latin, now that voice cried, "I shall light a candle of understanding in thine heart, which shall not be put out!"

All of the symbols of light within the chapel made sense now. Many of the members of the guild of the Holy Name of Jesus were chandlers and candlemongers. Of course their rites would employ light and dark, good and evil. Surely they didn't demand sacrifices beyond time, money, and secrecy.

"Soon we shall have the painting of the ten virgins come to life on our walls," the voice intoned.

Come to life, I thought. And how was that? Did they intend to present living tableaux or pageants, like those for the princess Catherine or the mystery plays the guilds gave each Christmas? The outlined virgins would never come to life, not without *Maestro* Firenze. I raised my hand to knock on the door until I heard the next words.

"And now we shall hear from our brother Christopher, who has obtained the artist for us."

Yes, the next voice was his: "Let us realize that the five foolish virgins are closer to life than the five wise ones. Womankind, unwed or not, has been weak and foolish since the days of Eve, when she tempted Adam to sin, taken in by the Evil One. And so it has been ever since that females, though they be made from Adam's rib, tend to evil and seduction and desperately need direction and correction from both God and man."

I jerked my hand down and stood up straighter. Of course, he spoke Holy Church doctrine, but it suddenly rubbed me sore. I had managed my shop quite alone for months between Will's death and Gil's arrival. I had hired Gil and was yet in charge of major decisions. I was rearing my son without a man, though Gil and Maud certainly helped. I could carve candles and fine effigies. But yes, I had been foolish too—to adore Nick, a man above my star. And foolish certainly to ever think of wedding and trusting Christopher Gage, however much I desperately needed his support now in what must be a wrongful-death inquiry. I could bear to hear no more, to wait no longer. I must find help here.

Knowing I looked a fright, but determined to stand up to these men if need be, I knocked on the partly open door and called in, "My name is Varina Westcott. A man chased me into the crypt after I brought your candles and I hid, but the artist Firenze lies dead outside this door."

CHAPTER THE NINTH

*C*haos ensued. Faces crowded the doorway, Christopher's among them. Though he looked appalled at my appearance, he swept me into his arms, even when the others came out with lanterns and, half-blinded by their lights, I showed them where the body lay.

After that, time became as endless as the blackness in the crypt had been. Questions came at me from the guild members, then the constable, next the high sheriff of the city, finally the crowner—all who entered the crypt to examine the body through the holy guild chapel. I hoped my tale made sense, as I was forced to cobble some of it together to avoid mentioning the queen. The ruling I overheard bandied about among the city law enforcement officials was that the Italian artist had fallen and broken his neck, or had been murdered by a man unknown. Most English thought Italians or artists were not to be trusted, anyway.

Talk of women being fools, I thought. All that was obvious. Did they not credit what I had told them enough to at least inquire about the man, talk to those above in the cathedral who might have seen him?

However protective Christopher had been this day, I would never wed him now. As for Nick, the man had deserted me without a fare-thee-well, and after that kiss and his words the day of the joust, I swore that I would swear off men! Oh, yes, that would be the clever thing to do.

At least several of the guild members said they would pay for Firenze's funeral, and I promised a waxen shroud and votive candles. Finally, they carried his body out. I sobbed at his loss, leaning back against the last thing he had ever painted, the wise women with their lamps.

Christopher, Gil, even Maud stuck tight to me that night, until I begged exhaustion and Maud took me upstairs to bed. Insisting I bid my Arthur good night, I sat by his bed to calm him, but I could not calm myself. Again and again, as I tried to sleep, the whispering man in black approached me in the depths of my dreams. Finally, I went back into Arthur's room and lay across the end of his bed, listening to him breathe, willing him to be safe always and have sweet rest. I had not been able to save my dear Edmund from death, but I vowed nothing bad would ever happen to Arthur.

Christopher had done just what I'd feared: insisted that this all proved I needed him to protect me. He said he'd used his influence to keep me from being questioned further. But my thoughts still raced: The mystery man had had a sword and perhaps a dagger, so if he had killed Firenze, wouldn't he have run him through or cut his throat? But I had overheard the crowner say there was not a drop of blood upon him, and his neck had been cleanly snapped. Cleanly? An accident? Only a fall? More like a murder. I warrant that if Roberto Firenze had not been what Londoners termed a stranger—a foreigner—they would have looked closer for a killer, unless someone with authority had told them not to. I only knew I wasn't going out into the city soon on my own again, not to graveyards, not to chapels or crypts.

With the winter weather, I would be a voluntary prisoner in my home and shop, as if I had been locked up for doing something dire, but I would cling to my work and my family.

And I knew now for certain one thing more: As soon as the time was right, or if he asked me first, I was going to tell Christopher Gage I would not wed him. Will and I had made a good marriage, but it was a binding of hands more than hearts. Nick Sutton had stirred my now celibate body—that was all, I told myself. I warrant men were not to be trusted in general. After all, Adam in the garden had the choice not to take that apple, and look who got blamed! Oh, yes, but for business matters, I vowed I was finished with men.

How soon my solemn promise was put to the test. The next day, I was preparing to close up the shop with my son's help, for, one way or the other, I intended never to be alone here now. To my amazement, I saw Nick Sutton dismount in the street, just as he had that first day we had met nearly two months ago. He was alone this time.

I froze where I was, my hand upraised to place a candle in the top ledge of the window for display. I snatched my hand down, so it wouldn't look as if I were waving or beckoning him in. I retreated to the counter and leaned against it for support.

My mind raced, yet went only in circles. I had not sent word of Firenze's death to the palace. I'd heard the court would be moving soon to Windsor for the twelve days of Christmas. On the morrow, the Prince and Princess of Wales were setting out for Ludlow Castle in Wales in a grand cavalcade. But Nick—why was he here? Why now?

"Mother, is it the bad man?" Arthur asked, tugging at my sleeve.

"No—a friend from when I was carving candles at the palace, the one who came to fetch me sometimes."

We stood together, facing the door as Nick entered in a blast of crisp air. It had started snowing, and his black-caped broad shoulders and cap showed a dusting of it. He smiled as his gray eyes took us both in.

"A fine boy," he said, removing his gloves and lifting off a leather satchel he wore on a strap over one shoulder. "Someday you will be taller than your mother, Arthur, but I am glad to see you are helping and protecting her even now."

I was touched that Nick recalled Arthur's name, but considering whom he was named for, it was not so surprising. Still not smiling at Nick in return, I bent him a slight curtsy, and Arthur bowed as he'd been taught to do when his betters came in to shop. Even after all that I'd been through, I felt my face flush at Nick's presence, the mere sound of his voice and kind words. I made proper introductions. Nick seemed to say all the right things, and the lad almost melted in his presence—as did I, who should know better by now.

"Varina, I heard what happened," Nick told me, speaking quietly over Arthur's head. "But before Arthur leaves us so that we may speak alone for a moment, I have an early yule gift for him."

"For me, Sir Nick?"

"Just Master Nick for now, Arthur. But yes, when I was a lad, I always favored tops and could get them to spin for hours—well, minutes—and this is a special one." He produced a large wooden top from his satchel, one carved and painted. "You see," he said, stooping to Arthur's height, "when you get it going just right, this painted hunt hound seems to chase this roebuck. They are fashioned so that they appear to go up and down a bit too. Now, here's the leather pull cord. I'm pleased you're here, because I'd rather show you, man to man, than leave it with your mother."

"I thank you! Can we try it here?"

"Some other time. You take it with you and let me know later, will you? I'm leaving on the morrow with the other Arthur—our prince—for Wales, and there's to be a fine parade out of town, if you might bring your mother and the rest of the family to see us off."

I heartily hoped Sibil Wynn was still with the queen and not with Princess Catherine. Still, the day of the jousts, I had felt she was flirting with someone below us when Nick had not yet appeared. Oh, what was wrong with me? I had no right to be jealous about this man! Yet, although I'd best forget him, I rued that he was leaving.

"Oh, yes, I'm sure we shall see them off and wave you away!" Arthur cried, standing on one foot and then the other in his excitement. "Is it all right to leave, then, Mother?"

"Yes. Yes, and thank Master Nick again for his kindness."

As Arthur obeyed and hurried off, I steadied myself for whatever was to come. I stared at Nick's black gloves, which he'd dropped on the counter. The queen's other guard she'd sent to me, Jamie Clopton, always wore black gloves. . . . My pursuer in the crypt had worn black gloves. . . . Christopher too had fine black winter gloves. . . .

"You've quite won him over," I told Nick as the door closed behind Arthur.

"But have I won you over?" he asked, as his eyes narrowed in perusal of my face and form, just the way I caught him watching while I carved the waxen images.

He was not jesting; he looked entirely serious. I could have fallen through the floor.

Nick always made my thoughts scatter. He was not merely flirting—was he? I hoped that if Arthur ran straight to Gil or Maud, they would give me a moment before rushing in. I could not believe that Nick was here. Was his purpose only to bring my son a gift and to tell me he was leaving and that he'd been moving up in the world? We had shared much of our sad losses and our goals those days we'd spent together. Though I must get over this man, a farewell was better than nothing from him.

"The lad favors you, Varina."

"Do you think so? If you'd seen his father, you would see him more in Arthur. The younger, Edmund, looked like me."

"Yes—I have not forgotten about Edmund."

"Nor I the losses of your family and fortune. So, did the lady at the palace send you?"

"With a gift for your Arthur when she's about to be separated again from hers? No. I regret I haven't come sooner, but I have been kept in almost constant attendance upon the prince or the king."

"That should please you. Now to Wales. And you said you heard what happened. You mean *Signor* Firenze's death?"

He nodded, his eyes still devouring me. "One of the palace guards who knows the sheriff told another—but how we heard doesn't matter. The lady knows, and she is grieved and concerned."

"Did you hear the rest? That I found his body? Nick, I swear, I was pursued by the same man! He spoke only once in a distorted whisper, but he claimed the queen had sent him. He said that the master painter was already on his way to the palace and I must go too."

Nick came closer and rested his hands heavily on my shoulders. Little waves of heat radiated down my arm, to my breasts and belly, even lower.

"I had not heard all of that. Maybe Firenze talked too much—the man talked all the time—and he was overheard by the wrong person. Although they have gone underground for now, even in the city there are some who hate the Tudors. I will see the lady knows that the assassin pursued and tried to trick you too. She is sending a groom to care for your horses, but in truth he is a guard to keep you safe. Varina, I wish it were me."

Now his hands gripped my shoulders, else I would have hurled myself against him and hung on tight. How foolish I had been to think I could forget or forgo this man—and he was leaving.

"Listen to me," he plunged on, his tone as hard as his hands. "You must put out the word that you have hired this man. He will sleep in this shop at night and go with you should you have an errand. Another mouth to feed, I know, so the lady is sending a purse of coins with him. She will be most interested in who the man in the crypt—the murderer, perhaps—was and how he might have known to target you and Firenze."

"Am I to tell no one who my new groom really is?"

"Your immediate family, if you must."

"Please thank her for us," I told him with heartfelt relief and gratitude. How could I ever have suspected the queen? "So you came today to tell me all that because she asked you to?"

"Yes and no. Though I seldom see her of late, she did send me because I know about what you have done for her. I'm to tell you that Jamie Clopton is the man I mentioned, and he'll be coming later today. But I also came because I had to see that you were well and to let you know I rue the day you finished your work and I could see you no more."

My eyes widened as he came closer; I held my breath as we both stood, slightly leaning on the counter and toward each other. "I brought something for you too, and I ask for a gift in return," he went on as he put his hand into his satchel again and drew out a flat wooden box the size of a handkerchief. I watched, transfixed, as he unhooked a tiny metal latch on it.

"Nick, I have no gift for you."

"Just your promise you will not wed—or so much as become betrothed to Master Gage you told me of, or to anyone else, while I am gone. I believe I will be back with the prince's retinue in the late spring or early summer, unless His Majesty summons me back before then. He told me that he might need me for something he has promised to look into. But will you promise me about denying Master Gage?"

"Has no one set her cap for you?" I blurted.

He grinned, then sobered. "I am pleased you are dismayed about that, but I am not going to wed anyone—not until I have done for the king and myself what I must do."

"Protect the prince."

"And, as I told you before, find Lord Lovell."

Oh, by all the saints, I thought, why did he have to talk of his passion for justice and revenge when I wanted to talk of promises and passion? I'd sworn off men, and here I was, ready to do anything he asked, queen's commands or not.

When I hesitated, he opened the lid of the box. A garnet necklace with black metal links lay within on worn green velvet, glinting in the glow of the shop lantern. Putting one hand to my throat, I gasped at the beauty and the impact of it. "Oh, Nick, I cannot."

"A gift of friendship, not ownership. It was my mother's, one of the several things my grandmother managed to snatch when we were turned out of our home and estate. When you wear this, whether openly or under your clothing against your bare skin, I want it to cheer you, to remind you that we have shared much and perhaps shall share yet more."

"It is so dear of you, especially since it was your mother's."

"She died in childbed bearing my sister, who came early and had weak lungs. Two of us Suttons, at least, Lovell did not as good as kill!"

"But if your grandmother lives in poor circumstances, should she not have it?"

"She insisted I keep it. Will you argue like a lawyer and turn me down?"

My chin and lips were trembling, but I mouthed the word "no." Would he think I was puckered for a kiss? I longed for one, not more words, so I closed my mouth and argued no more. I did not want to seem ungrateful, and I would have proudly worn even a piece of brass or tin he gave me. How much this must mean to him—*I* must mean to him.

"I will ever treasure it—and my time with you," I whispered, blinking back tears that welled up in my eyes as he fumbled with the clasp to put it on me. When he had fastened it, I turned, almost within the circle of his arms, overwhelmed by his gifts, his nearness. Surely no future lay ahead for us, but we had these snatched moments before he left London, left my life again.

"You see, Varina," he said, his voice rough with emotion too, "you remind me of her—my grandmother, for I hardly remember my mother. Not in appearance, but you are strong, despite fears and danger, loving and protective of your boy—your boys—as she was to me. And loyal, always loyal, whether to queen, or country, or a man—the right man, that is."

We embraced and held hard. How well we fit together, soft body to hard, his all angles and planes. My breasts flattened against his chest. Even through my lawn chemisette I could feel the press of the necklace below my throat. He kissed me there, his lips and the tip of his hot tongue sliding down to the fluted collarbones above the necklace itself. Then he took my mouth, possessively, just once, then seemed to pull himself away as if my lips opening beneath his in surrender had burned his.

"I'm late," he said, grabbing his gloves. "And if I stay a moment more, that counter will make us a very hard bed. I should be at Baynard's Castle now, overseeing the final packing. Varina—I know Jamie has a dour face, but he has a good heart. Keep him close, but don't you dare treat him as you would me. The necklace is beautiful, and you are too," he threw over his shoulder as he made for the door. "Keep it safe for me then."

He started out before a brief look back just as Gil hurried in. "Ho, Gil," Nick said, "keep a good watch over Varina!"

Gil gaped that he knew his name, and I recalled again how much Nick and I had shared about our lives those days in the little waxworking chamber at the palace. My body yet ablaze with his touch and gaze, I hurried to the window to watch him mount and spur his horse away into the thickening snow.

Queen Elizabeth of York

This very day the king and I would be en route to Windsor for yule, so it saddened me sore to be waving Arthur and Catherine away as they started toward Wales, far to the west. A cheer from the waiting crowds went up as their long entourage left the cobbled courtyard of Baynard's Castle and headed into the London streets, raked clear of muck heaps and strewn with straw.

"Uncap, knaves! Your prince passes!" came the cry from some of the guards, though I am certain that Arthur with his kindly heart would not have asked his people to bare their heads in the winter wind.

Arthur turned back in his saddle, looked up, and waved once more to us as we stood in a window of the gatehouse through which the procession streamed. Then, turning his face away to acknowledge the cheers, he was lost to my sight. Although Catherine would make the journey in a litter, she had opened the leather curtains to wave farewell too. It brought to my mind seeing my parents set out on several journeys, and how—at least in coloring, if not in strength—Arthur resembled his royal grandsire.

Though the king quickly turned away to talk business with some of his privy council—the first portion of Catherine's massive dowry had just been paid by the Spanish—I stayed at the window, watching the parade pass under me. Behind the initial yeomen guards and the royal couple came officers of their household, English advisers appointed by the king who comprised Arthur's Council of Wales and the Marches, then more guards. I spotted Nicholas Sutton, since he was tall and sat a horse so well. He was craning his neck, looking back and forth, evidently searching for someone. Many of the Spanish nobles who had come to England with the princess had sailed for home, but the ladies she had left came next, mounted and wrapped against the winter winds with their riding masks protecting their complexions. And then came the endless rattle and clatter of nearly one hundred carts and packhorses of the baggage train, overseen by guards and servants.

So far to go, one hundred twenty-five miles, days of waving and nodding at four miles an hour, perhaps just ten to twelve miles a day. Bitter weather, grueling roads, staying each night in different inns or homes, including several Arthur himself owned. Anger flashed through me that the king had decided now was the time they were needed in Wales. But he had promised they would be sent for to return to London for the summer season. How it grieved and fretted me to be separated from any of my children, especially my princes.

My heart was burdened too by the murder of the brilliant artist Roberto Firenze. Nick had said that the assassin had told Varina Westcott I had sent him to fetch Firenze and her. Plotting was afoot, and not just mine. I had suspected before that someone close to me was not to be trusted, but who? Who else might have known what Firenze and Varina had done for me? Granted, the Italian talked incessantly. While the king investigated the princes' demise in the Tower, should I do more than send a guard to help protect Varina? And how to do that from Windsor Castle, while I was away from London during the busy yuletide season? No, I feared I must trust that for now, sadly, but of necessity, Varina and Jamie Clopton were on their own.

CHAPTER THE TENTH

Mistress Varina Westcott

J amie Clopton, as serious as he was, fit well into our household, and, truth be told, I felt better with him sleeping in the shop below at night and staying nearby during the day. He was only twenty, not very bright but utterly loyal, and I had quickly put aside my qualms that he might have been my pursuer in the crypt. His presence assured me that Her Majesty had not meant me or *Signor* Firenze ill.

My only problem with Jamie was that young Arthur adored him and declared he wanted to be a hired guard someday too. Also, Jamie's brother was a guard in the Tower, and Jamie regaled my son with stories of ghosts and prisoners there, until I asked him to stop. I didn't need my boy having nightmares like I did.

Today I was pleased to see how much Jamie, like Arthur, was enjoying the mystery play the Christmastide mummers were presenting in the street a few doors from our shop, this one about the nativity of our Lord. Though it was hardly meant to be a comedy, Jamie was grinning and slapping his knee to see horses with false heads, long necks, and humps, portraying camels. The asses were real but kept munching on the hay under the Christ child, making the rag doll with the halo bounce up and down.

Many of the guilds presented tableaux or set pieces with some dialogue they took from place to place during these festive days: Noah's ark, King David's enthronement, our Lord's walking on the water or feeding the masses with but a few fish and loaves. Everyone this late in the day was filled with plum porridge, mince pie, and yule cake washed down by wassail, and much merriment ensued. Our family had already enjoyed our meal amidst the rich kitchen scents and the sweet smell of our bayberry candles.

Christopher had a chief part in this, the chandlers' mystery play. He portrayed one of the wise men, since, no doubt, he could hardly play the Savior Himself. This was their last stop, and he had asked to speak to me privily afterward. I knew what was coming: the ruby ring and the ultimatum about wedding him. He believed, correctly, that I was still shaken by my experience in the crypt and Firenze's death. But if he expected a positive answer, he was much mistaken.

I had thought he would spring the proposal on me quickly after the murder, since he kept claiming I needed his protection. I had steeled myself for this day and felt prepared. Besides, I could feel my garnet necklace under my gown and cloak, for I wore it daily, though usually hidden, and that gave me hope.

Christopher had been most annoyed that I'd hired a new groom, a frivolous female expense, he'd said, since I owned but four horses. I had told him that I had the money to hire and support Jamie, which was quite true, although it was coin from Her Majesty's purse. I told him that no one could keep death from the doorstep, so the continual sale of waxen shrouds and funeral and mass candles would pay for Jamie.

Though we made and sold more funeral candles than festive ones, everyone wanted Christmas candles to light their yule logs being dragged onto their hearths, so the chandlery was doing well enough. Our own hearth in our upstairs solar smelled not only of wood smoke but also of ivy, bay, rosemary, and laurel. Garlands of holly were strung along mantels and banisters as our own huge yule log crackled merrily each night. But how I wished I could rid my brain of one chorus from the yule log carol we oft sang. It seemed to haunt me, to warn me of something dire yet coming:

> *Part must be kept wherewith to light*
> *The Christmas log next year;*
> *And where 'tis safely kept,*
> *The fiend can do no evil here.*

Was that fiend who murdered Firenze still out there beyond my well-lit shop and home? Or even standing here in this small crowd? Her Majesty, who had resided for a time now at Windsor Castle, must believe so, or she would not have sent Jamie. Did she look over her shoulder as I did now, or gaze out of her windows and yet seethe with fury that someone had murdered her royal brothers? How I wished the king had not sent Nick with Prince Arthur and Princess Catherine to distant, wild Wales. Why did they need so many guards there? I'd counted nigh on sixty when my son and I had waved farewell to Nick as he left with the prince's entourage.

I sighed as the mystery play ended with bewigged men as angels blowing trumpets and everyone cheering the performance. Was Nick in Wales yet? I had scarcely been out of London and, like my father, longed to see more of the world. However, I did not long to see Christopher heading for me, his magi's crown in hand, an avid look on his face.

"Let's away up to your solar," he said with a smile, and took my arm to steer me toward my house. "We can have it to ourselves before everyone else comes up. I have a gift for you."

One, I thought, that was ruby red and would almost match the garnet necklace I so cherished. "Christopher, I regret I have not given you a definite answer before, but you really would not listen," I began as he hustled me through the shop and up the holly-garlanded stairs to traverse the hall that led to the solar.

It was here that I had walked lately at night when the house was silent, my pacing well lit by candles, anxious for Nick's safety and my own, trying to decide when to tell Christopher I could not wed him. By the saints, I was a bit of a coward, for he had said more than once that his vouching for me had kept me from being more stringently questioned by the constable about my relationship to Roberto Firenze—"When I know for certain that nothing untoward passed between you!" he had said, emphasizing each word.

"With all that has gone on in my life lately, I must tell you that I am not ready to wed," I told him now. "Not you, not anyone."

"Then we will set a day a month or so hence, so you can get used to it."

"You have been generous and kind, but I can put off my refusal no longer. It isn't fair to you."

"By hell's gates, it isn't, woman!" he said, though I had seldom heard him curse. His hand on me tightened so hard that I flinched. He hurried me along even faster. "Do you not know which side your bread is buttered on?" he demanded. "The benefits of our union and the guild for you? *Was* there something between you and that volatile Italian, you two artists always chatting about paint and colors? And in my own house, when I left you alone?"

"Of course not. Let me go. You are hurting m—"

"I'll not let you go! You've been hurting me. Everyone knows you've been putting me off, and it doesn't help my reputation! Or was there someone at the palace you favored while carving your pretty candles?"

"The palace is in my past," I insisted, shaking his hand off and turning to face him in the doorway of our solar, where the yule log snapped and crackled. Susan, our maid, who had been tending the fire, fled the room through the back servants' door before I could call her back.

"But your service to the queen doesn't have to be in your past—our past," he insisted, seizing both my elbows, pulling me toward him into the room, nearly lifting me off my feet. "Surely the queen will want more carved candles—the Spanish princess too. United, with the correct connections, we could have the premier chandlery of all England, catering to the Tudors, and our own children to follow in our footsteps. A Tudor dynasty—a Gage dynasty. Gil and Maud know what's best, and I'll win Arthur over."

"Christopher, you aren't listening. I am wedding no one now, perhaps ever."

"You do realize I can ruin you in more ways than one, Varina," he said, his voice a menacing whisper, his face furrowed in a frown. That voice—so like the man in the crypt. "Gil needs to be accepted in the guild; you need pardon for selling carved angel candles without permission—and if the authorities caught wind that you had a personal relationship with that dead Italian—"

"The crowner didn't rule for murder, but he should have!"

"That's my point—an inquiry can always be reopened. I said *if* they were to learn that you had a personal relationship with the Italian, they might just do so, and you just might be the one under suspicion."

"There was no personal relationship between us, but an interesting acquaintance!"

"Ah, I can see it now," he went on, his voice taunting, "a lovers' quarrel that day in such a holy place. You slapped him or mayhap pushed him away; he fell and broke his neck; you dragged him out where other bodies lay in the dark, interred forever."

I was aghast at his tirade, his implications. And at how such an accusation might force me to expose my duties for the queen. Would she help me or abandon me if I were arrested and sent to trial?

As frightened as I was, I was even more furious. "Leave my house!" I told him. "That is a pack of lies, and I will appeal it beyond the city authorities if I must."

He locked the door to the hall. He put his magi crown down on a table and slapped his gloves there too—black gloves. "Swear to me you will wed me, or I swear to you I will do all I said," he whispered.

Undecided whether to stand my ground to defy him or flee, I crossed my arms. "If so," I countered, "I will claim that you were the tall man in the crypt with the black gloves and the lantern. I will say you wrongly believed that the *Maestro* and I were having the relationship you claim, and your overweening pride was hurt. You had set it up that Firenze and I would be in the chapel alone together. You came back early from the beekeepers in Kent, not only for the secret rites but to kill both of us, only I fled from you. Take your lies to the constable, and I will swear you were that man."

He had stared at me all through that, his mouth agape. I warrant he had locked the door because he meant to make love to me, whether I was willing or not. He had certainly not expected a mere woman to turn his threats against him. And the fact that he had obviously thought all this out— could he be the killer? I needed protection indeed not *by* Christopher Gage, rather *from* him.

He leaped at me, and I ran. He yanked me back into his harsh embrace and ripped off my cape, nearly choking me as he tore the ties. I tried to scream, but he clamped a hand over my mouth, twisting my head back against his shoulder.

Why didn't the others come in? Perhaps Arthur and Jamie were having another snowball fight in the street. I needed Gil or Jamie or someone.... I feared he meant to break my neck—perhaps as he had Firenze's.

I bit Christopher's hand hard; he yelped and let go. I started to scream, but as if my panic had summoned him, Jamie leaped into the room through the servants' entry by which the maid had gone. He pulled Christopher off me and slammed his gloved fist into his face. Christopher's head snapped back. Blood spurted from his mouth as he slid to the floor, holding his jaw in his hand.

"Damn you, bastard, you broke a tooth! I'll have your head, you bootlicking cur!"

"This bootlicking cur," I cried, "is not only in my employ, but was once a guard from the palace!" I looked down at my former friend—my husband's former friend, at least. Regretful that I had given that away, I yet knew it was the only way to keep this man from causing me and Jamie—my family—more trouble. I put my hand on Jamie's sleeve to stay further violence.

"You—you still have ties to the palace?" Christopher asked me, spitting blood and a tooth into his hand. "I knew it! And you're keeping it secret from the guild."

"I am not in the guild; nor is a weak woman likely to be, and you've been keeping Gil out, haven't you? I repeat, leave my house now and admit this chandlery through Gilbert Penne into the Worshipful Guild of Wax Chandlers, even if he never becomes a member of your Holy Order of the Name of Jesus, our dear Lord who said to turn the other cheek and forgive seventy times seventy."

"You'll not preach Scripture to me, woman," Christopher mumbled, still bleeding. "Or hide behind the queen's skirts just because you carved a few pretty candles for her to give the Spanish princess."

"Nor shall I ever wear your bloodred ring. Just call me Eve, then, off on her own, gazing at the tree of the knowledge of good and evil—and I see a snake in the grass here before me."

Whether those words finally shocked him to silence or Jamie's hulking menace convinced him to leave, Christopher Gage rose shakily to his feet and stalked from the room through the servants' door. Jamie followed him down the steps to be certain he did no more mischief.

I felt both elated and rueful. I should not have invoked the power of the palace. The queen had given me permission to tell those closest to me that I had, at least, carved candles for her. But Christopher was no longer close to me—he had made himself my enemy. Perhaps that would force him to stay away, not to tamper with my life or with Gil's. And surely I had not spoken the truth when I'd accused him of being the man in the crypt.

Trembling, I went over to the hearth and braced myself against the mantel, stiff-armed, with both hands, staring down into the red-gold flames. As they slowly devoured the large log, I wished so bright a light could chase away the cold and the dark from my heart.

PART II

"And the light of a candle shall shine no more at all in thee; and the voice of the bridegroom and the bride shall be heard no more...."

—REVELATIONS 18:23

"In my true and careful heart there is
So much woe, and so little bliss
That woe is me that ever I was born;
For all that thing which I desire I miss,
And all that ever I would not, I have."

—"A COMPLAINT TO HIS LADY,"
GEOFFREY CHAUCER

CHAPTER THE ELEVENTH

Queen Elizabeth of York

"*E*nter!" I called out at the flurry of knocks on my privy chamber door at Richmond Palace, where we had resided since leaving Windsor after Christmas.

I knew something was wrong when Sibil Wynn rushed in rather than walking circumspectly. I glimpsed her flushed face before she nearly collapsed in a curtsy.

"Word from the king," she said in a trembling voice. "He wishes your presence forthwith. A courier has come from Wales."

It was April the fourth, just after dark. Dared I hope Arthur's bride was with child? "What news?" I demanded, striding for the door.

"I know not, only that the king sent for you in haste and—"

With Sibil and several other ladies scurrying behind me, I walked as fast as I could, covering the eternal length of corridors between us. What would it have been like, I thought erratically, to be a commoner, to live in a small place, to make one's own meals and clean one's house, to always share the same board and bed? Why, it took a retinue of attendants to pad the mattress, check for concealed weapons, perfume the sheets and blankets, and draw the curtains of the royal bed.

Fear stabbed me as others sank into bows or curtsies as I passed. Faces blurred by. Could someone who was cleaning Westminster have stumbled on my secret chamber with the wax effigies and sent word to the king? Perhaps he had news for me of who had harmed my brothers in the Tower? No, no, he was secretive about all that. Besides, I'd heard he had allowed James Tyrell to return to France, so surely he had questioned him and cleared his name. The courier from Wales—it must be something concerning our dear Arthur and Catherine.

My heart sank when I saw my husband, slumped, silent. Worse, his confessor, Father Martin, was with him, gaunt and grim faced. "My lord, what has happened?" I demanded.

Henry leaned against the back of a chair, gripping it with both hands. He opened his mouth to speak but could not. Breathing in and out, in and out, he had not yet looked at me.

In a soothing voice, Father Martin said, "As I have told His Majesty, if we receive good things at the hands of God, why may we not endure evil things? Your Majesty," he said to me, "your dear son Arthur has departed to God."

At first I was so stunned I could not catch his meaning. I gaped at him, even as the king shuffled toward me—

suddenly looking old, so old—and pulled my cold hands into his trembling ones.

"Arthur ..." he choked out. "Took ill—died. A chill, ague—I know not, but more details will come forthwith."

My knees gave way, but Henry held me up. My dear son, firstborn and heir—another lost child—the hope of England's future, the next Tudor king ... dead? Had he said dead?

Dry gasps racked me. I swayed on my feet; we swayed together.

"C-Cather-ine," Henry stuttered. "She t-took ill too, but is better. But so sudden—our Arthur ..."

I held him, tried to comfort him as I heard Father Martin leave the room and close the door. "My dear lord, we must see that he is cared for—a fine burial," I choked out.

"Not clear back here. At the abbey in Worcester. I swear it shall become a cathedral, a shrine! Now only willful Henry, a mere boy, stands between us and oblivion for the Tudor throne, for our daughters can never secure the kingdom. Fighting—battles—chaos again."

I know not where I found strength to so much as speak. "Do not say so. We are yet young, my lord. We have lost children but have hale and hearty ones. But there will never be another Arthur, so beloved, so—"

I needed to sit down. I felt ill, faint. I tried to get to the chair but instead fell into Henry's arms. He lowered me to the floor and sat beside me, both of us wailing and weeping and tearing our hair and clothes. Curse royal restraint or decorum, however much we were alone. My two brothers gone, my two babies, now our hope for the future in our dear

Prince Arthur. Despite his weak health, sudden, so sudden. Too sudden?

I sat up straighter. Had we—the king—sent our son into danger to a distant Welsh castle just as blindly as Mother and I had sent young Richard to the Tower with our young King Edward V? No, no, I must not imagine a traitor in every tower, and yet ...

"We shall make plans from here for his burial," Henry was saying, his voice not his own.

"Indeed we shall." I got to my knees to rise. "The necessary things must not go undone, and I shall see to that."

Mistress Varina Westcott

Though the early April breeze was brisk, I kept my bedroom window ajar so I would not feel so closed in. After many sleepless nights, fearing, despite Jamie's watchfulness, that the man who had killed Firenze would seek me out, I was sleeping somewhat better lately. As I had expected, Christopher had also become my enemy, though he was evidently wary enough of my court connection that he had proposed Gil as a guild member. Still, I had heard naught from the palace or Nick and steeled myself that I might never again. I'd gleaned no word from customers that the Prince and Princess of Wales and their retinue would be returning this spring.

As the night bells of St. Mary Abchurch and St. Swithin's ended their twelve tolls for midnight, I heard a horse. That alone was unusual, for there was a curfew and the night watchmen walked their routes. The hoofbeats came fast, close, on cobbles. A rider in our courtyard beneath my window? But had Jaime not locked the gate?

I slipped from bed and peered out into the darkness, kneeling in the new spring rushes on the floor. One wan lantern threw a square of pale light into the courtyard. Yes, a rider here, dismounted. Men's voices. Oh, thank God, Jamie was greeting him. He must know him and have let him in.

But who could it be? My stomach cramped. Jamie had said he would not admit anyone at night. Who would know to knock on the shop door where Jamie slept on a pallet he removed each day? Now the two tall men bent in huddled talk before they disappeared beneath my window.

He was letting the stranger into the house! No doubt through the door leading to stairs that came directly up into the back hall near the bedchambers!

All the fears I'd fought to keep at bay beat against me. That murderer who had pursued me in the crypt . . . I should not have trusted Jamie—was he just biding his time? I had believed that the queen had sent him to guard me, that she could have naught to do with silencing Firenze.

At least my Arthur's chamber was down the hall. Should I hide? No. Then they would search for me and rouse or harm the others. I had no weapon here but a heavy pewter washbowl and ewer.

I shot the bolt on the door and darted over to dump the rest of the wash water from the ewer, accidentally spilling most of it down my breasts so that my night rail clung to me. The floor was slippery, but I stood beside the door and lifted the heavy thing with both hands like a club. Though it came muted, the rapping on the wooden door thudded through me.

"Mistress Varina! 'Tis Jamie. You have a visitor from the palace!"

My pulse pounded so hard I shook. In the middle of the night? Did he mean to lure me out with the same lie my pursuer in the crypt had used?

"What's amiss?" I called, my voice not my own.

"Nick Sutton's here from Wales with sad news and a command."

"Nick?"

"'Tis I, Varina," came that unmistakable voice. "The Prince of Wales has died. I'm to take you to Richmond Palace as soon as you can get your things together. The queen needs funeral candles, winding sheets—and you."

I could barely take in his words. Her Majesty's son, the pride of the Tudors, dead? She wanted funeral goods for him, but why send for me too?

I unbolted and opened the door a crack, then looked out. Jamie held a lantern; I blinked into its light. Yes, praise God, Nick Sutton in the flesh, looking harried but handsome. When his eyes dropped from my face to my breasts, I remembered my sopped night rail clung to me. He swallowed hard and glanced back to my face.

"I'll have to dress," I said.

"We'll be riding hard and fast. I've brought boy's breeches, and you'll ride with me for now. I've packhorses and guards waiting in the street to carry candles and waxen cloths, and I'll leave a bag of coins to cover things with Gil."

He thrust at me a lace-neck shirt, breeches, woven cap, boots, and cape, all of blackest hue, perhaps to hide me at night but also for the formal period of mourning.

"I'll have to tell my family, say good-bye to my Arthur," I said, stunned at the sadness and speed of all these events. As much as I had yearned for Nick's return, was I dreaming, this time not about the loss of my own child Edmund? That is when it truly struck me that the death was not only of our prince but of Her Majesty's son, another of her cherished, lost children she so grieved. I wondered whether she wanted a waxen effigy of Arthur too. No, if I was reasoning all that out, I surely was not dreaming.

Keeping his voice low, Nick said, "I understand if you want to wake your son and then leave him. But Jamie and I think you'd best tell just Gil and let him and your sister handle things here. Waking your lad—saying good-bye—could confuse or upset him."

"Yes, all right. I've never been to Richmond, but it isn't far. I'm sure I can be back on the morrow."

I was certain he started to say something else but held back. I closed the door and scrambled into the clothing, which fit amazingly well, however foreign it felt to be garbed as a man. I pulled my hair back in a horsetail, tied it up, and pinned it as best I could beneath the leather cap.

Jamie had roused Gil, who gaped at me as I clomped out into the hall in my manly garb and unfamiliar boots. Tears trickled down my cheeks as we went downstairs into the workroom and storage areas below. Gil quickly pulled out and rolled six huge sheets of wax-impregnated cloth—far too much for one corpse, but I didn't say so, for perhaps that is what had been ordered and paid for. Among the forty votive candles we counted out, I wrapped six black candles, then added two angel candles, one for the queen and one for

Princess Catherine, a widow so soon, so young. Just think, I marveled: Westcott cerements would enclose the body of our dear Prince of Wales, and our candles would light his tomb.

"There's a certain way to wind these cloths," Gil was telling Nick, who hovered close, as if they'd been boon companions for years. "They'd better have someone skilled in Wales to do it lest they crack."

"I will see to that," Nick assured him. For once, I doubted something the man had said, but perhaps on the way to Richmond I could give him advice to pass on to the embalmers there.

Even though he was all brusque business, I drank in the sight and sound of Nick Sutton. He was truly here, and I was going with him to see Her Majesty. I'd somehow forgotten how tall he was and failed to recall completely his gray eyes and the way his eyebrows could slant when he frowned. His hair looked shorter, his face paler, and new frown lines seemed to furrow his forehead. Perhaps he had lost a bit of weight, for he looked leaner.

Gil and Jamie carried out what we had selected. "Jamie," I told him on his way back in, "please keep a special watch over Arthur—and no more frightening tales of torture in the Tower." He nodded and went to lug out another load as Nick came closer, watching as I stuffed a few more things in a satchel in which I had already put a day dress and a better gown, a hairbrush and slippers.

"I'm sorry things are rushed, so desperate," he said, lifting a hand to cup my chin and caress my wet cheek with his thumb. "You'll have to trust me on this, trust the queen too."

"I am honored to serve her in her dark hour."

"We'll talk later—on the barge from Westminster to Richmond," he promised.

"I've seldom been outside London."

I sensed he wished to say something important, but he only nodded, then said, "Clothing and goods will be provided for you if you are away a little while. Let's ride."

It became even more obvious that I had been sent for in all haste, for barges seldom plied the Thames at night. But the oarsmen were skilled and fought against the incoming tide. They bent their backs against the current as we headed westward on the Thames. It might have been the same barge in which Nick first fetched me, for we sat on a similar padded bench, close together in the chill April air, holding—no, gripping—each other's hands.

"Soon the entire city will waken to the dreadful news," Nick said, scanning the darkness on both banks of the river.

"How did it happen—his death?"

"Both he and the princess took suddenly ill late last month, over a week ago in Wales. Events and symptoms are yet unclear. Some sort of throat infection ... difficulty breathing, weak lungs, which he'd had all his life, of course, and had recovered from. He became unconscious and died on April second, and his body is lying in state at the castle, but needs better—formal—tending before his funeral and burial on the twenty-third of this month. There will be a huge funeral cortege between Ludlow and Worcester, with many nobles in attendance. Their Majesties long to be there, but protocol and tradition deem it otherwise, of course, even for lesser folk."

"I always thought it sad that the family are seldom the chief mourners."

"But the king and queen are making the plans," he said, as if to defend them.

"Yet it seems wrong that even Princess Catherine won't attend. When my husband died—little Edmund too—I cloaked and masked myself and slipped into the graveyard to watch the interment from a ways off. I've never told anyone else that."

"You brave and bold girl, my little iconoclast, yearning to be in the chandlers' guild, breaking in on that holy guild's secret service—and turning down a profitable marriage proposal from an influential man. Jamie told me about all that, and how Master Gage has reacted since then."

I nodded to all he had said and clung to his praise, however much I longed to know what "iconoclast" meant. A female who did not keep to her place? Someone who broke the rules? I did not intend to be any of that, but this was no time to argue, and I changed the topic.

"You brought the dreadful news back to Their Majesties from Wales?" I asked. "What a burden to have to be the bearer of that."

"At least they did not kill the messenger, as they say. I've been blessed that they have seemed to trust and employ me more and more."

He nodded proudly, but I saw light from the lantern in front of the barge reflected in a single tear track on his left cheek. Was he thinking of the royal family's losses or his own? Either way, I understood, and longed to comfort him.

"When I reached Richmond," he went on, "I told the king's confessor, and he related the tragic news. They both took it terribly hard, then sprang into action, making decisions. The queen sent for me and, again secretly, for you."

But why secretly this time, I wondered, if the funeral would be public and we were simply selling and delivering funerary goods for it? I did not ask that question. Rather, I yearned to tell Nick I had missed him and thought of him incessantly. I wanted to ask what it really meant to him that I had turned down Christopher Gage's ultimatum to wed. I wanted to throw my arms around Nick and hold tight, to climb into his lap, but we huddled together, almost cuddling. I felt strangely safe, my thigh pressed to his through my man's garb instead of my thicker skirts, my hands between his, skin to skin. The barge thrust on through the Thames, push, pull, up and down, my exhausted mind spinning 'round and 'round. . . .

I must have dozed, slumped against him. He started too as one of the bargemen called out, "Richmond! I can see the towers and turrets!"

The oarsmen had an easier time of it now. Not only was our destination in sight, but Nick said the tide turned here, which would help their rowing. Dawn pearled the sky, silhouetting the intricate, many-storied buildings and fantastical towers as we came closer. It was so rural here, the palace set among forests and orchards. A long row of flowering cherry trees stretched along the riverbank before the palace, so it seemed the rosy brick and stone buildings emerged from a sea of foaming white.

"The king was once the Earl of Richmond, you know," Nick said as I gathered the sack of my wrinkled garments and the wrapped, carved angel candle I would give the queen. "When old Sheen Palace burned on this site, he helped design Richmond, and, I warrant, loves it best of all his royal houses. It was finished only last year, and—the wonder of the age—has running water in the royal chambers. The wooden floors still smell fresh, and even the ceilings are painted and gilded to the hilt."

Indeed, the beauty of the palace awed me. When I had first entered Westminster, I had been excited. Now, soon to face the sorrowing queen—and for what secret purpose?—I felt reluctant. Perhaps she did want an effigy of Prince Arthur. But at least, through it all, Nick was with me.

"What is that mournful sound?" I asked him as, with unsteady legs, I disembarked upon the landing. "Could they be holding a funeral mass already? It's like distant voices humming or singing."

"When the wind is right, you can hear it rushing past the painted and gilt weather vanes that protrude from the onion dome cupolas on the towers—the singing weather vanes they call them. It always sounds eerie, and yes, it seems as if the palace itself is mourning."

Sunlight was peeping over the forest and tall stone walls when we entered the palace by the front gate, which guards flung open for us. I still clung to my sack of garments, for surely I would not be taken to the queen or even to one of her ladies looking like a lad. But evidently I was much mistaken—and mistaken about what else?

We strode across an outer courtyard, where only a few guards were astir. Beyond that enclosure, I glimpsed gardens with sanded paths adorned with clipped, low bushes and guarded by the king's painted and carved stone beasts as at Westminster. Nick kept one hand on my elbow, steering me along as we strode into the inner quadrangle, where a huge fountain splashed.

"The privy lodgings," he told me as we went through a door on the far side, "a labyrinth of them. We're to go straight to the queen."

"But I . . . Looking like this? I need a moment's privacy."

"I understand, but do not take time to change your clothes." Nick gave me a moment to relieve myself in a small garderobe, one decorated no less with golden griffins and dragons on the walls.

We went upstairs, then down corridors as my wide gaze devoured timbered ceilings painted azure between beams and Tudor roses picked out in gold. Huge bay windows opened to the outside. It staggered me to realize how bounteous must be the royal wealth, but then the prince's death, my summons here, and Nick's presence all stunned me the more.

I rejoined him, and we turned into a narrow hall, a back way in again. Did all the royal residences have secret doors and chambers, perhaps for trysts or for escape—or for servants to be brought in covertly for particular favors? How sad that after sixteen years of rule the Tudors could not rest easy that the throne was indeed theirs. Now to lose their future, though no doubt the young Henry, Duke of York, would be elevated to become Prince of Wales.

As Nick knocked on the door, I recalled how the guards had called out for the crowd to uncap when Arthur and Catherine rode past en route to Wales. I removed my cap, accidentally snagging my hair, which spilled down my back. I swear, it was my only proof I was not a lad. My old acquaintance, Sibil Wynn opened the door. Though she was attired in black mourning garb, not prettily gowned and jeweled as usual, for one moment I felt as if the clock had been turned back to my first royal summons. But the smile on her face when she saw Nick sobered me.

"She's been waiting," she told Nick with no greeting but a narrow-eyed glance at me. "She hasn't slept."

We entered and passed through two more small chambers, elegant but empty. Ahead, through an open door, I could see Her Majesty within the last chamber, pacing. She too wore black, and ebony satin draped the tapestry I could see from here. At least two lanterns glowed on a cluttered table. She heard us and turned. Her once beautiful complexion looked sallow and blotched; gray half-moons hung under her red, pinched eyes. Like mine, her long blond hair was loose and wild. Nick closed the door behind the three of us.

He bowed and I curtsied, though I felt my attire meant I should bow too. "Blessed saints, you are here," she said, drawing us both up by our hands. Her skin was clammy and cold.

Dared I speak before she said more? "Your Majesty, I was undone to learn of the loss of our dear prince. I have

brought you an angel votive candle in his precious memory."
I unwrapped and extended the candle to her.

She took it, cradled it as if it were a baby, then did not
look at it again, but only at me, then Nick. "Yes—yes—I
thank you. And Nick for fetching you. The best funeral
goods have been selected? Plenteous winding sheets for the
damp Welsh spring?"

"Yes, Your Majesty," Nick assured her. "Packed on fresh
horses and waiting to head west."

"Varina, I am in desperate need of your services again,"
she said, drawing me a bit away from Nick. "I greatly regret
that someone harmed the brilliant Firenze, and I vow to you
that I am—indirectly—pursuing who might have murdered
him and tried to harm you."

"I thank you for sending Jamie Clopton—and now Nick."

Merely nodding, evidently intent on her own thoughts,
she pulled me down beside her onto an ornately carved and
thickly padded bench. That intimate move shook me. We
were sitting close, eye to eye. Our knees almost touched. For
one swift moment it was as if we were kin, both with our
blond hair spilling over our shoulders, both in mourning for
lost sons. In that moment, I felt closer to her than I ever had
to my own sister, Maud.

Not only grief but desperation emanated from the
queen. As she had been in her compulsion to possess the effigies, again she seemed driven by demons. The little butter-
flies that beat in my belly turned to flapping bird wings.

"I am not asking for an effigy this time," she went on in
a rush, as if she'd read my mind. "Not now, at least. I need

someone I can trust utterly to attend the prince's body, oversee his doctors or rustic embalmers to be certain all is well-done in that wild place—a place still teeming with Yorkist loyalists, I vow. You see, Ludlow Castle, though it has been in Tudor hands for these years of our reign, was once the mightiest of York fortresses. Our enemy, my uncle King Richard, used it as his stronghold and headquarters from time to time in the battle against my lord's forces. Two villains we discussed before—Sir Francis Lovell and Sir James Tyrell—have been familiar with the area, as has the Earl of Surrey, whom His Majesty is sending to Wales as our chief mourner. It was a necessity that the Prince of Wales be sent there with his council to command the area, but it was a . . . a risk—I did not realize how much—and now . . ."

She hesitated as tears flowed again. Evidently, she realized she was still cradling the carved candle in one arm, and laid it down between us on the bench. For the first time, I caught a glimpse of what she might want from me. To personally take the Westcott funerary goods to Wales? To go *clear to Wales* to oversee the prince's embalming? I almost blurted out that I could not bear to leave my son Arthur without a fond farewell, but his very name almost on my lips made me sit mute.

And nod. Dear Lord in heaven, despite my reservations and fears, I had just nodded my understanding, which the look on her face said she read as my agreement!

She nodded too, pressed my hand in hers, and that was our bargain.

"Nick, to me," she said, raising her voice, and he came

over. Evidently to avoid towering over Her Majesty, he knelt before us, between us. "Varina has agreed," she told him, "to go to Wales to tend the prince's body and to accompany the funeral procession to Worcester and help to oversee arrangements for the service there."

I had? I had agreed to all that?

"I know you will guard her with your life, Nicholas Sutton. The king has agreed to this service from both of you. But there is one more thing I speak only to the two of you, and I need your sworn vow of secrecy for the task. This boon must be kept secret from everyone—everyone!—unless I give you permission otherwise."

She stared at Nick. "Yes, I swear it, Your Majesty," he said.

She turned her head toward me. However bloodshot her eyes were, they bored into mine. "Yes, I swear all secrecy, Your Majesty."

"I fear—I think . . ." she whispered, her voice breaking before she went on. She cleared her throat and began again. "It occurs to me that our son and heir could have met with foul play. Though the Welsh chieftains, untamed as they still are, are loyal to our throne, Yorkist remnants remain of those who do not wish us well. Having lost my dear brothers in what was surely vile murder, I must know the circumstances of the illness and death of Arthur Tudor. It . . . it could be the same villain, though I must have proof. I have written letters to his widow giving both of you access to her presence, permission to inquire for me about all that led up to . . . to their illness and his death. You must find someone to interpret her Spanish for you, so choose that one carefully, and do not overly distress the princess, if that is possible. She is, of course, like me, distraught."

"You fear poisoning, Your Majesty?" Nick asked.

"I fear evil, and I bid you both beware. If you can find what Their Graces did, where they went—yes, what they ate or drank that might have brought on ... brought on what happened ..."

She heaved such a huge sigh that I thought her already slumped form would deflate further. But she was strong even with the burden of this crushing loss, as I must learn to be, so that I too could bear my son's loss. So that I could take on this task she had laid upon us. So that, even though I would have Nick at my side, I could weather this dangerous duty in distant Wales.

CHAPTER THE TWELFTH

"*I* understand why she chose me ... to oversee ... care of ... his body." My words to Nick came out jerkily as we jolted along mile after mile on the same huge horse. "But I've never tried ... to find out why someone died."

Had I made a statement or asked a question? And it had sounded like a rhyme.

"Later," he said only. "Later for much more."

And what did that mean? I longed to ask. I had the strangest urge to laugh, though being garbed as a lad still sobered me. How I had yearned to be part of the all-men chandlers' guild and their secret society; now here I was, looking like one of a band of men in service to Their Majesties. I found a sense of heady freedom in all this. Freed from my long skirts, my daily duties, even from the confines of London, I dared to feel that I was momentarily free too of the rules that bound women. I was important. I knew I had some power, though I felt frightened and exhausted.

Still, Nick had not answered my question, and I could not even think beyond right now.

Even the horses we rode were able to rest, for we stopped for fresh ones every twenty miles or so on this route that Nick and several others had ridden only yesterday in the opposite direction. Then too, despite my initial excitement to see some of England, I barely knew where we were. So far, the ride had been a blur of hamlets, towns, fields, and forests.

Yet I adored the sweeping sensation of riding astride behind Nick in the big saddle meant for a man in full armor. I bounced against him with my thighs spread by his lean buttocks while my breasts rubbed his back and my arms held to his flat, hard waist. The garnet necklace he had given me slid up and down against the bare skin of my throat. It made my body ache for him, though, by the saints, I must not think so, for this was the most serious of ventures.

I had made myself save the repeated question of "Why me?" until we were dismounting again, for if Nick didn't turn his head, I could not hear what he said. Besides, I recognized that among our companions, we could hardly shout back and forth about our secret assignment. At least now we were hemmed in by the fifteen others dismounting amid creaking saddles and horse snorts, so no one would hear us.

"Nick," I whispered, "why did she choose to send me—to discover the reason for his death, I mean?"

"The queen trusts you, for one thing." He lifted me down before what looked to be a country inn. My knees nearly buckled, but his hand steadied me until I got my land legs. "Varina, you are known by but a few people, so that is of import to her, and—"

"So since I am of no account to those important enough to have harmed the prince," I said, hands on my hips, "I will not cause undue interest?" What was wrong with me? I suddenly sounded like a shrew.

"That is part of it. You are of interest to me, however, so be reasonable about this."

"Reasonable? Preparing the royal body for the grave is one thing, but to leave my son and family, searching for a mysterious man or men, suddenly does not sound reasonable."

Before he could scold me, I ran inside for some privacy to relieve myself and to grab some drink and sustenance. But the moment we were on fresh horses again, I pursued my query, this time hoping to keep my temper in check.

"And *you* will not cause undue interest either?" I asked, leaning around his shoulder to keep my voice down. I was becoming more fearful that I had agreed to all this, leaving my son, home, and shop. Jamie was taking word back to Gil and Maud—I had written a note to Arthur about riding clear to Wales with our funeral goods—but when would I be able to go home? "Are we," I went on when he didn't answer, "to play the parts of the sheriff and the crowner who questioned me about poor *Signor* Firenze's death?"

He turned his head so I could hear him over the thunder of hoofbeats. Even from his profile, I could tell he was frowning. "In a way, but without their blatant authority. I know it is a new and difficult challenge for you to serve Their Majesties this way."

"But you are used to such assignments?"

"I told you I yearn not only to prove myself but also to

protect the Tudors. You're exhausted, Varina. We all are. Best, like a warrior heading for battle, you learn to sleep in the saddle."

In other words, he wanted me to keep still, to go back to acting the way I had for years, doing what I was told by the male members of my family, then by the Tudors, and now by him. I leaned my forehead against his shoulder blade. "I must be both tired and mad," I said, quietly enough that I thought he could not hear.

"It may be a madman we're after," he said, surprising me. "We both have a stake in this, Varina. We shall phrase our inquiries carefully, if not covertly. I should tell you aforehand that the lady made me vow I would protect you and your honor, especially since you are unescorted by womenfolk on this journey."

My honor? Reputation, he meant, of course, the very thing Christopher had bemoaned about himself. I supposed Nick meant that he had taken some sort of vow, for the queen oft spoke in terms of those. Had he promised her not to lay an untoward hand on me?

May the Lord forgive my wayward thoughts, but that angered me at the queen a bit. I was irked at Nick too—at the entire world, including myself for getting into this—but I was not prepared for the next words he spoke. Perhaps he had waited until we were mounted and on our way again so he did not have to face me.

"She also said," he told me, "that should some question of impropriety between the two of us arise, I can say that we are betrothed, so tongues will not wag."

I sucked in a sharp breath. He said no more. Was he now silent because he assumed I *must* accept such an arrangement, since it came from the queen? Or because he was angry he must play that part? After all, anything between us of lasting value was impossible, with our different stations in life and his desire to live close to the Tudors—wasn't it? I felt as if cold water had been thrown on my yearning for him, my mooning over the two kisses we had shared. Despite the weight of his gift to me around my neck, there would never be a betrothal ring, so my desire for him must be tamped down. God's truth, I must not act the strumpet with him or become merely his mistress!

What was wrong with me? I asked myself. I desired Nick; I was honored to serve the queen. Yet this new sense of power and import had made me argue, made me challenge Nick, want to fight him. . . . I sputtered with frustration, perhaps with longing too, but held my tongue—for now.

As we entered another stretch of thickening forest, our guards pulled tighter to surround us and the ten burdened horses. I could only pray we'd packed the wax cerements and candles well enough for safety's sake. I heard at least two swords scrape from their scabbards lest we be beset by thieves. Night was drawing nigh, and thickening shadows shifted through the woods. Two more hours or so, Nick had promised earlier, and we would stop for a while to sleep. He, I realized, had not slept since leaving Ludlow with his dire news, yet he managed to remain calm and controlled, while I seemed to be losing that battle. I yearned for a soft bed, but not one with Nick Sutton in it!

Despite all that had just passed between us—our first argument?—I held tighter to him as the forest road down which we plunged closed in to resemble a tunnel. Dark bushes brushed our feet, and giant oaks loomed overhead, some with low limbs as if to grasp at us. We passed through deep, mossy banks where the faint smell of wood smoke from invisible chimneys or campfires wafted on the air. Erratic dirt tracks led from this main road into mazes of thickets. Whether such paths were beaten bare by beasts of the animal or human kind, I was not sure.

But despite my fears, I could not leave our discussion where it had ended. "Well," I finally said, "I hope it doesn't come to our having to claim a betrothal, even if we are in an untamed land."

Again he turned his head to speak over his left shoulder. "The idea would be distasteful to you?"

"Absurd, that is all. We must, of course, tell some lies of necessity, but I don't think that particular one will work. Why would a king's man on the Tudor ladder to power and popularity want his name linked with a mere chandler and candlemonger?"

"The lady has made you more than that. *You* have made yourself more than that, Varina, and you are more than that to me."

I held to him, my arms tight around him, my anger, if not my fears, dissipating a bit, yes, lifting away. I suddenly felt dizzy, but not from exhaustion or the continual bouncing. *You have made yourself more than that, Varina, and you are more than that to me.*

It was one of the most seductive, inspiring statements a

man had ever made to me, and from this man I so admired and—saints preserve me—also desired.

Queen Elizabeth of York

The king downed a few gulps of wine and nibbled a bit of cheese, then took a huge bite of bread and chewed quickly. Finally my urging that he take some sustenance was rewarded, though I sensed trouble coming. I had just told him what privy duty, besides delivering candles and shrouds, I had given to Nicholas and Varina, and I feared he wanted to fortify himself for battle.

"I cannot believe you took that into your own hands," he said, his voice low and slow. "Granted, foul play could have caused Arthur's death, but trusting the discovery of such to Nick Sutton and a female chandler?"

"Varina Westcott is talented, bright, and circumspect. Her chandlery makes the best waxen cerements. I had her carve some candles for me. You said I could care for ordering the candles and wax cloth."

"Yes, yes, that is not what I meant. To have the two of them, however carefully, inquire into what Arthur and Catherine ate, where they went . . . I could have assigned someone to do all that."

"But it has to be done now, while evidence—clues—are fresh, and by someone who does not seem official—not an arm of the king." I rose from my chair across the corner of the table in his privy withdrawing room and knelt before him, draping my breasts and arms across his knees as if to cling to him in supplication. "My dear lord, they can inquire sub rosa, go about the grounds or trace Their Graces' steps without drawing attention—at least I pray so, lest some of our enemies mayhap yet lurking about that area ferret them out."

"Such as whom?" he asked, lifting my face with his hand so that I stared up into his narrowed eyes.

"Wales still has wolves," I told him, my voice strong. "Not only the four-legged kind but also the two-legged Yorkist wolves in Tudor sheep clothing. You have said so yourself."

"But do you have someone specific in mind?" he demanded, his voice finally rising to its usual volume and pitch.

"You know there have been rumors about Lord Lovell returning from Europe."

"Only rumors. The way the bastard keeps disappearing, giving us the slip, causes wishful chatter about him. I've had some reports that he's been seen too, but the man's a damned chameleon, so no one knows what he looks like anymore."

"So you've heard reports also. Isn't it true that, as your sworn enemy, Francis Lovell used to spend much time in that area of Wales before my uncle was king?"

"But the point is, will you, a woman, go behind my back in political matters?"

"Political? I say family matters, and that is a woman's realm. Our Arthur is dead, and, despite his weak health, we're not truly sure how or why! And Catherine is recovered, so why is he not also? As for other suspicious persons, what about Sir James Tyrell? Oh, yes, I know he's back in France, but he has his minions too."

"Now you indeed overstep! He has been pardoned and is true to me!"

"My dear lord, I tried to speak with him during the wedding festivities, but he avoided me. He knows the region around Ludlow like the back of his double-dealing hand, since he was commissioner of soldiers in Wales under my uncle Richard. And you have sent the Earl of Surrey as our chief mourner to Ludlow when he was once a Yorkist to the hilt."

"By hell's gates! So were you, Elizabeth!"

"By birth, yes—not truly by choice!"

For one moment, my husband gaped at me, obviously stunned by my vehemence or my specific suspicions. However weak he had looked since we had heard the tragic news, he amazed me by standing in one swift motion and hauling me to my feet, so that I almost dangled before him.

"*I* will see to James Tyrell!" He spit the words out. "You are hell-bent on blaming him for more than siding with your uncle in the wars, are you not? More perhaps than being invited to our heir's wedding? I have told you I will undertake the inquiry into what certain men might or might not know concerning your other great matter from years ago!"

Could he not even put into words the loss—the deaths—of my brothers, and one a rightful king? *My great matter*, he called it. Although James Tyrell had been in London for Arthur's marriage and the joust—how I'd cheered when young Sutton had bested him—had Henry not yet questioned Sir James about his possible knowledge of my brothers' deaths? Rumors had been circulating for years that Tyrell knew something of it. And now for Henry to react so strongly against my need to know about Arthur's demise too, another prince perhaps done away with by foul play . . .

Henry's grip on my arms was hurting me, but his angry response to handling "my great matter" pained me the more. I wanted to rave at my husband. I wanted to yank away from his grasp and kick his shins and tear my headdress off again and scream. But I took the wisest way for now, a woman's and wife's way, because if I must work sub rosa myself, so be it.

"I rue that I broke my promise not to bring this up until you gave me the report you promised," I said, my voice trembling. I blinked back tears. "I know you are looking into all possibilities about the boon I begged of you, but I am so distraught over our dear Arthur's death that I am quite undone."

He pulled me to him in a strong embrace. With my throat pressed against his shoulder, I could hardly swallow or breathe until I turned my head away. "Of course, I too," he said. "I cannot bear to look ahead but only back, cherishing our boy, our heir, the happiness he had these last months. But I must prepare for the future; we both must. Once we are certain that Princess Catherine is not with child, I shall arrange for young Henry's investiture as Prince of W—"

A knock resounded on the door, and he slowly loosed me. "Speaking of which," he said, "I've sent for Henry. With his brother gone, he now needs his father and king for a tutor."

He cleared his throat and strode behind the table, setting aside the tray of food and drink he'd hardly touched.

"Enter!" he called out.

My lord's mother walked in with Henry in tow. "My lady," he addressed Margaret Beaufort, "sit with Elizabeth in her chambers for a while, if you please. The Duke of York and I have matters to discuss."

Both his mother and I curtsied. I wanted to hug young Henry as I left, but with a hint of a swagger, he'd gone to his father, who was already bent over an account book he must mean to show the boy, as he once had Arthur. I was not comforted to be given over into the care of my mother-in-law, but as she rattled on, I prayed silently for the soul of my son, for the safety of his Spanish widow, and for the two I had sent to discover the cause of Arthur's death—and mayhap his killer.

Mistress Varina Westcott

The second night on the westward roads toward Wales, we stayed on the fringes of Worcester, the town where the prince would be buried. I longed to have a chance to visit the Abbey of St. Wulfstan to decide on the placement of candles, even to familiarize myself with the location of the coffin during the funeral and interment site, but there was no time now.

We stopped the third night at Bewdley, one of Prince Arthur's manor houses, with its little half-timbered town nearby. How proud he must have been of this place he would never see again. Black mourning banners and draperies shrouded many doors and windows. As if the manor needed protection from winds or perhaps border raiders, it huddled at the side of a hill. A full staff awaited us with lit fires and food, but despite the lanterns and torches, the site still seemed foreboding. The deep Wyre Forest bordered the property to the west, a brook to the north, and the roaring spring-melt River Severn to the east, as if we were on a little island.

"At least there are many guards about," I observed to Nick as we finished our hearty meal, surrounded by others in the prince's dining hall.

"It is royal property, but the area's been in dispute for years. The argument is whether Bewdley sits in Shropshire or Worcester," he explained. "As a result, the area harbors fugitives and criminals. Now, don't fret about that. We'd best turn in, because at dawn's early light, we're off for the rest of our ride. No one will use the royal bedchambers, but you'll have a private one with a feather mattress, and I'll be right across the hall with some others. If you need me, just knock."

Everyone beat a quick retreat, and the house soon fell silent. I bathed in warmed water a servant had left, then slept the dreamless sleep of the dead—a sobering thought in this fine manor that now could belong to Prince Arthur's father, his widow, or his younger brother. I'd bet on the king.

The next morn, we ate a hot but quick breakfast of frumenty, then were on our way again. Nick looked much better, though he never looked bad to me. Yet I longed to smooth his hair, matted from his pillow, and the little creases imprinted on his cheek from a sheet or bolster. The linens and towels provided in my room, at least, had been most luxurious.

"No more questions?" he asked as we walked out to meet the others.

"Of course. Do you know what your nemesis, Lord Francis Lovell, looks like?"

"Why bring that up now? Women's intuition? Yes, if there has been foul play in Wales, I warrant he or his lackeys could be involved, though he has always seemed to disappear alone. Lovell's looks—no," he said, frowning. "Only by hearsay, and his appearance could have changed with age, of course—if he's still alive. If he is, and I find him, the bastard will not be around for long, at least, once he's delivered to the king for questioning!"

He mounted and another man boosted me up into our saddle. The long ride had done one thing for me, besides bond Nick and me a bit closer, and that to what end I knew not: Finally, putting aside personal fears and longings, I had found the strength to become fully committed to the dangerous, daunting task that lay before us.

Ludlow loomed ahead; at least I'd been told so. Even the wearied horses must sense it, for they lifted their heads and picked up the pace. Yet I saw no sign of walls or towers through the thatchy maze of forest. No one could miss the change in the terrain, though. The low green hills of England had grown before our eyes to rolling moorlands with the hint of mountains ahead, and fertile fields edged by hedges turned to bare, reddish bracken. Thick blackthorn trees were in early blossom, with dark, spiny twigs and sprays of small white balls. Now and then, we emerged from the forest and passed pastures with ewes and their young lambs as I squinted ahead around Nick's shoulder, looking for Ludlow.

He had described the castle to me as the mightiest of

the old York fortresses. He'd said it was originally one of the castles built by the early English kings along the Welsh Marches that bestrode the borderland between England and Wales. During the civil war that had placed first Richard, Duke of York, then our current king upon the throne, Ludlow had oft been Richard's stronghold and headquarters.

"Wales is known for its fierce fighters," Nick had said, "the skilled bows and spearmen of the English armies. But don't worry, Varina. It's no longer a barbarian place. Most of the local chieftains speak English, and, on the inside, at least, Ludlow is a residence of palatial grandeur now."

When we rode from the final fringe of forest, there it was, of gray-white stone, huge and bulky and primitive-looking, with thick walls, battlements, and a moat. It was only as we rode into the thin sunlight that I saw what looked to be a yellow sea lapping at the skirts on one side of the castle before a stretch of bogs began.

"Those daffodils have popped out since I rode away," Nick told me, pointing. "Their Highnesses had to search high and low for ones in early bloom when they ventured out."

"So they did venture out? We shall have to trace their steps. But first, I must see whether those who have begun to embalm the prince will heed the advice and commands of a city chandler, and a woman to boot."

"I've no doubt," he said as we clattered across the wooden drawbridge under the up-drawn portcullis that guarded the front entry, "that, with the queen's letters and your strong will, they will listen and obey."

CHAPTER THE THIRTEENTH

*A*lthough I suppose my tears were from grief and exhaustion, they were tears of gratitude too. I cried over the lovely, small chamber I had been given at Ludlow Castle, which overlooked the River Terne far below and blue-gray mountains in the distance, and for the box of gifts from the queen. Nick, whose chamber was just across the corridor from mine, had brought me the box once we were settled. Within lay two lovely gowns, warm stockings, a night robe, a hooded cape lined with squirrel, a hat with a veil—everything in black, of course—as well as two pairs of fine leather shoes and a leather purse puckered at its top with felt cloth and drawstrings.

In addition Nick had already delivered letters to the castle steward and the two doctors who were overseeing the embalming of the prince. Those letters, in Her Majesty's own hand, Nick said, gave me permission to oversee the final arrangements for the royal corpse.

But it was the personal letter from the queen in the box of garments that shattered my poise and bolstered even more my conviction to carry out the duties with which she had entrusted me. After Nick left me alone to change my clothes, I read the words over and over, hoping to memorize them:

> *Dear friend Varina, keeper of my secrets, I ask you to destroy this letter after you have read it. I declare you my mistress of mourning while on your journey. You must act in my stead—not, of course, when you oversee the preservation of my dear son's body, but as my chief mourner. The king sends Thomas Howard, Earl of Surrey, Lord High Treasurer, as the official royal mourner, but you also, having lost a son and understanding my previous woes, are the one who must represent me in grief and in discovery of what occurred.*
>
> *I charge you to be faithful to the vow you made and to seek answers, should there be answers to find. And, I pray you, look closely upon my son's face, even in death, so that you may create his sleeping countenance for me anon.*
>
> *Be wary and be safe, and bid my dear firstborn, the hope of my heart, a fond farewell for me, and see him to his eternal resting place. Please place this ring of mine upon his baby finger that he might wear it for all eternity.*
>
> *Elizabeth R, mother, queen, and friend*

Mother, queen, and friend, she had signed. As I had come to know her, she saw herself as a mother first. And so must I be to my own Arthur; yet here I was, charged to learn about the prince's death, and with Nick at my side and watching my back.

I examined the plain gold ring she had fastened to the piece of parchment with a ribbon stuck through it. Both ends were caught in a blob of wax in which she had impressed her signet ring with the initials E.R. and a blooming rose. I wondered whether Christopher's chandlery had sold the palace the sealing wax. After prying it off the page and putting it in my purse for good luck—for the queen's crest, not the wax—I put the ring upon my own little finger, so I would not lose it. It reached only to my second knuckle. How small, perhaps a ring Arthur had worn as a child, or one that the queen herself had from her own parents.

As tired as I was, I needed to wash and change, eat something from the tray that awaited me here, then hurry to the anteroom of the chapel, where the prince's body lay. I had been told that his two physicians had not left his side and had done some preliminary embalming, whatever that might mean. I skimmed the queen's kind letter one more time. *Friend Varina*, she called me. Her mistress of mourning. And so I would be.

Hoping I would ever remember her written words, I held the letter to the flames of the low-burning hearth fire—what a luxury here. How well Her Majesty or Nick had prepared things for me. I watched the paper catch the flame, then curl and burn to crisp, silvery ash.

I examined the two gowns, both splendidly made, one obviously more formal than the other. I put the brocade one aside and donned the day gown, of fine, fitted wool with double sleeves and a gilt belt with a link for keys, small tools, and my purse. Dropping the fruit knife from the tray inside my purse also, I gobbled down a chicken leg and most of a meat pie to give myself strength. In the hall, to my surprise, Nick awaited, talking low to a guard. I wondered whether, under other circumstances, the halls would be so full of men-at-arms.

"Let me escort you to the chapel," Nick said, as his gaze swept over me. He seemed to approve of my appearance, for he nodded and smiled. He looked elegant, finely attired in black with dark green piping, with a flat, feathered hat upon his head. He had shaved; the shadow of his beard that had darkened on our full-tilt ride here was completely gone. "Time to beard the doctors in their den," he told me, playing off the thought I had not spoken aloud, as if once again he had read my mind.

"Will the doctors be difficult, do you think?" I asked him as he tucked my hand in the crook of his arm, and we started down a narrow, curving stone staircase, just wide enough for two abreast.

"Not with the queen's letter they have received. Not with me hovering in the background. And should they be, just give them that quelling look you have perfected and go about your business."

"My quelling look? No, I shall save that for you. But do you know them?"

"Just these last months, and from a distance. Dr. Matthew Martlet has the most experience and has been with the prince almost since his birth. He's the one with the silver hair. I know it's been a huge burden for him that Arthur was never as robust as his younger brother. I've seen him cringe every time Arthur coughed. The younger one, William Enford, is a climber, ever looking for ways to get closer to the king, but how can I disparage that?"

I squeezed his arm in understanding and sympathy. How honest Nick had always been with me about his ambitions. But those were one of the things that must mean we could never be everything to each other, for he would spend his life closely serving the king. I had not a doubt that Nick Sutton would someday regain his lands and family prestige, whether through finding and besting Lord Lovell or not. And I . . . I would be blessed just to see Gil become a member in the chandlers' guild and to be allowed to carve my angel candles, perhaps once in a while for "my friend," the queen.

Nick led me through the huge, high-beamed great hall, where servants were setting up tables and benches to feed many. Each long plank table was being draped with black cloth, and the dais, where no doubt the prince and princess had presided over festivities, was bare.

Nick steered me down halls with tapestries draped in black. Where did they get all of that dark cloth so quickly? That reminded me of something. "The wax cloth has been delivered to the embalming room?" I asked.

"It has."

Inside the chapel with its vaulted ceiling, I could see the four-foot-tall bier erected near the altar with the open coffin atop it, awaiting the body. Voices came from a small anteroom across the way. We traversed the chapel, where local and visiting mourners would file past and pray before the long funeral procession to take the prince to his resting place at Worcester Cathedral would set out.

So much to do, for he was to be interred on April 23, and this was the ninth already, and he must be prepared to lie here in state by the morrow. With a procession hauling a coffin down dirt roads, how many days would it take us to get back to Worcester for the funeral and burial? I reckoned a week, so we had barely a week here, both for the prince's lying-in-state and for Nick and me to learn what we must, to tell the queen. Would she share that with the king, I wondered, or would her secrets from him continue?

At the door of the small anteroom, Nick introduced me to the doctors. Though both wore black shawls, they were decked out in their traditional red-and-gray robes lined with taffeta and their round, brimless hats with lappets. I could tell instantly that Dr. Martlet was the senior physician, because his robe had a wider fur band than did Dr. Enford's. Both looked extremely nervous and, the moment they spoke, seemed defensive.

"We did all we could for him, of course," Dr. Martlet told me as Nick moved away to stand at the door. Despite the aroma of sweet herbs and aromatics, I could see why Nick retreated for fresh air. However chill it was in here, the embalming and encoffining needed to be completed at once.

"I do not question that," I told him. Noting that the rolls of waxen cloth had been, as I had ordered, stood on end in a row rather than piled, I moved past them to view the prince.

They had covered him with a black velvet pall that draped itself to his thin form. His pointed-toed slippers peeked out the bottom as if he had been covered up in bed to keep warm.

Dr. Martlet spoke again. "Despite the prince's ever choleric humors—so light faced and slender, with his excess of yellow bile—I fear it was noxious vapors felled him. The princess too. Of course, diseases spread by airborne vapors can be absorbed through open pores of the body, and you might know the prince and princess insisted on venturing outside the castle on a womanly whim. Who knows what noisome vapors lurk on the walls as cave damp?"

"Cave damp?" I said. "The prince and princess were in a cave?"

"I knew curiosity could kill the cat, but what could I do?" Martlet said, with an elaborate shrug. "They did not even take us along, nor many guards. Prince Arthur wanted to see the old burial place of a king, and the princess yearned to traipse through the boggy meadow, looking for early flowers. Then too, but a few days ago, there was word of a man contracting the sweat in the village."

Caves and bogs forgotten, my head jerked up. "The sweat? My family died of that! Could the prince have contracted—"

"I was going to say, it was simply rumor," Enford put in, as if to take over for his medical partner. "We sent an apothecary to examine that man, and it was merely fever and ague, not the *Sudor Anglicus*."

Yet I tucked that tidbit away, as I did the fact that Arthur and Catherine had ventured out into damp areas. I had never heard of noxious vapors seeping into pores, but I meant to examine every possibility. If sweat could go out, could not vapors get in? I oft felt fogs from the River Thames creep up all clammy on my skin. But I knew this puzzle must become clear from a hundred scattered little pieces.

And why had Nick not told me about caves and bogs, if he was one of their guards? Even if but a few had accompanied them, did not Nick at least know of it?

"So," Martlet was saying, "of course we prescribed herbs, pomanders, and scented cloths for both the prince and princess, for she became ill too, though her stronger constitution pulled her through. She has her own physician, of course. A great, great tragedy that, despite our Herculean efforts, the prince sickened so quickly."

"With what specific symptoms?" I asked.

"Everything went awry after their day outside the castle walls, traipsing about," Martlet said, not answering my question. "Of course, he always took poorly to drafts and was oft racked with coughs."

"Which we routinely treated with all sort of elixirs and bleedings," Enford added.

"Of course, if you must know, the more ill he became," Martlet went on, as if the younger man had not spoken, "the more His Grace became listless and had trouble breathing. Nausea, running of the reyns—"

"The kidneys. You mean heavy urination?" I asked.

"Exactly, and at the end, swift organ failure."

"But the nausea," I said. "How does that relate to a breathing infection?" I meant to pursue that more, then saw that Nick had advanced into the room, shaking his head so only I could see him. Evidently neither physician was going to answer my question. Was Nick implying I should not ask it, or that I had best turn to tending the body? That decision was settled by Dr. Enford's slowly lifting the shroud from the prince, who was clothed only in a nightshirt.

For a moment, in the blazing candlelight, I stood in awe of dreadful death. My parents, my beloved son—like this, the shell here and yet the essence, the soul, departed. Arthur Tudor, Prince of Wales, looked like a waxen effigy, one I could have carved for the queen. His face was blessedly serene, his features gone slack, and I would tell Her Majesty in all honesty that he looked peaceful. And yet so young, so much promise gone because of an attack of noxious vapors he and the princess caught when they ventured out? *We shall see about that*, I thought.

"What have you done so far?" I asked the men.

"Removed the soft organs, of course," Dr. Martlet said. He sounded more annoyed by the moment at all my questions, but the man irked me too, with his "of courses," as if he condescended to so much as explain things to me. "We are trained as full surgeons, not like the barber-surgeons, who had best stick to cutting hair, pulling teeth, and bloodletting. And, of course, the embalming, of commoners with occasional help from you chandlers. It has been decided that the prince's heart shall be buried here, in the castle churchyard. We have it in an alabaster-covered jar—over there—and thought you could wrap it with your waxy shrouds too."

"Yes, *of course*," I said, though I'd never wrapped an organ before and had to steel myself at the thought.

"As to what we've done," Martlet went on, "we washed the body cavities with sweet wine and aromatic fluids, oils of turpentine, lavender, and rosemary—not all easy to get right now, but the village apothecary was of some assistance." He wrinkled his nose in disdain, so I assumed the ongoing battle between London physicians and apothecaries about prescribing cures tainted their attitude even here.

"Also," Enford said, picking up the narration, "we rubbed his skin with preservative spices and balms. The chest and belly cavities we stuffed with herbs, so we are ready for the clothing, then the wrapping of him."

"Do you have his burial garments?"

"They have been entrusted to us."

"Then I shall unroll the wax cerements while you dress him."

"Save some wrapping for his heart."

"Yes, there is plenty. Her Majesty insisted on that."

I moved away and unwrapped one roll of the wax-impregnated cloth and approached the jar, which had been pointed out to me as holding Arthur's heart. It sat almost inconspicuously on the stone floor in a corner. Bless Nick, for despite the crowded quarters in this small, close chamber—it almost reminded me of the room at Westminster where I'd carved the effigies—he must have recalled how tight spaces affrighted me. He knelt at my side to help me lift the heavy lid from the jar. I moved a wall torch to the sconce directly over it. Within, brown and purple, still and soft, lay the heart that had beaten for the prince's body, for his wife and family, for his future kingdom he would never rule.

I had expected blood, but there was none, not a trace. How I wished the heart could whisper its secrets of what had happened to him. Together, Nick and I lifted it out—I thought I would be ill at the task—and laid it on the waxen wrapping. With Nick's dagger, I cut a circle in the cloth around the heart, then wrapped the sides atop, and we slid the organ back into the jar, then sealed it by wrapping the entire alabaster vessel.

I jumped when Enford, evidently leaning close over me, said, "I warrant they will put it in a little coffin of its own, but best to keep the water out every which way. It rains here as if Noah's very flood were loosed again. Here, he's ready."

I cleaned my hands in water and wiped them on a piece of cloth and stood to regard the kingdom's onetime Prince of Wales, garbed in fine fashion, as if he would arise for a council meeting or a wedding feast.

"I told the queen I would say a prayer over him," I told the men. "If you would step out for a moment . . ."

Frowning, muttering, the doctors did, and Nick hovered in the doorway. I slipped the ring Her Majesty had sent onto Arthur's little finger and whispered to him, in the queen's stead, "Your mother loves you and ever will, Arthur. And she will embrace you again someday in heaven."

I added a silent prayer. It had to be enough. Time was fleeting. I was certain the doctors had not done a good job here, either with embalming or ferreting out what had killed him.

"Let's finish," I said, and Nick called them back in.

We rolled and tucked and wrapped the body in double what I would have used for any other mortal shell. Then the doctors summoned guards, and six of them lifted the body and carried it out, shoulder high, to where a black velvet–lined coffin sat upon the bier. Several priests appeared to pray and chant as Arthur was laid in the coffin and the top was closed, bolted, and covered with another black velvet pall.

Over the coffin, workers raised a canopy of black cloth stitched with a white cross. Banners of the Trinity, the Lord's cross, the blessed Virgin, and Saint George were put in place, each adorning a corner of the coffin. The bier was guarded by six other men with shiny breastplates and halberds facing outward. I quickly oversaw the placement of votive candles on and around the altar, and the castle steward arranged the flaming torches along the walls in huge sconces.

Side by side, Nick and I knelt at the coffin as others of the household were permitted to come in, then were slowly, silently ushered out. Many wept openly; some whispered prayers and crossed themselves. I told myself I must remember details of the scene to tell the queen.

When Nick and I stepped out of the little chapel, despite the mood of mourning, I whispered to him, "Did you go along or, at least, how much did you know about the royal couple's foray outside the castle? Cave damp and bogs—"

"He used me for an emissary to the Welsh chieftains, who should soon be here. I was out for two or three days at a time, so I missed that. They had both already taken to their beds when I returned, and I did not know they'd ventured out."

I scolded myself for my frustration at him. Surely he would have told me already if he'd accompanied Arthur and Catherine outside the castle. Ah, but I understood feeling imprisoned by the weather and the walls, for after the horror of being chased into the lightless crypt at St. Paul's and finding *Signor* Firenze's body, I'd felt a prisoner in my own home. And to always have the added strictures of servants, attendants, and guards, the royal couple must have suffered from spring fever and become a bit headstrong and careless. But were they to blame for their own sudden illnesses or was someone else?

As we walked back into the great hall, a dark-haired man with a short beard beckoned us off to the side. "One of the princess Catherine's closest advisers," Nick whispered, and escorted me over to him.

Before Nick could introduce us, the man spoke in such a rush I could barely understand his Spanish-accented English. "I am Alessandro Geraldini, *sí*, the *Infanta* Catalina's chaplain, as you say here, eh? I sent to say Her Grace did read the queen's letter and she see you now."

So, I thought, as Nick nodded and we followed the man's quick steps, the next path of our inquiry had just been decided for us.

CHAPTER THE FOURTEENTH

*P*rincess Catherine did not rise to greet us, and I quickly saw why, for she appeared wan and weak. At least she was out of bed, dressed in a black brocade robe and sitting in a chair. Except for her chaplain, the lean and sallow Alessandro Geraldini—Nick had whispered to me that he was actually her confessor—she was alone.

We sank in a bow and curtsy and stayed there, heads down, until she said in English, "Rise." The priest indicated we should sit on stools that had been drawn up, while he stood behind her high-backed, carved chair.

Although I had the feeling she understood most of what we said, Father Geraldini translated everything after her single English word. The queen had counseled that we must choose our translator carefully, but it was done for us, and surely we could trust a priest.

"Her Grace," Geraldini told us, "says she thank you for bringing the letter of comfort from the king and especially the one from the queen. She thinks of Her Majesty always as her English mother and by the name her people call her, Elizabeth the Good. And for your duties to the prince here, much gratitude to Master Sutton and now to Mistress Westcott."

Tears in my eyes, I nodded. Given permission to speak, Nick explained our hurried trip and added comforting words about my care of the prince's body for burial. Through all that, as her confessor translated, Her Grace's eyes moved back and forth from my face to Nick's. Finally, she put up her hand and spoke to Geraldini words he translated, frowning.

"The princess welcomes the death mistress and does know she is trusted."

The death mistress! What had the queen written to her daughter-in-law, or was that a misunderstanding of "mistress of mourning"? Had the queen told her outright that Nick and I would look into the circumstances of the prince's death?

Geraldini's Spanish, Catherine's Spanish, then Geraldini's English made communication slow. Longing to ask my own questions, I shifted in impatience on my stool.

"The princess Catalina, she been ill also," Geraldini said. "She is grieving her royal husband's delicate health not survive the attack."

Nick and I shot each other a sideways glance. I sensed he was reacting to the words "the attack." But it had suddenly occurred to me to wonder why the king had been so adamant that his heir, in poor health as he was, make the grueling winter journey this far. I decided I would speak.

"Do you refer to the attack of bad air or vapors, Your Grace? The prince's doctors mentioned a venture outside the castle and into a cave and bog."

"Oh, *sí*," she blurted out, directly to me in Spanish, as her lips lifted in a ghost of a smile, "*era un día bonito, buscando por flores!*"

"It was lovely day," Geraldini translated, "looking for flowers. You see, we had long, wet winter. The thought of daffodils cheered her, though they found few before going into the forest."

It seemed I was questioning him now. "Into the forest too? To search for more flowers, since they were not yet in bloom around the moat?"

"Prince Arthur wanted to show her the place the Welsh hero Owen Glendower has been," Geraldini told us on his own, as if he should be answering for her after her impassioned outburst. "They did go into the forest near the ancient Welsh stone tomb, not far from the old herb woman's hut they did visit. Time and again, Princess Catalina said it was a day they shared she will ever remember—and then they both took ill."

Catherine—obviously her Spanish entourage still called her by her Spanish name, Catalina—spoke to Geraldini again in a rush of words. Then it seemed her strength was gone, for she leaned back in her chair and closed her eyes. I saw she was crying unashamedly, gripping the arms of her chair and not covering her face.

"They had a sudden parting, she to her doctors, he to his," Geraldini said. "Messages sent, even a flower he begged be picked for her. But never did she see him again, and now outside, the flowers are in all bloom. . . ."

The man's voice broke. Nick sniffed. I blinked back tears as Catherine's confessor pointed to a small metal vase with a single flower in it, a daffodil, quite slumped and dead.

"Perhaps more conversation another day," Nick said, standing. We both bent at the knee, but the princess did not gaze on us again as we backed away and left her chambers.

Huddled over the small table in my room, Nick and I supped together as if, I thought, we were wedded. We were making plans around the necessary duties we must perform here. We had been informed that at first light, the prince's heart would be buried in the churchyard with the attendance of several Welsh chieftains, English Marcher lords, and senior officials from the royal household and council. Both of the prince's physicians as well as Nick and I were to attend.

"We need to find someone who was with them the day they went out," I said as we finished our repast with cheese tarts and cream. "They must have taken someone along, and I'd rather not have one of her ladies in tow as a guide when we retrace their steps."

"I hear they did not take an entourage, only two guards. I hope I can find one of them who recalls exactly where they went in the forest and the bog. It's a big, wild area, though I've heard of the tomb they must have visited. It's called a cromlech. Although it's the burial place of an unnamed king from centuries ago, the folk hereabouts claim their ancient hero Owen Glendower's spirit visits there. As for an old herb woman in the forest—well, I'll go to the guardroom when we're finished here and ask around. So, *are* we finished here?" he asked, and his voice shifted from quick and crisp to slow and sweet.

"After the week and the day we have had, I believe so," I said. "That bed looks inviting." I felt myself blush the moment I blurted that out.

His eyes held mine like a magnet. "I was thinking the same thing, but business first, right?"

I could only nod mutely, even after all my earlier questions and opinions. He stood and came closer, so close I had to look up at him. I realized I did look up to him too, in admiration of his strength and in gratitude for his kindnesses to me.

I went willingly as he drew me up into his arms. I lifted mine over his shoulders and linked my hands behind his strong neck. My heartbeat kicked up, thudding in my ears. As I was pressed so close to him, did he feel that too?

He kissed me. Not just kissed me, possessively and thoroughly, but caressed me at the same time, back and waist, even cupping my bottom through my skirts as if to lift me. My hands stroked the crisp hairs on the nape of his neck, and I clung to him while the entire room and castle tilted and swayed. My breasts tight to his chest, the heat of my blush turned to fire. He tipped me back a bit and I clung to him, my mouth open to his sweet assault, which I wanted desperately and gave back mindlessly.

I could not think, could not breathe, would never have said "stop" had he laid me on the bed across the room and possessed me there. Somehow, we turned and whirled together as if in a dance, and I found myself pressed to the wall next to the door while his lips raced down my throat to the tops of my breasts.

He tugged one sleeve off my shoulder to lower my neckline and his tongue darted there in the valley between my breasts. Like a green girl, I gasped for air, for sanity. My legs went weak as water, but he held me up.

Breathing raggedly against my damp flesh, he whispered, "Later. I know not when, but later!"

Did he mean this night? After we went home? After—

"I need to get to the guardroom before most of them go to bed. And before I gainsay the queen's orders that I am to protect you, to keep anyone from laying a hand on you. I am certain she meant that to include me. I know you do not want to give out falsely that we are betrothed, and if we are found together alone in the night or at morn—I thought to risk it this one time—I will have to answer to her, despite my own hunger for you. I will see you in the morning for the burial of Arthur's heart—and so now, somehow, will bury mine."

After that tirade of words and passion, though he was breathing heavily, he merely pecked a kiss on my cheek, opened the door, and went out, closing it carefully behind him. I leaned against the wall for a long time, not trusting my legs, savoring the memory of his touch, grateful the queen cared for my safety but furious that Nick had applied that promise to himself.

It was a large crowd, I thought, for the burial of a heart, so what must the coming funeral be? Big-shouldered Welsh chieftains, some wrapped in bulky furs, with heavy beards and wide, solid swords at their sides, stood cheek by jowl next to finely attired English lords from the borderlands or London.

The king's chief mourner, the Earl of Surrey, had arrived with his large retinue and seemed to command everyone's attention and respect. I watched him closely as he presided over this sad event. Though Nick had said Thomas Howard, Earl of Surrey, was nearly sixty years old, he looked younger, with his alert face, clipped auburn beard, muscular form, and upright, almost regal posture.

Nick had told me he'd once been loyal to King Henry's rival, Richard III, and had even fought against the Tudors in the Battle of Bosworth Field. After being confined to the Tower for a time, he was released, pardoned, even rewarded for his skills as a soldier against the Scots. Like James Tyrell, Surrey had been taken back into the king's good graces because he needed men like that. No doubt Nick hoped that, on a lesser scale, he could earn his family's way back too.

I pulled my eyes away from Surrey as the alabaster jar Nick and I had wrapped in Westcott wax cloth was lowered into a metal box already placed in the ground.

Evidently in order of precedence, beginning with the Earl of Surrey, the major English and Welsh mourners shoveled soil atop the metal box, then individually took their leave, heading inside the castle. The hollow thuds echoed at first, then became more muted. In my trembling hands I held a spray of daffodils delivered to me by the princess Catherine's confessor, with her request that I place them on the ground above her husband's heart. Poor Catherine was mourning alone, as was customary, and too weak to attend anyway.

Why, I wondered, was I blessed—or cursed—with the trust of royal women? Who would have thought an angel candle someone took to the queen, one such as I had sent to the princess this morning by her confessor, Geraldini, could have begun all this and put Nick in my life's path?

When the Latin words were spoken, the benediction said, and, but for two guards, Nick and I stood there quite alone, I realized that I had been the only woman present. Ever the mistress of mourning, I told myself as I approached the burial spot in the walled churchyard, which could be seen from the ramparts of the castle. I would leave these flowers not only for the prince's young widow, but also for his mother—yes, this would be something else I must tell the queen.

Under the gaze of the two guards and Nick from behind, I placed the flowers, adjusting them prettily upon the freshly turned soil. Stepping back, I bowed my head in silent prayer, then took another step away, as I had learned to back away from the presence of royalty before leaving a room. I thought not only of the queen's loss of her son but also of the loss of my Edmund. How I missed my dear boy Arthur, and prayed that he was well with Gil and Maud, and that no harm would ever come to him.

As I looked up at the cloudy sky, my eye caught figures on the battlements, evidently watching. Three women together, the princess herself between two others, peeking between the jagged-toothed crenellations. I was tempted to wave, but—since they might not want to be seen—I resisted. What had it cost Catherine of Aragon in strength and courage to climb up there to see at least a part of her husband buried?

Nick looked up and obviously recognized her too. "She's

still weak, and the queen needs her back in London. Someone else is watching too," he added as we both noticed a man on a different part of the battlements, quite alone, and not clad as one of the guards.

"I see him," I said. "But is it a man? Hard to tell when the cloak flaps like wings, as if he could swoop down here in a trice."

"It's a man," Nick said. "He has his hand on a sword and it glinted in the sun a moment ago. I think it might be the Earl of Surrey, gone up there to make certain all is accomplished that he's been bound to oversee."

I started to walk away, but Nick didn't budge, and that pulled me back.

"What?" I said. "It's not the earl?"

"I'm not certain—but . . . I'm just imagining things."

"Like the ghost of Owen Glendower?" I teased, trying to lighten both our moods. "The Welsh maid they sent me this morn says he's still alive after 'only' one hundred years. She boasted that her brother is a *brudwry*, some sort of prophetic poet the Welsh love, and believe what they say too. The *brudwry* have poems and songs about how Glendower disappeared into the mist of the mountains when his rebellion against the English was put down, but that he is still alive and will return someday to avenge himself on Wales's English conquerors."

"Perhaps by striking down the heir to the English throne?" Nick held my hand as we left the church graveyard and headed toward the castle. "That gives me chills," he said with a noticeable shiver. "Not that they believe in a ghost, but that's what they say about Lord Lovell: that he vanished into a mist and that he'll be back to fight the Tudors any way he can. But let's not fear poems and rumors. I've found a lad to lead us tomorrow in the steps the prince and princess took the day they went out on their venture, so we shall have one too."

"And, I pray, not contract noxious vapors. Nick, the fact the prince was nauseous . . . I wanted to ask the princess whether she was too, but when she became so tearful, I dared not."

"I know. We need to learn what the prince ate that day."

"You said you found a lad. So, not a guard who went with them?"

"They took two guards and a local Welsh guide, the village apothecary's son, Rhys Garnock. Both guards have, unfortunately, been sent ahead of us to prepare resting stops for the funeral cortege, but the lad will probably be most useful for getting us around, finding the same spots where they stopped."

"He's the apothecary's son?" I asked. "Can that mean anything? The prince's doctors said they had the apothecary examine the man who may have had the sweat, but it was only fever and ague."

"They admitted they got some embalming herbs from the village apothecary. But so what if the boy was the one who brought the herbs to the castle? All that was after the prince died. I warrant our illustrious doctors would not have used the lowly apothecary—a rural one at that—for their own prescriptions after His Grace took ill.

"I'll call for you about an hour after mass tomorrow," he went on. "Come garbed as a lad again. I'll bring a horse for you, and let's hope that a rustic-looking man and two lads won't attract any undue attention from someone watching."

"Like that caped man on the battlements? We could have rushed up there to try to see who it was."

"Not worth the effort. If it was Surrey, he'd be annoyed. If it was someone who doesn't want to be discovered, someone who knows his way around the castle, despite all the guards, he would not be there when we arrived. If he's someone dangerous, we don't need to tip him off that we're looking for him, or for information about the prince's death."

"And if it was the ghost of Glendower up there," I put in, swinging his hand a bit in the sheer joy of being near Nick anywhere, "he will just have to meet us in the forest."

"Don't jest like that." He frowned and gave my hand a little squeeze. "I've lived for years with ghosts—ones who were betrayed and slaughtered—and I cannot rest until justice is done for them."

Queen Elizabeth of York

It was not often the king came to my quarters, but here he was, unannounced and alone. I turned away from gazing out the window at the blank gray sky over London, for we had returned to our capital. How I wished I could be one of the seagulls screeching and wheeling over the rushing Thames and fly to Ludlow. But I would have to let my emissaries, Nick and Varina, be my eyes and ears—and heart—there.

"My dear lord," I blurted as he closed the door behind himself and strode into my presence chamber, "not more bad news?"

"In a way," he said, glancing around the room, evidently to see whether I was alone. I was solitary often lately, for loneliness and melancholy suited me, despite how my ladies fussed when I dismissed them. By the Virgin's veil, at least Henry had not come looking for me when I was with the sleeping images of my other lost children but two chambers away, for then he would have thought me demented indeed.

"Our son Henry is all right?" I asked.

"Yes, hale and hearty as ever and quite aware of his elevated circumstance. But I have come to give you news of your 'great matter' before you hear it from someone else," he said, and drew me by the hand over to the table, where he seated me, then pulled another chair close. Elbows on his knees, he leaned forward and took my hands in his again.

"Hear it from someone else? You have told someone else that I want answers about my brothers' murders?"

"Of course not. I meant you would hear of the fact that I have had to besiege our own castle in Calais against Tyrell. You were evidently right to suspect him," he said, shaking his head, "at least of duplicity in his loyalty to us. And after all I've done for that man! I had ordered him home for questioning, but he refused, claiming he could not leave his command at the fortress Guisnes in Calais right now—and saying he had been to London so recently for the royal wedding."

"He must have guessed he is suspect in the loss of my brothers. And if he has a guilty conscience . . ."

"I fear the base-hearted churl has no conscience. He has hoodwinked and defied me. I've received word on the best authority—my spies in France—that, though claiming and pretending to be loyal to our reign, over the years, even recently, he has housed and abetted various Yorkist rebels and sympathizers there—there, where I have entrusted him with that command!"

"I knew he did not deserve to be at Arthur's wedding or the joust thereafter. He was even at my coronation years ago. When the throne was first yours, why did you not confiscate his lands or attaint him, as you did other Yorkists? Why did you pardon him!"

"Keep your voice down, Elizabeth; he had been in France during the Battle of Bosworth, so had not helped King Richard there. Besides, I needed someone like him—just as I used the Earl of Surrey—who was willing to change his allegiance to us. Both men were Yorkists who saw the righteousness of my claim to the throne, or so I thought. I believed I needed Tyrell as a shining example of that. But what I came to tell you is that a fortnight ago, when I heard of his defiance, I ordered English troops to take the castle and deliver him to me. There was a siege and still he defied me. He was promised safe passage, but when he came out, he was arrested and is being sent back here under guard to be thoroughly questioned."

Wide-eyed, my heart pounding, I nodded through all that. Tyrell's true colors had come out at last. The rumors that he had known something about the murder of my brothers could now be examined. Declared a traitor, he would be questioned, no doubt under duress in the Tower, the very place where my brothers had met their fate. I might finally have answers, have some balm for my guilty soul.

But, I reasoned, as my husband took his leave and I was alone again, was making Tyrell a shining example truly why the king had seemed to favor, even to coddle the man over the years? And until I begged of him to find Richard and Edward's killer, had he never doubted his liege man?

At least, I thought, with my head on my arms, facedown upon the table, if Tyrell was the one behind the vilest of crimes and had been holed up in France, he could not have sneaked off to Wales to harm Arthur. If there was foul play in Wales, someone else was to blame—perhaps someone Tyrell had sent or encouraged, even sheltered. But the biggest puzzle of all was this: Since it appeared Sir James Tyrell had ever been a Yorkist at heart, why would he have harmed the two young Yorkist heirs, unless someone else had bribed or forced him to do so? Yes, my uncle Richard could have urged Tyrell to be that killer, to clear his way to the throne. The dreadful thing was that their deaths had also cleared the way for Henry Tudor, my beloved husband.

CHAPTER THE FIFTEENTH

Mistress Varina Westcott

I suppose my feelings that day Nick and I ventured outside Ludlow were much like Princess Catherine's when she and her husband went out on their last day together. I could not wait to escape the confines of the castle, and it was a partly sunny day with a fresh breeze after the smell of dank, centuries-old stones and dusty tapestries and draperies—and the heaviness of death and grieving. With a sense of adventure and freedom, despite our terrible task, I too would be with the man I loved.

Since Nick evidently knew the area surrounding the castle fairly well, I wanted to be somewhat familiar with it before we rode out. I rose and ate early and attended an early mass, for it was the Sabbath, though it would be no day of rest for me. With my Welsh maid, Morgan, I went up on the battlements where we had seen the princess and the man with the cape looking down on us yesterday. It was windy but deserted up there. Though I studied the area where we had seen the man, I had come to survey the countryside. Ah, how *Signor* Firenze would have appreciated this view, however much his great skill had been portrait painting.

Below the rocky escarpment on which Ludlow Castle had been built, the very view from my chamber window, rushed the wide River Terne, leaping with white water over boulders in its way. From another side, I gazed down on the village of Ludlow, mostly gray stone buildings that looked like toy houses from here. Our guide, the apothecary's boy, Rhys Garnock, would have a steep walk up to the castle to meet us today, for Nick had said he had no horse of his own and we must provide one.

Around the village lay fertile fields, separated from one another not by English hedgerows but by two plowed furrows and a grassy path, though in areas where sheep or cattle grazed I saw some stone fences. A dense forest edged the fields, and the vista beyond was misty moors, mountains, or marshes, the latter referred to as bogs here, mostly of peat and grasses. I saw nothing that could be called a cave, though Nick had said we would visit the ancient cave tomb called a cromlech where the ghost of the Welsh freedom fighter Owen Glendower was said to be seen. I almost asked Morgan its location and whether she knew of an old herb woman who lived in the forest, but it was best to trust almost no one.

When we returned to my chamber, I sent Morgan away and changed into my boy's attire, including my riding boots. Nick knocked shortly thereafter and rocked my poise again by whispering on the stairs, "Prettiest boy I've ever seen."

Actually, I thought that young, thin Rhys Garnock was

almost as well-favored, with his light brown hair, fine complexion, and rosy cheeks. I guessed his age at about twelve or thirteen. He seemed eager to please, and it did please me that his English was so good. I silently scolded myself for thinking that, just because these people lived in the wild borderlands, they would speak only Welsh.

"If'n you wish to catch the old herb woman at her hut afore she wanders out foraging, we should go there first," Rhys said to Nick.

"Perhaps she will stay at home on the Sabbath."

"Doubt it. Too far to come to the village church and needs each day to forage, so she's said. But best go 'stead of Glendower's cave. 'Tis not actually a cave—just seems like one."

"But on the day the prince and princess rode out, they went to the Glendower site first, then visited the herb woman?" Nick questioned.

"Oh, aye, but a storm came up that day, so the old woman returned early, that she did, and 'tis a lovely day today, so she'll be out and about all hours."

I rode between them, making us three abreast on the road. Rhys knew I was a woman in disguise, but he had not so much as blinked at that. It made me wonder whether he sometimes worked sub rosa for others. "You seem to know the old woman's habits well, Rhys," I said.

"Been sent to buy herbs for my da oft enough, ones he couldna find or grow," he told me. "Besides, Da says she was a friend of my great-grandmother's, all the way down to us."

"So she is old, indeed," Nick said.

The boy rolled his blue eyes. "Claims to be near old as

Glendower, that she knew him once, but canna be." He lowered his voice. "No one lives that old, so it's Glendower's ghost seen in these parts, not the man himself, but Da's not sure 'bout Mistress Fey. That's one reason the princess Catherine wanted to meet old Fey, 'cause she didn't believe the prince 'bout the woman's age, and they were laughing that day and made a bet of it. As for the prince"—the boy lowered his voice again—"I hear tell he been talking of buying wild garlic from her, spice up his winter fare at table, but 'specially said it be an aphro . . . aphro something—like a love potion. Da says it be good for breathing problems too, so he prob'ly knew that and just boasted 'bout the love potion."

Nick and I exchanged glances again. If the prince sought an aphrodisiac, did that mean he and Catherine still had not bedded?

"How did it happen that they knew to take you for a guide?" I asked him. "Had they bought herbs from your father?"

"Don't Da wish! Some Ludlow village folk loved the prince, bringing hope and power back to the Welsh people, eh, what they not had since Glendower's rising. No, one of the chieftains here'bouts musta told Prince Arthur I knew old Fey and how to find the cave. Don't mean to brag, but I even know the bogs like the back of my hand. Know how to hide in the water, breathing through a hollow reed to get close to the ducks, where I can grab one or two if my bow and arrows get too wet, then just wring their necks."

"As for the other folk in the village," Nick said, obviously trying to keep Rhys on track, "did they not love the

Tudor Prince of Wales? I've heard tell that some are still loyal to King Richard and the Yorkist cause in these parts."

"Well"—the boy drawled out the word as if hesitant to go on—"when Richard was Duke of York, he was oft here, his loyalists too."

"But not hereabouts anymore? Those loyalists who don't live nearby, I mean. Any coming in from other parts, maybe even from eastern or northern England?"

"Don't know of that, milord, for I'd sure like to go t'other way—from here to the east. See, I been out and about oft in the woods for my da, even though I not be wantin' to be an herbalist like him, but a knight's squire or page in London Town or duck hunter for the royal table, if'n I must. The prince, milord—I swear on my life 'tis true—if he would have lived"—the boy gave a huge sniff and wiped his nose with his sleeve—"said he'd take me back to London with him, and find me a place with a real knight of the realm too. That's what he said, with a real knight of the realm."

I'd heard the Welsh had excellent singing voices and endless verses to their songs, but this lad had a fine, singsong one for talking endlessly, once he got going. Nick told him, "You help us now, and we'll see about all that, if your da is willing."

"I reckon if I didna have two younger brothers coming on, he'd never let me go, but if'n I vow to send back coin now and then, I'm hoping for it."

Vows and hope, I thought as we rode into the fringe of the forest. Vows to the queen and her hope we could mourn for her here and discover something of foul play—if it was to be found.

Suddenly both sun and sky disappeared, and shadows gathered as we rode, single file, Rhys first and Nick behind me, under the huge branches of age-old trees. Birds flew silently, but squirrels screeched loud enough to make me jump. The sudden shift in temperature chilled me more than it should as I looked all around, despite the shrinking vista. I had heard wolves still roamed these woods.

Even within the forest, our mounts waded through a bog. It wasn't deep, and there was an obvious path through it, but last year's hollow brown reeds stood as tall as the horses' withers and clacked against our boots and stirrups. "Those reeds," Rhys said, snapping one off and looking through it, "see—the very ones I use to breathe through when I'm edging closer to the ducks, 'specially like now, in the spring, when the water could completely cover me. Bet old Fey knows tricks like that too, but I never asked her."

I didn't believe those rumors of an ageless herb woman, I told myself. It sounded like one more fantastical topic for a Welsh bard's song. And if she lived anywhere beneath these dark, shifting trees, how would she know whether the sky was to bring sun or rain anyway?

When Rhys led us back onto solid ground, I saw, rising above the thick grass, a thin finger of fragrant wood smoke as if pointing out our way. We rode into a clearing where sat a squat stone cot encircled by rows of plants. Most stood like corpses of themselves, blighted by winter frosts and not pulled up or replanted yet. They leaned against stakes or cords, as if strung up by their spindly arms, slumped with their heads down. As we rode a bit closer, I noted that some had sprouted anew with the spring weather.

Despite our silence and the thick-leafed carpet under our horses' hooves, perhaps the herb woman heard us, for out she came—no, that could not be the old woman. Unfortunately, she must have another visitor, though I saw no horse. The woman who emerged stepped into an errant splash of sun. She was as blond as I and wore a muted blue gown that clung to her ripe body. She was beautiful too, standing erect and graceful as she lifted a hand to cover her eyes and gaze our way.

But as we came closer, I saw her gown was gray and hung loose on a bony frame, her hair snow-white and her arm wizened, her face cobwebbed with wrinkles. Had the sun and shadows played a trick on me? I dared not ask Nick or Rhys now or she would hear me.

She nodded in greeting as Rhys gave our names, and we dismounted. Rhys spoke to her in Welsh, but with a scratchy voice she said to us in English, "Are all the lovers from Ludlow come to visit me then? An' I hear the last two didna fare so well."

My insides lurched as Nick and I exchanged a lightning glance. "It is for that reason that we are calling upon you," he told her. "By visiting you and the Glendower cromlech, we are honoring the last day the prince and princess had together before his death."

"Ah—make no mistake," she said, shaking a crooked

finger nearly in his face, "Glendower is not buried there. Oh, no, his lordship visits only when it takes his fancy. I've seen him up on the castle ramparts too, sword flashing, cape flapping."

My legs went weak as water, but Nick barely flinched. "When Their Graces were here, did they buy any of your fine cooking herbs?" he asked.

"Not a bit, though I gave her sprigs of dried lavender for her hair. The boy—the prince—was seeking fresh wild garlic, a particular favorite, but it's too early. Will you step inside then, and I'll give your lady"—she glanced at me, obviously ignoring my costuming as a boy—"a bit of lavender too, since you are wanting to imitate the others, eh?"

Everything she said unnerved me. Despite my inherent curiosity and my desire to learn all I could for the queen, I did not want to go inside this woman's cot. But we three shuffled in and, as she snatched a sprig of dried lavender from her low ceiling, which was an upside-down garden of dried, hanging flowers and plants, I darted a look around. And stared at what Nick and Rhys were gaping at too.

"You have a fine banner with the red dragon of Wales," Nick said, stating the obvious. Spread against the wall, it stood out like a gold-and-crimson beacon amidst the pale stone and baskets of herbs, the simple low bed and table and two stools.

I noted well that she had what the London chandlers called peasant candles, field rushes dipped in fat, which smelled and smoked. How disdainful Christopher had been of those. It was dim in here, because her two small windows were covered with linen soaked in resin and tallow to keep out drafts, so she could not have seen us coming. The entire cot seemed dank and dusty. I could not help myself; I sneezed.

"God bless you," she said. Much relieved she had invoked the Lord's name instead of some pagan deity's, I nodded and forced a small smile. "The boy prince gave it to me," she said, somewhat proudly, "in exchange for his lady's lavender. Since it's the Welsh dragon, I took it. Glendower will like it too."

She was mad, I thought, and that was that. She was old but claimed to be older, mayhap believed she was. But did she have visions of Wales's onetime would-be deliverer from English rule, or did she make all that up to either bring others here for business or to keep them away? I was intrigued by her but disturbed too.

Yet I accepted the fragrant lavender from her. "That for you," she said. "And for the new widow, I shall give you some rue in a black ribbon, for in the future she will rue her future, her marriage to the king."

Yes, she was crackbrained, I thought. "You do know the prince died?" I asked, wondering whether she was hard of hearing or forgetful. "The princess is now not wife but widow, so will not wed a king."

"Ha! Wait and see. For Glendower lives, at least our new Glendower, eh?"

"And who is that, the new Glendower?" Nick asked, his voice rising.

"Why, one and the same. I must be off to my gathering now, but this lad will show you where to look for him, eh, Rhys?"

"Aye, Mistress Fey. And Da says if you pack up some rosemary to ward off bad dreams, he has need of such to sell, and I'm to fetch it on the morrow."

"Canna have enough of that, eh? Everyone has bad dreams." Turning her head away from Nick and Rhys, she looked straight at me. Her pale blue eyes seemed to brighten, to bore into mine, and I fancied for one moment in the dimness that she was young again. Was she a witch or sorceress? Gooseflesh skimmed my arms, and I shuddered.

In my free hand, I took the small bouquet of rue, indeed wrapped with a black ribbon, as if she had known we were coming and that we could take it to Princess Catherine. It resembled a small bough of grayish evergreen and smelled pungent—bitter. Nick took my elbow and steered me outside. He turned back only to give the woman an entire gold sovereign with the king's likeness on it, which she squinted at as if trying to make it out—or, I thought, to give him the evil eye.

Nick and I thanked Mistress Fey, and Rhys told her something in Welsh that made her chuckle. Was *I* the one going mad? I had feared for my sanity after I had lost my child, even that day in London, when I fancied the angel dangling above us for Catherine of Aragon's parade was my Edmund as he would look in the future. Was the queen's obsessive nature, to refuse to let go of her dead, rubbing off on me?

"Don't cling to that too hard," Mistress Fey said, pointing at the rue. "It will rub off on you—leave a rash."

I could only nod. Had she just read my mind about the queen rubbing off on me? No, mere coincidence, happenstance, all of this. Or had this woman cast a spell on me? I should stop sniffing the lavender she'd given me too; we must discard the gift of rue for the princess. For when we rode away, even after I whispered to ask Nick whether she had looked young to him until we came close to her and he said no, I glanced back. And I swear by all that's holy, I saw a young, comely woman standing there again, just watching us.

As we headed for the ancient cromlech, I suddenly dreaded seeing it. The strange old woman's claim that Glendower was seen near this ancient tomb or on the battlements of the castle made me want to flee. I pictured again the man Nick and I had seen there, his sword flashing and his cape flapping, as old Fey had said.

Yet I did not want to discuss my feelings in front of young Rhys. How did I know he wouldn't tell Fey or someone else what I had said? Hail-fellow-well-met the lad might seem, but I was more than ever convinced that evil lurked here and could have harmed the prince and princess. How would I ever explain that old herb woman and such nebulous fears to the queen? Though I had leaned back and twisted around in the saddle to drop the lavender and rue into my saddle pack, their scents clung to me, curled into my nostrils as if they would reach my brain.

"Tell us about this cave tomb," Nick was saying to Rhys. He also leaned over to put a quick, steadying hand upon mine on the reins, so he must have noticed I was trembling. I had to buck myself up. I was with Nick and a Welsh lad he trusted. Surely all would be well.

"I heard tell," Rhys answered Nick, "the Irish call such tombs giants' graves, but here'bouts we call this Glendower's cave. 'Tisn't truly a cave but a chambered tomb cut back into a hill, and folks say if'n you pull out a small stone from it, it grows a new one. But it's mostly huge stones, with a portal to go in, like to another world—you'll see."

We did see, as the massive blocks, one balanced on two upstanding others, emerged from behind the next scrim of trees. The tomb was indeed built against a hill. Two protruding stones made a small forecourt entry. A square stone partially blocked the entrance. I suppose it once could have been moved to block it entirely.

"Amazing," Nick said. "There are huge, ancient standing stones in England, though I've not seen them. What a fine monument this is to some ancient king or chieftain."

"And to Glendower," I heard Rhys mutter under his breath, but I saw him cross himself as if he too were anxious about going in.

I had a good nerve to stay with the horses, for I realized it would be an enclosed area in there, a dark coffin of sorts. I wished we had brought lanterns or candles, lots of them. But after my time in the crypt of St. Paul's, how dark could this be? Some light must filter in. And I would be with Nick. Obviously, the prince and princess had survived being here—or had they? Noxious vapors seeping into the body's pores suddenly did not seem so silly as when the doctors had first mentioned them. Cave damp? And with bogs nearby?

No, I was being female and foolish, I scolded myself, and straightened my backbone as Rhys held my horse and Nick helped me down. Rhys led the way in. "Takes a bit for your eyes to see," he said. "Course, the lordship's body was buried way back in, but this here chamber's the one where Glendower sits or paces sometimes—some folks got a glimpse of him and his cape, heard his sword scrape on the walls."

After dealing with Mistress Fey, I almost expected to see the old Welsh warrior here, but, of course, there was no one.

"I saved it for a surprise for you," Rhys said, extending his arm at the portal of the next chamber. "When Prince Arthur was here, he left battle flags, Tudor ones as well as ones of the Welsh griffin and dragon, like the one at old Fey's. Till he died and folks figured it be bad luck, they been coming out here to see them. Some say it's an honor they been left by the Prince of Wales, but some who don't like it say it's sacrifice—or, ah, sacrament—"

"Sacrilege?" Nick said.

"That's it. See, in here."

The boy started into the narrow passage to the final chamber, but he jerked back so fast he bumped into Nick. "Can't be!" Rhys muttered.

"What?" Nick said, and stepped forward, tugging me close behind him with one hand and drawing his sword with the other.

Nick gasped, and I saw for myself what must have recently happened. The banners Arthur had left—the two bright green ones, at least, with the Tudor and York roses entwined—were slashed to shreds. The Welsh ones with the dragon and the griffin seemed to have fared better but were spattered with what looked to be blood, no doubt the same in which was written on the wall in huge letters, *GWELL ANGAU NA CHYWILYADD.*

"What does that say?" Nick demanded of the shocked lad.

"'Death rather than dishonor,'" Rhys said, his voice trembling. "'Tis Glendower's old curse 'gainst English rulers."

Nick gasped, then turned to mouth the words to me alone: *In English, that's Lord Lovell's motto too!*

CHAPTER THE SIXTEENTH

Staying to guard the cromlech, Nick sent Rhys and me back to the castle to summon the king's representative, Thomas Howard, Earl of Surrey, to view and assess the damage to the prince's property. I quickly changed into my woman's garments—was I right to wear my best brocade gown to attend an earl?—then rushed to see him, flushed and out of breath, with my hair poorly pinned and only half-veiled.

I had to ask directions to his suite of chambers. At his door stood a guard to whom I gave my name and said I had been sent to give His Grace immediate information about the ruination of the prince's royal banners. My legs shaking from my haste, and from facing an earl—the Lord High Treasurer of England, no less—I was quickly admitted. I curtsied as he rose from behind a desk in a small anteroom. Up this close I could see that his narrow face, lofty eyebrows, and aquiline nose gave him a haughty look. He was nearly as tall as Nick.

"Ah, the young woman sent to oversee the prince's burial," he said as his gaze swept over me once, then again, much the way Christopher used to scrutinize me. He came around his desk and stopped but a few feet away. "Trouble outside or inside the castle? Say on, mistress."

I blurted out all I knew—how the Welsh claimed the ancient tomb was haunted, how the prince and princess had visited it, and how it had now been defaced with Glendower's old curse against the English—though I did not mention that Nick had said it was Lord Lovell's motto too. I explained how the banners were all shredded and bloodied. "And, my lord, a Welsh lad named Rhys Garnock is waiting in the outer ward to be your guide to join Nick Sutton there to assess the situation," I concluded breathlessly.

"I'll go at once. I am here as the king's emissary, and we will brook no insults to the prince's memory or the right of Tudor rule. Sirrah, to me!" he shouted so loudly that I jumped. When the door behind me opened, he said to his man, "My horse, ten armed guards, all in breastplate and helm!

"I would take you along, Mistress Varina," he said, all business now as he donned a leather jerkin from the back of his chair, "but it will not be a proper place for a young, fetching woman—and you did come to fetch me, did you not?"

Despite his haste, he shouted a little laugh and gave me a tight smile as he assessed me again. I wondered whether it was obvious I had dressed in great haste. Should I not have worn so grand a gown in the midafternoon? I should go, but he had not dismissed me. Instead he kept talking, perhaps to himself. "It's worth knocking a few Welsh heads—just as hard as the Scots, I wager—to have a pretty lass come calling. That is all—for now, mistress," he said as his man rushed past me with boots and spurs. I curtsied again and backed away.

Well, I thought, the lad Rhys could not do much better than to work his wiles on a more powerful man about serving in London. I just hoped that my carelessness in dress and flushed face had not given him ideas that I wanted to work my wiles. No doubt a man of his power and place, however long wed and with the large family Nick had mentioned, was used to "young, fetching women" vying for his attention.

As I returned to my chamber and paced there—six steps to the window, six to the door—I felt powerless, and that would not do. I had been sent on an important mission, and I had thrived on my brief taste of action to fulfill it. I stopped and changed to my woolen day gown with difficulty, but I did not want to summon my maid.

So here I was again, a mere woman on my own in a man's realm, a woman to be sent back to the castle, one who could not join the Worshipful Guild of Wax Chandlers or ever hope to be a member of the guild of the Holy Name of Jesus—oh, no, not those who blamed women alone as far back as Eve in the garden for the sins of mankind! It wasn't good and it wasn't fair! I took to hitting my fist on the window ledge each time I passed, as my mind leaped from thought to thought about what I had seen today.

I realized now that the most telltale thing old Mistress Fey had said was something that had slipped out and then slipped right by all of us. "Glendower lives," she'd said, "at least our new Glendower, eh?" At first Nick had picked up on that and asked her, "And who is that?" Though she swiftly changed the topic, I swear a living man she knew had slashed the prince's banners and left that curse in the cromlech. Perhaps there was a method in her madness to mislead us.

I had thought she was a soothsayer to know we were coming, for she had that bundle of the rue herb tied up for the princess. But she could have meant to deliver that to the castle herself when she went out to seek herbs. Had she read the wishes of my heart, to call Nick and me lovers, or was it just observation on her part, mere coincidence?

I jolted at the rapping on my door. Nick back already? I ran to open it. My maid, Morgan, stood there. I was about to tell her I did not need her services when she said, "Mistress Westcott, the princess Catherine requests you attend her at once. Her confessor priest sent word and says you know the way. And what's happening that all the men rushed out?"

"I—I'm not certain, Morgan. We shall have to wait until they return."

"Rhys Garnock says you didna see Glendower at the cave, but that he's back! Oh, wait till I send my folks in the village word of it!"

"Morgan, Glendower is not back. He lived and fought nearly a hundred years ago. He was a man. Men die."

"Well, my folks always said if the old herb woman could live that long, he could too!" she replied, and flounced away.

I went into the hall and closed my chamber door, then, on second thought, went back and locked it with its big iron key, put that in my purse, and wended my way through the maze of corridors to wait upon Princess Catherine. Both Nick and I must be more careful, even here at the castle. I was not certain whom we could trust. And since I didn't believe the man up on the parapets had been a ghost, but flesh and blood, that meant he somehow had access to this well-guarded fortress.

The Princess of Wales—though I reckoned she would not hold that title long, since Prince Henry must surely be named to take his brother's place—looked much as I had left her. Same chamber, same chair, same black velvet robe with the priest Geraldini standing behind her. However, she had ordered a chair pulled up for me in place of the lower stools on which Nick and I had sat. And I was more used to the slow pace of having to use an interpreter, though now and then she interjected some English words of her own.

"Tell me what did happened at the old cave tomb," she bade me in English, so I told her. She replied, "The prince loved those banners, loved the Welsh, and they proud of him, their Prince of Wales." Tears gilded her eyes, but her voice was strong.

"I warrant this was done by one person, one enemy," I assured her, "not the Welsh people he well served."

"The angel candle you carved is lovely," she said, surprising me with her sudden change of subject as she switched back to her interpreter. Geraldini translated her Spanish: "I shall take it back to London, and it will be on my privy altar wherever I go. I believe you wished to ask me more yesterday about when the prince and I went out, two young people in love. Only wed six months and now a widow."

"Yes," I said before melancholy could overtake her again. "And I must tell you that I have also met the old herb woman named Fey."

"What a wonder—and a puzzle. Not a witch, I suppose, for the holy words say, 'Thou shalt not suffer a witch to live,' and she has lived long among these Catholic people, despite their folktales."

"At times, I thought she could read my mind," I confided in her, despite the fact Father Geraldini raised his eyebrows and shook his head. "And at first, when I saw her from afar in the slant of sunlight, I thought she was young and pretty—but then . . ."

"I too. I too!" the princess said, leaning forward as Geraldini translated. "But I asked Arthur, and he said it was mere woman's fancies. Ah, he had such plans that day, plans for us, for our children, though everyone here whispers we had not yet performed the conjugal act. Have you heard that talk?"

I was astounded she had brought that up. Making love, making a child—had she or Geraldini called it "the conjugal act," as if it were some legal or political maneuver? But then, to royalty who were expected to reproduce themselves to hold the throne, perhaps that is exactly what it was.

"I . . . No . . ." I floundered. "I came not to inquire of that."

She gave a hearty sigh, and Father Geraldini looked much relieved not to have to pursue it further too. "Since you came from the queen," she said, her pale cheeks coloring, "I thought perhaps you were here to learn of that. They will wait to name Arthur's brother, Henry, Prince of Wales until they are certain I am not with child, but I am not—sadly. Whatever will become of me? Shall I go back to Spain or stay in my new land?" she asked, but I knew she did not expect or want my opinion.

Tears glazed her eyes and, fearful I would be dismissed, as Nick and I were before, I addressed the key question among the many I wished to ask: "Could you please tell me what you ate the day you took ill? And I beg you, Your Grace, though I had it from the prince's doctors, can you tell me the progress of your illness and what you know of the prince's too?"

"Ah," she said. Then, not going through Geraldini, she added in English, "You or Her Majesty think poison? My parents, Their most gracious Majesties Ferdinand and Isabella, always they have food tasted twice and we here too. But when Arthur and I go out, we take some things—bread and cheese, wine—all tasted, nothing else."

She ticked off on her fingers and had translated what they had eaten for breakfast and the noon meal. My mind racing, I nodded to encourage her. "Oh," she added, with Geraldini still speaking for her, "we did both eat the wild garlic, both had to eat it or the breath, it kill you when you kiss, yes?"

Wild garlic? Old Fey had mentioned that but said it was too early to gather. Had she lied?

"You got it from the herb woman?" I asked.

"Oh, no—she have none of that," she answered for herself. "From the man across the bog—our horses splashed our clothes, and we did laugh so hard."

222

"What man across the bog? Which bog?" I asked, sliding forward on my chair seat.

"The one close, that way!" she said, pointing to what I figured was westward. I could tell that she was tiring again. Her voice, which she had raised in excitement, was slowing, and her gestures seemed to exhaust her as she dropped her hands in her lap.

"I should like to get some of that garlic too," I told her. "Do you know the man's name? Does he have a cot there?"

Geraldini was translating again, and looking alarmed as he did so. I could tell he was hearing this for the first time. "I know not. But he was a poor man with a wooden box of herbs carried before him, and a leather thong around his neck to hold it up."

"An itinerant?" I asked, but Geraldini didn't know that word. "A traveling peddler?" I reworded it.

"Oh, *sí*—yes," she blurted, speaking for herself again. "The man, tall and speak well. Clear from somewhere with name Colchester."

"The man's name was Colchester?"

"No—the place where he come. A kind man and did tell to us wild Welsh garlic make men sire many children, so Arthur eat a lot and I a little and we all laugh. But it rain then—we come back. The last time I see him, my husband, he give me a sweet kiss. Coming back through the bog, Arthur have mud spots on clothes, but I remember him always in shining armor in my heart. And then we sick—stomach pain," she said, pressing her hands to her flat belly through the robe.

"Nausea, vomiting, diarrhea," Geraldini put in.

"And hard to get breaths, so bad for the prince!" Catherine added. "Ah, it still so hard to get breaths when I think all I lost."

The men still had not returned from the cromlech when I finished my interview with the princess. I went back to pacing, to thinking. Morgan had left me a tray of food. I considered sending for her and insisting she eat it with me, but was I becoming too suspicious?

What to do? What to do with what I had just learned? The royal couple could indeed have been poisoned—but with wild garlic, which Arthur evidently loved and had oft eaten before? With wild garlic, old Fey said, that would not be ready to find about the area yet? And Prince Arthur had kissed his wife good-bye with a sweet kiss. That must be because she'd eaten the garlic too, so she could not smell or taste it on him. Was it true that wild garlic made one fertile, or was it just an old wives' tale—or a strange peddler's? Perhaps Nick and I could ride into the village to question Rhys's apothecary father. But something else was troubling me. The peddler from across the western bog had spoken well and told them he was from Colchester. That didn't make sense, yet there was something just out of my reach about it that I could not recall.

I decided not to eat this food but to get something from the great hall, where the visiting mourners were being fed. A herd of beeves had been brought into a field near the castle to provide for everyone. Surely their meat could not all be tainted if someone was out to harm those of us who were mourning the prince's death.

Then I would go outside garbed as a lad again with one of the guards who had ridden in from London with us. Nick would no doubt have much to tell when he returned, but I would have much—even more than what Catherine had told me—once I took a look around the western bog. Lovell's motto might be "Death Rather Than Dishonor," but I was going to take for mine the new chandlers' guild claim, "Truth Is Light." And come hell or high bog water, I was determined to learn the truth.

I changed my garb yet again, back to a lad's garments. Sim, perhaps twenty years old, a brawny but kindly royal guard who had come with us from Richmond Palace, was willing to go out with me. "So long's we don't lose sight of the castle," he said.

"Just across or, hopefully, around the bog to the west," I assured him, but I was having trouble assuring myself. At least, I prayed, Nick would be pleased when he heard I had taken an armed guard. Time was of the essence in all we did here. On the morrow, we had promised to help the Earl of Surrey plan the order of the funeral cortege. Lest I let that honored task go to my head, I told myself that we were simply included because the queen had singled us out. And, I told myself, we needed to both interview Rhys's father about wild garlic and revisit old Fey to see whether she would change her story about when it grew. Either she was wrong that it was not available yet or she had told some fellow conspirator that the prince wanted such and he had managed to slip the royal couple tainted—poison—garlic.

We urged our horses onto the well-worn marsh path of

beaten-down reeds that served for a passage here. This moss and peat bog seemed to merge with a distant meadow and then rolling moors. The area we traversed bore patches of knee-high, new spring grass but also pockets of last year's dead, hollow reeds standing as tall as bushes, with their new growth pushing up between. Our horses' feet made a sucking sound.

"Did you ever harvest wild garlic as a child?" I asked Sim.

"Wild garlic? No, mistress. Or should I call you 'boy'?" he said with a chuckle. "I like garlic and onions too, though, and my grandmother made fine rabbit stew with 'em, God rest her soul."

"Did the wild garlic ever make you sick, especially if you overate it in the spring?"

"No, but burped it bad for hours; that's sure."

"Do you know what it looks like?"

"Oh, aye, gathered it many a time. In the spring, green leaves but no blossoms. Flowers come in the autumn and bulbs dug in the spring, but reckon it's a bit too early now. Still, I've not been to Wales afore, so not sure."

You might know, I thought, a storm would come up. Gray clouds clustered on the westward horizon, creeping over the mountains in the direction we were riding, and I heard the faint rumble of thunder. By the saints, I tried to buck myself up: Rain would just make this jaunt more like the day Arthur and Catherine came this way. They must have come out of the forest from Fey's cot nearly at the edge of this bog, so how could the old woman possibly have had time to tell someone to find early wild garlic and approach them with such? Pieces of the puzzle were not fitting yet, and I must be careful not to force them into the wrong places.

Now and then a frog croaked or jumped out of our way. Despite our reedy path, our horses often sank into fetlock-deep water. The swishing sound was constant. Finally, we emerged on the far side of the bog, onto a grassy path with solid soil beneath and occasional new-leafed trees offering shade and shelter if the storm came. But not one with lightning in it. At the first sign of that, I would have to make this quick and head back. Besides, I had no doubt that, despite the fact that Nick had shuffled me aside today, he would be panicked or irate if I were missing when he returned to the castle. He and I must find time to return here early on the morrow if I had to leave in haste because of the storm.

"Don't see hide nor hair of anybody. Where to now, mistress?" Sim asked, keeping one hand on his sword.

"I'm not sure. I want to look around for signs of some sort of cot, maybe an herb patch or two, even a small planted field."

The thunder seemed to roll off the distant mountains and echo in the Terne Valley. Disappointed and frustrated, I realized we should start back. And then, beyond a scrim of hawthorn bushes, I saw the ruins of a small building, perhaps once a cot.

We rode closer. Sim's saddle creaked as he stood in his stirrups to scan the area, but I approached the cot. Barely half of the walls stood now, and those were of tumbled stone. But within was a place in the grass where someone had lain;

a small iron cooking pot and a spit stood over the silver ashes of a fire. A large hunk of pink meat was yet speared by the spit, partly cooked.

I dismounted to take a closer look while Sim stayed in the saddle, still gazing around. The ashes and meat were cold. "The meat is starting to smell," I told him. "It's beef, I think. I hear wolves are in these parts, so why didn't this meat draw an animal to eat it? Someone's eating well out here, sleeping out at night, perhaps, too. Look, Sim! Against that stone—an empty wine bottle."

"Stars and moon been bright lately," Sim said, but I was hardly listening. "It hasn't rained for a while," he went on, "but it's coming up one now. We'd best get back, mistress. It could be anyone passing through—'cept for the fancy eating."

"I think these words on the wine bottle are French," I said. "Imagine that, brought clear to Wales. Yes, yes, you're right. We need to head back. I'll return with Nick so we can—"

I gasped and screamed as an arrow whizzed over my head and struck Sim in the neck. He toppled backward off his horse and hit the ground with a thud. I heard the sickening snap of a bone—his neck? Both of our horses started, then shied away. If I tried to get my mount now, I'd have to run out into the open. I ducked behind the toppled-down wall, holding the empty wine bottle as if it could be a weapon. Then, when I heard and saw nothing more, I crawled to Sim.

My fault, my fault, my brain kept repeating. I should not have come out here, not brought one of the royal guards. His neck was bent at an odd angle. He was gushing blood from the throat, and thrashed for only a moment before he lay completely still, his wide eyes staring up at the darkening sky. I touched the side of his bloody throat to see whether life yet beat there. No. Not even enough to move more blood. By the saints, this was my fault, and now I could be killed too.

Queen Elizabeth of York

"Elizabeth, something has come in a metal box for us from Wales," the king told me as I joined him in his withdrawing chamber. "Perhaps some memento of Arthur's that Catherine has sent. No, it's marked as coming from Nicholas Sutton and Varina Westcott. It came in by another fast courier."

My hands were trembling. Could Nick and Varina have discovered something of foul play already and sent some evidence? Or was it indeed a remembrance of our beloved son?

"I knew we could trust them to be clever and discreet," I said.

The king cut the cords, and I helped to pull the parchment away from the box. I expected papers, a report of how things were going there, other than the official reports we received daily. Inside, I recognized the wrap—waxed cloth like I had insisted Varina take in plenteous amounts to wrap Arthur's body and shield his coffin should it rain during the slow, doleful journey to Worcester for his burial.

Henry pulled the paper open. It was stained pink in

places. Something painted. Surely not a newly carved or colored candle?

But it smelled. The stench was nearly overpowering as we both gaped down at . . . a heart! Years ago I'd seen deer's hearts while out hunting with my father.

A human heart? Our Arthur's? But it was to have been buried in the churchyard at the castle. Had someone not understood? Were these dread contents some sort of demented insult? Had they gone mad in Wales?

The king cursed and collapsed into his chair, while I gripped my stomach and turned away to retch on the floor.

CHAPTER THE SEVENTEENTH

Mistress Varina Westcott

Another arrow pinged off the wall and fell at my feet. I grabbed it—I know not why—and, terrified to remount where I would remain a target, I bent over and fled headlong into the reedy bog. I had not gone more than a few yards, splashing, panting, when I stumbled on a large carcass.

Horrified, I fell to my knees and felt my boots fill with water. It was a dead beef cow, maybe one poached from the herd to feed the castle mourners. Had Sim and I stumbled on a poacher's camp? The bottom part of the big body lay in the bog, but most was exposed to the air. Not a fresh kill, for the blood from it was dried, and flies buzzed upon its rotting flesh. But I saw that someone had hacked the heart right out of it.

Keeping low, I slogged my way around it. If the archer—the murderer—pursued me, I was making too much noise. I blessed the next rumble of thunder until I heard the crackle of lightning nearby. Another arrow zinged close past me and spiked into the water. My stomach clenched and my throat tightened. Again I pictured Sim, shot through the neck.

Lightning or arrows, I had to go on. I could hear someone sloshing through the shallow water behind me. If he trapped me here, I'd end up like that carcass—like Sim. Why had I thought I could come out here without Nick, without more guards?

In what must be the center of the bog, the water went thigh-deep. Taller reeds and grasses grew here too. Dared I try to hide, hoping my pursuer would pass me? If I could only catch a glimpse of him!

I tried to kneel and peek out, then realized I would have to sprawl to be hidden. I heard him coming slower but nearer. Should I scramble away again, run a zigzag path, and pray his arrows would not hit me? No. From the way big, strong Sim had fallen dead, this man must be an expert shot. It could be any poacher or Welshman who still resented English rule, for more than once I'd heard of the prowess of the local bowmen.

If only I could hold my breath and hide *in* the water! But with the storm . . . the lightning . . .

And then it came to me, how the boy Rhys had said he'd hidden underwater and crawled close to hunt ducks, breathing through a hollow reed. Those grew in abundance here. Then too, that would get me lower so that if lightning did strike, it might go to something higher in this flat bog.

I seized a reed that looked about the right length—not quite as long as my arm from elbow to wrist. My heartbeat kicked up even more. I did not know how to swim, and to breathe underwater seemed a frightening fantasy. I told myself I did not have to swim but only put my body and head under the surface, then breathe, just breathe. . . .

The reed had a crack in it, so I seized another. Thunder shook the very earth, and the wind kicked up, bending and bowing the grass and reeds. He could see me if I didn't get down, get under. What seemed like years must be only a few moments as I put one end of the hollow reed in my mouth and sucked air through it. No choice—no choice. I thought I could hear a man swishing grass aside, slogging closer. But what if he stepped right on me, drowned me or shot me at close range?

Faceup but my body lying sideways, I pulled my legs tight to my chest and I forced myself under the water with the reed in my mouth. Dangerous. Desperate. I found I had to pinch my nose tight, but I did pull in air. How long? How long could I stay here before I would panic and burst to the surface? After peeking once at the wavy, greenish world overhead, I kept my eyes tight shut.

The water felt good, I tried to tell myself. Cool against my sweating skin. Sopped peat moss lay under me; sedges and grass shifted against me. My knees, my entire body felt as weak as water. My panic of being enclosed in a tight, small place assailed me. *Just breathe.* It wasn't dark, at least, not like being in the crypt. Could this be the same man pursuing me? Did he want to harm me, kill me because I served the queen? Was it because Nick and I had been sent to probe into the prince's death? But no one here knew of those tasks, did they?

Just breathe. This was like washing my hair or dipping

my face in the washbowl, I tried to tell myself. Rhys had done this for years and boasted of it. I would tell Nick of it, boast of it. Then I must bring him and others back to retrieve Sim's body, to show them the animal's corpse with the heart cut out.

It seemed I lay there for an eternity, the water turning cold against my sodden garments and quaking flesh. My very soul screamed at me to get up, to suck in fresh air, to flee. But if the man were still near, all this could go for naught. If he hadn't found me now, would he head back, away from the castle where he could be seen? Guards should be on the castle ramparts. They should see and send help.

I suddenly pictured the silhouette of the caped man standing on the castle walls while we buried the prince's heart in the churchyard. Cape flapping, sword flashing ... Surely not Glendower reborn, as the Welsh wanted to believe, but flesh and blood—and full of hate.

Again, a rumble seemed to shake the very earth, the water in which I lay. Closer thunder? Horses' hooves? The man's footsteps nearby? Perhaps he was beating the reeds for me with his bow.

Water began to seep into my mouth and throat. Mayhap all these last year's reeds were delicate. I was shaking so hard that I was bending or breaking this one. I must risk sitting up before I gagged or coughed.

Though I wanted to leap up to suck in air and tear out of this bog toward the castle, I rose slowly, holding my breath until I thought my lungs might burst. The sky was gray and roiling overhead. Windy but no rain yet.

Hearing no one, I parted and peered through the grass.

A good distance away, headed back toward the end of the bog where Sim's body lay, walked a man almost as quickly and steadily as if he trod dry land. He was either tall or seemed so from my vantage point. I believe he had light hair. He wore a dark cape but the hood had fallen back.

Quick! I needed to get help before he got too far away to pursue.

But as I ran for the castle, glancing at him once more over my shoulder, he seemed to disappear into the fog and mist. It might be a trick of my eyes from water running in them, of course. Or perhaps he had knelt down or hidden himself in the grass. And where was the arrow I'd taken as some sort of evidence? I had lost it back there. Could I not do anything right?

Deliverance, for I saw partly armored men on horseback, streaming into the castle over the drawbridge! It might be Nick returning from the cromlech. At least they were king's men, ones I could send after Sim's killer right now. I shrieked and hallooed and waved.

The men halted and the rider at the head of the band turned back and rode toward me. My heart fell. Not Nick but the Earl of Surrey. He reined in and stared down at me, glowering. Heedless that I must look like a drowned rat, I told him, pointing, "I rode out with a guard to the far end of the bog, but an archer killed him and chased me! A poacher, I think, for there's a beef's body too, quite cut up. The murderer is wearing a black cape."

I believe it took the earl a moment to recognize me and to credit what I said. He lifted himself in his stirrups and raised a hand. Four men immediately thundered toward us, their hoofbeats matching the next rumble of thunder, while the others rode on into the castle.

"Ride around or into that bog," Surrey shouted to his men, and pointed outward. "Bring back under arrest any man you find there, caped or not."

"Be careful, for he's skilled with a bow and arrow," I added. "He shot the royal guard Sim right through the throat, and his body's on the ground!"

"Mark the spot where he fell and bring his body and any horses back," Surrey ordered his men. They immediately rode away. I went limp with relief until I saw the way the earl was regarding me. No wonder, for my wet garb clung to my shaking body, and my hair had come loose and dripped everywhere like a sopping gold curtain. Then I realized the look he gave me was not one of disgust—but lust.

"The queen's woman," he said. "Ah—Mistress Westcott, Veronica."

"Varina, my lord."

"Just so," he said, walking his horse closer. With one arm, he leaned down and snatched me off my feet, pulling me sideways before him onto his saddle and turning us for the drawbridge. His chest armor hurt my shoulder and hip.

"I am grateful for your help," I told him, trying not to hold on to him but find a place to grasp his big saddle. "I ran from the man and hid in the bog."

"I guessed such from your appearance. My men will find him, and we shall question him together. You do manage to attract trouble, mistress. For one moment I thought I had my own little selkie emerging from the water."

"A selkie, my lord?"

"A changeling from the sea, a seal in water and an alluring woman on dry land. The Scots say they shed their skin and seduce human men. Selkies live with their lovers for years, especially if the man can find a way to hide their sealskins so they cannot escape back to the sea." He said all that pleasantly enough, but put his hand right on my thigh and stroked me there with a heavy thumb through my wet breeches.

As cold as I was from the water and wind, I felt frozen by his touch. Sim's murder—my fear and headlong flight— all seemed a nightmare—then this?

In the courtyard, where the rain had finally started pelting down, I tried to slip off the horse, but Surrey had a good hold of me as he dismounted and lowered me into the circle of his arms. "You'll catch your death of cold," he said, obviously used to giving orders and being obeyed. "I'll send for your maid, but you need a warm fire and a proper bath—and to tell me in more detail what happened."

"I am grateful, my lord, and will call upon you later," I said, and tried to back away, but he scooped me up into his arms, bouncing me once against his steel chest armor to get a better hold.

"We should have a physician examine you too," he said, and, holding me tightly, carried me into the shelter of the arched entryway.

A new sort of panic set in. Did one blatantly refuse an earl or gainsay his wishes? I kept recalling that Nick had once told me that King Edward, our queen's father, had amused himself by taking lovers from the city merchants' wives. But the earl had vowed to summon my maid and a physician. One of the prince's doctors, or his own? In his suite of rooms, who knew what could happen? Or was I misreading all of this? No, I was no green girl. I'd seen that look on my husband's face, especially the first few years of our marriage, and I had accepted it. On Christopher's face, and hated it. And on Nick's face, and desired it.

"Please put me down, my lord. I am fine and wish my own chamber."

"Then I'll take you there to see you are well tended."

Nick had said the Earl of Surrey, the king's Lord High Treasurer, was nearly sixty, but he was as strong as a strapping lad of sixteen. Did he know or care that his hard hold on me was bouncing my arm and bum against his armor? Nick, I thought. Where was Nick? Had Surrey left him back in that cave?

As if my frenzied thoughts had summoned him, I heard his distant voice. "Nick!" I shouted, despite that Surrey swore under his breath.

I heard footsteps. Nick skidded to a halt before us, nearly bumping into the earl. "Varina, are you injured?" he demanded, ignoring the necessary courtesies of greeting Surrey. "His lordship's men said you were running through the bog. You could have been killed!"

"Crown business," the earl said, as if to brush Nick aside. "I need to further examine her and have sent my men to see to her attacker—who evidently killed the guard she took, someone named Simon."

"Sim?" Nick said to me. I could tell he wanted to pry me out of Surrey's arms. "Sim Benton?"

"Yes. Nick, you weren't back, so I knew I must take a guard."

"Was all this for a mere woman's whim to see that damned bog?" Surrey demanded. I could tell Nick wanted to interrogate me too, but he held his tongue, bless him, for I could hardly tell him what the princess had said in front of the earl without revealing our secret task here in Wales. "Stand aside, Sutton," Surrey ordered. "You consider the puzzle of who defaced the cave, and I'll deal with Mistress Varina. I'll send for you if—"

"I need to go with her," Nick insisted as I squirmed to be put down despite Surrey's grip on me. "It's only proper, my lord, and the queen would wish it, for by her command, I am responsible for Varina's well-being. By Her Majesty's permission we are betrothed."

I fear I gasped a bit too loud. The earl's arms tightened and his chest armor pressed even harder into me. "Why was I not informed?" he asked as Nick stood his ground, half a head taller than the earl and much angrier. I knew clearly now that Surrey had indeed intended to possess more than whatever knowledge of treachery I had.

"It is a secret engagement," Nick said, staring hard at him and not so much as blinking. "Such could hardly be announced or celebrated in this tragic time of mourning."

"And here I thought you were a clever climber, Sutton," the earl said with a slight sneer that made me dislike him all the more.

I truly think I had lost my voice; my brain and emotions seemed frozen. I had hoped Nick would not have to use this ruse, a last resort merely to protect me so I might do my duty. And to be haggled over—indeed, lied about so that Nick could keep me out of Surrey's clutches—or more like so we could keep our investigation into the prince's death a secret . . .

"Mistress, I did not know," Surrey said, and finally deposited me on my aching, soaked feet.

Nick put out a quick hand to steady me, though Surrey still held my other elbow. I felt like a fragile breastbone from a yuletide goose about to be pulled apart by two people to see who won a prize. Nick did not want me for himself, but only to keep me from Surrey, and to protect me, as he had promised the queen. Because I wished the lie to be true and knew that could never be, I wanted to collapse and cry. But they were looking at me, and I must play my part.

"I . . . we needed, as Nick said," I stammered, "to keep it private—for now, for the period of mourning."

The earl finally loosed his hold on me, removed his helm and held it almost ceremoniously in one arm. Frowning deeply, he said, "Sutton, I suggest that you keep a better eye on your betrothed. It sounds as if she could have been killed out there today, which I will look into. Now, I have much to do."

He turned and walked away, his spurs jingling.

As soon as he was out of earshot, Nick exclaimed, "How was I to keep an eye on you when I was with him all afternoon and then he left me there until the contingent of guards arrived?" He gestured wildly, most unlike himself. "You could have been killed indeed!" he repeated when I expected at least tender concern. He pulled me off into an alcove.

Hands on my wet hips, I shot back at him, "You could have let me handle him so you didn't have to forfeit your trump card of a false betrothal!"

"Oh, yes, I could see how you were handling him! Rather, he would soon have had his hands all over you, and you would have ended up on your backside in his bed like some doxy!"

"You—in the midst of all this danger, of our inquiries—just acted out of jealousy, didn't you?" I demanded. "Well, I warrant I understand that. At first I thought you and Sibil were lovebirds."

"Sibil? No, the queen just asked us to work together for a while. Sibil is mad for a courtier, a handsome devil, Nigel Wentworth, another former Yorkist who has pledged to serve this king."

Strangely relieved, and recalling Nick's goal to earn his own way with the Tudors, I felt my anger ebb. Perhaps Nigel Wentworth was the one Sibil had been waving to from the parapet the day of the joust. I realized I was not really angry at Nick, but at Surrey, and mostly at myself for getting Sim killed and nearly betraying our secret mission. Upset with myself, I tugged free of Nick's grip and started for the stairs.

"Not the main staircase," he said, pulling me back.

"Oh, that's right!" I spit out, shaking him off, my temper on edge again. "I'm ever to be sneaked in the back way!"

"Keep your voice down! And I recall you, not me, are the one who dubbed the ruse of a betrothal between us 'absurd.'"

With my sopped boots squeaking, dripping a trail of water, I darted down a corridor that led to a back staircase, Nick in hot pursuit. "Never mind that fantasy," I insisted, feeling on the edge of tears again. "I was not just out in the bog to admire the scenery, you know," I threw back over my shoulder as we thudded up the stairs. "The princess summoned me again and told me the prince and she had been given wild garlic by a peddler at the far end of the bog." I lowered my voice and slowed my steps. "Despite that we were told the herb was not to be found this early, some from last year could have poisoned them."

Wide-eyed, standing on the same stair with me, he nodded. We said not one word more until I reached my chamber, where I jiggled the latch until I recalled I'd locked it and realized I'd lost the key in the bog as well as the arrow I'd meant to bring back as evidence.

"By the Virgin's veil!" I muttered the queen's favorite curse and burst into tears. "What else can go wrong today?"

Nick tugged me across the hall into his room and sent his servant to find someone to get my door open. Feeling a complete ninny, a failure—and by the saints, I missed my home and son!—I sat in the chair where Nick put me and sobbed. When he stood me up again, then sat down with me in his lap, I wanted to jump up and be strong on my own, but I just held on to him as if he were the last solid thing in this swaying world.

"So tell me about Sim's killer, besides his being a good archer," Nick said much later, after my chamber door had been unlocked with the castle's master key. My maid, Morgan, had been summoned to help me bathe and change into my burgundy woolen day gown. My aching limbs and the terror of the day made me desire nothing more than to sob myself to sleep in my own bed, but Nick and I sat across the small table from each other in my chamber.

"From all you have told me," he went on, "I agree Sim's killer could be the peddler-poisoner or a poacher. He might be one and the same."

"I caught a distant glimpse of him as he walked away," I told him. "Tall, I think. Caped but not hooded. I think he had light hair—blond, white, or gray, though I know that's vague. I realized it was about to rain and was foggy and misty, yet he seemed to simply disappear, and—"

Nick jumped to his feet. "Disappear? This place is getting to you," he said, pacing to the window and then back again. It was still raining; water sheeted down the thick panes of glass. "You thought old Fey looked young at first," he accused. "Your eyes are bothered by tricks of the light. I don't want to hear drivel like they claim about Glendower coming and going in the mountain mists, or Lord Lovell vanishing into thin air during battles against the king!"

"Lord Lovell? You're the one obsessed with Lord Lovell! But you saw the man on the parapet of the castle when we buried the prince's heart," I insisted, hands on my hips. "Not a ghost of Glendower, but perhaps the same man who defaced the prince's banners and the walls of the cromlech. The new Glendower, as old Fey let slip."

"But who the hell is he? He's flesh and blood, and we have to find out who he is!" Nick raked a hand through his hair and lowered his voice again. "Varina, you nearly got yourself killed—and by a damned ghost, the way you tell it. I wish you could have brought that arrow back that you said you had. If I could find that, I'd try to trace the fletching, though that won't be easy, since everyone's some sort of bowman around here! I'm tempted to lock you up in this big stone fortress of a castle, but no doubt you'd still find a way to put yourself in danger."

"That's not fair. Now you're the one acting like this place is getting to you!"

"No, you're getting to me. I need your help; the queen has sent you, but I don't want you hurt! All right, let's calm down," he said, sitting back in his chair, "and assume the poacher-peddler somehow poisoned the prince and tried to kill Princess Catherine too. Killing the Tudor heir is a victory in battle. Sly, clever—not even an obvious murder." Wide-eyed, he whispered his words now. "And Arthur's killer might be willing to dispatch anyone who gets in his way, including you."

"Me?" I asked. "Otherwise, why would he pursue me when I didn't see his face and can't identify him? What if the man who murdered *Signor* Firenze in the crypt and came after me then is this same man now? Perhaps he wants to murder anyone who serves Their Majesties, or he thinks I know something that I don't. But how would he have so much intimate information about me? I was once fearful the queen wanted to silence me about making the effigies."

"I believe we can trust the queen. But we must find the peddler whether it's the archer or not. It could be any disgruntled Welshman who still wants freedom from the English or is a York loyalist, since these parts bred so many of them. At least we know it wasn't Surrey, since he was with us when we buried Arthur's heart and then he was with me at the cromlech."

"But he's a man who likes to be in charge, to know everything. Maybe Surrey wanted to take me off alone to his chambers to interrogate me about what you and I are doing here."

Nick shook his head. "He had other plans in mind for you. I know that look he had."

"So we absolutely can trust him?"

"I would risk it. Surrey's Yorkist loyalties are over. He knows his future lies with the Tudors, and, however angry I am with him, I believe he has hitched his star to the king. Just keep in mind that he is a rank opportunist and is used to taking what he wants, his wife and a large brood of children notwithstanding. You are not to be alone with him, whatever excuses he concocts on the morrow to 'examine you' further. You are a beautiful, desirable woman, Varina, even dripping wet with bog mud in your hair."

In the midst of our arguments and reasoning, that warmed me to the very pit of my belly. "I do see his lordship for what he is," I insisted, trying to keep on track. "He didn't even get my name right at first, when I'd gone to him about the cromlech. He called me Veronica."

Nick reached across the table to take my hands. The hint of a smile crimped one corner of his mouth, but his voice was deadly serious. "If I haven't said clearly so before, *Varina*, I value you for much more than your beautiful face and body."

Why did this man always manage to disarm me with straightforward statements that seemed not a bit flowery but made my insides cartwheel and my thighs and breasts tingle? We swayed slightly toward each other, and I antici-pated another kiss. Instead I nearly jumped out of my skin when someone pounded on my door. Reluctantly, I answered it to find one of the Earl of Surrey's men, the one who had brought him his armor in his chambers earlier today, standing there. He had been with the four men who had ridden off into the bog. Nick came to stand behind me in the doorway.

"I'm to tell you, Mistress Westcott," the man said, "that the earl's men found no sign of the several things you described. Sim Benton's body and your two mounts are nowhere to be seen, though we spent a goodly time combing the area. I'm to ask, are you certain he was dead?"

I gasped at his stunning news. "I'm positive," I told him. "I felt for the pulse in his neck, and he was shot through the throat, so he could hardly have wandered off."

"But we did find a steer stolen from the royal herd, partly butchered," he said. "And two more items of interest the earl says you are to have." He lifted from the floor an open-topped wooden box with a leather neck cord nailed to it. "Some sort of a peddler's box, we take it, with nothing inside—rainwashed. We did find two arrows in the bog. One we gave to the earl and one he sends to you." From his belt he plucked an arrow with a wet shaft and fletching, and extended it to me. "Good even to you both then," he concluded, and walked away.

The moment I closed the door, Nick took the two items from me. He studied the arrow closely. "I don't think we even need to have the peddler's box identified by the princess," he said. "Our prey is unpredictable, cleaning up after a murder but leaving the blood-spattered ruins in the cave, if it's the same man. Let's hide these under your bed for now."

"No—no, I don't want them in here. Take them with you."

"All right. We'll talk more about everything tomorrow, when we ride into the village to visit the apothecary. Business first, but as for our betrothal—"

"Our playacting betrothal," I interrupted. "We shall let it serve our purpose for now, but I won't hold you to it, of course."

"Yet maybe I shall hold *you* to it. I'll sleep on it now— and then later, maybe we can sleep on it together," he said. But his expression was still grim, and he had a tight grip on the arrow and peddler's box. He kissed me quickly, then quietly closed the door behind him.

My knees shaking, I shot the bolt to lock myself in. Then, to steady myself, I leaned against the solid wood, torn between hatred of our unknown enemy and my growing love for Nick.

CHAPTER THE EIGHTEENTH

"*V*arina," Nick said, "I am placing you in the funeral procession next to me with the other guards. We'll be riding directly behind the coffin. You'll need to oversee keeping it dry if it continues to rain like this."

"And that way you can keep a good eye on her too," the Earl of Surrey said with a little smirk. "If this damned weather doesn't let up, the road out of here will be even deeper than the bog I found her in."

I ignored the fact that Surrey had hardly found me *in* the bog. Nick frowned but plunged on with explaining his plans. I don't know how he found the time, but he had made labeled drawings showing the order of marching and riding mourners for the prince's funeral procession. He had even drawn in a few horses, banners flying, and the draped coffin on its cart.

Today, in a corner table in the great hall, despite the mourners streaming through to pay homage to the prince,

Nick had laid out his ten papers. With a lantern held for him, the earl bent over each drawing as Nick named the order of those in the cortege.

Occasionally, Nick would shoot a question at me, such as, "Unless the skies turn fair, it will be pointless for anyone to so much as carry the unlit tall tapers before the coffin, right?"

"Yes," I said, staying on the other side of the table from the men and the earl's hangers-on. "Soaked candle wicks would not light for the funeral in the cathedral itself. But I do understand the reason I should keep the coffin in sight. After being jostled on rutted, muddy roads, it may need to be rewrapped. I'll need at least one extra packhorse to carry the long tapers and the rest of the waxen shrouds."

With a sharp look at me instead of Nick, Surrey interrupted. "You'll see to that extra horse for your betrothed and her other needs, will you not, Sutton?"

I saw Nick bite back a comment with a clenched jaw. Why did the earl have to bait him like that? Did he not like anyone in charge but himself, or was he upset to be taking orders from a man of lesser rank? Or even, perhaps, because Nick had arrived in time to pry me out of his lordship's arms? At least I looked like a woman today, for I had decided to abandon my ruined clothes and pretense of being a lad. And to stand up more for myself with the earl, just as I had finally done with Christopher. Surrey was still full of lusty glances my way when Nick was pointing out this and that on the paper, so I simply ignored him, the king's official royal emissary or not.

Finally all was approved, we were dismissed, and Nick

and I met in the corridor between our rooms. He told me, "I wish you could wrap both of us in that water-shedding cloth, if we're still heading for town to see the apothecary. The rain's not hard but it doesn't let up—nor does the earl."

I agreed heartily but did not wish to argue. We yet had work to do for Her Majesty. "Do we need Rhys to show us the way, or do you know where the apothecary shop is?" I asked.

"I doubt whether there's more than one of them in that little town," he said, his voice yet on edge. Besides being in a snit over Surrey's attentions to me, he was obviously feeling the grip of the vise we were in, to be leaving soon and not to have found the evidence we needed.

When we rode through showers and mist into gray stone Ludlow village, I realized again that Wales seemed such an otherworldly place that it cast spells on outsiders. Even now in the misty village, the stone walls running with rain seemed to weep and scowl. Since we'd arrived, strange things had begun to seem commonplace: Heroic ghosts from the past came and went, an aged woman sometimes looked young, and men appeared and disappeared at will. The past blurred so with the present that I had begun to imagine what it must have been like here when Glendower fought for freedom and when the Yorkist Richard of Gloucester, later to become king, lived at Ludlow with his loyalists who still might prowl these wet woods and spongy bogs.

Nick was on edge too, for the way our enemy here seemed to appear and disappear reminded him of his archenemy, Lord Lovell. At least if the man was supposed to be hiding out on the Continent, he could hardly be the one causing havoc here. Despite the fact that we could not yet answer the queen's questions about her son's death, I was now counting the days until we could leave Wales.

I soon saw that other things that we expected would be as they were in England were different here too. In this outlying area of the Tudor kingdom, there was no such thing called an apothecary like in London. When we asked the location of the Garnock apothecary, a woman said, "A what? Oh, ye mean the herbal? Percival Garnock is an *herb-a-list*," she said as if we were dolts. "Down that way then." Nor did I see the familiar phoenix rising nor an extended tongue with a pill painted on the sign over the door, but rather the picture of a crudely drawn plant that I could not name.

Once we knocked on the door and introduced ourselves, Percival Garnock, balding, thin, and not as talkative as his son, swept us a bow and gestured us in. As we stepped into the herbal shop, a wave of yearning for the familiar things I loved hit me hard. The work counter held scales and weights, as in my chandlery. On the shelves, among pestles and vials and syrup bottles, I saw blocks of beeswax, though hardly for the purpose of molding candles.

"To make chest plasters, mistress," Master Garnock told me when he saw me staring.

"Do you keep your own bees?" I asked as my eyes took in rows of small drawers and more shelves with glass carboys, funnels, and flasks displayed. I explained, "We can't have them in the city but have our wax brought in from the country to make candles."

"Oh, aye, right out back, hives by the brook where my sons like to fish—aye, they do," he told me, gesturing toward a window running with rain. I knew I must forgo my feelings of longing for my son and shop, for Nick was standing on one foot, then the other.

"Your son Rhys was a fine help to us as guide," Nick told the man.

"He was honored to be there," Percival Garnock said with a sigh. "To see the words of Glendower painted on the cromlech walls—such an honor."

I could tell Nick was going to put his foot in his mouth with the man. He'd been upset that Glendower and Lovell used the same motto, and that the Welsh stood in awe of their "ghost" when he hated his nemesis. A sharp approach wouldn't do to get us answers or to ask for Rhys's services in the future, so I quickly put in, "We came hoping you would share some of your vast herbal knowledge with us, Master Garnock."

"Wish the prince's physicians would have thought o' that afore he died. All they did was send for embalming herbs after he was gone."

"What would you have recommended for his cure?" I asked.

"What I had little of but could have found fast from old Fey in the woods. Rosemary, aye, for coughs and breathing troubles. Sent Rhys to fetch some from her for others, but he's not back yet. Why, the prince's physicians also asked me after the fact if the single case of the sweat in the village could have hurt the prince, but Narn Romney didn't even have the sweat!"

Nick spoke up. "Master Garnock, what do you know of wild garlic in these parts? Can it be gathered this early?"

"Soon. A week or two—less if some was in a sunny spot, but doubt it."

"Do you know of a local peddler who might sell it?"

"Not likely. Besides, you'd need someone with my knowledge of herbs—or old Fey's—to be sure this time o' year to get the right thing. I swear, but that woman's been around so long she might know everything; aye, she might."

With a shudder, recalling our interview with Fey, I forced myself to keep to the topic. "What do you mean, 'to get the right thing'? Can it be confused with wild onions?" My conversation with Sim yesterday haunted me. He'd said his grandmother used to make him rabbit stew. But did his mother still live to mourn the loss of her son? She had no doubt been proud of his service to Their Majesties. Back in London, should I seek her out and comfort her—pay her something? Should I tell her I rued the day I'd taken him with me, and I understood the agonizing loss of a son?

But my thoughts crashed to a halt when Master Garnock said, "Once in a while, wild garlic gets confused with meadow saffron, which pops up even earlier than the garlic. They look alike—aye, they do. But the latter's deadly, so's one must be sure what's what. More'n once, horses or cows graze it and get sick or die quick."

Nick's wide gaze slammed into mine. Deadly? Get sick and die? What if . . . what if the prince's death was an accident? A peddler mistook meadow saffron for garlic and the prince did too? Or not really a peddler but a poisoner, one who knew the difference and had heard from Fey, from someone, that the prince was seeking garlic, a favorite spice and aphrodisiac. The horrid specter of the dead steer in the bog flashed through my mind. Could the peddler-poisoner have killed it with meadow saffron too? But then why eat tainted meat? Or was that meat from something else and, for some reason, the heart from the big beast was the only thing the man wanted?

Master Garnock walked to his wall of small wooden drawers and went immediately to one, lifting something out with a wooden pincer he had hanging on the wall. "It won't harm you a bit from touching it, but I like to keep the flora pure of skin flakes or soil. Dried meadow saffron—the last of last year's," he said. He showed us the dried plant he had plucked out. It looked like a dead crocus flower without a bloom.

Nick asked, "What are the specific symptoms of ingesting meadow saffron?"

"In small doses, measured out by an herbalist, it can help fight the smallpox. But too much—dreadful belly pain," he explained, dropping the plant in a small paper packet and handing it to me. "A burning mouth, then thirst and great difficulty swallowing. Nausea, running of the kidneys, slowing breath, then death, depending on the size, strength, and health of the victim. You . . . you don't imply the prince . . ."

"No, nothing of the kind," Nick said. "We are simply inquiring, and appreciate your wisdom and your discretion." Nick pulled two gold sovereigns from his leather pouch and placed them side by side on the counter with a finger yet on each coin, surely a fortune in a shop like this, even in my London shop.

"Payment for my silence?" Master Garnock whispered, wide-eyed.

"Not at all," Nick said. "For your consideration that we might take your son Rhys with us in the funeral procession and so on to London. I will try to place him in the king's household or, failing that, take him on myself. He said you had two younger sons more suited to the herbal trade and you might be so kind as to give him leave to try his luck in London for a year or so. You have been very helpful to us today, and I know your fine lad would be an asset to those of us who serve the king. Rhys is blessed to have a father who would consider letting him follow his head and heart."

At that, strangely, Master Garnock glanced from Nick to me. I thought he would ask whether we were wed, or why I had been garbed as a boy yesterday, but perhaps Rhys had not told him so. If he could keep his tongue on that—though maybe the cromlech visit of Glendower's "ghost" knocked everything else from the boy's head—he would be a welcome help to Nick or the king indeed. I noted well that Nick made no mention of trying to place the lad with the Earl of Surrey. And I saw the apothecary kept the coin Nick had offered.

Percival Garnock said he would think on it and must speak to his wife. When we went back out into the rain, Nick told me, "I'm going to deliver you to the castle, then ride to talk to old Fey again. With this rain, she'll be there."

"I'll come too. You shouldn't go alone."

"You were distressed near her last time."

"I was not distressed! She was just strange, that's all, but then so are most around here. Besides, I want to hear what she says about meadow saffron—if she told someone that the prince was searching for wild garlic. It could be what poisoned Their Majesties. But accidentally or on purpose? We are to work together on all this—you said so and the queen did too!"

"Come along then. I'd best keep my eye on you, since I've ever been ordered to—and wanted to—from the first."

With that, he gave me a quick boost up on my mount, and we were off to see someone I was certain was a witch, or perhaps, at the very least, just an everyday Welsh sorceress.

Queen Elizabeth of York

Despite how the king and I shared our grief for Arthur's loss, it finally helped me to have my ladies about me too. I had wanted only to mourn alone at first, but their chatter and obvious care for me kept my mind occupied. Yet nothing could erase our being sent that horrid heart. Not a human heart, the king's physician had said, but that of a cow or horse. Still, the king had written a missive to Nicholas Sutton demanding to know why it was sent and what he knew of it. The king had included in that missive a warning: An informant the king greatly trusted had heard that Lord Francis Lovell was back in England—but no one knew where or why.

"I have a question to ask, Your Majesty," Sibil Wynn said as she looked up from her tapestry frame. The two of us were momentarily alone, as the others had gone out to walk the lapdogs in the courtyard. "I heard that Nick Sutton returned to Wales in a rush. Will he be back soon?"

"I thought you had your cap set for Nigel Wentworth."

"Oh—yes. I inquire about Nick only as a friend."

"I should think so, after Nigel has given you such fine gifts," I told her, eager to get her off the subject of why Nicholas had been sent back to Wales. "It is obvious to me where Nigel's heart—and, I pray, his future—lies. Even His Majesty has noticed how your suitor dotes on you."

"Oh—His Majesty too? I hope he knows how fine a man Nigel is, and that he is fully loyal now and wishes to serve with all his heart."

"Exactly what I was saying. With all his heart—which I hope is set on you, Sibil. You must be careful to guard your maidenhood until you are certain he wants a wife and not a liaison. Before all this unhappiness, I was waiting for Nigel's request for a betrothal with you, but I warrant he will wait now for the period of mourning to end—to end formally," I added with a sigh. "For me, it will never really be over."

"I do understand," Sibil went on in a rush, her needle poised above her work. "It's just that Nick and I worked together for Your Majesty's special task, and I wondered what he is doing now."

"I value and appreciate your discretion on your fetching Varina Westcott to the palace," I said, trying another tack to shift the subject.

"I'll never tell, but can you trust the candle merchant? Surely she must be proud of what she's done, such beautiful carvings. She and Nick got on overwell, I thought, considering her position here—and in life. Of course, that is all past now, since she's gone back to her shop, but I just hope she resists the temptation to boast of what she did here."

I said nothing for a moment and folded my hands in my lap. I had noted a certain camaraderie between Varina and Nicholas. He was ambitious, so I had always imagined he would try to make a prestigious marriage. I did not want him simply toying with my wax woman's affections, and had told him he might mention their betrothal in Wales only if he needed to protect their reputations or further their investigation. Should I not have overstepped there? Had Varina or Nicholas overstepped with each other?

I said only, "Varina Westcott is of service to me. She is a fine wax candle carver and candlemaker. And do not pass on gossip in general, as it is most unbecoming."

"As you say, Your Majesty," Sibil said, looking not a bit contrite as she bent back over her needlework. But, frowning, she looked up again. "Do you mean gossip such as that Sir James Tyrell, who is in the Tower, is being questioned for terrible past crimes even beyond his recent defiance of the king?"

I nearly dropped my book. No one was to know what Tyrell was being examined for! Could someone have spread the word that he might be complicit in my dear brothers' murders?

"What is being noised about?" I demanded. "Exactly what and by whom?"

She looked startled at my outburst. "I can't recall who said it. I just heard Tyrell's in the Tower for questioning about more than refusing to return to England when ordered to do so. Oh, Your Majesty, I only wanted to ask about Nick, and now I'm quite undone and you are too. Forgive me."

"I will if you leave me alone just now. And do not listen

to or spread tittle-tattle about Nicholas Sutton, Varina West-cott, James Tyrell, or anyone else!"

"Yes, Your Majesty." She stabbed her needle back into the tapestry, stood, and flounced out her skirts. Looking suddenly pleased with herself, despite my scolding tone, she bent me a quick curtsy and was out the door.

I regretted I had lost control, but too much seemed to be spinning out of my control. If word was out about Tyrell's questioning, would his answers become public knowledge too? And though Sibil Wynn had heard such bandied about, would I be the last to know?

Mistress Varina Westcott

We found the path toward Fey's clearing after two wrong starts. The rain was turning the forest path into a bog, which unnerved me. Worse, we heard someone singing strangely, coming toward us. Rhys had indicated that Fey did not venture out in bad weather, but could it be she?

"Stay back," Nick whispered, and drew his sword ahead of me. Thank the Lord, it was Rhys who emerged from the tall grass, head down, slogging along on foot toward us and singing in a strange falsetto. He was walking in water nearly up to his boot tops and, despite a felt hat, was dripping wet, with his hair plastered to his forehead.

"Oh, milord—and milady," he said as Nick's sword scraped back into its scabbard. "If you be looking for Fey, she's not there. Went to get rosemary from her. And"—he lowered his voice so I could hardly hear him in the patter of the rain—"it looks like she just flew away."

"Flew away?" Nick demanded. "What do you mean?"

"Her footprints are in the mud and then—whoo—just gone."

I had no idea what he meant, and Nick must not either, for, frowning, he turned back to shake his head at me, then told the lad, "We've been to see your father and asked about your services, which we could use now. Here, I'll give you a hand up, and you ride behind me."

"What did he say, milord? Can I go with you to London Town?"

"He said he'd talk to your mother and think on it."

He hauled the lad up, and we were off again. By the saints, my heart pounded so hard it muted the rain. Rhys began to thank Nick for talking to his father, then just went silent too.

"Fey!" Nick shouted when we reached her clearing. "Fey!"

At Nick's voice, two vultures sitting on her smokeless chimney took flight. Rhys pointed at a spot on the ground, and we rode slowly over, leaning from our saddles to look at it. The rain pattered down less here, since a large oak with new-budding leaves leaned over us.

"See?" the boy asked. "The rain's pounding them to pieces, but her footsteps—she drags one foot—come over from near her cot to right there, then nothing. She walks to this point and vanishes."

"I see a single horse's hooves in a parallel path," Nick observed. "She must have walked to this point and then a horseman picked her up to ride, just as I did you a moment ago."

"No," I said before Rhys could answer. "The horse's prints are too far from her—unless she . . . she leaped far."

"Or flew," Rhys put in.

"Was there anything amiss in her cot?" Nick asked.

"Not that I saw, milord. Well—'cept the Welsh banner the prince gave her was gone, maybe packed away for safe-keeping."

"Maybe someone came here to steal it," I suggested with a shiver, as a rivulet of cold rain ran down my back despite my cape and hood. Would that someone then cut and deface that banner like the ones we found in the cromlech?

"Doubt a theft," Rhys said. "Not someone from these parts. No one wants to cross Fey—she's like a special thing here, like Glendower."

We dismounted and searched Fey's cot. The ashes in her fireplace were barely warm, but they could be left from yesterday. On her cluttered worktable Rhys found a half-bound bundle of dried rosemary, no doubt meant for him to take to his father's herbal, but the battle banner was nowhere to be seen.

"Not that she kept things neat in here, but I see signs of a struggle," Nick noted.

"I agree," I said, pointing to a tipped basket that had spilled its leaves—which looked like dried meadow saffron.

"Wait!" I told Nick as he looked under her bed. I pulled out the packet of the herb Percival Garnock had given me, then compared my sample to the spilled herbs more closely. "It could be the same," I whispered. "Rhys, do you know what is in this little basket she had?"

The boy leaned down, sniffing and squinting in the twilight of the cot. "Looks a bit like wild garlic but doesn't smell like it. Sorry, but one reason Da might let me go is I'm not so good at the roots and leaves."

Nick and I were hardly listening to him. "Maybe Fey was connected to the peddler," I said. "She was the supplier, but was she in on why he wanted the herb? Maybe she's fled because he came back to warn her we were looking around, getting too close."

"But she must have figured that out from our first visit."

"We didn't know to ask the right questions then."

"Despite the rain, let's search the area a bit more," Nick said, and led us outside.

The vultures that had flown before were back on the roof, this time with two more of their ilk. "Something's wrong here," Rhys said, stating the obvious as the big birds glowered at us and didn't budge this time.

Nick walked over to look even closer at the footprints, which the rain was erasing slowly, since the oak partly sheltered them. I went with him while Rhys stood a bit back, holding our horses. Strange events or not around here, I thought, she didn't just fly away. We were not reading these prints correctly. Witches flew, but that couldn't be the answer.

I tipped my hood back and looked up, blinking into the raindrops. In the tree directly above us, hanging from a limb by a rope around her neck, was Fey's drenched, dead body.

CHAPTER THE NINETEENTH

A scream died in my throat. Nick came to stand behind me and looked up too, then grabbed my shoulders. I heard Rhys run over to us. "Hanged?" the boy cried. "Who dared do that?"

I could not look away from Fey. Her sodden gray gown clung to her thin form. Partly hidden by the foliage, hands bound behind her back, she looked as if she danced in the breeze. The rope by which she had been hoisted was tied to a limb just over our heads.

"Rhys, take Mistress Westcott's horse and go fetch the sheriff in Ludlow," Nick ordered. "Tell no one else. Bring him here. Now!"

As the boy obeyed, Nick said to me, "We're going to leave her there for the sheriff to see. He can summon the earl or castle bailiff for this. I'll be damned if I intend to be interrogated by Surrey again. The queen committed her burdens to us, not him. For safety's sake, get into the cot."

"I'm staying with you."

"We're both going inside and we'll guard her from there. We could be targets out here—of a hangman who is also good with a bow and arrow. Let's go," he insisted, and steered me directly back into Fey's cot, pulling his mount so it blocked the open doorway, though we could peer out above and below the horse's body.

"You think he did it—the peddler?" I asked, my voice shaky.

"I don't know what to think, but I'm working on it. I've had men search the entire circumference of the castle to see whether they could locate a secret way in—for someone to stand on the parapet and watch us bury the prince's heart. A lot of castles and manors have old, hidden siege escapes. But they found nothing. I have inquiries out in nearby farms and villages with sketches of the fletching on the arrow from the bog, to see whether we can trace it to anyone so fanatically loyal to the Yorkist cause who would dare to kill the Tudor heir."

"But you and I are supposed to be working together. I didn't know any of that."

"I'm telling you now. I feel helpless to be able only to keep those vultures away—the birds, I mean," he added under his breath, and, holding his horse's reins so he would not bolt, shouted at the lurking birds, which were now nesting in the oak tree. They flew again but only circled and came back.

"Nick, I realize I shouldn't have gone out into the bog without you. I regret that Surrey happened to be there. But that doesn't mean I don't trust you or—"

"It means you might have been killed, and on my watch!"

"Oh—you're worried that the queen would hold you responsible. Now I see. Your duty, your future is at stake, especially since you're in the awkward and regrettable position of having told the king's Lord High Treasurer, Surrey, that we're betrothed."

"I don't want to hear such nonsense. If you want to argue, save it."

He kept looking out the door instead of so much as glancing at me, which made me even angrier. "It's true, isn't it?" I demanded. "Well, I agree with you that our duty to Her Majesty is more important than some mock betrothal."

Scowling, he glanced at me, then away again. "I swear, woman, you drive me mad. With frustration, with desire. Now keep quiet so we can hear more than the rain on the roof, lest someone tries to sneak up on us."

Whispering now, I plunged on anyway. He had my ire up, and I was panicked at the way events were unfolding. Firenze and Sim murdered, and now this. I easily could have been the third death. "Nick, we've had two dreadful turns of events—two terrible deaths here in Wales. I understand that, but must you attack me?"

He turned and seized me by both my upper arms. "Attack you? I'm trying to keep you safe. And that motto on the cave wall—the way your pursuer disappeared without a trace when Surrey's men searched—the poisoning of the prince—now this . . . Varina, what if Lord Lovell's back, within my reach, planning harm, and I can't find him, let alone stop him?"

It shook me even more to realize that Nick, my strong,

stalwart Nick, was afraid. I nodded in understanding and lifted my hands to grip his wrists, even as he held me. It was as if we propped each other up in the midst of a sweeping storm, and I knew, at the very least, we were a solace to each other.

While Nick and I stood like silent statues but for when he shouted to keep the flesh-eating birds at bay, the sheriff rode in pell-mell with Rhys. Nick and the sheriff, a burly man with a black beard named Cargon Dylan, lowered old Fey to the ground. I went outside despite what Nick had said.

"I ne'er thought to see the end of her," Sheriff Dylan said with a shake of his head and a loud sniff. Both men—Rhys too—kept looking around the clearing and into the trees. "I swear but it'd be like her to leap up again and dart off into the forest." He snatched off his cap, and, despite the weeping of the skies, Nick and Rhys did too. Not to be outdone, I threw back my hood. The rain felt good, washing me despite the chill of it.

"I'll send for the crowner straightaway and look into who could have wanted to silence or hurt Fey," the sheriff promised. "With the rain making the road nigh on impassable in places, the procession will be leaving on the morrow, so's not to be late for the funeral at Worcester."

Nick's head snapped up. "Who says?" he demanded.

"Got word from the castle, sent from the earl. The whole village been told to turn out to line the road just after dawn. I'm to see to it, so looking into old Fey's murder will have to wait. Hope that don't give the one who did this time to flee."

Nick's and my gazes met over the man's shoulder. I could

just hear Nick thinking, *The one who did this wants to do more than flee.*

But more startling than the sheriff's announcement was the fact that, just before he covered Fey's face with one of her own herb bags, I was certain I saw not sopped silver hair but gold, a wrinkled face gone smooth, and a soft white throat instead of a creased one gone purple from a hangman's rope.

When we returned to the castle, all was in chaos. Despite the rain, the Welsh and some English visitors still streamed over the drawbridge and into the castle to file past the casket in the chapel. People were packing; servants were running hither and yon. Despite the downpour, goods were being assembled in the courtyard. Nick saw me to my room, then, much dismayed that he had not been present when the earl ordered the departure moved up, went off to be certain everyone knew the order of the procession.

In my chamber I found Morgan folding my garments and putting them into saddle packs. Once again I ignored the food and ale waiting for me on a tray and went downstairs to find some sustenance from the common kitchen, though I could barely force food down. Fey's face—her fate—tormented me. Again I had mentioned the illusion of her youth to Nick.

I went into the small chamber off the chapel where we had wrapped the prince's body, to be certain that the tall, black funeral tapers and the extra waxen cloths were packed, wrapped in that same rain-repellent cloth. All was well, just as I had ordered and checked twice before. I stayed until the goods were carried off to be divided between saddle packs and a cart. Despite the suddenness of our looming departure and the wretched conditions outside, I was happy we were heading toward home.

I felt exhausted, but I was so tightly strung I knew I'd never sleep. Yet I needed my rest. Sadly, our leaving a few days early meant that the princess would be left here alone until she was well enough to travel to London. Was she yet too weak to bid farewell to her husband either publicly or privily? I prayed she had a strong contingent of guards left to protect her.

I thanked Morgan for her help, gave her several groats, with which she seemed pleased, and dismissed her early. I lay down in my riding gown so that I could be ready quickly when the cry came in the corridors for the funeral participants to awake. I would take my saddle packs downstairs and find Nick, for he'd said he might be up all night. I would also be certain I had the samples of meadow saffron from Percival Garnock and the one I had taken from Fey's basket. . . .

Fey, swinging in the tree with the vultures after her, after us all . . . in the darkness of my room where I was fleeing a man chasing me . . . chasing me through the bog and shooting arrows at me so I couldn't breathe . . . and poor Sim had his throat pierced, and that big beast had its heart cut out of him, just like the prince . . .

Now the darkness surrounding me was that of the crypt under the cathedral. I heard, echoing in my head, the voice of that man who wanted to kill me, who had killed *Signor* Firenze. He wanted to murder me among the tombs and monuments to the dead. His cape flapping, he pursued me through the cemetery where my son lay buried, not the queen's son....

I sat straight up in bed with a gasp. Trying to run, I had churned my sheets to waves. A dream, a nightmare, that was all! But ... but did I at least now know who the man was who had chased me through the crypt that day? His voice ...

I had to tell Nick! I scrambled barefoot across the cold stone floor to fumble with my door lock. I'd left a candle burning, but it had gutted out. Darkness. I had dreamed about the dark, about being closed in by death. If Nick was in his room—however late was it?—I had to tell him what I'd just recalled.

I swung open the door and took a step into the hall, only to trip over a body in the dimly lit corridor.

I fell to my knees with a gasp. Nick! It was Nick!

Queen Elizabeth of York

"My dear Elizabeth, of course people, servants and nobles alike, are going to talk," the king said, trying to calm me when I explained what Sibil had told me. "Now that I've made the move to have James Tyrell examined, if he's found guilty or is even implicated in your brothers' demise, I'll have it shouted to the rooftops. Though I was wary of so much as broaching that subject again, I've changed my mind. Justice must be served, and your continued torment over the royal lads' disappearance must be eased. I believe Tyrell will tell my inquisitors all under duress."

"Duress. You are going to have him tortured to make him talk?"

"I'll have him threatened with it first, then order its use if I must. Considering what you've been urging me for weeks, I warrant that can hardly displease you."

It was the first night we had lain abed together since we had heard of Arthur's death, but neither of us was in the mood for anything but sharing what mutual strength we could muster. It had helped us to speak of our lost son and of our new-fledged hopes for our heir, Henry. The boy would not be invested as Prince of Wales until we had Catherine back from Ludlow and were certain she was not with child, for any issue of Arthur's would keep Henry second in line for the throne. But I could not keep from asking about Tyrell, despite the king's telling me earlier to leave it all to him.

I swallowed hard and said, "Torture displeases me, Henry, but I see its necessity. Tyrell defied you by refusing to come out of his stronghold, and he must be made to confess whether he harmed my brothers."

Henry's hand gripped mine under the covers, like talons rather than fingers, for he had suddenly lost weight. "You must let go of your guilt for your brothers' loss, this . . . this witch hunt for who might have been involved, or it will make you bitter and ill, Elizabeth. Huge, sweeping events pay no heed to people's hearts, not even if you are the most powerful people in the kingdom."

"Or even, I suppose, if you are the lowest stable boy or kitchen turnspit and lose the ones you love."

"Elizabeth the Good, they call you for your tender heart. Sleep well, my love, for we have difficult duties ahead to preserve Crown and kingdom. There—did that sound as if I were addressing my privy council or the entire Parliament?"

"It sounded like wisdom to my head and heart. At least we have the children and each other. At least, whatever else befalls, we have that."

But as I lay stock-still so as not to disturb Henry, who soon fell into labored breathing, fear gnawed at me again. That I might never know what had happened to my dear brothers, for I must blame someone besides myself. That since I had lost three children now, I might lose young Henry and his sisters too. That someone still lurked in the darkness who wished us ill, but who waited to strike again.

Mistress Varina Westcott

Thank the Lord, Nick sat up from a pallet he'd evidently placed in the hall. He half caught me as I fell over him. He'd been sleeping here! I'd seen far too many dead bodies of late.

"What is it?" he demanded. "I've been here for hours."

He was guarding my door! Sleeping on the hard, cold floor to protect me. How could I have mistrusted him, been angry with him? I wrapped my arms around his neck like a child affrighted by demons.

"I had a nightmare—but I think I know who chased me!" I blurted as he stood with me yet clinging to him and quickly shuffled me inside my room, coming close behind.

"A nightmare of being in the bog?" he asked.

"And in the crypt at home. I don't know whether what he told me was true, but I remember what he said."

"What who said? Slow down and tell me all."

"It was in the cemetery where my family is buried, and he was there—a strange man talked to me. But now I think he must have followed me on purpose. He may have been the same as the man with the cape on the castle parapet, maybe the man in the crypt and the bog, but why? What am I to him?"

"Varina, you've simply had a nightmare. You're not making sense. Just because the man on the parapet and in the bog wore a cape—"

"No, it's more than that. Yes, I had a dream, but I'm awake now."

Nick dragged his thin straw pallet into the room, then closed and bolted the door behind us. He sat in one chair, but when I moved toward the other, he pulled me into his lap.

"Listen to me for a minute," he said. "We must think logically, not emotionally now—both of us. As for the man in the bog, I've learned the fletching on the arrow was what they call antique, used by King Richard's Yorkist loyalists hereabouts years ago, and that would have included Francis Lovell."

"Now who is being emotional, speaking mayhap only from his deepest fears?"

"All right, I admit I'm obsessed with finding the whoreson traitor. Say on about your dream—your nightmare."

"Perhaps when I was at rest my mind spoke logical truth to me. I remembered—I dreamed of an encounter, mayhap not by chance, in the graveyard of St. Mary Abchurch, not far from my house and shop." I was speaking quietly, but my right temple lay against his shoulder, so he could hear me well. I felt secure in his arms, which made the telling easier. I had not felt real fear in that graveyard encounter, but my unconscious, dreaming mind must have recognized the danger or the evil that reeked from that man.

"It was in mid-November, the day I took candles to St. Paul's for the service celebrating Catherine's safe arrival from Spain. I stopped by to visit my son's grave on the way, and a man came in through the cemetery gate, close behind me. I did not recognize him or think much of that at first. He nodded to me, then went off a ways. I recall his hooded black cape flapped in the breeze and snagged on his sword."

"It's not just the cape and sword that are similar, setting you off on this track?" Nick asked again. "Did he have a quiver of arrows on him, besides a sword?"

"No, but while I was at Edmund's grave, he approached me, saying I seemed familiar with the area and that he was looking for his cousin buried there, by the name of Stoker."

"Stoker?" Nick repeated as his arms tightened around me. "Go on."

"He introduced himself as Alan Bainton from near Colchester. And I'm thinking now that the princess said that the peddler told her and the prince he was from Colchester."

"What did he look like?" Nick demanded, his voice suddenly urgent.

"His hood was pulled up against the wind, but I saw he had a gray-and-white speckled beard, a strong nose—almost hooked at the bridge of it. Silvery hair, I think, though he kept his hood pulled up. It was blustery that day, so I gave it not a thought. I could not guess his age, though the hue of his hair and beard says something. But his voice—unusual, a bit raspy, just like the man in the crypt. It was nearly a whisper, but it commanded attention. I saw no horse but he wore fine spurs, and his boots were shiny. He said he had an ill cousin he would need to bury soon. Nick, you're hurting me, squeezing so hard. Nick!"

"Did he say aught else?" he asked, loosing his hold on me slightly. I sat up straight on his lap as another terrifying thought assailed me.

"No, but . . . if you're thinking it could have been Lord Lovell, have you ever heard his voice? Is it raspy?"

"I've never heard it, but I have been told such. That though he spoke that way, his orders were always obeyed, a sort of inbred leadership, even in the din of battle. A relentless man for his cause—and, of course, one who seems to come and go at will. Anything else you can recall?"

"Yes, I—I think he said something like he thanked me for my . . . my future assistance," I said, almost stammering.

"Future?"

"I had mentioned the chandlery to him, for candles and shrouds if his cousin died. Oh, I rue the day I told him where to find me, though he never visited, as far as I know."

"Of course we can't be certain it was Lovell. He could be dead or in Europe yet, for all I know—if he ever went there in the first place. But if it was Lovell, I'll wager he knew who you were before his pretended chance encounter, at least that you were going to the palace, working for the queen. Mayhap he was lurking around to try to harm Arthur and Catherine then, or maybe to get access to the queen, Prince Henry, the king himself—hell, I don't know! Damn the dangerous demon, if it was him. He could not harm the Tudors in London, so he came to Wales. . . . I don't know."

"But so few knew about my ties to the queen. Even if he

followed me to Westminster, how would he know whom I went to serve or why? Could Jamie have told someone, such as maybe his brother, who serves the king at the Tower? But why would the stranger, Lord Lovell or whoever he is, try to harm me either in the crypt or the bog?"

"I know not, but if your Alan Bainton from Colchester said he was looking for the grave of a Stoker, perhaps it was in reference to his pride in arranging, then escaping capture in the Battle of Stoke. These things may be circumstantial, but some of the pieces fit."

"I . . . Yes, it seems far-fetched, but so is believing in a ghost. How devious! As if he's playing a game, enjoying all this."

"There's more. Bainton was the name of one of Lovell's favorite properties in Yorkshire, forfeited years ago, as all his possessions were once the king attainted him. After he fled the Battle of Bosworth Field, promising to fight the Tudors another day, it was rumored that Lovell fled first to St. John's Abbey in Colchester. Later—rumors again—he left the abbey to lead another revolt against King Henry. All of that . . . I'm not sure, and was too young to do anything about it. When that rebellion failed, word was he found sanctuary in the Netherlands, but now I'd bet my life, which indeed I may be doing, that he's back with a vengeance and intends violence against the Tudors."

"Or has committed it already against the prince. So perhaps he hates those, like us, who closely serve them."

"Or he needs to stop us, especially because he may have heard how I hate him in turn, or he fears we are onto his game. Yet I would wager all I have that he wouldn't bother with the likes of us unless it could serve his ultimate purpose to harm or kill the king."

"But even if he somehow learned I have access to the queen, could he know for what? Could he know about my carving the effigies—that the queen was deeply disturbed by the loss of her brothers and her children? No, how could he? I think we're reading too much in. Maybe my dream was full of foolish fears."

"I still say too much fits. But if he's really back in England, the king must be warned."

'Round and 'round we went, until our voices trailed off from exhaustion. Just where we sat, I clung to Nick and he to me that night, both with our own thoughts and terrors, dozing, then jolting awake again. It took not only a rapping on my door but also the crier in the corridor, calling, "Rise and make ready! Rise and make ready!" to rouse us fully.

When the crier had passed, Nick slipped out to his own room, and I, still stiff and sore from my flight through the bog and sitting up most of last night, donned my cloak and lifted my saddle packs. I could hear the rain beating on the window, and I dreaded going out to face the long, mournful journey. Even more, I dreaded being out in the open, where our mystery murderer—be he Lord Lovell or, for all I knew, Glendower's ghost—could shoot an arrow at me. At least we were leaving Wales and would surely be safer soon.

PART III

"How oft is the candle of the wicked put out? . . . How
oft does their destruction come upon them?"

—JOB 21:17

"This love, that has me set in such a place
That my desire it never will fulfill,
For neither pity, mercy, neither grace,
Can I find; and yet my sorrowful heart,
I cannot erase."

—"A COMPLAINT TO HIS LADY,"
GEOFFREY CHAUCER

CHAPTER THE TWENTIETH

*I*t was easy to find my place in the waiting funeral procession, close behind the hearse, draped with black velvet and now covered with Westcott waxen cloth to protect it from the rain. How I wished that my departed husband as well as my hardworking sister and brother-in-law could share this moment of pride with me. I would tell my dearest boy, my own Arthur, that the chandlery he would inherit someday had made the covering and the candles for Prince Arthur, the boy who would have been king.

As I adjusted the cloth to be sure it was tightly tied, I noted that Rhys Garnock was on a horse, back in the group of guards. His father must have agreed that he could go with us. Had Nick known and forgotten or forgone to tell me that too? And where was he?

As if I'd shouted his name, he appeared at my elbow and pulled me back under an archway out of the rain. "Just before the last London courier arrived, I was given a letter for us from the king and queen," he told me. He had to raise his voice to be heard over the hubbub. He patted his leather pouch, so I assumed he had the missive there. I could not have read it in this gray, rainy dawn anyway. "It seems that, under our names, a package was sent from here via the same messenger who goes back and forth. The package held a heart."

I gasped and clapped a hand over my mouth before lowering it to ask, "A human heart?"

"They thought so at first. But the royal physician deemed it the heart of a beast. And another beast is back in England—Lovell. The king's informants have it on good authority."

I grasped his hands hard, but he didn't so much as flinch. He was looking at me but through me, perhaps seeing his enemy in his mind's eye, though he'd said he was not certain what he looked like. But was I?

"Then," I whispered, "that could have been Lord Lovell or one of his lackeys who shot those arrows at me."

"Probably not a fellow conspirator, as Lovell seems to be working alone this time. Having failed more than once in open rebellion, perhaps he's now a lone wolf, damn him! Killing the prince, trying to poison the princess. But yes, why try to capture or harm you—twice, or even three times?"

"Yes. If the man in the cemetery and in the bog is the same one who chased me in the crypt, I vow he killed *Signor* Firenze too! But why should he be after him and me? Because we served the queen? And how could he know of our sacred, secret task of creating her wax effigies? Could he have killed Fey too?"

"I don't know, and we can't tarry now." Nick exhaled

hard and stared out into the gray morning mist. "All I know is that with his tricks and treacheries, Lovell's back, and I'm going to get him, whatever it takes."

"The heart of a beast," I whispered, picturing the horrid package Their Majesties had received, and under our names. Nick had started away but turned back. "Do they think we would do such a thing?"

"I sent a brief message back explaining we knew naught of that outrage. As for the messenger who delivered the package, he recalls nothing of its donor but that a tall man with a sun-browned face and silver hair—a deep cleft in his chin, more like a scar, also—caught up with him just outside the castle as he rode last time for London and gave him the package from us."

"Alan Bainton from the cemetery! Probably the poison peddler from the bog!"

Nick nodded solemnly. "In my reply to Their Majesties, I said only that we would have news to report to them about what I called our personal preparations for the funeral. I signed from both of us but dared not say more in writing. I'm not sure whom we can trust anymore."

"Except each other," I said. I felt Nick was distancing himself from me again, but I could hardly blame him for being caught up in the rush of duties for this departure. And surely Their Majesties must know we would do nothing like that. Had not the queen realized that I, who agonized over my lost son, would never be a party to such a horror?

"It was the heart cut from that steer in the bog!" I insisted. "It must have been, and that peddler devil meant for them to think they'd been sent the prince's heart."

"Or it was some sort of message to them—a clever threat. 'You have had, or will have, the heart cut right out of you'—something like that. Varina, what if Lovell has them on his death list next? As bad as all this news is, I wanted you to know. We need to leave. I just pray that those six black-draped horses can pull the hearse on these roads. I'm taking a team of oxen along just in case. Keep an eye on that coffin—and be careful. I'll be near."

Rhys appeared to help me mount, giving me such a strong boost up that I almost catapulted off the other side. "Sorry, milady," he said. "Not so used to horses yet."

"Rhys," I said, leaning down to him, "you must call me 'Mistress Westcott' and call Nick 'Master Sutton,' instead of 'milady' and 'milord.' You have a lot to learn, including that titles and rankings matter. Keep your eyes and ears open and your mouth a bit more shut until you have been around for a while."

"I'm grateful, Mistress Westcott. Many thanks to you and Master Sutton for taking me on."

I was going to ask him what Nick had told him about whom he was to serve, but a sudden hush fell over the assembled entourage. Hearing muted gasps and whispers, I sat up straight and looked around. From the shadows where Nick and I had just stood emerged a woman I thought at first to be a nun. It was the princess Catherine in black formal mourning attire, including a nunlike barb headdress that covered all but her face. Had she come to bid Godspeed to her husband's coffin?

Men nearby who recognized her in the dim light snatched their caps off, then dismounted to help the women dismount and kneel. The princess was supported—propped up, more like—by two of her women with hooded capes. She whispered to them, and they stepped back as she gazed up at the coffin on the hearse, blinking into the rain, which soon streamed down her wan face. If she was crying, I could not tell.

Not waiting for Nick or Rhys, I slid off my mount and went to the cart that held the extra wax cloth. I had two rolls of it separated from the rest, lest I needed to grab them fast to rewrap the coffin en route. Nick had appeared again as word of the royal arrival spread up and down the entourage, and many others dismounted and knelt on the wet cobbles. The Earl of Surrey appeared from his forward position in the procession, bowed, then took Her Grace's hand.

Nick rose from his bow, saw what I was doing, and hauled Rhys over to me. "Rhys," I whispered, not waiting for Nick's order, "hold high the back of this cloth behind the princess while Nick and I cover her with the front."

Having freed herself from Surrey, the young widow was now standing with both hands flat upon the side of the coffin, stroking it through the layers of waxen cloth and black velvet. She pressed her forehead, then her mouth there in a farewell kiss. Tears blurred my eyes as we three held the covering over her. "*Adios, adios, mi esposo, mi amor,*" I heard her whisper over the patter of the rain on the cloth above us. Then she added, "*Que te vayas con Dios.*"

As she turned toward the castle, her gaze caught mine. I think she saw for the first time that we held the shelter over her. She seemed to simply nod her thanks, and I thought she would pass on, but she gripped my wrist with amazing strength and said, "I never forget your kindnesses. Like an angel, guide him to his rest."

Her two women were instantly at her side again. How much she seemed to have aged, but it was probably that close-fitting black barb that made her look so pinched and pale. My heart went out to her, one young widow to another. *Like an angel*, she had said to me. Like the carved angel candle I had given her . . .

In that moment, despite my fears, I made a vow: Even at great risk to myself, I would help Nick find and stop Lord Lovell.

Despite the initial inspiration we mourners took from the people of Ludlow village lining the road—I saw Rhys's family wave him farewell—the journey was arduous. The roads that we had covered so quickly heading west had been churned to mud and mire as we plodded east. All along the way, my eyes scanned dripping foliage, the dark places of the forests. In the open fields I felt we were being watched too, though I could see no one riding abreast, even afar. Looking for a tall, caped man, I scanned the faces of the mourners from villages and farms along the way. When I saw one or two such in the dreary miles, I jerked alert, my eyes searching for Nick if he rode not beside me, until I saw the humble roadside mourner was not the very devil himself but another man.

The skin on the back of my neck crawled as I remembered poor Sim flying backward off his horse when the arrow pierced him. My throat tightened at the memory of the sight of Fey's scrawny, ravaged throat. *Signor* Firenze's neck had been broken. Each one murdered at the neck, yet in different ways. Was it the mark of one killer who was skilled with strong hands and a bow?

I sat erect in the saddle, though I wanted to duck, to cling to my horse for protection. Had the poisoner taken my other horse and Sim's so that he could keep up with us on fresh mounts?

Even the support we felt when we stopped at manor houses or inns along the way, and finally when we reached the town of Bewdley and stayed in the prince's own manor house again, did not lift our spirits. By the third sodden day, when the horses could no longer pull the weight of the hearse, Nick ordered them replaced by four white oxen he had held in reserve at the rear of the procession. They were slower and not so fine-looking, but otherwise we would have all bogged down.

Nick oft rode by my side but elsewhere in the long procession too, making certain all was well. Each time he disappeared, though I rode amidst guards and with Rhys behind me, I began to tremble. At times it seemed Nick simply vanished into the crowd or the scenery, when I wanted to cling to him. I took to watching the prince's riderless horse, carrying only his armor and poleax. It was as if the prince too, like the man on the castle roof, in the cemetery, in the crypt, and in the bog, had simply vanished into the mist.

At each comfort stop, I scrutinized the wrappings over the black velvet coffin, retying or adding layers when the rain soaked through cracks in the cloth. I prayed that the deluge would stop before we reached Worcester so that the torches and my tall black mourning tapers could be lit and carried in the procession. For still the skies, like those who lined the roads, wept.

One day out from the abbey where the prince's body would be interred, Nick leaned over from his horse to squeeze my gloved hand. "I need to stay with the entourage, but since your charge from the queen includes preparing the funeral candles, would you be willing to ride ahead with a contingent of guards and your packhorses? I'll send Rhys as your errand boy and see you at midday on the morrow."

"It would help me to have time there to see things are arranged, though I'd rather stay near you."

"A great compliment, since that means you'd be out in this cursed weather almost an additional day. Varina, I don't want us to separate either, but I've given orders that the men guard you well, both in the abbey and at the inn where you will sleep this night. And Surrey, of necessity, must stay with the cortege, so you—I—won't have to worry about him harassing you."

Nick's face was so intent. Just as all of us, he looked like a half-drowned cat rescued from a well. "No," he said suddenly, as if to himself. "I've changed my mind again. Rather than your spending an entire night there, I'll send a contingent ahead with you when we are closer to Worcester on the morrow."

"But you just said—"

"I know what I said. But lest our archenemy is targeting you somehow, guards or not, I will keep you here, and that's that."

I was both relieved and upset. We were all exhausted, all

on edge. Without another word, Nick spurred his horse to ride back into the well-ordered ranks of armed guards. Such indecision was so unlike him. But I concluded that, in this instance, it was also another of his indirect compliments to me, further proof I meant something more to him than an assignment from the queen.

After nearly five grueling days on the road, I knelt at the high altar of the Abbey of St. Wulfstan in Worcester and gave thanks for my safety in all I had been through since leaving London. Then, because the funeral entourage was but a few hours behind me and my guards, I put them all to work unpacking the eight tall black funeral candles, which I set in spiked holders, four on each side of the altar. They would be lit just as the procession with the coffin came up the long central aisle. Other candles had been sent from London for this mournful occasion, so I oversaw their placement in holders and sconces too.

When all was well inside, everyone went outside to await the funeral entourage in the street before the abbey. Why the king had decided Arthur was to be interred here, I was not sure, but perhaps so that he lay forever between the realms of Wales and England, both of which he would have ruled. Folk from the town, surrounding villages, and farms had turned out in force. The crowd looked like a dark lake lapping around the abbey, and as many as six people deep lined the main street as far as I could see.

The rain had let up a bit, so I was glad to see the torches had been lit as the procession made its way into the city. Standing a bit apart from the Bishop of Lincoln, who was visiting to conduct the service, and a small crowd of priests with the abbot, I scanned the cavalcade, checking the wrapping over the coffin, searching for Nick. With a sideways glance, Surrey looked me over as he rode past and dismounted to be greeted by the church dignitaries.

I walked to where the hearse halted and, with the help of several others, cut the cords binding the waxen cloth and pulled it away from the black velvet pall. No sooner had eight guards carried the coffin inside than the crowd edged forward to tear off pieces of the wet, wrinkled cloth that lay upon the ground. I thought to protest the frenzy at first, but it was in honor of the prince, for they wanted a token of this event to cherish. Soon, nothing of the yards of Westcott cloth was left.

I hurried back inside, passing the procession waiting to accompany the coffin up the aisle. At the front of the church, I gawked and gasped. Each one of the eight tall black mourning candles I had carefully transported from London to Richmond Palace and then to Wales and now back again was broken or hacked off halfway down. Most upper parts lay on the floor, but two were bent over, held dangling by their sturdy wicks, which had not quite been severed. I was aghast at the destruction and then at what it meant.

At the back of the abbey, I heard the mourners streaming in and ran forward. Nick was suddenly at my side, picking tops of tapers from the floor, cutting free with his sword the wicks that made the others dangle.

"He's here!" I said as I scrambled from candle to candle. "He's inside!"

"I warrant he's gone now. He's careful to strike, then flee

to fight another day, and it's not his way to be trapped or caught. He always retreats, the whoreson coward. It's Lovell; I swear it is!"

Without another word, we worked desperately to place the top halves of the candles in the holders where the entire tall tapers had been. When I saw they were different heights, I moved a few so the higher ones were at the outsides and seemed to slant toward the altar near the catafalque where the coffin would be placed. I was so furious that, for once, I felt no fear.

As if nothing were amiss, the funeral procession started up the center aisle, the presiding bishop with a censer of incense leading the coffin, then priests, next Surrey, a boys' choir, finally other dignitaries. Perhaps they had not seen this mess and would not realize what had happened. I prayed no one would tell the queen.

Nick and I hastily snatched up the bottoms of the tapers, which we had dropped to the floor, and, out of breath, scrambled back behind the choir area and altar screen. Only then did I realize that two of the bottoms of the tapers were missing. Had we left them in plain view at the front of the church? It was too late to go back for them now.

Panting for breath, burdened with candles in our headlong rush, we nearly fell into the gaping hole prepared for the lowering of the coffin into the crypt. Nick grabbed my arm, and we threw ourselves back from a ten-foot fall where the tile had been removed. And there, below, lay the two bottom pieces of the missing tapers, crudely hacked by knife or sword into some sort of shape.

My skin crawled with horror, and I nearly threw up as

we gaped down into the dim crypt together. Nick drew his own sword quietly, though the droning dirge that echoed through the nave drowned out the sound. With his sword raised to strike, he searched the area behind the altar—thank heavens, hidden from the service—and found nothing.

"We're going to have to be lowered down to retrieve those for evidence to show Their majesties," Nick said. "Besides, when the prince is buried, it might look like some sort of curse and I won't allow that. Let's tie my belt and your girdle chain together." We did that, but the resulting "rope" was not long enough. We ripped the ties from our capes and knotted them to the cord.

"The thing is," Nick whispered as the Bishop of Lincoln's voice rolled on in Latin, "my weight might rip these ties, and you won't be strong enough to haul me back up. You'll have to go down."

I did not argue or delay, but what if it was a trap? What if Lovell was lurking in the crypt below, waiting for one of us to descend? He'd hacked apart my candles, so did he plan the same for me?

Bracing his foot against the corner of some long-dead abbot's tomb, Nick quickly lowered me down. The queen and the princess both had asked me to help guard and guide their prince to his resting place. Now I stood within it.

I refused to look into the sharp shadows. Several caskets or stone sarcophagi sat on shelves in the dust of the ages down here. I began a fit of sneezing, but threw the first two-foot-long piece of black candle up to Nick. He caught it handily and leaned over for the next. I shuddered to think our archenemy had handled it, hacked at it in his hatred.

Nick caught the other, then managed to haul me up until I could claw my way and scrape my belly over the side, where he could pull me up the rest of the way. Each holding a piece of candle before us, we hurried back around through an alcove to stand in the nave behind the mourners. It was then that I saw, even in the dim light of torches and other candles, what was carved into the once smooth black wax. In perhaps a mockery of my prettily carved angel candles, it was a grotesque, ugly face of a demon, perhaps Satan himself. No, no, I saw it now: Someone had crudely carved a crowned man—the prince, or mayhap the king—his face twisted in the agony of being poisoned, or perhaps in the torments of hell itself.

CHAPTER THE TWENTY-FIRST

During the long funeral ceremony, I was so exhausted, I nearly swayed on my feet. Just after the Bishop of Lincoln ended his prayers and sermon, the prince's riderless horse, decked out in pieces of his armor and weapons, was brought in. The animal snorted, and the whites of his eyes showed his fear of the crowd and strange setting. The sight of that poor beast saddened me even more, for surely one touch from his lost master would have calmed him.

I scanned the crowd, looking for a face I did not really know, might not recognize unless the person spoke in his rasping yet commanding voice; someone tall, of course, but many were, especially the guards. Then too, so many of these mourners had grizzled beards and hair. With the dreadful weather, some wore black cloaks.

Was our enemy here? Was he watching and plotting more poison, or was he a murderer who took any way to eliminate his enemies? A hangman's rope. Bows and arrows.

A broken neck in the blackness of a crypt like the one wherein the prince would soon rest? Or was his ultimate goal the assassination of another Tudor prince, or even a queen or a king?

Finally, guards carried Arthur's coffin to the south end of the altar, where it was lowered into the crypt. As many of us as could crowded in behind the dignitaries. The heavy coffin was lowered by twelve men and the ropes pulled back up. As the bishop sprinkled holy water and then dropped a ceremonial clod of earth upon the coffin below, I felt Nick's arm around my waist. Had we not both held the horrible candle carvings at our sides, I might have been momentarily content.

The king's chief mourner, the Earl of Surrey, then each of the prince's household and council broke their staffs of office over their heads and cast them down. They clattered into the tomb where the beheaded black Westcott candles had lain. Woeful cries of mourning rent the air. How I hoped I could do it all justice when I told the queen of this, I, the queen's chief mourner here, though none knew that but Nick and I.

Yet was Her Majesty's grief any greater than mine when others had buried my dear son and I had watched from afar? Or was her joy deeper than mine when we bore our sons and first looked upon their tiny faces? Not a bit, I swore to myself. And that was why, queen or citizen, highborn or low, we women were sisters under the skin no matter what befell us.

The mourners greatly disbanded after the funeral service, though some, including Nick and me, stayed on at the Two

Roses Inn nearby for the night, planning to head to London on the morrow. Rhys was content to fill his belly, then sleep in the stables with the men guarding the remaining horses. I was relieved when the Earl of Surrey departed, with a kiss on my hand no less, and whispered, "No other London merchant I have met could hold a candle to you, Varina." I was relieved he was gone, and I did not even mention the incident to Nick. What the earl would report to His Majesty—would he so much as mention Nick or me?—I did not know and was too exhausted to care.

I kept nodding off as I sat at table in the common room, eating tough roast beef with Nick and several other guards I'd come to know. Besides, each bite reminded me of that dead steer in the bog. I soon excused myself and went off to the small third-floor chamber I shared with two women from Prince Arthur's former household, who were being returned to London. At least they were both English, but it was sad to see how severely the princess Catherine's household was being reduced.

I collapsed in the single large bed, lying with my face to the wall while they whispered together near the hearth about hoping to find positions with someone else of import at court. I hadn't shared a bed with anyone for such a long time, but the three of us would fit in this one well enough. If only, I prayed, we would not have to share it with bedbugs, or even the mice I could hear in the thatched roof above.

I drifted toward sleep the wiser that night, glad I had no part of Surrey . . . and his mistresses . . . for I was counting not coins but the hours until I would be home and see my son again. I could not lose my dear boy, though the queen had lost hers and so much more. . . .

Queen Elizabeth of York

His Majesty and I had been forcing ourselves to eat, for we had no appetite. Sleep came no easier. I could tell he was restless too. I punched my feather pillow in the vast royal bed and said, "I do feel a bit better to know Arthur has now been laid to rest. Better, that is, unless we discover foul play, and that horrid gift of the heart seems to indicate that. My father used to say a spirit did not rest easy if it had been cruelly dispatched until his or her murder was solved and the perpetrator punished."

"In other words, if someone dies in battle or is executed for a crime, they lose more than their life? They are haunted, or haunt others, for all eternity unless their murderers are repaid in kind? I don't want to hear such heresy, and not from you. It isn't civilized, and it isn't Christian."

"My dear lord," I said, fumbling for his hand in the dark, "let's not argue or have a philosophical discussion tonight." He had been more than testy lately—entirely on edge. I understood that people mourned differently. A king cannot weep and wail, nor cling to painted waxen effigies of those lost as if they were flesh and blood.

"Nor is it Christian to torture someone in the Tower. Elizabeth, besides the loss of our heir, I realize you aren't happy that I said you should not ask me about James Tyrell's inquisition in the Tower—that I would tell you when there was something to tell."

My heartbeat kicked up. "Then is there?"

"On the rack, Tyrell admitted several things. On the initial line of questioning, he confessed that he gave shelter and succor to several Yorkist enemies of our Crown when they passed through France—gave them food, drink, and a bed. I have no doubt that he offered encouragement and mayhap funding too"—his voice rose—"in *my* castle there, when he had vowed to be *my* man! That alone is enough to bring treason charges. And Lord Lovell was one of those men."

"Not him again! Like a ghost, he keeps arising from rumors of his death. So they could well have been in collusion for other dreadful deeds. I vow they sound like a pair, Tyrell and Lovell! But you said Tyrell admitted to something else?"

"Your instincts were right about him. At first he merely confessed he was in and out of the Tower at the time of your brothers' demise, and insisted that so were others and he knew naught else on the matter of the princes in the Tower's disappearance and fate. And then, I believe since he knew he would be accused of treason anyway, he evidently decided to cleanse his filthy soul. Without further torture, he admitted that he and two rough fellows, now both dead, did enter the boys' chamber in the White Tower and smother them with the down pillows and coverlets on their beds."

I gasped and sat up in bed. Henry held hard to my hand, but with my other I instinctively threw my coverlet off and my down pillow to the floor. I wanted to collapse in sobs and beat the wooden headboard, but I continued to clutch Henry's hand and stared into the darkness of our chamber, seeing it all, the horror and the children's helplessness. In their last moments of life, did they think of their mother and me? Had Arthur, too, thought of me?

"Done, I assume," I finally choked out, "at my uncle Richard's orders to strengthen his claim to the throne?"

"Yes. I am so sorry to tell you all this now, with our recent loss, but it seemed so important to you. . . ."

"Seemed? Yes. Yes! And my brothers' bodies?"

"He swears he does not know. That the other two accomplices—"

"Tell me their names!"

"A Miles Forest and one John Dighton, both deceased. I looked into it."

"And now we can tell the world what happened!"

Though I sat stiffly away from him, he sat up and tugged me into his arms. "No, Elizabeth. Listen to me. I do not want all this brought up again, noised about to churn up rumors and lies. Publicly, we will let Tyrell die for his treachery in France, not for this, but we will know the truth. Now is the time the nation must mourn our Arthur and soon enough celebrate Henry as the new Prince of Wales, once I think he's really ready. We must move forward, and now that you know what happened, the past must be dead."

I did not argue, though I disagreed with him completely. He had done what I had asked, learned who had murdered my brothers, who should have been the king and the next in line to him. But did he not know that, for me, the past was not dead? And though I might never have their bodies— bones and dust now, who knew where?—to bury with pomp as we had our Arthur, I had their waxen and cloth forms hidden away, so real they seemed almost to breathe.

I breathed too, letting out a huge sigh. I let my husband hold me as my mind went back over all he had said.

"Tyrell's to be executed?" I whispered.

"Very soon, but not too hastily, not right on top of Arthur's burial today. Beheaded on Tower Hill and that will be the end of that for him—for you too."

I nodded, but, by the Virgin's veil, I wondered whether Tyrell's losing his head could really keep me from losing my mind.

Mistress Varina Westcott

When we arrived back on Candlewick Street in London, I dismounted in the chandlery courtyard and, leaving Nick and Rhys behind, burst through the door and ran into the shop. This was April the twenty-fifth, and I had been gone three weeks when I had thought I was going away only overnight.

No one was in the shop. Surely Arthur was home from school by now. I thudded down the hall and up the stairs to our living quarters. "Arthur! Mother's home!" I shouted, and heard his voice and footsteps as he ran to meet me.

Heedless of how big he was getting, I swept him into my arms and spun him around the way I did when he was smaller, planting wild kisses on both his cheeks before I remembered that I hadn't so much as invited Nick and Rhys in.

"My precious boy!" I cried, and set him down to hold his hands out from his sides to examine him. "My, but you've grown!" I cried as Gil and Maud ran in and gave me hugs, then began to rattle off all that had occurred in my absence.

Faithful Jamie, hat in hand, appeared from somewhere and waved to me before, I supposed, heading out to the courtyard to talk to Nick.

It was so good to be home, but I knew I could not stay, even now. Not after all that had happened. I had a half hour to bathe and change my clothes, for we were going to see the queen.

All the way on the barge to Westminster, as Nick frowned into the river and Rhys gawked at everything and held our horses, I kept silently rehearsing what I would say to Her Majesty. I planned first to give her the comforting news. How the Welsh and English alike had mourned and honored Prince Arthur. How Princess Catherine had seemed deeply grieved and in love with him. Perhaps then I would describe the funeral service—saving, of course, the news about the two crudely carved candles for last. Nick carried them even now in a saddle pack over his shoulder to show her. How I wished I could be giving her another of my carved angel candles instead, one with Arthur's fine features etched in it, but I'd had no time or tools to make it.

We left Rhys with the horses, since for now he was to be Nick's squire. With a nod from the guard at the outer door, as ever we went in the back way, up stairs, down narrow hallways, and entered the chamber where I had spent so much time carving the four royal effigies. The queen, who had been sent word we were coming, awaited us there, pacing among her waxen kith and kin. Full well I noted that a large, new block of fine beeswax for carving stood in the dim corner, but I said naught on that.

Nick bowed, and I curtsied. Her Majesty stepped forward and raised us. She was garbed all in pearl-studded black satin that whispered when she moved. "I thank the saints and the holy Virgin you are safe. I must hear all you learned, but the king is coming to my withdrawing chamber so that you can explain to both of us. Is there . . . is there much to tell of the special charge I gave you . . . of the prince's death?"

"There is," Nick and I said almost in unison.

I watched her expression change from hopeful to vengeful—I swear that is what I saw as she clenched her fists and her nostrils flared. I noted she was thinner, paler, with little crow's-feet perched deeper at the corner of each blue eye.

"I knew it," she said through gritted teeth. "And the king must too."

It had been staggering enough for me to meet the queen six months ago, but to be called to explain all this to the king! My knees were shaking, but Nick seemed only eager as we followed Her Majesty to her suite of rooms. I tried to buck myself up that, after all I had been through in Wales, this was nothing to fear. The one to fear was the man who murdered anyone who got in the way of his treachery and vengeance.

As we entered the queen's withdrawing chamber, I was shocked by the king's appearance, but calmed by it too, for he seemed genuine in his grief. In processions and parades, he had looked great and grand, with broad padded shoulders and fine, flashing garments as he rode or strode past. Now he seemed shrunken, gaunt, his skin sallow and his hair lank.

How he must have suffered Arthur's loss, not only as prince but also as son.

My heart went out to both of them, for I understood their pain if not their position. Why, if I learned my sweet Edmund—or my own Arthur—had been poisoned, I would hunt his killer to the ends of the earth! Yet how relieved I would be when they sent others besides me out looking for their son's poisoner.

"Rise," His Majesty said as we both bent before him. "The queen has told me of your covert mission in Wales, so what say you? Nick?"

Nick began to recount what had happened at Ludlow. I warrant it was best he spoke, for I would have colored it all with more emotion. But he stopped after telling them of our first visit to Fey and what we found in the cromlech, turned to me, and said, "Varina, why don't you explain what happened when I wasn't with you—the second interview with the princess and what happened in the bog?"

My voice trembled at first but picked up speed and pluck. I told of all that; then, with a nod from Nick, I explained my encounter with the mysterious man in the cemetery of St. Mary Abchurch in London nearly six months ago. I went on to what had happened to me in the crypt, omitting that Firenze and I had created the queen's effigies, implying only that the artist and I were linked by the chandlery guild's painted coat of arms. I included the best description we had of the peddler, broached the topic of the wild garlic, and mentioned the carcass of the king's beast found cut open near the bog.

The king interrupted. "That's where the traitor got that

heart he sent us! I believe this story can only get worse! Arthur was poisoned, wasn't he? Our Prince of Wales was poisoned, and someone's going to pay!" He crossed his arms over his chest, then grasped his shoulders as if to hold himself up. "Why in God's precious name didn't Surrey suspect any of this? But Arthur—out on a quest for a garlic love potion and with only two guards? Why did he think I sent all those guards along?"

"Your Majesty," the queen interjected, "he was only a young man in love who wanted to make us proud by begetting a son. At least he had his wife's love and ours too—he knew that, so it made him bold, bold as you have ever been."

The king snorted and began to pace. He almost made me dizzy. Nick picked up the tale again, adding information about our visit to the herbalist and how he gave us the link between the harmless wild garlic and deadly meadow saffron.

"And, Your Majesty," he added, "the peddler-poisoner's knowledge of local lore and of the lay of the land suggests he was someone who used to live in the Ludlow area."

"As did a huge rat's nest of Yorkist loyalists, the ones who served Richard and were there with him before Bosworth Field and some at Stoke! Say on. Is there more? We owe you much in gratitude and payment, but is there more?"

With a nod at me to explain, Nick withdrew the two pieces of black candles with the grotesque faces on them. I told of how quickly and cleverly they had been hacked apart, crudely carved and thrown into the crypt, even how we had retrieved them.

"In and out of many a scrape, eh, Mistress Westcott?"

the king said. I vow there was a hint of admiration in his voice.

Each of them took a candle from us and gaped at it. The king swore a string of oaths and heaved his into the cold ashes on the hearth. "It's . . . it's worse than the heart," the queen whispered, and, as if it burned her, she thrust her candle back at me and collapsed into a chair.

"We'll get him!" the king vowed with clenched fists. "We've faced opposition before, but somehow, none as covert or insidious. Instead of raising rebellions around impostors or leading men in battle, the cowardly churl's gone underground! It's Lovell; I swear it is!"

He raised his head to look me straight in the eye, then back at Nick. I had no time to realize I should have lowered my gaze.

"Nicholas Sutton and Mistress Westcott, you have served us well," the king said. "Nick, can you give even more information about this tall, caped, white-haired, bearded man with the raspy but commanding voice who dared to walk about our capital city and perhaps stalked Prince Arthur even then? And for some reason, he accosted Mistress Westcott in a city cemetery and a crypt—both places of mourning and the dead. Either or both of you, speak up again."

As if he must spew out that name before it poisoned him, Nick cried, "Yes, I concur it is Viscount Francis Lovell, Your Majesty."

"Varina?" the king said.

"Yes, I agree. But why he has an interest in me, I am uncertain."

My eyes met Her Majesty's wide gaze. I could read her

thoughts: *If you believe it is because Lovell knows about the effigies and hopes to hurt them or me, say nothing else.*

"Perhaps," the king plunged on, "it was because you carved a few candles for the princess, and he thought he could bribe or coerce you to gain access to the palace. What a spider's web! We have recently learned that Lovell was housed and hidden in France at our castle by another dangerous"—he looked at the queen—"and murderous man, Sir James Tyrell, who has long deceived us with his true loyalties. Tyrell has just been executed for his treason. But Lovell, that slippery serpent, was not there when we recently besieged and took the castle. Perhaps he was in Wales, eh?

"Nick, I must call upon you for another dangerous quest. I told you in the missive I sent to Wales that Lord Lovell was back, but my people may now have discovered the lair wherein he hides himself between his vile deeds. Bold and wily as ever, he goes to a site he loves and knows, but a place so obvious he must be betting we'd never search there: His own long-forfeited Minster Lovell, the castle where he grew up. I've had spies in the area, for I once gave the estate to my dear uncle—which no doubt galls Lovell all the more. My informants there have caught distant glimpses of someone they believe might be Lovell outside the place, near it, walking toward it—but then he vanishes, and they can't locate him."

"As ever," Nick said, "the ghost who wreaks havoc and disappears."

I could see that his hands were trembling. I too stood aghast at how the pieces came together. Nick had been right about Lovell, not merely obsessed with him. While the queen and I stood silent, Nick told the king how Lovell had led on, then deserted Nick's beloved brother, Stephen, in the Battle of Stoke, and then melted into the mist. For a moment, I thought Nick had made a massive mistake in reminding the king that the Suttons had fought against him once, but I had misjudged Henry Tudor.

He gripped Nick's shoulders and told him, "Besides your loyalty to your country, we have a cause in common then. Before Lovell does us more harm, we must find and stop him, and I swear that God has set you before me as the man for this righteous task! And, Varina—Mistress Westcott," he said, turning to me and taking my hand in his cold one, "because Lovell is a man of disguises, a man of deception, and you have evidently seen him of late more than once, I ask you to go along with Nick, not to put yourself at risk, but to identify Lovell once he's caught. Both of you, get a good night's rest while I assemble your guards and lay plans. Be back here day after tomorrow to ride to Minster Lovell. And, of course, you will both be well rewarded."

"My reward will be justice at last," Nick said.

My heart was beating so hard at the mere thought of facing Lovell again that I could only pray we'd capture him easily and he would kill no one else. And since I had been given a day's precious leave, I was going to spend it with my own beloved Arthur.

CHAPTER THE TWENTY-SECOND

The driving rainstorm reminded me of Wales, and delayed us so that it was the next afternoon before Nick and I rode into the chandlery courtyard. As the skies cleared and the late-afternoon sun came out, I prayed good weather boded better things to come. I was so anxious to see my boy again. I knew he would not be back from school yet, so I would surprise him with open arms.

Nick dismounted and went out back looking for Jamie, while I greeted Gil. "Don't fret now," he said, and patted my shoulder. "Maud left in plenty of time to accompany Arthur home. He's missed you sore and will be jumping for joy."

"If I'd been a bit earlier, I'd have gone in her place and wouldn't he have been surprised?" I said, clapping my hands in excitement as if I were a child myself. Surely, after a short journey to Minster Lovell—and facing down that demon who had been bred there—I could return to my family and all would be well. Well, that is, if I could only keep Nick in my life.

While Gil turned back to overseeing the apprentices, I went outside and led my horse toward the stables where Nick had gone to find Jamie. I was approaching the door when Nick stepped out and gestured to me: *Keep quiet and come here!*

I let go of my mount's reins and tiptoed to him. *What's amiss?* I mouthed.

He thrust a finger over his lips and pulled me inside. I heard men's voices, Jamie's and another I recognized, that of his brother Silas, the Tower guard who had told Jamie dreadful stories of what went on there. I peered around the beam of the first horse stall. Yes, it was Silas Clopton, a hulking man with ragged-cut hair. He had bright blue eyes, but I shuddered to think what those eyes had seen in the depths of cells or dungeons. Jamie had told Gil that Silas oversaw some of the torments, the dreaded rack and who knew what else.

"Aye, strange indeed," Jamie was saying. "Why wasn't Tyrell allowed to say a word afore he was beheaded? 'Tis tradition."

"Ne'er heard the like. He chattered like a magpie in the Tower. Guess the first time being racked was all he could take."

"So then, you heard him talk when he was tortured?"

"Aye, and it haunts me still, when none o' that usually frets me. I be so used to it, and prisoners are mostly villains to the core."

"And Tyrell wasn't?"

"Oh, aye—the worst," Silas said, and lowered his voice so I had to strain to hear. Nick seemed to be holding his breath, and he gripped my wrist hard. "The king's inquisitor asked him what he did the night the two young princes in the Tower went missing. I wasn't turning the screws that first day, but I heard it all."

"They think he hurt those royal lads back then? If so, maybe he died for that, as well as for disobeying the king's order to give up the French castle and come back to London."

"Oh, aye, the wretch admitted he hurt those boys, 'stead of swearing by all that's holy he was guiltless like he done at first. He'd confessed real easy to other things, like hiding some other blackguard name of Lovell. He kilt those boys and must have got rid of their bodies, but on whose orders? Why didn't they ask him who put him up to that, aye?"

Nick scowled, and I pressed a hand over my mouth. Tyrell had murdered the princes in the Tower! But why had that not been trumpeted far and wide as a major reason for his execution? No doubt the princes' evil uncle, King Richard, had them killed to clear his way to the throne, but why would the Tudors not want to proclaim Richard's guilt in the most public manner?

I leaned against Nick, shaking, picturing the waxen images of those young princes I had carved for the queen. They had looked so real after *Signor* Firenze painted them and she'd had them garbed and wigged that even I would swear they merely slept. Finally, she must know who had killed her brothers! A conspiracy against the Crown, indeed.

Lovell, following in Tyrell's footsteps for dispatching heirs, had murdered Prince Arthur. Now that Tyrell was dead, if Nick could capture Lovell and he was executed, would not the Tudors finally rest easy on their throne?

Tears in my eyes, I was about to tiptoe outside again when Jamie cracked out, "If Tyrell killed those lads, he deserved to be racked and beheaded! Why, two young boys, just like us years ago, Silas. So why should it fret you if he got what he deserved?"

"'Cause of the way he confessed," Silas said. "On the rack, he kept saying to the king's inquisitor, who come special for the task, 'Just tell me what you want me to say! I'll say anything he wants if you'll just stop. God will know the truth, God will know the truth, and the king does too!' You know," Silas added, "once he said that, the king's man said to halt the torment and asked Tyrell for no more details, like they usually do. Not about how he did it, not about where the bodies been hid. And since Tyrell wasn't allowed to give no speech from the scaffold 'fore he lost his head, I been thinking . . ."

"Listen to me!" Jamie said, his voice tense and desperate. "You'd best not think about it more, best not be telling me this, not anyone. Let it be. He confessed, he's dead, and that's that. You go talking more about this and you'll be losing your own head!"

"I had to tell someone. I do good work there, have a strong stomach, but this time—something's strange, that's all."

On trembling legs, I slipped out of the stables with Nick right behind me. As we hied ourselves toward the back door of the house, I said, "Silas is right. Why would the king keep all that quiet? It sounds as if his inquisitor tried to make Tyrell say something that wasn't true."

"I know not, but we have another task. We must concentrate on finding Lovell—letting him share Tyrell's fate. Jamie's right that it's best not to question all this, at least not now and not aloud. Varina, I'm off to Whitehall, but I'd treasure a moment with you first, and I know your boy will be home soon and then I won't get so much as a hug or a kiss."

He pulled me into the house and closed the door behind us. We hurried up to the solar, where I was hoping to surprise Arthur when he and Maud returned. They were a bit late.

"Since you will have all day and night with Arthur, I'd covet a bit of attention right now," Nick whispered into my wild hair. He seemed hurried, almost panicked by what he'd heard in the stables, and I was distraught too. We clung together, trying to shut out everything but our last moments for a while.

He crushed me to him as his lips took mine. I lifted my arms around his neck and held on hard. Nick's hands went everywhere, caressing me, moving, cupping, grasping until I thought I would go mad. We did not break the kiss, our mouths open, our tongues dancing and demanding. If he had taken me there, standing, I would have welcomed it. This was madness, after all we'd been through, in midafternoon, soon to be facing danger again. But it was a wonderful madness.

He laid me flat on the floor and threw himself down

beside me. I arched my back as he stroked, then kissed my breasts right through my gown. My entire being sprang alive as he slid one hand up my leg, ruffling my hem above my knees. His lips skimmed down my throat, down— And if Arthur and Maud rushed in . . .

"We can't—right now," I said, breathing as hard as if I'd run miles.

"I know. Besides, I can't tarry. Varina, at the last moment, the king asked me to go ahead without you, and you'll follow with guards on the morrow. I didn't want to tell you before— have you worry or argue. He didn't want to wait another day before I searched Minster Lovell. And that will give you more time with Arthur, if not me."

Nick sat us both up and lifted me to my feet. He held my chin in one big hand to stare down into my eyes. "I vow to you, Varina Westcott, we will find the time to make things right between us. Then will you say yes?"

I would have said yes to anything he wanted, because I wanted him at any cost. Our different stations in life, our unfinished quest, and Lovell lurking aside, I would have ridden out with him to fight the world bare-handed if he had but asked.

"I know not to what question," I whispered, "but yes. Yes!"

He kissed me hard, set me back, and stomped out.

Leaning breathless against the inside door to the once familiar solar, I listened to Nick's quick boot steps fade. I heard his horse's hooves strike the cobbles as he rode out of the small courtyard. I ran to the street-side solar window to watch him go, but the latch jammed, so I saw him distorted by the thick panes of glass as his form shrank and disappeared.

And what would Nick ask of me? I wondered as my skin still tingled from his touch. To let him possess my body? To be his mistress or—dared I dream so—his wife? But now, where were Maud and Arthur?

Queen Elizabeth of York

I was praying on my knees before the block of wax from which Varina Westcott would carve my beloved lost Arthur when I heard quick footsteps in the corridor. Fearful of anyone rushing about, I turned and rose as my last living son, Prince Henry, burst through the door.

"Mother!" he cried before I could say a word. "What's all this?"

He was out of breath and red in the face. I was shocked to silence, and flushed that he had stumbled on my secret place.

"Oh, you can't be here," I cried foolishly. "This is my privy room, and whatever are you doing running hither and yon, as if someone's chasing you?"

"Margaret and Mary are, but they'll not find me. Never do when I give in to their pleas to play hide-and-seek. It just allows me to be free of them for a few moments. But this . . . I—I didn't know—obviously . . ." he said, gawking at the figures.

It was too late to thrust him from the room or try to cover the obvious with a lie, not to clever Henry. But how to keep him from telling his father? Or was it time to tell the king so that he understood the depth of my brokenness in these children's loss, even before Arthur's murder? My son didn't understand, of course. Would my husband?

While I wrung my hands as if I were of no account at all in this, Henry gaped at each waxen figure. "These are my dead brother and sister—but these?" he demanded, pointing at the carvings of my young brothers. "Are these the princes in the Tower—my lost uncles?"

"Yes. Yes, they are. All as dear to your mother's heart as you are."

"Especially now, since Arthur is gone too," he said, and it hurt me to hear that so plainly, politically expressed. "The king does not know, does he?" Henry asked, still looking at the effigies and not at me.

He seemed older than a lad who would soon be twelve. Even without his moving again, his stance had a bit of a swagger. "Ah, no," I said, "but, of course, I planned to tell him when the time was right."

"And would that be now, since it's been proven that terrible Tyrell killed them, though I warrant word of that is still a state secret?"

I frowned at him. Had he figured that out himself or had his father explained it to him? I still could not fathom why the king wanted the murderer's identify kept secret except, he claimed, so the murders would not become a topic of contention again. Those who hated the Tudors had tried to say that Henry himself had wanted the boys out of his way too.

"Fine work, by the way," Henry said. "As fine as that of Phidias, I've no doubt. I warrant the wax woman did these as well as candles?"

I had no notion of who Phidias was, but my son's fine education and quick mind were no solace right now. "Yes, she did."

I knew not whether he even heard me. He could not take his eyes off the effigies. He bent close, scrutinizing them from each side, every angle. My heart was pounding as he stared at my closely guarded treasures. Should I bargain with my boy for silence on this, even though I'd said I would tell the king?

Henry finally straightened to his full height, tall, robust, and well-favored for his age, older than his years in body as well as mind. His shock had dissipated now, and a little quirk crimped the corner of his full mouth, but not in a smile.

"You know, my lady mother," Henry said, "perhaps it is best this not be sprung on Father at this time. I could keep your secret, if you wish, especially if we could trade favors."

"Trade favors?"

"As you know, Father believes my investiture as Prince of Wales should be put off for a time, because of mourning for our dear Arthur. And so here I am, despite my school lessons and more time with the king, doing things like running from mere girls and stumbling on your secrets. But if the king could be encouraged to officially name me his heir, I wouldn't have time to so much as mention this—and you could tell him in your own good time."

I gasped audibly and stared at my son. A bribe. A threat. And yet, by the Virgin's veil, I was tempted to take that brash bargain.

"Best neither of us tampers with king's business, but I can see your point," I said. I was stunned, floundering. Even

Prince Arthur could not have come up with this carefully couched demand.

Henry looked suddenly uncertain I had called his bluff. "Then I shall rely on that," he said as if we'd agreed. He bowed, backed away, then said, "I swear by all that's holy, you will never have a death carving of me! I will live for the others, Mother. Live for you and be a strong prince and someday a great king!"

He spun away and was gone.

Mistress Varina Westcott

I heard a boy's voice downstairs and tore out into the hall. Why greet Arthur in the solar? I'd hug him the moment he came in the shop door.

I thudded down the steps, but where was he? Where was Maud? I saw only a lad I did not know hovering near the door. A friend of Arthur's? Had he fallen and been hurt and Maud had sent this boy for us? I pushed past Gil and rushed to the door.

"This is my shop. May I help you, boy?" I asked.

He said naught but thrust a folded, unsealed note in my hand and was off like the wind. Someone wanted an order to be picked up later, I thought. Or a note from the palace perhaps?

While Gil muttered under his breath about Maud and Arthur dawdling in the shops when she was needed here, I stood in the window light and opened the note and read:

> *We must hope another Arthur does not disappear*
> *from the face of the earth. That will be so unless you*

> *meet me where we met before by your other son's*
> *grave in one hour. Tell no one besides Gil and Maud,*
> *especially that guard, and be there absolutely alone.*

It was not signed, but it did not have to be. I was so distraught that, for a moment, I could not fathom the meaning of the words. Then it came to me cold and clear. Someone— I would bet everything I held dear that it was Lovell—was going to murder my son if I didn't meet him in an hour. No, no, this must be a nightmare caused by the loss of Prince Arthur. I would wake up. Maud had gone to fetch my boy from school. If I followed these directions, I would be facing this phantom alone. Could any of this be true?

My hands shook so hard that the paper rattled, and I pressed them together so Gil would not notice. "A problem?" he asked from the doorway on his way out toward the workroom and courtyard.

I could not bear to tell him now. I had to think clearly. "Just a disgruntled customer. I'll go out shortly and settle this."

How quickly I had made that up. Why was I not lying flat, screaming, beating my fists on the floor? Had I changed so much then, some from my own trials, some from watching Nick? Had I learned to do what I must, at any cost? I could only pray this was some terrible trick intended to keep me in line, but I feared it was true. Yet if Arthur had been taken, where was Maud?

My desperate hope that this was a hoax was shattered when Maud came in the shop door alone, weeping and panicked. Jamie had gone out to the stables, and Gil wasn't here.

No Nick, no chance to catch him now. I must take care of this alone, save my boy above all else. I knew the worst of it before Maud opened her mouth.

"It's Arthur!" she shrieked. "He's gone! Varina, we started to walk home, but a woman came up to talk to me about a big order of candles, and when I turned, he was gone. I should have been holding his hand, but he said he wasn't little anymore. Then the woman disappeared too. I—I couldn't find him, but I don't think he ran off with friends. He wouldn't do that to us; he wouldn't—so I dashed home, thinking he'd be here, wanting to show me he could come home alone."

"He didn't. Lock the door, because we have to go tell Gil what's happened."

"But—but what's happened? We have to look for Arthur!"

"Lock the door, I said, and then both you and Gil will have to help me by doing nothing."

We sat, all three of us, huddled over the note. Maud rocked back and forth, moaning, blaming herself. I was in agony that it had come to this. Lovell had outfoxed the king and Nick: He was in London abducting my boy, not at Minster Lovell. What did he want of me? What had he evidently wanted from the first? I saw clearly that I must do as the note said: handle my meeting with him alone, *absolutely alone*.

"I swear I've seen the woman somewhere before, but I can't place her," Maud said for the tenth time, grinding the heels of her hands into her red eyes.

"You must calm yourself and try to remember," I urged her. My voice was deadly calm, but I was seething inside. We weren't dealing with someone who wanted ransom for my boy, but rather someone who wanted information or my help in something evil; saints preserve me, for I would do anything to save my son.

"Could she be an infrequent customer?" Gil asked. "Someone from church?"

Frowning, Maud shook her head.

"How was she dressed?" I asked.

"Brown garb, neither fine nor poor. She was pretty, her reddish hair covered by a hood and veil. She was rouged and had a rather long nose, blue eyes, I think—yes, I'm sure. A cloak clasped around her, despite the warm day. She said she wanted to place a huge order," she repeated again, her voice almost a wail. "I turned my back just for a moment—the area was not crowded then—and . . . and he vanished."

I did not tell either of them that I had received a note telling me to meet Arthur's abductor alone—now, in a mere quarter of an hour. I had no choice but to go to the St. Mary Abchurch cemetery where my other son lay. How terrible, how clever that Lovell, who had accosted me at that site months ago, would make me meet him there again. I did not think for one moment he would have Arthur with him. If I crossed the abductor—the demon who did not think a thing of murdering boys, even royal ones—I feared I'd never see Arthur again. How frightened he must be. But not as much, I prayed, as I was.

Now I fully understood the queen's passion to keep any remembrance of her dead children about her, how her loss of her son Arthur had stunned and shattered her. I pictured my Arthur laughing at Christmas, stuffing his mouth with candied plums. He'd been so proud when he'd shown me how he'd learned to use an abacus. I heard his reedy voice telling me all he had done in school each day. I felt the lack of him in my arms, regretted the times I'd told him to pipe down or not twirl his top across the dining table. I was a horrid mother to have left him to go to Wales, however much I'd been commanded to do so, however much I had loved to be with Nick.

The words of the note I'd read privily without showing Maud or Gil—especially not Jamie, who was out in the stables—had read, *We must hope another Arthur does not disappear from the face of the earth.* Disappear from the face of the earth to be buried . . . like the prince whom Lord Lovell had poisoned . . . dead and buried, like my little Edmund. If I lost Arthur too, I myself might as well disappear from the face of the earth!

CHAPTER THE TWENTY-THIRD

I lied to Maud and Gil, saying I was going to Christopher for advice—without Jamie, since Jamie had struck him. I also said they were to wait in the shop lest a ransom note be delivered. I was surprised they believed that I would go to Christopher, but they knew I was desperate. At least there was no chance of my old suitor coming into the shop, for since yuletide he had been avoiding me like that plague. I also made Gil and Maud promise they would not tell Jamie, and I would be back soon.

But as I made ready to set out for the graveyard, Maud seized my hands in her cold ones. "Sister, dearest Varina, forgive me! You have ever been kind and good. I was jealous—resentful—all these years. You are so skilled with the wax, like Father, and so pretty. Then with children I so long for. But I love Arthur too. I would not harm him, and now I thank you for not blaming me when it was all my fault—"

"No—mine too. I didn't realize the depth of evil, that it could strike my son also."

I hugged her to me hard. We were both shaking. I rued the fact that our precious conciliation was marred by this tragedy. "I swear I'll get him back, Maud. I must go now. Keep a stout heart for me and Arthur, and do not tell Jamie where I've gone, even if he rants and raves."

I slipped out the front door with a wax-carving knife hidden up my sleeve. After pretending to start out for Christopher's, I turned my steps toward the graveyard where I had met the demon Lovell before, and no doubt not by chance.

Though the day was mild and sunny, the familiar shops and houses seemed to frown down on me, casting shadows. People, even ones I knew, passed in a blur. Quickly moving clouds overhead made it look as if the church tower would topple on me. My horror of small, closed places leaned hard on my heart again.

The gate squeaked as I entered. The breeze rustled trembling leaves and graveyard grass. I scanned the area and saw no one. Was I early? Was he watching to be sure I came alone? He could be behind one of the tall, thick yews hunched over as if guarding the mossy stones. I walked quickly to Edmund's grave, hoping to have a few moments of prayer to calm myself, whispering, "Oh, Lord Jesus and our holy Virgin, protect my boy, and guide me to get him back. Oh, Lord Jesus and our holy—"

From behind a large stone monument, a cloaked man emerged as if rising from a tomb. I gaped at him as he came closer. Yes, it was the one who had spoken to me here before, this time with his hood thrown back. But I wasn't sure he was the one who had chased me through the bog at Ludlow, because he seemed older now, even a bit stooped, with the hint of a limp. Was that put on, or had he been injured? His silver eyebrows were sleek and angular over dark eyes that seemed to burn from within. A grizzled, shovel-shaped beard cupped his long face, but it could be fake facial hair. So this was the man of many faces, the ghost who came and went at will.

"You shall be of help," he said without greeting. Yes, that raspy voice, assured, even commanding. The man in the crypt. And the slant of his shoulders, the turn of his head—yes, the man in the bog! Firenze's killer. Sim's too. I must not accuse him of the murders, or of even stalking me before. I had to play along. He had my Arthur!

He went on. "I regret taking such extreme measures to be certain you would assist me, but this is a matter of utmost import."

"To me it is. I want my son back first, and then we can bargain."

"I knew you were strong. Your lad is too, right now, at least, so you will do as I say."

Though smooth and calm in words and manner, this man was a fiend from the pit of hell, the enemy of the Tudors, ravenous to harm their heir Henry and destroy their future.

"Do you recall," he said, "that when we met here before, I thanked you for your future assistance? The future is now, so let me explain. I have learned that you have easy access to our queen, going to her apartments through a back way. And

I believe few in the palace—perhaps even the king, eh?—know of your longtime free access to her.

"Fear not for her safety," he continued, as if he'd read my mind. "I wish to help her, but not only would she not see me if I asked for an audience, but it would endanger me."

"I could take her a note in exchange for the return of my son. I cannot do aught else," I insisted. Did he actually think I would trust him not to harm the queen?

"Are you so foolish to refuse me or order me about? God as my witness, I only wish to tell the queen in person who really murdered her brothers in the Tower."

I gasped. "But Tyrell—"

He gave a sharp laugh that chilled me. "Heed me carefully, Mistress Varina Westcott, for I have your son tucked away in a distant place only I know well, all safe and sound—for now."

My mind raced. Did he know Nick and I had discovered he had poisoned Prince Arthur? And that Nick would soon be looking for him at Minster Lovell? Though the wretch stood before me now, could he have had Arthur sent to Minster Lovell? A distant, safe, and sound place only he knew well, he'd just said. If his boyhood castle, which he must know inside and out, felt safe to Lovell, and he appeared and disappeared in that area, could he not make my boy disappear there too?

I told him, "Although I have access to the queen's chambers, I must pass by guards. They would never let me take someone with me whom they did not know."

"You will tell them I am the new artist to replace *Signor Roberto Firenze*, the one she favored to paint your pretty wax effigies. Sadly, she, like you, suffered his loss sorely."

He knew about my waxwork and Firenze's painting of them! He was gloating over Firenze's death! My voice broke as I fought for control. "Did you know the artist?" I dared to ask.

"Indeed, he once did a portrait of a king for me—the king who should be on England's throne even now."

Signor Firenze had painted King Richard for this obsessed loyalist? Then perhaps my artist friend had not panicked or suspected danger when Lovell first approached him in the crypt. Or perhaps Firenze had refused to help him gain access to the queen, and so . . . he had killed him. For two reasons now—my son's safety and my own—I must at least pretend to help this blackguard.

To make everything worse, there must be a palace informant who had told him about what Firenze and I did for the queen and how I had access to her. Surely Firenze had not given that away. Nor Nick. Sibil?

I nearly fell to my knees at that thought: The woman Maud had described, who had distracted her so that someone could take Arthur, could have been Sibil! That man whom Nick said Sibil was madly in love with, Nigel something, had once been a Tudor enemy. Could he be an enemy yet, and Sibil too? And in league with Lovell?

I pressed my arms tight to my midriff and felt the carving knife I'd secreted there, but I dared not use it. I couldn't disobey or betray this man. I could only say, "Yes, I can try to pass you off as a new artist. But I must go to the queen to arrange that, so there will be no snags when we try to enter. If I go to see her yet this afternoon, you must trust that I am not giving anything away to her."

"Arrange it for me then, and I shall contact you soon to learn the timing."

"We can meet back here to discuss it."

"No. You will hear from me about the next time and place. Comfort your heart that you will have your boy back and you will be helping to serve the cause of justice—God's justice, not this upstart Tudor king's version of it. Tyrell did not murder the queen's brothers, the princes. But I know who did and, more important, at whose command, and Elizabeth of York must know it too. And keep your guard away, or I'll dispatch him as I did that other poor bastard who was supposedly protecting you in the bog."

I was astounded he had confessed even to that, but he was desperate too. "And poor old Fey?" I blurted.

"Poor old Fey? I'll have no one else, besides me, working magic in Wales, changing appearances, telling me what I should do."

The man was mad. I was dealing with not only a demon but a crazed one. I could have plunged my knife into his chest if I were not desperate to protect my Arthur.

"Why did you not kill me in the bog?" I dared.

He gave a derisive snort. "If I had wanted to put an arrow through your pretty neck, I would have done so. The arrows I shot at you were a warning to stop, but you did not heed them. I wanted to have this talk then as well as in the crypt, but you eluded me and disappeared. Bright girl that you are, perhaps you have learned that imitation is a form of flattery, for everyone knows I can vanish on a whim. Now, we have tarried here long enough," he added with a scowl and a glance at the gate.

"Will you speak your name?" I asked, just to make him think I did not know his identity.

He swept me a mock bow. "A worker of justice and right, and Henry Tudor's worst and most recurrent nightmare."

He started away, then spun back with a swirl of cape. "Find a way to make it all happen soon," he said, pointing at me, "or I swear there will be another lost lad named Arthur, also buried in a very special tomb."

I agonized each step I took toward the palace, going directly from the graveyard and hiring a common river barge. Ah, I recalled the happier times when Nick and I—and Sibil, who might be a spy and traitor—had taken the royal barge to Westminster.

Staring into the murky Thames, I agonized over what to tell the queen. The truth? Should I beg her for help in seizing the man who must be Lord Lovell? But then how would I be sure my son was safe? I was no doubt expendable too, yet I had no choice but to abet his plans—did I? Or perhaps they could put the madman on the rack as they had Tyrell and let Silas torture him until he told where to find my boy so he could be rescued. Maybe Arthur was at Minster Lovell, and Nick would find him. If only I could send for Nick to come back, let him know the man he sought was here in London and would contact me again.

And above all, did Lovell really mean to merely talk to the queen or did he mean to kill her? I felt torn asunder. Hot tears coursed down my face, blinding me. I gripped my hands so tightly together that my fingers went stark white. Leaning over the side of the boat, I feared I would be sick to my stomach—to my very soul. It would be easier to cast myself into the swirling Thames than to betray the queen or lose my dear son. If Lovell harmed her, it would be my fault. If I lost my dear boy, I could never bear it. I now faced the greatest dilemma of my life: risk the queen or risk my Arthur and myself?

I was admitted by the guards. How easy it would be to get Lovell access to her. I waited briefly in a withdrawing room for Her Majesty. My hands shook as I heard her familiar quick footsteps, the swish of her gown.

My stomach in knots, tears in my eyes, I turned, expecting to see her stoic, sad face. But Her Majesty Elizabeth of York looked radiant, smiling as I had not seen for days— ever. I blinked back my tears and curtsied.

"My joyous news may have preceded me if you spoke to anyone in the palace today," the queen told me, pulling me quickly up. She clapped her hands, then pressed them between her breasts as if she were praying. "I am with child!" she announced. "The Virgin of miracles has blessed His Majesty and me with a great gift for the Tudor dynasty! Of course, that joy cannot heal my heart from other losses, but here I am, with the hope of a new child, one to be born next February, almost on my thirty-eighth birthday!"

"Your Majesty, I am so happy for you, for His Majesty too."

She grasped my hands. I said naught of all I had rehearsed. To risk the queen's life was terrible enough, but now that she carried a child in her womb—two lives and so much in the balance, perhaps an heir to back up Prince Henry—I could not risk their futures, the very future of the realm. So then I must indeed risk my own life, and Arthur's too. Silently, I begged the Virgin of miracles to help me find another way to save my Arthur and to outsmart Lord Lovell.

"But why are you here, Varina?" she asked, sitting on a padded bench by the window and patting a place beside her. My knees were quaking. I dared to sit down as if we were equals. "Are you not to ride to Minster Lovell early on the morrow?"

"I—I came to warn you to keep a good eye on Sibil Wynn, Your Majesty. I believe she might be in league with Yorkists who do not wish you well. And that she might have told some of them about our effigies—for I swear it was not me!"

She seized my hands. "I believe it was not you, and I have had suspicions of that girl. But if the king's enemies know of your carvings, they may try to sow discord between the king and me. I must tell him before someone else does, perhaps someone close to me."

"Close to you? Do you mean Sibil might dare?"

"Prince Henry has discovered our secret and admired your work, my dear, bright lad that he is."

Our eyes met and held. Now was the time I should follow Lovell's commands to somehow gain him access to the queen, but I had made up my mind. Before daylight on the morrow, Jamie and I would be out the back door of our stables and heading for Minster Lovell, even without the king's guard, for Lovell, if he was watching my house, would notice that. At least Nick would be at Minster Lovell to help me, and he must be informed of Lovell's latest ploy to harm the Tudors.

I had wild hopes that not only Nick but also my Arthur might be there. Snatching at straws I might be, but I had naught else but this: Lovell had let slip that my son was being held somewhere distant, someplace Lovell considered safe and knew well. And if I disobeyed—as I intended—my Arthur, like the poisoned prince, would be buried in a very special tomb.

Swearing Gil and Maud to secrecy about where I was headed, and warning them to be wary of strangers, I dressed as a lad and set out with Jamie before dawn for Minster Lovell. I had told Gil that when the king's men arrived to escort us, he was to say I was indisposed and would go at a later time. Hopefully that would throw Lovell off. Yet I shuddered to think that he was a man of surprises. More than once, it seemed as if he had read my mind.

At least I had finally filled Jamie in, and he claimed he knew the way. We went by the Great North Road toward a part of England where I had never been. I prayed every mile of the way that Nick would still be there, and if Arthur were there, Nick could help me find him. Women's intuition? A great gamble. When Lovell realized I had crossed him, what if he headed back to his family's estate? Once a ravenous beast realized it had been deceived by its prey, where else would it run but to its lair?

Despite my harried state, I thought the area called the Cotswolds was as gentle and peaceful as Wales had been rough and wild. Surely nothing dire could happen in such a calm, pretty place. But late afternoon on the second day we took a wrong turn and got lost. So Jamie hired a local lad named Hal to guide us through the thatch-roofed village of Witney and the last three miles toward the smaller village of Minster Lovell. The lad reminded me of Rhys, talkative and proud of his home area.

Beyond the cottages and marketplace, I could make out the sprawling, bone-white stone estate, Minster Lovell Hall, on the River Windrush. How could such an evil soul as Francis Lovell have been bred amidst this beauty of gentle hills and spring fields dotted with sheep? How he must have cherished the home of his ancestors and become even more bitter when the new king gave it to his uncle Jasper Tudor, who had helped him win the crown from King Richard.

I asked Hal to tell us about the manor, so we would know its basic layout. He said he had two uncles who had once worked in the kitchens of Minster Lovell Hall. According to the lad, the Lovells had built the manor house at least two centuries ago and had passed it down from lord to lord, this viscount, Lord Lovell, being the ninth.

"A family home," I had murmured, thinking how dear my home and shop were to me, and I'd not even lived there two decades. Yes, I could believe even a vile wretch like Lovell could cherish his home.

"Aye, Minster Lovell's big and grand, right on the river where me and my friends swim," Hal said. I wondered if they hid underwater, breathing through hollow reeds to snatch at ducks, but I needed to get more information.

"But you feel no loyalty to the Lovells for all that, no soft feelings?" I asked, for well I recalled loyalists to the Yorkist cause in Wales.

The big-shouldered lad drew himself up even straighter in the saddle behind Jamie. "I be loyal to my master, King Henry!" he declared. "The Lovells done wrong and went wrong. My uncles worked in the kitchen when Jasper Tudor held the estate too, see, and a good master he was too."

And yet, despite the tranquillity of the place, I swear I felt the wind shift and a chill set in as we approached the open fields surrounding the estate. I reined in, and Jamie pulled up beside me, with Hal sitting behind him.

"What then, mistress?" Jamie asked.

"Despite that Nick Sutton and other men loyal to the king should be here, we cannot be seen riding directly in. If our quarry left London, it's possible he has beaten us here and could notice us, at least as strangers. See that man herding sheep?" I asked, pointing. "I think we should make him an offer to let two of us on foot help herd them close to the entrance so we can slip in, while Hal holds the horses here and comes in through the main entry with them after nightfall. There's a pretty penny in it for you, lad."

"All right," Hal said, "but 'tis said that it's not Lord Lovell here'bouts, if that's who you be seeking. It's only his ghost comes and goes."

With a shudder, feeling I was caught in a whirlpool of time back in Wales, I dismounted. It was no ghost who had accosted me more than once or who had killed the queen's Arthur and taken mine.

CHAPTER THE TWENTY-FOURTH

I had never herded sheep before and was surprised how they smelled when woolen cloth did not. They didn't seem very smart or to know their way, but then, they were not usually brought this close to the gatehouse of the large manor house. Lem, the sheepherder, said it made them nervous, especially the sharp shadows thrown by the walls and buildings when they were used to sun and open fields. I felt like one of the animals, not quite sure what I was doing, not very bright, shoved this way and that in my dark quest to find Arthur and Nick.

Tears filled my eyes in gratitude when, as we approached the manor entrance I had my eye on, a priest suddenly appeared, on his way out. I prayed that was a good sign.

"May we go in this way, Father?" I asked, before realizing I should trust no one except Nick and Jamie here. But this man could not be Lovell in disguise, for he was short and squat, quite young too, so he could not have been here when Lovell was growing up. Unfortunately, I was so on edge I had also forgotten I was garbed as a boy and should have sounded like one.

"Do I detect a woman in lad's clothes?" he replied, tipping his head to peer under my cap. "Most unseemly. Friends of yours, Lem?"

"No, Father. Visitors."

"Not friends of Lem's," I put in quickly, "but of Nicholas Sutton, king's man. Is he here?"

"Oh, aye, everywhere about the area and grounds for two days now. I was just blessing the manor hall—God's mysterious ways are far better than man's. I believe his guard Finn is just inside, and you can't miss him. If you can get by Finn, you are welcome to enter. But to be so in disguise, when they are looking for a man in disguise, is most fool-hardy and wayward, mistress."

"They have not found Lord Lovell?"

He frowned at me, and I could almost hear his thoughts behind those watery gray eyes: How dared this woman dress like a male and assert herself like one too?

"Best you ask Finn and Master Sutton of that and not include Lem in your schemes. Lem, my lad, I warrant you have not been inside the estate since we closed up the narrow way, eh?"

"Aye, Father Mark."

"You see, mistress, and . . . and your man here," the priest said, frowning at Jamie too, "there used to be a narrow back escape gate from the early days, lest the hall came under siege, but it's been bricked up. I gathered nigh the entire village here last year to preach on the 'narrow gate, for broad is the way that leads to destruction and there are many who go in by it.' Take heed then," he concluded with the sign of the cross made directly at me as if I were accursed.

I had no time to argue or explain but hurried through this wide gate without another word. And I saw there, as the priest had said, a guard, hopefully Nick's companion, for he was the tallest, strongest-looking man I had ever beheld. He had been about to close this door when I pulled my hat off, shook my hair loose, and told him, "We are sent by the king and are looking for Nick Sutton. And, just like you, for Lord Lovell too."

I barely had those words out than two other men appeared and then, from across the cobbled courtyard, Nick!

Queen Elizabeth of York

As I was being prepared for bed, I was surprised to see the king enter my chambers unannounced. He nodded to us, then asked me to send my ladies away, so of course I did. I had already dismissed Sibil Wynn from my service and was having her questioned by the king's men, though I had made them promise they would not physically harm her. Whatever the poor girl, besotted of a former Yorkist loyalist, had done for him, I still had a tender heart for everyone—except for Lord Lovell, whom I saw as Satan incarnate.

"Do you have word of Lovell's capture?" I asked Henry.

"No word yet. I need to ask you about something Sibil Wynn said during questioning."

"You vowed you would not have her tortured!"

"Only threatened with ruination and imprisonment—

and torture for her lover, Nigel Wentworth. But she said the strangest thing, so I'm told, in her hysteria. She claims that Varina Westcott was carving for you not only what she called angel candles but also life-size death effigies of our lost children—and your brothers. And that they are secreted here, near these very chambers."

My heart careened to my feet. I was caught! But then, I should have known he would find out, and I had been trying to muster the courage to tell him myself. At least Prince Henry had not betrayed me, perhaps because I had asked the king to invest him as Prince of Wales sooner than he had planned. But now—this.

"I was going to tell you, show you," I said, floundering, "but you had so many things on your schedule and in your heart."

"It's true then? My dearest, why?" he demanded, and his voice had an edge to it now.

I stared at him, not seeing him for a moment as I rested my hands on my flat belly, so flat it seemed a dream that I carried a child there. Could my monthly flow have stopped for other reasons? No, I knew the other signs. Though I was stunned by this turn of events, my thoughts circled back to what he had just asked.

"I needed to have them near me," I said in a voice calm and quiet, not my own, not the tone I thought would be mine. "To tell them I'm sorry I failed them."

I saw Henry was keeping a tight rein on his temper, that he wanted to rail at me. "But you never failed them," he insisted. "These cruel, unfair things happen in a world of woe." He took my warm hands in his cold ones. "You must let the past, all that pain, go or it might harm the babe you carry—harm us."

"You won't order the effigies destroyed? They are beautiful, peaceful."

"But to hang on to death that way—especially your brothers. With Tyrell's death, I thought we settled all that, put it to rest."

"To rest? If my own uncle Richard ordered their deaths, I hope he is rotting in hell, but I will never rest!"

"I want to see the figures now. Will you show me or shall I go alone?"

I nodded jerkily and pulled my hands away. With him behind me, I walked the narrow corridor toward the closed door.

"We'll need a torch," I told him, taking one from its sconce on the wall. "It's dark in there."

I had almost told him, *I keep it dark so they can sleep.* I actually thought of it that way sometimes, that they were still alive. If he tried to take them from me, I would lose control, and our next—our last—child would be born to a guilt-ridden madwoman.

"Amazing," I heard him whisper as I held the torch aloft and we gazed at the waxen images. "So real. When the shadows shift, I can almost imagine—"

"Yes. Yes!"

"But if you wanted funeral effigies near their tombs, we could have done that."

"Hardly of my brothers' tombs, for they have none. Only God knows where their bones lie." I shook so hard the torch wavered, and he took it from me and placed it in a sconce. "I wanted them near me—with me," I whispered. "And I want one of Arthur too—see that block of wax there and—"

"No, I forbid it, forbid this! It isn't healthful for you or the babe you carry. I don't want you reminded of all this! Your brothers' losses especially, long ago and over now."

"Over?" I said. "Never over for me, never past!"

I could tell he was furious at my defiance. Oh, yes, I could read him and knew he would try to distract me from this big bone of contention. "She's a genius, isn't she, your wax woman?" he asked. "Elizabeth, if you keep these of our children here, I can accept it, but those of your brothers so long lost, what good is that?"

"It helps me atone for my sin, my guilt about them. I should have told my mother, 'Don't let them go. Beg that they be guarded better in the Tower!' You don't understand how hard all that sits yet upon my heart, for I was born and bred a Yorkist, though I am true Tudor now!"

I broke into sobs, my face in my hands. He pulled me to him, his trembling arms wrapped around my shaking shoulders.

"Yes, believe me, my dearest," he whispered, "I do understand your grief and guilt. By all that's holy, I swear I do!"

Mistress Varina Westcott

Despite everyone staring, I was in Nick's arms, telling about Arthur's abduction, Sibil's possible treachery, Lovell's orders to me. I admitted I had fled London under the cloak of darkness, so Lovell or his spies would not know I had come here.

"Damn Lovell! Sibil too," Nick muttered as he steered me into the manor house itself. Following behind, Finn and

Jamie gave us a little distance as we crossed the great hall and ascended a staircase. "But what made you think Lovell would hide Arthur here?" he asked.

"From some things he let slip. Even if the king's uncle once owned the manor, Lovell would want to be here—wouldn't he? He was reared here. It was his family's home for centuries. He must know it well, the perfect place for him to hide a boy."

"For the last two days Finn and I and two others—all king's men—have searched each inch of this place. But we'll look again now for a boy as well as for the man himself. I have no doubt he has been in London of late, but once he sees you've fled, he might reappear here—come back, I mean. But listen now. There's only a skeleton staff, since the king has not given this place to someone else since his uncle died. Rest here in my chamber, and I'll send someone up with food," he said as he opened a door to a large room that must have been the master's suite, perhaps Lovell's once. If so, I would rather have slept in the stables, but I nodded and obeyed, as Nick shouted, "Men, to me!"

"I'm going to help search too!" I called after him as he rushed into the hall. "And do you know," I went on, as he turned back to me, "that there was once a small gate for escapes during a siege somewhere here—the priest said so."

"I know where it is, but it's bricked up. The red brick stands out in the white stone on the side by the river."

"And Lovell mentioned some sort of tomb. Could he be hiding or have hidden Arthur in a church or cemetery?"

"We've searched both—the entire area—but I'll look again."

338

"I'll help! I want to help!"

He nodded, then huddled with the men. Two of them drew swords. It comforted me to see that they were acting quickly. I must find someone to send for Hal, who was holding our horses near the woods, so he could help search too. I prayed that if Lovell was still alive, he'd keep Arthur alive too, even if only for a bargaining chip.

In teams of two persons, we searched until nightfall and then by torch and lantern. We all met briefly in the great hall each time the church bells tolled an hour. Even in the maze of rooms, the pealing bell was clear, since the church stood cheek by jowl with the manor's outside wall. How I wished we had some Westcott candles, large ones. Each empty bedroom, storeroom, pantry, larder, and garderobe we searched in futility made me more frenzied.

I could hear my heart pounding each time I opened another door of a dark, dusty room or peered into a cobwebbed cubbyhole in the old church. No tombs there seemed to have doorways or entries. I felt continually sick to my stomach. What if I never knew what had become of my boy? Would that be worse than closing a coffin on him as I had on sweet little Edmund? To lose one son and then another—again I felt close to the queen, almost as if she were with me.

"Tomorrow at first light, we'll search the town and surrounding farms again," Nick had promised about ten of the clock before I lay down to rest. "It seems to me that Lovell's gone to acting alone, but we can't be sure, and some lackey could be hiding Arthur."

Sometime before the midnight bell tolled the new day, I

took Jamie with me and went to find Nick and Finn. They had gone to search in the vaulted cellars again, full of dusty hogshead casks and empty racks for wine. Our torches made the shadows jump at us, and our voices echoed as we called Nick's and Finn's names.

"Find something?" Nick asked as he answered and we approached them.

"Can't we search the church again?" I asked. "It was here when Lovell was growing up, even if Father Mark was not. Since Lovell said Arthur might be buried in a very special tomb, there must be a hidden cellar or some access underground."

"Varina, you know we went through the church, tower to floor, but we'll search again in the vault. The small crypt there is sealed. But considering how our prey has operated before, it's worth a try, even at this hour, at prying it open. You've got to get some sleep. Go back to your room and stay there with Jamie outside your door. Finn and I will roust out Father Mark and take a look at the crypt, which is no doubt full of dead Lovells."

"As this one should be," Finn muttered.

Snatching at that glimmer of hope—a new place where they had not looked before—and absolutely exhausted, I went back to the master's suite Nick had made his own. I lit four candles to push back the dark. I refused to lie down until he returned with his report—oh, if only he could find Arthur there!

I sat slumped over the table with my head on my crossed arms, trying not to grieve, trying to stay awake, thinking of that day we closed the coffin lid on my second son and how

I'd feared closed places since then. The thought of a dark crypt, smaller than the vast black one at St. Paul's, pressed in on me. But I would gladly search it for my son. . . . However long I had gone without sleep, I should have gone with them. . . . *Please, dear Lord, don't let my Arthur be closed in some dark place where he is afraid. . . . Please, I beg you, send my love to him; save him. . . .*

I must have slept. I thought I heard something bumping in the hall. Footsteps? Nick must be back. I rushed to the door and opened it. The hall torch had guttered out, so I went back for two candles, though a torch farther down the hall burned low. Jamie was not in sight, only the bench he'd dragged there earlier to sit outside my room.

"Jamie?" I called, trembling at the memory of losing my guard Sim at the far end of the bog. "Jamie! Nick!"

At first I thought I heard a squeak or a strange echo of my own shrill cry. Or was I dreaming? For at the end of the dimly lit corridor, a boy in a white shirt gestured to me, calling, "Mother . . . Mother . . ."

I gasped and squinted to see better. What it a ghost or a trick of my eyes and ears? Perhaps I was still asleep. For certain, a boy's form and face, but my boy? As it beckoned, I heard again, "Mother . . . Mother . . ." and was certain it was Arthur.

Whether the half-lit image of my son was the work of angel or devil—or Lovell—in that blinding moment I knew not and cared not. I dropped the two candlesticks but, with a candle in each hand, raced down the long, dark hall so fast that molten wax puddled by the wicks burned my wrists and spattered onto the wooden floor. When Nick returned, perhaps he would see that and know which way I had gone. And where was Jamie?

As I ran, one candle flamed brighter and one flickered out. Just before I reached the end of the corridor—it looked like my Arthur; it must be!—the boy was seized nearly off his feet and disappeared. So I was not heading to a dead end of the hall, but to a turn.

I pressed the candle wicks together to have two lights and let more wax fall to the floor. Yes, I glimpsed a tall, dark figure and the flash of the lad's white shirt when I peered around the dim corner. Arthur! It must really be my Arthur!

"Arthur? Arthur!"

The man was tall. He lifted the now silent boy over one shoulder, so he held the backs of his legs and his head dangled. He turned away.

"Stop, Lord Lovell!" I shouted. "I will bargain for him! I knew you'd come back here. I would have done the same. Loose him, and I'll help you escape."

"I *have* escaped—again. I learned to swim in the river outside years ago, how to move under the surface, hold my breath. The king's men looked for me after Stoke, but I escaped partly underwater. As for Minster Lovell Hall—*my* hall—I know each nook and cranny here. And blow that damned candle out!"

I did as he said, making certain I got more wax on the floor. It was not as dark here as I thought. I fancied I saw a crack of light—a doorway behind Lovell where there seemed to be no door.

"Mother, Moth—"

"Hush, boy!" Lovell said, and gave Arthur such a hard bounce I heard the air whoosh out of him.

"Don't hurt him! It's all right, my Arthur," I said in a soothing voice, edging closer. "This man is going to let you go."

"Come with me then," Lovell said. "I must know some things; then I'll set you both free."

I did not believe him, but I saw no other way. Perhaps I could find a ploy to stop him, to free Arthur, at least.

"Yes, of course," I told him. "Whatever you say."

I knew Arthur's life meant nothing to him. As desperate as I was to leave a trail of wax, now with my candles out, all I could do was pick at them with my fingernails and drop the pieces of cold wax upon the floor each time I moved.

"Come then," he repeated, and pushed at a wooden wall panel that slid inward to reveal a dimly lit, narrow opening. He put Arthur down. The child grappled himself to me, arms tight around my waist, smothering his face against my belly. I clutched him against me. "Oh, my boy!"

Lovell pulled me forward with Arthur, who was still clinging to me. I dropped one candle but held the other, and held on to Arthur. Before I could right myself or fight back, Lovell yanked Arthur from my arms and dragged me by the neck of my man's shirt toward the door, then shoved Arthur after me.

I was afraid that if I screamed, he would harm my son. To my amazement, Arthur kept quiet too. If I could pull him after me, could we flee back down the corridor? Nick or someone must come soon.

I did not fight Lovell but picked frantically at the single candle I still had, dropping the pieces behind me as he pushed me into the doorway and pointed down a flight of dusty, narrow stairs. I heard him close the door after himself. I went first. Lovell dragged Arthur behind us.

Once, twice, I scraped the base of my candle along the rough wooden wall. That time I had descended the stairs into the meeting room of the secret society of the Guild of the Holy Name of Jesus flashed through my mind. I'd expected to find *Signor* Firenze there, still painting, but he'd been dragged into the crypt and murdered by this man.

At the bottom of the stairs, Lovell shoved me against a musty stone wall and thrust Arthur against me. We clutched each other. Our captor produced a large dagger and said, "Not a sound, or it's over. Do you understand, Mistress Westcott?"

"More and more. Lead on."

"You first, that way," he said, pointing with the blade. Ahead I saw a dim, distant light. Did this place have a spider's web of hidden passages? The weight of the castle, of the world, seemed to be collapsing on me, and it was all I could do to keep from screaming.

Gripping Arthur's hand, I led the way. I was sweating and gasping to breathe, but I could tell the air was getting colder, danker. It was as if we had descended into a narrow, black tomb, and my fear of enclosed places terrified me as much as did this man. Had Nick returned from searching the sealed crypt yet, and had he found Hal and me missing? Would he think we had gone out searching somewhere again, or would he look for us and find the wax trail I had left him?

"Halt here!" Lovell whispered, then pressed Arthur between us to reach ahead of me and shove and kick at another panel, this one outward. It was heavy, a thick and rough substance—bricks? With my thumbnail of my free hand, I tried to pick at the wax of my single, shrinking candle, then ran its waxen base along the rough brick to leave a mark. I tried to do it at the level of my hips, not looking down, hoping he would not notice.

As Lovell shoved me through the opening, I sucked in fresh air. Somehow we were outside! I saw scudding clouds and stars above. Did I hear the river? If only Arthur and I could flee to freedom now!

"In here," Lovell said, and as if he'd heard my panicked thoughts, he held the dagger to Arthur's throat. I gasped but my boy hardly blinked. Somehow Lovell shoved at the brick wall, which rotated inward—another hidden door. Had we just emerged from the so-called narrow way the priest had mentioned, the old escape tunnel? Nick had said he'd examined it, but it would have looked solid, and he'd hardly go along pushing at each part of it.

"Where are we?" I asked as Lovell swung closed the brick door behind us. Lit by a single lantern, it was a small room roughly hewn from stone with one brick wall. I reckoned it measured six feet by six, with a ceiling that nearly scraped Lovell's head. It was silent and stale in here. A small table with paper and writing utensils, one chair, a bench, and a chamber pot filled it. Several small kegs were stacked in the corner. I saw a straw pallet on the floor.

"My sweet, simple sanctuary, oft for days at a time," he said. "Sit and listen to me carefully. Boy, back to your cot."

It horrified me how quickly Arthur obeyed him. What

had he done to him, or had he simply told him that he would kill me—kill us both—if he disobeyed? I was certain now, since he was showing us his lair, that he intended exactly that. If I could get his knife and stab him—but I had no illusions I could wrestle it from him.

"I'm listening," I said as he leaned back against the brick wall we had come through. I could not see where the door had been, or a handle to move it in or out.

Our captor drew himself up to his full height, keeping a tight hold on the knife. "I am an honorable man," he told me, "who has been forced to live in dishonorable times because a conniving cur with no rightful claim to the throne clawed and cheated his way to it. Henry Tudor as good as murdered my liege, Richard of York, the true king, and others."

"Killed in battle, you mean? At Bosworth Field and Stoke?"

"Keep quiet, I said. I only want you to know that what I do, I must do to stop the spread of Tudor poison. And so it was most fitting that Henry Tudor's whelp, Prince Arthur, was dispatched that way."

Was there no means by which to stop this murderer before he harmed us? My only hope was that he was telling me this so that I could justify him to the king or queen. But I had the sickest feeling he was going to use that dagger. Necks—he had always killed people by breaking or shooting their necks, and he had already held that weapon to Arthur's.

Despite his admonition to keep quiet, I blurted, "I will do whatever you say to help your cause and then—"

"I knew you were a woman who could not follow orders. Yet how I would have valued one like you on my side, at my side, just like poor Sibil Wynn! For once, I almost regret what I have been driven to—what I must do. But everyone is merely a means to my end, a prince, an old herb woman ... anything to cover my path and hurt the hateful Tudors, even rob them of their kin and allies."

"You'd best flee directly back to France. There is a hue and cry out for you, so—"

"Silence, woman! I am not to blame for any of this! I did not kill the princes in the Tower, and those who did were following the devil's orders. You have ruined your chance to help atone for that, but I have another way to gain access to the queen and her children—perhaps even the upstart king himself. Before I fled London, I heard she is breeding again, another heir to dispatch, eh? So I have found a woman who quite resembles you and, in the dusk or dark, that will have to do."

Before I could grasp his meaning or argue more, he huffed the lantern out. Blackness flew at me, enveloped me. I felt fresh air waft in, glimpsed Lovell's silhouette against the stars outside—and then the brick wall slammed shut.

I leaped to my feet and felt Arthur's arms come hard around my legs in the utter blackness. Lovell had left us in this tomb to die, the very special tomb that he had told me my Arthur might be buried in.

CHAPTER THE TWENTY-FIFTH

At first, I held Arthur in my lap, rocking him as if he were a baby, telling him how much I loved him, how I would get him home somehow. In this small, dark place, I was also trying to comfort myself.

"He's a mean man," Arthur murmured more than once, but I had no time to learn how my boy had been treated. The air was growing increasingly stale.

"We must find a way out of here," I said, trying to sound calm when I wanted to scream. So closed in, so dark, these walls, the heavy ceiling pressing down, that man's black hatred suffocating me, as indeed our lack of air in here might. And time was precious: Lovell had a plan to use someone who could pass for me to gain access to the royal family. And, God help me, I could almost believe that he could spirit himself back to London before anyone could catch him.

"Arthur," I said, "when you saw him go in and out, could you tell how he worked the door?"

"Just pushed it, but I tried and tried before, when the men who brought me here left me untied. It didn't work for me. I think it's magic."

"Nonsense. It's evil. We still must try. Nick Sutton is here at the manor with some of the king's men. They will find us, or catch Lovell and make him tell where we are."

"He comes and goes, disappears like he can hide anywhere."

We stood and I felt my way to the brick wall that held the doorway, running my hands along it, pushing, then beating my fists on it in my frenzy. I broke out into a cold sweat, and tears coursed down my face, but at least Arthur could not see. I had to keep control for him, for a possible escape.

"How long were you here?" I asked. "Were you brought right away when you were taken from Aunt Maud?"

"A long ride, but straight to here. One man stayed with me, but when Mean Man came, I never saw the other one again."

"There must be a source of air here, or did someone open the door now and then to get fresh air from outside?"

"No, it smells bad like this, but I think the air comes from behind those kegs, like a little breeze from there."

I felt my way along the rough-hewn walls until I found the curved corner where I'd seen several small kegs. Maybe we'd have something to drink to keep us alive until Nick found us or . . . or until we starved or I went stark, raving mad. But when I tried to move the kegs, they shifted easily, and I could tell they were all empty.

Yet a glimmer of hope revived in me—fresh air! There

was a crack here, though narrower than my hand. We had nothing with which to enlarge it, and it was stone anyway. As well as feeling fresh air coming through it, I thought I heard sounds. If this vented to the outside or even to the back staircase and narrow halls Lovell had brought us through, could someone hear us if we shouted? Even though the halls were dim, would they not see the wax trail I had left? They must be combing the building for us, perhaps even searching outside. Again I heard sounds, wind sighing or even the river close outside. I longed for it to be voices, but I feared we were alone. Would someone, even years hence, find our bones here—perhaps the way someone might stumble on the bones of the little lost princes in the Tower?

Now I heard no sounds but moving air. Mayhap I had imagined the other. My hopes collapsed. Even if Nick and the men found my wax trail, those hinged panels on Lovell's doors must need some trick to make them open. I wished heartily that Arthur were free, but at least his being here with me kept me sane, kept me thinking. Compared to the vast crypt at St. Paul's, this space was knowable. Never mind that it was closed in like a coffin. Yet even with this fresher, cooler air to breathe, I felt as if I were suffocating.

Arthur said, "Mean Man said even if I screamed and screamed in here, no one would hear me 'cause of all the stone. Beating on the brick wouldn't do a thing, he said. Course, we could yell anyway. Unless that would use up too much air."

Did he sense I was losing control? He was trying to take over, keep me going. How brave and dear. How much I loved him. Whatever happened, he would be with me.

"A good idea," I told him, wiping tears from my face lest he kissed me or touched me there. "Let's take turns and shout. I'll go first."

I shrieked and screamed into the air vent until I had to cover my own ears. At this rate, I would lose my voice, but what did that matter when I might lose my life? I felt dizzy, ill. I was going to be sick.

Arthur tugged on my sleeve. "Mother, stop! Stop! Don't you hear that?"

"Hear what?"

"I don't think it's an echo," he said, pressing his face down next to mine. "I think it's a man's voice, and I hope it's not Mean Man again!"

We both screamed into the vent. And heard an answer. Nick's voice? I wasn't sure. "Quiet!" I ordered Arthur when he started to screech again.

Summoning the last shred of my strength, I shouted again and again. "We're in the narrow gate. Brick wall! We're in the narrow gate. Brick wall!"

"Bricked in!" Arthur yelled into the air vent when I got a coughing jag from inhaling dust.

"Keep shouting!" I cried. "I'm going to try to hit the table into this side of the brick wall! Keep shouting!"

I thought my arms would shatter, even as the table split and mortar dust mingled with the stale air. Time crawled onward toward eternity. And then came a rumble from the other side of the wall that I was trying to batter. I stood back. Arthur, bless him, kept yelling. And Nick and the big king's man Finn knocked a small hole in the brick wall, while Arthur and I hugged each other and cheered.

I suppose it took a good half hour for them to bash a hole big enough for us to climb out. I shouted to Nick what Lovell had said about his new ploy to reach the queen—and who knew who else he might try to harm. When we emerged into the fresh air, into the starlit night, I saw only Nick, with his arms outstretched, and big Finn, holding a stone mallet. Praise the saints, there sat Jamie, with his head wrapped though bloodied from when Lovell must have knocked him out.

They thrust water at us and we gulped it greedily. Then, after I hugged Arthur hard, I gave him to Finn and Jamie, who vowed they'd protect my boy with their lives and have him back home waiting for me.

"How far ahead of us can Lovell be?" I asked Nick. "We must catch him before he tries to enter the palace, for I fear the worst."

"I'm not sure, as no one saw him leave—again. Probably an hour, maybe more."

"Or," Arthur piped up, "maybe he's there already. He told me he's a ghost and he really scared me. Can ghosts fly?"

"He's not a ghost, my boy," Nick told him, and ruffled his hair, "and we're going to prove that once and for all."

Hal got unsteadily to his feet and stood by Arthur. They both waved farewell as Nick, despite the darkness, lifted me onto a horse and mounted another, with two of his other guards behind us. "Arthur, all will be well!" I called to him. "I will see you at home and all will be well. . . ."

My horse leaped to a gallop almost instantly. I looked back once, then only ahead as we rushed into the dark of night. At a speed that made our hurried trip to Wales seem slow, we pounded down the road back toward London to warn the queen.

Queen Elizabeth of York

Nicholas Sutton had been gone to Minster Lovell for five days and Varina for nearly three, and I was anxious to hear from them. I could not rest, I could not sleep, and that could not be healthful for the child I carried in my womb— another prince. I was certain of it. I was also sure that, if I had not been breeding, the king would have been more openly angry with me over the effigies of my brothers than he already was. He was seething, and I lived in dread that he would order me or someone else to destroy the images of my brothers.

"Your Majesty." A voice broke into my agonizing. I saw it was my lady-in-waiting Sarah Middleton, who had taken on more duties for me since Sibil Wynn had been arrested. "I know it's after dusk, but the guard says Varina Westcott is asking to see you."

"Yes! Yes, of course, send her to me at once."

"She's with her brother-in-law, a chandler, Gilbert Penne, who has not been here before. They said something about his being able to color wax candles the way your previous artist did."

"She's not with Nicholas Sutton? But then, he may have sent her back ahead. Yes, send them up forthwith!"

I began to pace. Answers at last, ones that I prayed were good. Oh, if only they had found and captured Francis Lovell, that would lift the king's dark mood and keep us safe. Tyrell gone, then Lovell . . . Dear Lord in heaven, justice for my dear Arthur's death at last!

Varina was cloaked and veiled, which I found strange. And she seemed not as light-footed. My hopes fell. Had her son been lost; had some new catastrophe occurred? My stomach cramped in fear, but I trusted her and so I stood my ground to welcome them. Her brother-in-law was much older. I had just told Lady Middleton to leave us and the door closed behind her when I saw it was not Varina at all. A woman of the same size, blond and pretty but—

"Do not call out, for I have but one thing to say and then we shall be gone," said the man—no doubt not the chandler Penne at all—and he pulled out a dagger from the depths of his cape.

I gasped and longed to flee, but fear and that knife kept my feet rooted to the floor. Instinctively, I lowered my hands over my belly, clutching them together so hard I heard my bones crack. I wanted to shriek from the very depths of my soul, but I stared at him, stared like a dumb rabbit stares at the serpent before it strikes. I did not know for certain, but I feared who he might be. I had heard the king inquire of both Varina and Nick about this man's description. That raspy, commanding voice was a harbinger of doom.

"Say your piece then and be gone," I said. I lifted my chin in defiance, but my voice quavered.

The woman actually curtsied to me, but the man only glared. Yes, he had eyes like an adder's, ready to strike.

"I thought," he said, "you should know the truth of who ordered your brothers dispatched in the Tower—smothered, to be precise, then their bodies done away with on special orders."

"I—I already know and regret that ... that," I managed to get out, "it was my uncle, who was then king, king when he had no right."

"Had no right?" The man—now I was certain it was Lord Lovell—exploded, coming closer with his dagger in his hand. "The man who ordered them murdered had no right; that is true—but it was *this* king, your husband, for the boys stood in his way too!"

"Liar! Yorkist lies!"

"And you," he hissed, his voice low now as he bent over me, "a Yorkist born and bred. An arranged marriage, I know, but to wed the murderer of your brothers, and now you breed his children."

"And you murder them!"

He snorted and dared to smile. "Arthur. A mere milksop. Now, Prince Henry," he said, and I watched his fingers go white as they clenched the handle of the dagger, "there's a worthy lad, but one I shall deal with in due time."

Dear Lord in heaven, what if he was here to harm Henry? Or knew I was with child? I would not doubt for one moment he would kill me to kill the child, so was that his plan with dagger poised? Had the news reached him? And a terrible thought: Could this man be speaking the truth about my brothers' murders? Some pieces of the puzzle fit. The king's quick execution of Tyrell, who had confessed but under duress. The king's command that Tyrell not be allowed to cleanse his soul on the scaffold with a public confession. The king was always disturbed when I broached the subject of the boys' deaths. But no—it must have been Richard's orders that sent them to their deaths! Yet the king knew the names of the two lackeys who had actually done the deed and that they were conveniently dead.

No. No, I loved my husband, the father of my children, living and dead. My lot in life had been cast with him. This was Lovell, the devil incarnate, and he was lying.

"You've said what you wanted," I told him in the strongest voice I could muster. "Now leave before there is a hue and cry sent out for you."

"Jane, your belt," he said, still staring close into my face. He put the knife point to the side of my neck. I felt it draw a trickle of blood there. Varina had said Firenze's neck had been broken, that her guard in the bog in Wales had been pierced through the neck.

Lovell stared close into my eyes as his companion bound my hands behind me and shoved me into a chair. "The scarf," he said. The woman pushed some of it into my mouth and tied the ends behind my head. It made me start to gag at once. And Lovell still held that knife in his hand, and I was so fearful. I longed to break free and cover my belly, to scream, to run. I was helpless. Just as helpless as those who were exposed and stretched upon the rack in the Tower.

"You see," he said, "Sibil—yes, the Sibil and her Nigel you have under arrest—told me weeks ago where to find Prince Henry's chamber. As soon as I am finished here, we will pay your prince a little visit. Not poison this time, but just a good, old-fashioned dagger, eh?"

I began to buck as he knelt before me and raised the

knife, pointing it toward my belly. Oh, yes, he knew I carried another prince. He would destroy the Tudor dynasty by destroying all our heirs and the one who carried them, and then Henry Tudor would be alone—unless Lovell found a way to kill him too.

I screamed through my gag and kicked, landing a good blow on his shin, even as the door to the room exploded inward. Nicholas Sutton was the first to rush in with sword drawn, though I saw others behind him. A battering ram fell upon the floor and rolled away from the door it had breached. Lovell's companion screamed and tried to run, but a boy yanked her back by her hair. Oh, not a boy but Varina herself! Lovell raised his arm again to stab at my belly, but Nicholas slammed into him, knocking the knife away.

The king with even more guards crowded into the room as Nicholas yanked Lovell around by his cape and slammed him to the floor. My husband ran to me, removed the gag, and sliced through my ties as Nicholas hit Lovell in the face again and again, then slammed his fist into the man's belly. I broke into tears of relief, sobbing, gasping for breath.

The king pulled me into his arms as Nicholas dragged Lovell out into the corridor. The guards there parted for them as for Moses at the Red Sea. The woman—Jane was her name—was pulled out by guards too. Varina strode boldly to me and, still in the king's embrace, I held out my hand to grip hers.

Varina told me, "Lovell abducted my son Arthur to gain my cooperation, which I would not give. My boy is safe and now yours too. We rushed back from Minster Lovell as fast as we could."

"God be praised," I said only, my voice breathless. Then, despite being queen, I could not hold back my sobs of relief as the room cleared of guards. I could hear Lovell shouting curses as he was hauled away.

"What did he say to you?" the king demanded of me. "Lovell—what did he say?"

"That he came to try to kill Prince Henry, and our unborn child," I told him, and no more. I could not bear to repeat or to believe the message that horrid man had shared with me, and I would die with it never spoken. It could not be true. He was our enemy. He had lied to make me hate my husband. That was all; that must be all.

When Nicholas returned, looking mussed but not a bit bloodied, the king told him, "We have our archenemy now, Nick. And I don't want him brought to trial or even questioned to spew his . . . his poison. I want a slow death for him—time for him to realize all he has lost."

"I know a place where we can imprison him at Minster Lovell," Nicholas said immediately. I saw him take Varina's hand. "A place that he intended to make the living tomb for Varina and her son."

"God's will then," the king said with a loud sniff. "Nick and Varina, we owe you both a debt of gratitude, which will be paid. Nick, I know you've been through much, but I cannot think of a better man to see to Lovell's demise. And be sure he's guarded well, so he does not pull one of his resurrection acts. No angel will come to roll the stone away from his burial vault, I vow."

As if we were equals, the four of us stood in a small circle. Varina appeared stunned that the king had addressed her by her given name. Ah, this wax carver and I, this merchant chandler . . . We had shared lost sons, common dangers and enemies, despite the chasm of rank and station that loomed between us. And there was another chasm—the doubt in my heart that my husband was a murderer too. Just how far had he gone to secure the throne? And yet my life was embedded in his. And I would say naught.

One hand protectively on my belly, I pulled gently away from the king's embrace and held out my arms to Varina, my sister of sorrows, my mistress of mourning. And we leaned on each other, holding tight, drawing comfort.

CHAPTER THE TWENTY‑SIXTH

Mistress Varina Westcott

*A*s dreadful as his fate was, I felt that Lovell's death was just. When Nick returned to London after several days, he told me Lovell had railed against the king until the last brick and mortar silenced him.

At least our rescue from that place had ruined Lovell's clever two-touch door. Nick said that one had to hit a certain brick at waist level and also push a lower brick with the foot at the same time for the spring mechanism to work. At least my strewing wax along our path had led them to the first trick door in the hall, though they'd had to break through it to get near enough to hear us shouting through an air vent that came into the tunnel itself. I had questioned Arthur, and it seemed Lovell and his henchmen had kept the boy cowed by telling him that if he didn't obey them, they were going to kill me.

But blessedly, that—and Lovell—was all in our past now. Losses and tragedies too, I prayed.

"I always felt affection for your son," Nick told me when we were alone in the solar of my home, "but what he went through because of Lovell—I feel even closer to him now. And to his mother."

"I suppose the king will want to question both of us again."

"I think he wants everything buried and forgotten. Jamie received word the court has moved to Windsor, and only I am sent for. Best you stay here at home with Arthur and your family and wait for my return. And then I intend to ask you to be my wife, and pray you will give me a hearty yes."

"Oh, Nick!" I cried, throwing myself at him so hard he almost toppled backward. "But can you manage it? I used to fret that marriage would mean you can't be advanced the way you want at court."

"Better you worry whether wedding me will slow *your* rise to favor with Their Majesties," he said with a smile. "But, all that aside, what I want is you. I am certain the king and queen will permit and sanction our union, so consider this a proposal of wedlock."

"Wedlock—a sad word for such a blessed state, my Nick."

"I hate to bring this up after all we've been through, but does the solar door lock from the inside?"

"Yes," I told him. "Both the hall door and the backstairs door, and I don't think anyone will break them down."

We each shot the bolt on one door and met in the middle, all kisses and caresses. He threw four plump pillows on the floor from the chairs and we lay there, entwined and entranced.

Everything evil, everything frightening fled that night in our mutual trust and love. Arthur slept on; Maud and Gil left us alone, though the remnants of the night were much too short. Nick's strong body hovered over mine like a protective roof against the terrors of the past. Not only had I come home, but my dear love, Nick Sutton, had too.

The king made Nick a knight—Sir Nick, I teasingly called him. 'Twas not unheard-of, a gentleman or knight wedding a merchant's widow or daughter, to make her a gentlewoman. It truly mattered not to me whether I had been named a scullery maid, for I had Nick and Arthur safe. Then too, Gil received a gilt invitation to join the Worshipful Guild of Wax Chandlers, and Maud finally was with child. The only thing that hurt my happiness was that I was not summoned to make a waxen effigy of Prince Arthur. Later, I learned why.

Nick and I made another journey out of London, taking Arthur with us. We carried a deed and charter from the king—and a fat purse Their Majesties had given to both of us—so that Nick's ancestral home could be returned to his family. We met his elderly but spry and sharp grandmother and saw that she was reinstated in the home she had missed so much. I liked her instantly, even though, when she looked at me a certain way and the light slanted on us in her refurbished solar, I swear she reminded me of old Fey.

Once we returned to city life, Nick was away when the court was at Windsor or Greenwich, but home each night when they were at Westminster, so I was quite content. Then, just when my being summoned to the queen almost three years ago began to seem like a distant dream, Nick brought a royal summons for me, just after the queen had been delivered of a sickly girl child in February of 1503.

"Is she fearful the child will die and wants another effigy?" I asked Nick as he escorted me—not by the familiar back entrance—toward the queen's suite of rooms in Westminster Palace. Like dear Maud, I was showing a pregnancy, four months on, I reckoned, but I pulled my cloak closer around my slightly swelling form. If Her Majesty was going to lose another child, it wouldn't do to flaunt my happy state.

I was surprised to find the king sitting by her bed and no one else about. He motioned us over and rose. We curtsied and bowed. "Mistress Sutton," he said, and nodded a greeting—a surprisingly humble gesture. "And Nick. Come with me," he added to Nick, "for the queen would speak with Varina alone, about something that has my full approval."

Either I was going to finally begin Prince Arthur's effigy, I thought, or—God forbid—carve a new one for their sick infant. And yet, when the queen's eyes opened and I noted how ashen pale she looked, I held my breath.

"Varina, no one is to know yet . . . but you are good at . . . keeping secrets."

I could barely make out her words, her voice was so faint.

"I am ill," she went on. "Childbed fever. I feel . . . I am told I may not recover."

"But you are strong in your heart and mind and soul, Your Maj—" I protested, until she gave a slight shake of her head and gestured me to bend down to her. With one hand lightly on her bed—her sheet was soaked with sweat—I did as she asked.

"In a way, I gave you Nicholas," she whispered, gasping for breath. "And you gave me some peace. Now . . . the king has agreed . . . that you shall carve my effigy for my funeral. Come each day . . . so it will be ready soon. And make me—at last—look content."

I opened my mouth to protest, then closed it again. I nodded, kept nodding until I realized it and stopped.

"And do the one of my Arthur after. The king . . . he's seen them. He knows . . . and now accepts. He will pay you."

"I will do it, Your Grace, but as a labor of love."

A wan hint of a smile lifted the corners of her mouth. "Ah, yes—love. Our lots in life so different—but we are so alike," she said, then seemed to slip away, to sleep instantly.

The moment I straightened, the king came back to her side. "I knew that would tire her, but anything she asks—anything that I could do for her—almost, I would. Nick, I'll give others your duties for now and ask you to bring your wife to her old haunt to carve the new wax image. Make her beautiful, Varina."

"As she is and ever will be, Your Majesty," I choked out as he walked us to the door.

"And carve it quickly," he said. "I must summon back her physicians and her ladies now."

I left, stunned, but determined that I would make my dear friend look as lovely as she had been the day she told me she was with child again. I subtly stroked my own belly as Nick led me out.

Queen Elizabeth of York

As Henry hovered and the royal physicians tended me, I soared and slid, in and out, up and down. Prince Henry came in, and I gave him my blessing. His cool lips lingered on my hot cheek before he left, Henry now our only hope to be king. *Be a good and loving king*, I longed to tell him, but I was not strong enough to form the words. My dear, sweet daughters came and went, weeping. My mother-in-law, who would now really rule the royal roost, muttered something about how I had been a good wife for her son.

And then, as I closed my heavy eyes and drifted again, swimming in sweat, burning with fever, the Archbishop of Canterbury—what was his name?—gave me the final rites. Then I saw them all again, those I had so long sought. Was I in paradise already?

My mother was crying but said she forgave me. My brothers, so thin and pale, but hanging over my bed with wings, like angels. Who had hurt them? I still was not sure and did not want to know anymore. I just wanted to be with them all. My father, King Edward, strong and blond, was lifting me now, lifting me up to ride before him on his horse through London's streets. Yes, we were going to buy a book, and I was so proud to be his daughter, a princess. And then—and then the man named Henry Tudor, who had been our enemy, took me to his bed, and then there was a crown. . . .

A man I did not know held my hand, sobbing. I smelled incense, or mayhap it was sweet herbs or roses, white and red roses. A bright light was burning in my brain, a lovely angel candle. I began to rush toward it and then I flew.

Mistress Varina Westcott

Her Majesty Elizabeth of York died on her thirty-seventh birthday, and all of London mourned. Her newborn girl, Katherine, outlived her by but a few days. The king, Nick said, was inconsolable.

I was summoned to Westminster Palace on February 12, to oversee the embalming of Her Majesty's body—another final wish of the queen. Royal physicians did the work, but I, in tears, wrapped her gently in Westcott Chandlery waxen cloth. I stood with her ladies as her physicians carried her body from her bed. After they changed the linens, they placed the flexible body with the wax face and hands I had labored over upon the bed until it would be placed atop the black satin–draped coffin, then be regally seated next to her tomb in Westminster Abbey.

Once I saw the effigy was placed in the bed, its robes of velvet and cloth of gold arranged, its ornate hood fitted properly over the long blond wig—the king had found a painter to color the cheeks, lips, and eyes—I walked down the narrow corridor to bid farewell to the effigies I'd carved. It seemed but yesterday that I had first been summoned here. Nick would be meeting me soon, but I took a moment, touched each face as I had seen Elizabeth the Good do in her love for these, her lost children. Then I turned and, since I was not to use the back entrance to this room anymore, I went back toward the queen's now deserted bedchamber.

Lost in memories, I jolted to a halt at the sound of sobbing. Someone must have come in to mourn at the image of the queen, so I must go out quietly.

But I stood frozen in the door of her bedchamber. The king himself lay prostrate on the bed next to the queen's effigy, his face buried against its neck, his arm over the waist. It took me a moment to catch the meaning of his broken words, and when I did, I shuffled carefully back down the narrow corridor I had just trod.

"Forgive me, forgive me, my dearest, but I could not tell you—could not, and you so loyal. I was terrified you would know, would turn on me. It was . . . it was"—he gasped for air, near hysteria as I came to a halt in the shadows of the hall—"just something that happened."

What was he speaking of? I feared I knew.

"I caused it, but it wasn't my fault!" he wailed. "I—I said aloud one day in the hearing of some loyal men that my path to the throne would be clearer, faster if the princes were to disappear from the Tower. I didn't mean what happened. It was . . . it was like when King Henry the Second said to some knights, 'Who will rid me of that turbulent priest?' and they went and murdered Archbishop Becket! I had your brothers' murderers dispatched on trumped-up charges, so only I knew—all these years, I knew!"

I nearly fell to my knees. The king was confessing that he—even if indirectly—had caused the murders of the queen's young brothers! But he'd publicly claimed it was her cruel uncle, Richard of York, who wanted those impediments removed and commanded their killing. Tyrell had been blamed, and Lovell must have learned or guessed the truth somehow and meant to tell the queen so she would hate her husband and turn on him.

I could hear Henry VII, king of all England, sobbing, his mutterings incoherent. I tiptoed all the way back into the tiny closed-in room in which I'd carved the children's effigies. At least Nick's presence had helped calm my claustrophobia then. Nick had always helped. Would I tell him what I had overheard, or would that ruin his loyalty to the king? And would His Majesty's broken confession to a cold wax effigy of his dead queen ease his grief and guilt?

When I stepped out into the hall a good while later, all was silent, and I prayed it was now safe for me to pass through to the withdrawing chamber to meet Nick. Yes, the effigy lay alone on the bed. I fancied for one moment that I should make it frown and let the king wonder about its change of expression. But I was only, as ever, being wayward, the woman who ran her own chandlery shop and, thank the Lord, had turned down marriage to one of the most influential waxmongers in London. The woman who dared to share much with the queen, who dared to ride astride in men's garb to Wales and to Minster Lovell Hall and—

I gasped as a man, still in shadow, emerged from behind

the draperies. The king still here? Or had Nick come in and didn't want to be seen by others?

No—it was Prince Henry, so tall for his age. I bobbed him a curtsy. How long had he been secreted there?

As if he heard my thought, he asked, "Mistress Sutton, how long have you been here?"

"I was closeted in the far chamber, saying farewell to my work," I told him.

"Your best work is there," he said, pointing at the bed with his mother's effigy, "for the best of women. I shall never forget her."

"Nor I, Your Grace."

He came closer. "I might have need of your services for a full array of special candles at my investiture as Prince of Wales," he said, surprising me by his change of topic. "The king was putting it off for a while, but I think it will be soon now. Very soon, I'm sure."

I stared at him as my mind raced. Had he overheard his father's confession? And would he use it to— No, surely sons, even royal ones, were not like that. Not this queen's son . . . but then, he was his father's boy too.

I curtsied again, and he gestured that I could leave.

A mere week after the queen was buried with all pomp— when her effigy was moved along the streets, it trembled as if it were alive—Prince Henry Tudor became Prince of Wales, heir to the Tudor throne.

I decided then that although I had once named my dear son Arthur after a prince of Wales, this child of Nick's I carried, should it be a son, would never be named Henry. Carved candles for King Henry VIII's investiture, candles for his marriage to Catherine of Aragon, candles for his coronation but six years later—yes, our chandlery provided them all at the young, handsome king's request. But knowing Lord Lovell had made me realize that some men—cobbler, king, or in between—were not to be trusted. And so, over the long years of the rule of King Henry VIII, I cherished even more my beloved Nick.

Ebury Press Fiction Footnotes

Turn the page for more information on THE QUEEN'S CONFIDANTE, including an exclusive interview with author Karen Harper . . .

Author's Note

The two mysteries this novel probes are yet unsolved today and have grown in fascination over the centuries.

First, was Arthur Tudor, Prince of Wales, murdered or did he die of natural causes? Christopher Guy, Worcester Cathedral's archaeologist, says there are puzzling questions about Arthur's death. Why, he asks, was a man reputed to be in poor health sent to the cold remoteness of Ludlow? Peter Vaughan, of the Worcester Prince Arthur Committee, who researched Arthur's funeral for its reenactment in 2002, believes there is evidence of foul play. In Vaughan's words, "He wasn't a strong character, unlike his younger brother. Could it be that his father was strong enough to see that the best interests of the Tudors were to be served by Henry, Duke of York, rather than Arthur?" (From an article by David Derbyshire, science correspondent for the *Daily Telegraph*, May 20, 2002.)

I find it difficult to believe that King Henry VII intentionally had his own son done away with, but the "upstart" Tudors had so many enemies it is highly possible someone else murdered Arthur. And Francis, Eleventh Viscount Lovell, was repeatedly a thorn in their side.

Others have investigated Arthur's death through examining his grave site. Ground-probing radar has been used to pinpoint his final resting place beneath the limestone floor of Worcester Cathedral. Professor John Hunter of Birmingham University has completed work on this investigation, although so far the current queen has not given permission for the exhumation of Arthur's body to perform toxicology tests. Professor Hunter says, "Of course, if it's discovered he was poisoned and shouldn't have died, his brother, Henry VIII, would not have been king and subsequently we wouldn't have the Church of England." (See David Derbyshire reference above.) And so a small stone thrown in the pool of history can create many ripples and waves.

As for the tragic fate of the princes in the Tower, many theories about their disappearance and demise have been argued. It is strange that no search for their bodies was made after they went missing.

However, during the reign of King Charles II, in July of 1674, during some rebuilding in the White Tower, the bones of two children were found in an elm chest that was covered by rubble at a depth of about ten feet. This was under a staircase that led to the king's lodgings. At King Charles's request, these bones were interred in a white marble urn designed by Sir Christopher Wren and placed in the Henry VII chapel at Westminster Abbey, close to the tomb of their sister, Queen Elizabeth of York. In 1933 the bones were medically examined by Professor William Wright, who concluded they were those of two boys, approximate ages twelve and ten. Were these the poor murdered boys their sister must have agonized over?

And did King Henry VII order the execution of those boys? I have given him the benefit of the doubt by his not making it a direct order, but their loss cleared his way to the throne just as surely as it solidified King Richard III's claim. Tudor propagandists (like Shakespeare) blamed "hunchback Richard" and tried to clear Henry's name. But why was Tyrell not allowed to make the customary death speech on the scaffold?

More than once, rumors were rampant in London that King Henry had been behind the princes' deaths, as well as Arthur's. Perhaps these were just vicious smear campaigns, for the king was hated by many pro-Yorkists. It was not until England fell in love with the handsome, athletic young king Henry VIII that the reign of the Tudors stabilized, and even then, Henry and his children were paranoid about the claims of others to their kingdom.

If King Richard was behind the boys' murders, perhaps it is some sort of justice that, during the Reformation, his bones were thrown in the River Stour and his tomb was used as a horse trough and later broken up. Except for the eldest of the princes in the Tower, he is the only English king not to have a splendid tomb.

As visitors to Westminster Abbey have no doubt seen, the beautiful effigies and tomb of King Henry VII and his wife, Elizabeth of York, lie behind the altar in the Henry

VII chapel. The Tudors always did things with great pomp, perhaps because of their "inferiority complex" that they won the throne by might, not right, as many claimed. What partly inspired Varina's "angel candles" in this novel is the fact that Their Majesties' magnificent gilded effigies are surrounded by beautiful cherubs.

I must admit, as I watched on television the wedding service of William Windsor, the future Prince of Wales, to his bride, Catherine Middleton, I recalled the wedding of the Tudor Prince of Wales to his Princess Catherine of Aragon in long-ago London.

As in all my historical novels, I have tried to stay as factual as possible, even forgoing my temptation to call the long civil war that put the Tudors on the throne "the War of the Roses." Many novels set in medieval times use this memorable, picturesque title, but it was not actually coined until 1762 in David Hume's *History of England*, so the people of that day would not have known or used it.

Discrepancies in historical documents abound, forcing a modern writer to make frequent choices. I've read that Arthur's body at Ludlow Castle was displayed in the great hall and in "his chapel." Reports claim that Henry VII and his queen were at Richmond or Greenwich when they heard of Arthur's death, but I have chosen to use Richmond. The one setting I did change was that, for purposes of the plot, I have the queen die at Westminster Palace instead of at the Tower of London, where she had gone into childbed.

Standardized spelling is also a challenge. The *Infanta* of Spain who married both Tudor brothers has her name spelled both as Katherine and Catherine; however, since her

Spanish name was Catalina, I have gone with the C spelling. I have also seen Frances Lovell's name spelled Lovel, but as the family home was Minster Lovell Hall, I have gone with the double L. Francis Lovell is not to be confused with Sir Thomas Lovell, Henry VII's chancellor of the exchequer and constable of the tower, whom I, fortunately, did not have to use in this novel. Two real-life villains Tyrell and Lovell (a song-and-dance team, a law firm?) were confusing enough.

Research for this novel sent me into quite a study of the merchants and guilds of medieval London. There is yet today a Worshipful Company of Wax Chandlers, which has had a hall at 6 Gresham Street (originally called Maiden Lane) in London since 1501. The current, beautifully furbished hall is the sixth on the site and is available for hire for banquets, parties, and ceremonies. The guild's coat of arms is much as I describe, and their motto was, indeed, changed from Richard III's "Loyalty Binds Me" to the current "Truth Is Light."

Waxworking has a fascinating history, going back at least to ancient Roman times, and I was intrigued by the wax chandlers' part in medieval embalming. As for wax funeral effigies, the one of Elizabeth of York was part of the collection of the wax or wooden figures at Westminster Abbey (in the Undercroft Museum there) for years. I toured this museum several years ago. The original waxen one of this Elizabeth had a rich crown, a gown of gold satin edged with red velvet with a square neck, splendid robes, rings on her fingers, a long, jeweled wig, and a scepter in her right hand. Evidently, the waxen parts of the effigy were later replaced by a wooden head and hands. It once had a leather body stuffed with hay. Now only the head remains.

One more interesting bit of Tudor trivia about this woman sometimes called Elizabeth the Good: It is said that the queens on decks of playing cards, even modern ones, are modeled after her beautiful face.

Minster Lovell Hall, like most of the important sites used in this book, can be visited today, although the manor is in ruins. It is in a section of the lovely Cotswolds somewhat off the beaten path. The fascinating thing is, as it is described on the Web site of this manor hall (www.historic-uk.com/DestinationsUK/minsterlovell.htm), "It is said that, in the early 18th century [1708], during building work at the Hall, an underground room or vault was discovered. In this room was found a skeleton, sitting upright at a table, surrounded by books, paper and pens." According to those who discovered the bones, when the air entered this space, the skeleton and papers turned to dust. Was this the eleventh Lord Lovell? Perhaps we will never know, as no underground room has ever been found since then, but Lord Lovell was famous for disappearing, and his body was never found anywhere else.

The Guild of the Holy Name of Jesus was closely associated with the Worshipful Guild of Wax Chandlers and did have a chapel in the crypt of St. Paul's. Its remains survive under the paving around the apse of the present cathedral. One of the most fascinating, off-the-usual-track places I've found in London is the crypt of St. Paul's, said to be the largest in Europe. It is chockablock with who's-who memorials, such as Lord Nelson's, the Duke of Wellington's, and that of the creator of the current cathedral, Sir Christopher Wren, but also the antique tombs of many other, older unknowns.

I want to thank Dr. Barbara Hanawalt, professor of history at Ohio State University and author of the fascinating book *The Wealth of Wives: Women, Law, and Economy in Late Medieval London* (New York: Oxford University Press, 2007), for sharing information with me about merchant widows in medieval London. Several historical women in her research inspired Varina's shop, home, and circumstances. Also of interest were *Medieval London Widows, 1300–1500* (ed. Caroline M. Barron and Anne F. Sutton; Hambledon & London, London 1994) and *The Gilds* [sic] *and Companies of London, 4th ed.* (by George Unwin; London: Frank Cass & Co., Ltd., 1963).

The best biography I found of Queen Elizabeth was *Elizabeth of York, the Mother of Henry VIII,* by Nancy Lenz Harvey (New York: MacMillan, 1973.) On pages 190–195 the book contains a very complete account of the queen's subjects' mourning her death and of her funeral. The king's biographer, Bernard André, wrote of the queen: "She manifested . . . devotion toward God; toward her parents . . . toward her brothers. . . ." From such an accolade I have expanded on her guilt and grief over her brothers' deaths.

Thanks to my wonderful editor, Ellen Edwards, and the great support team at NAL. As ever, I appreciate the advice of agents Meg Ruley and Annelise Robey. Friend and fellow author Kathy Lynn Emerson generously answered questions and shared her knowledge of Tudor-era women. And always, to Don, proofreader and travel companion.

—Karen Harper

A Conversation with

Karen Harper

Q. The Queen's Confidante *is as much a novel of mystery and suspense as it is a novel of history and romance. What inspired you to go in that direction?*

A. The subject matter drew me to the suspense and crime solving. In dealing with these first Tudor rulers, King Henry VII and his queen, Elizabeth of York, a writer immediately stumbles over murders that have long been debated. Who killed the boy princes in the Tower of London? (Or who absconded with them—highly unlikely, I think, despite some claims of that.) Did Prince Arthur, Henry VII's heir apparent and older brother of the boy who later became King Henry VIII, die of natural causes or was he done away with? These mysteries are not only fascinating but they shape England and Europe for many years to come. For example, obviously Henry VIII would never have been king had Arthur lived. No six wives, no next three rulers: Edward, Mary, and Elizabeth. Perhaps no Protestant revolution ... on and on.

There is a second key reason I incorporated strong threads of suspense in the novel. That is what I love to write. In a way, all fascinating characters have their secrets, no matter the genre, but I love to read and create whodunits and whydunits. I've written a nine-book mystery series in which Queen Elizabeth I (who was named for her grandmother, the Queen Elizabeth of this novel) is the amateur sleuth. I also write contemporary suspense novels, so the bent toward suspense is just the way I write, and I was able to give that free rein in this book.

Q. Varina's chandlery business provides her with a fascinating background. How did you come to learn about the use of candles and wax effigies during this period?

A. Since I have written other novels set in medieval and Tudor times, I've always been aware of chandlery and wax effigies. In one of my visits to Westminster Abbey, I was fascinated by the Undercroft Museum, which displays death masks of British monarchs. These were used in their funerals and paraded through the streets of London. The idea of a woman who deals with death in an artistic way and solves a crime was too good to pass up.

Q. How common was it for a woman to inherit and run her own business in the early Tudor period?

A. My research shows that, sadly, about the only way a woman could have her own business at this time was to inherit it at the death of her father or husband, or possibly her last living brother. There were exceptions in the "broidery" (embroidery) trade, but in general, it was not a period where women held financial power or were admitted to the powerful trade unions. Marriage meant economic and social control by the husband, a fact I tried to bring out in this novel. My Author's Note mentions an excellent book on this subject, Dr. Barbara Hanawalt's *The Wealth of Wives.*

Q. Varina and Queen Elizabeth share a deep sadness over the loss of their young children. Most of us are aware that child mortality remained high until the twentieth century, but just how high was it during Tudor times? How did mothers (and fathers) cope with their grief?

A. Of course, this novel takes place in early Tudor times (the transition from the medieval era), not the high Tudor of the later rulers; however, mortality statistics during these years seem to be consistent. These are sad, indeed, and rather shocking. It is estimated that 25 percent of infants died in their first year; 12.4 percent of those remaining died between ages one and four, and 6 percent more between ages five and nine.

No doubt parents coped with these dreadful losses in every human way possible: resignation, depression, keeping busy, focusing on the next or remaining children. There are records of parents grieving greatly, so Varina and the queen illustrate that. I would surmise that the religious faith of the day also kept some parents strong through such trials, especially the belief that their child was in a better place and they would meet him or her again someday in heaven.

Q. You describe a fairly complicated embalming process for the royal dead. How was the common man treated in death during this time?

A. Commoners were simply wrapped and/or put in a plain wood coffin and "laid to rest," often in a shared grave. The wealthier the deceased, the higher their social class, the more embalming, altar candles, and formal grieving. And, of course, during plague or disease times, bodies were quickly gathered and dumped in mass graves, as I show in my novel *Shakespeare's Mistress*. I think it's especially fascinating that those who provided the funeral candles often worked with or as the embalmers.

Q. Nicholas Sutton works for the king and queen in hopes of reclaiming the land and position his family lost during what we now call the War of the Roses. Was royal patronage the only way to gain wealth and prestige during this period? What other avenues might he have pursued?

A. Royal approval and support was the main and quick path to recoup lost wealth and power under the Tudors. Economic strength was the other major avenue to recovery, but that could take generations. An interesting point here is that the Tudors, since they had gained their throne by "might not right," always tried to control who had power and who didn't. They carefully watched and often pulled down those who became too popular or powerful. So it was of key importance in rebuilding one's reputation to serve the ruler.

Q. Elizabeth of York has been portrayed in several recent novels. What particularly interests you about her?

A. I read an excellent biography of this queen (*Elizabeth of York, the Mother of Henry VIII*, by Nancy Lenz Harvey), but I have not read any of the novels, as I did not want them to influence my analysis of her character and personality. Above all, she was a strong woman—a survivor, yet she must have suffered greatly from the losses of her brothers and her children. What really interested me is that she is the mother of King Henry VIII, so what of her was in him? He evidently adored her. Those who think Henry saw women either as saints or whores always say that his mother was the ideal image in those opposing views of females.

Also, I was interested in Elizabeth of York's marriage dynamics. Most records reveal that her husband was cold and calculating; yet these Tudors obviously had a strong marriage, unlike their son Henry. Was her strong marriage possible only because of her good traits? She is a fascinating character, and I hope I have done justice to her. I always find that the bedrock traits of a person lie in his or her childhood, and her closeness to both her parents served her well. She knew she had been loved, so she was able to give love to her husband, her children, and her subjects, who dubbed her "Elizabeth the Good."

Q. Will we ever know what happened to the princes in the Tower?

A. Never say never, because documents do turn up from time to time, but I think the question was answered when the bones of those two young boys were found. I believe they were smothered in their beds and interred immediately, but on whose orders? Ah, there's the rub—and this novel's researched but debatable premise.

Q. Most readers might best know Catherine of Aragon from a later period in her life, when Henry VIII sought to divorce her and marry Anne Boleyn. She is often portrayed during that time as obsessively Catholic and embittered by Henry's treatment of her, but in The Queen's Confidante *she is sweet and brave, and so very young. How did she go from one to the other?*

A. Catherine's life story begins as a fairy tale, crashes into her young widowhood and tough times for a while, then turns to fairy tale again when the young, handsome King Henry VIII weds her. Her failure to produce a male heir is well-known, as are her later trials. But Catherine had a backbone of steel, partly from her strong religious faith, partly from the fact that she had powerful parents, partly just because she was built that way.

The set-in-her-ways, ultrareligious Catherine often portrayed in the Anne Boleyn stories does not do justice to how she was adored by the English people from the first. It does help explain, though, one reason the common people detested Anne Boleyn. They dared not blame Henry for his horrible treatment of Catherine, so Anne was the target. Catherine was a fascinating woman, but she had so many unhappy chapters in her life—which she handled as best she could—that most modern readers fail to understand or admire her. I would contend that, as the quote goes, that which did not kill her made her stronger. The tragedies of her life did not break her, so how did she go from one stage of life to the other? With great bravery, faith, and what modern people would call "class."

Q. Are you getting tired of the Tudor period yet? Have any other periods captured your writer's fancy?

A. I will be a Tudor maniac until I die, but I think the "high Tudor period"—Henry VIII and Elizabeth I— has been pretty well covered lately, not only in novels and nonfiction but also in movies and on TV. I was pleased to find these first Tudor rulers a bit fresher ground to research and write. As for other historical periods, my second love is the 1930s and 1940s. I have written one novel set in Britain and Italy in that era already, *Almost Forever*, and may write more in the future. Time will tell.

Questions for Discussion

1. Whom did you find the most interesting character in *The Queen's Confidante*?

2. Who would ever expect tyrannical Henry VIII to have had such a beautiful, loving mother? Do you know of children who have turned out very differently from their parents, in personality, values, and general attitude toward life? Does a parent really have so little influence over his or her children?

3. If Prince Arthur had lived, how might English history have turned out differently?

4. Viscount Lovell is identified as the villain of the novel early on, and we read to find out whether he can be stopped before implementing his plan to destroy the Tudor succession. What devices does Karen Harper use to create suspense around Lovell?

5. Did you notice that although Queen Elizabeth has power, Varina has the freedom to act? Discuss the pros and cons of being royal versus being a commoner, for

both men and women, during this time. Which would you rather be?

6. Do you have any sympathy for Christopher Gage, Varina's suitor? Is he justified in being angry when Varina finally turns down his marriage proposal?

7. Do you have any sympathy for Viscount Lovell? When does faithfulness to a lost cause become terrorism? What line does he cross?

8. What do you think happens to Nick and Varina after the book ends?

Also by Karen Harper:

Shakespeare's Mistress

Is the dark lady of the sonnets William's secret wife?

When Queen Elizabeth's men come looking for William Shakespeare – a rumoured Catholic in a time of Catholic-Protestant intrigue and insurrection – they first question a beautiful, dark-haired woman who seems to know the playwright exceedingly well. Too well.

She is Anne Whateley, born in Temple Grafton, a small town just up the river from Stratford-upon-Avon. And as parish records show – were anyone to look for them – Anne Whateley was wed to one William Shakespeare in a small country church just days before he married Anne Hathaway, the woman the world regards as his lawful wife . . .

Also by Karen Harper:

The Queen's Governess

'I could not fathom they were going to kill the queen. Nor could I bear to witness Anne Boleyn's beheading . . .'

Katherine Ashley, the daughter of a poor country squire, is lucky enough to secure an education and a place for herself in a noble household. But it comes at a price. Thomas Cromwell, King Henry's ambitious courtier, has plans for Kat. When she finally achieves her ambition of becoming a lady in waiting, it is because Cromwell needs a spy in the new Queen's court . . .

Kat witnesses Anne Boleyn's fall from grace and, as a favour to the doomed queen, agrees to become governess and confidante to the young Elizabeth Tudor. Together they suffer bitter exile, assassination attempts and imprisonment, barely escaping with their reputations and lives intact. But when Elizabeth is eventually crowned, Kat continues to serve her, faithfully guarding all of the queen's secrets, even the one that could bring down the monarchy . . .

Praise for *THE QUEEN'S GOVERNESS*:

'Harper's diligent research, realistic portrayal, and insider/outsider heroine will hook those who can't get enough of England's turbulent history...bestseller Harper maintains her focus on the roles of women – both powerful and powerless – in Tudor England, resulting in another enjoyable historical romp' *PUBLISHERS WEEKLY*

'Well paced and full of pitch-perfect detail, Harper's novel brings new life to an old subject and, as good as the best of Philippa Gregory, is sure to be a big hit with historical fiction fans and book clubs' *LIBRARY JOURNAL*